SHARKPUNK

An Anthology of Original
Killer Shark Stories

EDITED BY

Jonathan Green

SNOWBOOKS

Proudly published by Snowbooks

Snowbooks Ltd
email: info@snowbooks.com | www.snowbooks.com.

A catalogue record for this book is available
from the British Library.

Paperback ISBN13 9781909679962
First published May 2015

SHARKPUNK

EDITED BY

Jonathan Green

INCLUDING STORIES BY

Jonathan Oliver, Den Patrick, David Lee Stone, Ian
Whates, Amy & Andy Taylor, Toby Frost, David
Tallerman, Josh Reynolds, Alec Worley, Richard Salter,
Kim Lakin-Smith, Andrew Lane, C L Werner,
Laurel Sills, Jenni Hill, Robert Spalding, Steven Savile,
Kit Cox, Gary McMahon, Al Ewing & Sarah Peploe

Contents

Introduction

JONATHAN GREEN

SHARKS.

They have demanded our fear and our respect ever since Man first braved the oceans. Great whites, hammerheads, makos, tiger sharks… they are the ultimate predators, masters of their watery domain, an environment more alien to our species than the surface of the Moon.

Indeed, we are so in awe of these creatures that they have entered the mythologies of countless sea-faring cultures, taking on terrifying forms. Forms such as the shape-changing Hawaiian Kamohoali'I, and the Fijian fish-god Dakuwanga. Even the Ancient Greeks had their legends of Lamia, the child-guzzling daughter of Poseidon, god of the sea, while the Babylonians believed their own Persian Gulf-dwelling Oannes taught mankind wisdom – possibly the wisdom to stay out of the water when sharks were about.

And we, in the 21st century have our own modern myths of these oceanic hunters, myths that take the form of movies – movies such as Steven Speilberg's *Jaws*.

I would like to be able to say that it was all planned from the start, but it was pure serendipity that led to *SHARKPUNK* being publishing forty years (almost to the month) after the seminal shark movie was released to great critical acclaim in 1975 – a film that has left its psychological scars on mankind's psyche ever since. Perhaps it was something in the zeitgeist.

It was a happy accident – a throwaway comment made on Facebook, seen at the right time by the right person – that resulted in this project coming about in the first place. And serendipity has played its part in the formation of the stories within the anthology too; writers working independently of one another – on opposite sides of the globe in some cases – scribing stories that mirror each other's.

Take, for example, Jonathan Oliver's opening tale, *Peter and the Invisible Shark*, a sinisterly psychological piece that could almost be read as a prelude to Gary McMahon's equally unsettling *Silent Waters, Running Deep*. Then there is the pair of future war-inspired stories; Amy and Andy Taylor's *Shirley*, and Robert Spalding's *Rise of the Übershark*. One is a dystopian tale with a heart, while the other is an unashamedly pulp tribute to the film that inadvertently kick-started this whole enterprise.

There are also the darkly, not to say violently, comic *Sharkcop 2: Feeding Frenzy*, by Alec Worley, and *Swimming with the Fishes*, by Steven Savile, crime stories, viewed from opposite sides of the thin blue line. The former is an homage to 1980s' buddy cop movies, while the latter is a love letter to the noir thrillers of the 1930s – albeit it one soaked in blood rather than perfume, and crimped with serrated teeth marks rather than sealed with a kiss.

Other stories continue with the crime theme, likening the personalities of psychopaths to the ruthless natural instincts of the great white and its ilk, in the case of Jenni Hill's *The Serial Killer Who Thought She Was a Shark*, while Richard Salter's *Sharkbait* is a heist-gone-wrong page-turner of an entirely different kind.

Man's hubris when it comes to nature and science, and the price he will ultimately have to pay, has always had a riptide pull on writers of speculative fiction. *SHARKPUNK* has its fair share of such stories too, including Den Patrick's *Blood in the Water*, Andrew Lane's *Blood Relations*, and Kim Lakin-Smith's SF thriller *Goblin*.

Several authors have written brand new stories featuring perennially popular characters of theirs for the anthology. Toby Frost's hero of the British Space Empire, Space Captain Smith, encounters a shoal of deadly space-sharks in *Deep Black Space*; Josh Reynolds' Royal Occultist, Charles St Cyprian, hunts a ghostly menace beside the seaside in *Deep Red Bells*; Kit Cox's monster hunter, Major Jack Union, finds himself dealing with the aftermath of illegal whaling activities in *Ambergris*; C L Werner continues to chronicle the adventures of the samurai hero Shintaro Oba in *Feast of the Shark God*; and David Lee Stone returns to the world of *The Illmoor Chronicles* with his tale, *The Lickspittle Leviathan*.

There are other stories that are harder to categorise, such as David Tallerman's *The Shark in the Heart*; a tale of boys, bullies, and the corrupting nature of power. Ian Whates' story, *Sharkadelic*, considers the shark as art, as well as perfectly evolved killing machine, while Laurel Sills' *Le Shark* is a Faustian tale that plays with one of the many idioms that have been birthed from the likes of Jaws and his selachian kin, that of the loan shark.

The anthology concludes with *YOU ARE THE SHARK*, by Al Ewing and Sarah Peploe, a story that taps into the shared memories of a generation; inclement British seaside holidays, amusement arcades, and teenage alienation.

Twenty stories, twenty-two writers at the top of their game, and a host of sharks. But why gather them all into one book under the catch-all subgenre styling of *SHARKPUNK*?

Well, the shark part is easy, and has been covered in detail already, but what of the 'punk'?

The term 'punk', particularly when used as a suffix, has come to mean the subversion of whatever comes before it. The Punk movement of the 1970s was a reaction against the status quo at the time, characterised by anti-establishment views and the promotion of individual freedoms. More recently the

Steampunk subculture has rebelled against the deteriorating manners of a generation, and a perceived drop in standards in society at large, focusing on the fashions and etiquette of an earlier age as a way of reacting against deteriorating modern social mores.

SHARKPUNK takes the glut of ludicrous shark-themed monster movies of recent years – such as *Sharknado*, *Sharktopus*, and the proposed (but never made) *Gatorshark vs Zombie Cheerleaders* – and subverts them, dragging up to the surface, from the unplumbed depths of the collective subconscious, stories that are intelligent, stories that have emotional depth and weight, stories that have something to tell us about the human condition. Stories that make sharks frightening again.

So what are you waiting for? Come on in. The water's fine…

Jonathan Green
May 2015, London

Peter and the Invisible Shark

JONATHAN OLIVER

WITHIN THE HEART *of the dark, sleeps the shark.*

Peter stopped typing. Outside, something had just *shushed* past the window. He was sure of it. He turned in his chair and looked into the night, at the street below, but of course there was nothing. At least not the thing he was imagining – that he would hold within his words.

The glint in the trees is the light on the eye of the shark.

He'd met with his illustrator a few weeks before and Jane had laughed when he'd told her the title of their new book.
"I like it. Perhaps we can go for a Doctor Seuss thing with the illustrations."
"I was thinking Edward Gorey. It has to be scary."
"But funny, too?"
"Yes... yes, I suppose it had better be funny."
But, in the writing, this book hadn't made him laugh out loud like some of the others. The story was perhaps a little too close to him – the shark a touch too near.

Again, Peter's fingers stuttered to a stop on the keyboard. He watched as the shadow moved across the wall above his laptop, from left to right; a sinuous, yet muscular shape.

Outside it was quieter than before; not even a whisper of traffic from the nearby ring road. Peter's chest tightened as he thought about all those miles of air above him; and here he sat, on the ocean floor, the pressure of an entire world pushing down.

I hear him
I hear the shark, within the night, amongst the trees.

Peter typed as quickly as possible, keeping the circling shark within the text, holding it to the page.

*   *   *

WHEN HE GAVE it more thought than he was comfortable with, Peter had to admit that it was a silly thing to be haunted by – a shark. And not even a real shark, at that. Instead, it was the model of a shark he had encountered in an aquarium as a young boy.

It hadn't been during the school holidays, so why he and his father – not his mother, he wasn't sure where she had been – had undertaken the trip, he couldn't recall. There were so few visitors to the aquarium that day, it felt as though they had the whole place to themselves.

Peter's father stopped in front of a large tank to watch a turtle swimming up and down the glass, rising and falling. For a time he followed it, his head rising and falling, until his eyes became unfocused and he seemed to be looking far beyond the glass. When his father was like this there was nothing that he could do.

Peter let go of his hand.

At the far side of the room was an archway, beyond which ripples of green light played across the dark walls. Whale song echoed from within the cavern, calling to Peter. When he stepped beyond the arch, for a moment he really felt as though he was standing at the bottom of the ocean, and he held his breath.

Vast forms hung beneath the ceiling, dappled with the constantly shifting aquamarine light, which made it difficult to tell where the floor ended and the walls began. The clicks and squeals of a school of dolphins drew his gaze to the far corner, where they were frozen in flight, their toothy smiles forever open. In the centre of the room hung the great blue whale, its sides encrusted in barnacles, its tail upraised as though it were about to come down and propel the behemoth across the aquarium. Arresting as these forms were, however, it was one in particular that made Peter let go of his breath in a shocked gasp.

The shark hung just above the entrance to the next room, daring Peter to approach. Even though he could see that it was attached to the ceiling via two metal rods, the creature was no less terrifying – or maybe it was its unreality that made it worse, somehow. Whereas the whale boomed and the dolphins clicked, for the shark there was a strange, watery *shushing* noise.

Peter walked back to where his father still stood watching the turtle, and took his hand. Even though his presence offered little comfort or reassurance, there was no way that Peter was going to walk beneath the shark on his own.

His father didn't look up as the shadow of the shark passed over them. Again there was that strange noise – *shush, shush, shush* – as though the shark were trying to calm Peter, to reassure him, before it attacked.

*   *   *

THAT NIGHT, AS he slept, Peter returned to the aquarium.

This time there were no dolphins or whale in the submarine grotto, though their calls haunted the space they had occupied. Peter could see the metal rods that had secured them to the ceiling, their ends ragged and torn.

The shark, however, was still there – the Great White with its rows of sharp, incurving teeth and its alien eyes. Soon, the strange *shushing* sound was the only noise in the room, and then that too fell silent.

It's just a model. Just a big toy.

But Peter couldn't move, could barely breathe – a warm, wet trickle ran down his leg.

Two bangs in quick succession shocked him out of his torpor. The shark had broken free of its metal rods and drifted silently towards the floor. There was no sign of life in its pure, black eyes but, with a flick of its tale, it surged towards him.

Peter ran, charging past the tanks of neon fish and slowly undulating sea anemones, bursting through the gift shop, overturning racks of cards and stumbling over stuffed toys in his haste to get away. The shark made a further chaos of the shop as it barrelled through after him. *Maybe*, Peter thought, *I'll be safe outside*. But as he hurried out through the doors the shark was close behind. With a sound of glass shattering and metal tearing, it threw itself into the night.

Peter didn't look back, he just ran.

He couldn't remember the aquarium being close to their house – in fact he knew that it was at least an hour's drive away – but all of a sudden he found himself on his street. Hearing nothing behind him, he chanced a look back.

There was no shark.

At least until that soft, watery sound made him look up.

There was a shadow on the moon and Peter watched as it grew, the shark descending out of the night sky like some strange alien craft.

It stopped before him, hanging only a few metres above the road. The shark drifted slowly forward and nudged Peter with its head, pushing him back towards his house.

Peter didn't want the shark in his house. He didn't think that there would be anything his mother or father could do to stop it.

He stumbled away and ran for his front door, slamming it in the creature's face before lunging for the stairs. Again, there was the sound of breaking glass and tearing metal as the shark invaded their home. Peter ran for the only sanctuary he knew – his bedroom. There, he did what he always did when there was something to be afraid of: he dived under his bed covers and cowered in their womb-like warmth.

Peter sheltered within his duvet cocoon for what felt like an age, before he finally risked a peek above his blanket, only to find himself looking directly down the gullet of the shark.

It was dark within the shark.

* * *

THE DREAMS HAD persisted into his late teens. They were in no way a nightly occurrence, but each time they came, they always ended with Peter screaming himself awake, drenched in a cold sweat. Once, when he had been fourteen, he'd asked his father to check his wardrobe for him, convinced – even in the light of a bright morning – that the shark was hiding amongst his clothes. Of course, there was nothing to be found amongst his shirts and trousers, but Peter had slept in the living room for a week before daring to return to his bedroom.

Eventually, he found a refuge in writing. Encouraged by one of his teachers, Peter discovered that making light of the things that scared him diminished them, made them more manageable. In his early twenties, Peter discovered an aptitude and then a passion for poetry, leading him to regularly perform his comic verse at poetry slams and open-mic nights.

On his twenty-first birthday, Peter's father had come to see him perform. Peter hadn't told him where he was going to be that night, but just before he took to the stage, he saw his father sitting down at a table towards the back of the bar. Afterwards, Peter had brought him a drink, perhaps in the expectation that he would tell him how proud he was. Instead, he messily downed the whisky before snarling directly into his son's face, "You've made a joke of me!"

Peter replied without thinking. "No, Dad. You did that yourself."

*　　*　　*

ON THE BUS home after the gig, the shark returned.

Peter tried to convince himself that someone had spiked his orange juice. But he had watched the barman pour the drink from a freshly uncapped bottle, and though there were certainly some strange characters within the poetry scene, he didn't think any of them would have stooped so low as to drug him.

No, the fact of the matter was that after the gig he had got onto the bus stone cold sober, the argument with his father still making his guts churn, and fifteen or so minutes later, while sitting on the top deck, Peter had looked out of the window to see the shark drifting silently alongside the vehicle, almost touching the glass.

He was the only one on the top deck, so there was nobody Peter could ask, "Do you see that too?" He wondered whether it was some sort of prank, whether the creature outside was a remote-controlled helium balloon.

But there was no mistaking it; this was *his* shark.

This time, however, the creature elicited little terror, more a sense of curiosity.

The shark was damaged. Its flank had been slashed open, revealing the fibreglass structure within; one of its glass eyes had been cracked, and several of its teeth were missing.

Peter knelt on the seat and opened the window. As soon as he did so the strange watery *shushing* noise filled the bus. The shark butted up against the glass a couple of times; making a hollow plastic sound each time it struck.

Putting his arm through the window and leaning out as far as he was able, Peter tried to reach the shark. His fingertips had just barely managed to brush its fin when the creature drifted away. It turned on the spot and ghosted towards the park. He watched it thread its way through the trees, occasionally bumping against a branch, before the bus turned a corner and the shark was lost from view.

* * *

IT WAS ONLY when he woke up screaming in the bed he shared with his fiancée early one morning, several years later, that Peter finally told someone else about the shark.

The dream had been particularly horrific this time. Lying in their bed, Peter had watched as the shark ate his legs. The shark took its time over its feast and, in any case, Peter couldn't move. He could only watch as his feet disappeared between those vast jaws. The blood washed up against him and Natasha; a warm tide that lifted his fiancée's hair and fanned it out over her pillow.

The shark moved further up his body, almost lazily snapping a femur in two as it slowly bit down. Peter found that if he concentrated he could move a little. He reached out a hand to push the creature away, but his hand met not with living flesh, but slick, cold fibreglass. Peter could see the two broken metal stanchions protruding from the shark's back.

Peter hadn't understood that he was within a dream, convinced that this time the shark really would consume him. He could never be sure with this haunting, especially as he had seen the shark outside of his sleeping hours several times over the years.

When the scream that had been trapped in his chest finally emerged and shattered the nightmare, Natasha held him as the terror faded.

"I don't think it's odd at all," she said a short time later, as they sat in the kitchen in their dressing gowns, sipping tea. "Lots of people are scared of sharks."

"Shark. Singular. Not sharks generally, but a specific shark. The model of a shark in an aquarium."

And Peter told Natasha about his childhood trip to the aquarium and the encounter that had, inexplicably, filled him with a lifetime of fear.

"Maybe you should get an outsider's perspective on the matter." Natasha said. "It may be worth your while to go and see a councillor. It certainly helped me when I went through that dark patch last year. A good therapist can help you unpack things, see them for what they are."

Peter agreed to give it a go, but after three sessions of being told that he harboured a lot of anger for his father, he decided that that was quite enough of that bullshit, though that wasn't quite how he put it to the therapist.

"He's just making stuff up, Natasha!" Peter said. "I never even think about my father these days. It's like he's not even real."

"Okay," Natasha sighed. "How about, in that case, you write about the shark?"

"Because my books with Jane are supposed to be fun. Sometimes dark, yes, but always silly and fantastical."

"So make this thing that has a hold on you silly and fantastical. Peter, I'm sure that with Jane's help you can untooth the bastard, and produce a fun story into the bargain."

Though Peter loved Natasha, and though he had listened to what she, and, to a lesser extent, his therapist, had said, he chose to ignore their advice and push the shark to the back of his mind.

*   *   *

SIX MONTHS LATER, during a flight to Chicago that he and Jane were taking to promote their latest book in the US, Peter looked out of the window and saw a dark speck moving against a brilliant white cloud. The speck quickly grew as it flew towards the aircraft and Peter hurdled over Jane in his panic, lurching into the aisle and shouting, "It's going to hit!"

The thing that struck the plane, however, was not a missile or another aircraft, but the shark. It pressed its eye up against the window before darting away, disappearing back into the cloud that was now pregnant with the promise of thunder.

After the air stewards had calmed the other passengers and assured them that nothing had struck the aircraft, Peter was put under restraint. The only thing that alleviated what had turned into an awful flight was the presence of Jane, who remained by his side throughout the ordeal even though, on her face, he could read an expression that said – *I think that my co-author is having a massive nervous breakdown.*

The slew of questions Peter faced once they reached the United States, and the hours spent in small brightly lit rooms drinking indescribable coffee, finally convinced him of the wisdom of Natasha's words. He'd write about the shark.

It was only when they finally got to their hotel that Peter found out that his father had died while they had been somewhere over the Atlantic.

*   *   *

You cannot see
You cannot hear
But I tell you that he is drawing near
He's in your room
Beneath your bed

Peter re-read the last two lines again before deleting them. This book was supposed to be fun and writing those words had made him feel queasy. He didn't intend to traumatise his readers.

He had drawn the curtains several hours ago, but that had only brought the shadow into sharper definition, outlined on the cloth by the light of the full moon.

Natasha had long since gone to bed. He wanted to wake her, just so that he had someone *normal* to talk to, someone who would tell him that the shark was most definitely not drawing near. But he was so close to finishing the book and once the words were written then perhaps the haunting would be over.

Even so, when he hit Save and closed down the laptop there was that sound —

— *shush shush shush* —

and when he climbed into bed it followed him down into sleep.

* * *

PETER AND JANE wouldn't normally have gone to see one of their books being printed, but this was part of the publicity, tied in with a wider campaign by the publishers to raise awareness of the book industry amongst children.

The event was almost a wash-out, literally rather than figuratively. That winter had seen the worst flooding in the UK for almost two-hundred years. Many of the roads surrounding the print works were under water and the car that delivered them had driven down a narrow tarmac causeway which appeared to be in imminent danger of disappearing. Both of them were, therefore, keen to get the visit over with as quickly as possible, in case they were stranded.

A handful of school children had been bussed in for the occasion and Peter and Jane had even been asked by some of them to sign their books; the majority, however, looked as bored and anxious as Peter felt, distinctly underwhelmed by what they no-doubt thought of as the outdated technology that surrounded them.

"How have things been?" Jane asked when they had retreated to the relative quiet of one of the offices, though even here the boom and rattle of the machinery made her have to raise her voice. "Natasha told me that you've been through a rough patch lately, but you seem pretty good to me."

"Actually, you know what? I am."

Peter was telling the truth. After he and Jane had signed off the proofs of the book, he finally felt that he could breathe again; it no longer felt like he was at the bottom of the ocean, under the shadow of those creatures that roved the depths above. He was even starting to look forward to the school tour. And, despite his earlier misgivings about writing the book, he was pleased with what they had produced, especially Jane's illustrations. Her shark was so unlike his own that it had dispelled much of his fear concerning their latest collaboration.

The printing press finally wound down. Outside, Peter watched the racing clouds begin to fragment; weak, milky sunlight fighting through. In a flooded field he saw a fin emerge from the water. But that was okay, because this time the shark didn't surface, and Peter was pretty sure that was the last he would see of his nightmare.

The door to the office opened and the print manager entered.

"Are you two ready to see the finished product?"

"Yes," Peter said. "Yes, we are."

*   *   *

JAMES LIKED STORIES, but he wasn't sure that he liked this one. The man telling them seemed nice enough, but from the tone of his voice he was enjoying reading the story about as much as James was enjoying listening to it. The pictures projected onto the wall behind the man made things worse. The drawings showed a shark, but the creature was more than a normal shark; there was something sad and angry about it that James really didn't like.

He closed his eyes but that didn't stop him from hearing the words, and when the man shouted,

"You cannot see

You cannot hear

But I tell you that he is drawing near,"

James opened his eyes to see the man pointing. None of the other children turned – they seemed to be enjoying the story far more than James – but James couldn't help following the direction of the man's finger.

And it was there, outside, hovering beside the bike sheds. It had emerged from the man's words, swum out from the pictures, and now it was watching James, the rain pattering from its blue-grey fibreglass flanks.

BLOOD IN THE WATER

DEN PATRICK

Day One

There was blood in the water.

In my dream there was blood in the water, crimson tendrils dissipating in the cold depths of the ocean. I was so cold, crushed by deep places, made small by the roil and swell. But it was just a dream and I am awake now.

I do not know what day it is.

I do not know where I am.

There are scars beneath the medical dressings that make me shake and weep. What happened to me? This is not my nightgown.

I found the pen and notebook on the floor under the bed. There is writing in the front about blood types but nothing else. The end of the pen has been chewed. I will hide them beneath the mattress when I finish writing. It will be my secret from them, whoever they are.

The bedclothes are very clean, the cell not so much. It is a metal room; there is no window. A small air conditioning box brings heat and the smell of diesel. I do not think this is a hospital.

I tried to stand and reach the door but I am so weak. I sank to my knees the moment I left my bed. I wonder where my father is. Is anyone checking in on me? Have I been forgotten in this little room?

I will sleep now.

* * *

Day Three

I did not write yesterday. A man and woman in white coats came and gave me an injection. I was barely awake when the needle entered my arm. I tried to ask questions but they ignored me. They had no faces, just serious eyes above surgical masks. Eyes unwilling to meet mine. The man asked the woman a question and she said she had lost the information.

'That's the second notebook you've lost this month,' he complained.

The woman checked my pulse and for a second I saw a shadow of sadness cross her face.

'Sleep now,' she whispered to me. I tried to ask her where I am but I began to fall asleep the moment the door clanged shut.

Today my mind is not working. Just writing these words takes every ounce of my concentration. I have trouble remembering anything or putting my thoughts in order. I must put the notebook and pen away in case I pass out. They must not find my writing. I hope my father comes for me soon.

* * *

Day Four

I think it is day four. I cannot truly know. The man and the woman in the lab coats returned. I began crying, asking for my father, asking if I was in a hospital. They said that I must not be scared, that I must eat something. The man shone a light into my eyes and checked my pulse. He made me open my mouth like a dentist and told the woman she must look inside my mouth.

What are they seeing?

The man left the cell and called over his shoulder, 'Don't spend all day in here. We have much to do.'

She smoothed the hair back from my face then pulled down her surgical mask to reveal a small smile. There is much that is small about her, her hands, her nose, her eyes. Her shoulders are narrow, her waist the same.

A burly porter with black hair offered me a bowl of chicken solyanka. It took me a long time to eat. My mouth feels different somehow. The woman said the sedatives had reduced my appetite, but that I must try.

'Have I been in an accident?' I asked. 'I cannot remember anything.'

'Just try and eat,' she said.

'Where is my father?'

'He is coming. Soon, little one.'

'Have I had surgery?'

She evaded my questions for the most part, telling me only that I was safer here than on the mainland. I do not understand what she means. It was only after she left that I realised: I did not ask where we are. The drugs are making me stupid I think.

I ate the solyanka and asked her what her job was. She began to say 'biologist' but stopped herself, then looked out to the corridor.

'We are weapons designers,' she whispered. Her face became hard.

'Where are the weapons?' I asked. She looked at me, then asked if I wanted more solyanka. I told her my name but she would not tell me hers. I must have fallen asleep because when I opened my eyes she was gone. My surgical dressings have been changed. I am too afraid to look beneath them.

*   *   *

Day Five

I do not remember much today. Food arrives, brought by the porter with black hair. He needs a shave and a wash. I can smell him coming before the door unlocks. I sleep a lot, and when I close my eyes I see a girl. She is called Olesya I think. In the dream she is a year older than me, sixteen perhaps. I think we were friends. Yes, for a long time we were friends, then something happened. I imagine her lips and the outrageous things she says. I am so confused. Am I remembering or merely dreaming?

I am tired again. I must hide the notebook and pen. I must keep them secret. I must keep Olesya secret.

* * *

Day Six

More food came yesterday. More food than I have ever seen. Father is poor, we have little. Not so here. I think there must a be vast kitchen nearby making many good things. Perhaps they will let me work there when I am better. I would like to learn to cook.

The porter who brings the food will not answer my questions. He will not even speak to me. Only the female scientist speaks, and only in whispers. She does not answer my questions but brings small things; chocolate, candles, an old book. The story is about a man called Gregor who changes into a beetle. It is as ridiculous as it is boring.

My father has not visited me, unless I was asleep when he came. I hope not. I miss him very much in spite of the things we have said to one another.

I slept after lunch and dreamed of Olesya again. I kissed her and we touched with cold fingers. I was so nervous that

I shook as her hand stroked my face, more when her lips brushed mine.

The woman in the white coat returned and woke me. She shone the little flashlight into my eyes and took my pulse. I do not like it. She looked inside my mouth and her eyes widened in surprise. She covered her expression when I pulled back. I knew she would not tell me if I asked her what she had seen, so I tried a different question instead.

'Is Olesya hurt, is she here too?'

'There is no one here by that name.' The scientist looked confused, then sat on the bed and smoothed my hair back tenderly.

'I am Larisa,' she said, 'Tell no one, or we will both be in trouble, little one.'

'Where am I?'

'I cannot say, little one. Far from Vladivostok.'

Then she left. No more injections at least. I feel different somehow. Just blinking my eyes feels strange, the texture of my skin is not the way I remember it. My fingernails have a tinge of blue, yet I am not cold. I must stop writing now. More food is coming. They must not see the pen and notebook.

* * *

Day Seven

One of the porters left the cell door open. It must have been after noon. I have no way of knowing the time, not by watch or clock or by the rising of the sun. I wish I had a window. I have buckwheat porridge at breakfast, lunch is pirozkhi with vegetables. Dinner is always meat, usually fish. This is how I know it was midday.

I did not think to escape, rather a fierce curiosity took me over. The corridors are metal and dimly lit. Rust climbs the walls like an infection. Puddles of water stagnate, stained with multicolour chemicals, petrol I think. Pipes run along the walls and the low rumble of machinery is everywhere. Perhaps it is a furnace.

Two times I nearly stumbled around a corner into a scientist. They did not see me, locked in conversation or consulting charts and notes on clipboards. I took a rusting staircase upward, avoiding a man in thick white boots and blue overalls. I could smell him before I saw him; the thick musk of sweat so strong it was as if I were stood beside him. Finally I found a window, a small circular window like they have on ships. The window was set in a door with a broken lock. I pushed through, desperately afraid of what I would find on the other side.

We are in the middle of the ocean. On every side there is the vast green swell of endless seas. I cannot see land, only the washed out grey of the sky where it meets the distant blue of the horizon. I looked down at my feet; the ship did not rise and fall and we are high above the water. The wind was cruel and chased me along gantries, around blocky buildings. Windows are boarded up. Signs declare the structure abandoned, dangerous or both.

This is no ship. This is an oil rig.

Larisa saw me on the way back to my room. She said nothing, following me into my cell before checking my eyes with the light and taking my pulse.

'You must be careful, little one.'

'Where am I?'

'They will not tolerate you leaving your cell.'

'Where am I, Larisa?'

'I will bring you another book soon, I promise.' Her eyes were framed with tears. 'but you must stay in your cell. Please.'

* * *

Day Eight

I woke today to find much of my hair has fallen out. It looked very dark on the white pillow case. It has never done this before. I am scared. My nails are still blue and translucent. My skin feels smooth when I trace my fingers over it, yet when I run my hands in the opposite direction it is rough. I cut my tongue on my teeth often, my jaw aches constantly. All I taste is blood.

I tried to tell Larisa but she told me there was no time.

'You must start the training program today, little one'.

She removed my surgical dressings and said I was 'healing nicely'.

I asked why I had been operated on but she led me out of the cell and told me to be quick.

At first they asked me to walk a few laps of the room. It was a large chamber. The floor was a metal grille and the electric lights above flicker and buzz. It smelt of salt water and diesel. I panicked when I saw the needle. I assumed they would sedate me again but they took a blood sample instead. Again they took my pulse and looked in my mouth. I told them I could taste blood and they brought me water to wash it away, but without explaining why. Larisa held a stethoscope to my chest and told the male scientist it was 'satisfactory'.

'I don't think any of this is satisfactory', I said, 'I think I am a prisoner. Where am I? Where is my father? What have you done with Olesya?'

'Your father will be here soon', said the male scientist.

I was grateful for the food when it came. I am so hungry. I ate alone in the training chamber. When the scientists returned they seemed happier. I was made to run. They prepared obstacles and gave me a skipping rope. I hate skipping. I am not a young girl, I am a teenager. I did as they asked and each time they gave me food in return. I am hungry all the time now. I hope I do not get fat. I do not think I will.

I asked them what I had done wrong, asked them why I was a prisoner. Larisa said I was making 'fantastic progress' and 'not to worry'. The man looked at her. Even with his surgical mask on I could tell he was annoyed. He never removes it.

'Am I a prisoner?'

'No,' said the man, 'But you are safer here than you would be in Shkotovo.' He stepped closer and I could smell something hard, like oil and metal. 'The authorities are being very ruthless right now. Your father had little choice but to...'

He said no more. It was Larisa's turn to look angry now. They escorted me back to my cell.

I will sleep now, I am very tired.

*　　*　　*

Day Nine

Today I trained with a soldier. He put a big clock up on the wall and grinned like a crazy man. He has blond hair shaved down short. The lobe of his right ear is missing and his neck has a wide scar, pale and straight. He taught me Krav Maga and a lot swear words. Most of them are English. He said his favourite swearword is 'motherfucker' as the Americans say it in every film they make. I am certain this is not true. He also told me he used to be a spetsnatz. I shrugged. I have never been impressed by boys bragging, less so when they are men. He thought he was clever by putting vodka in a mineral water bottle. I could smell the alcohol before he unscrewed the cap. I can smell everything these days, diesel, rust, food, unwashed bodies and sometimes soap. The only thing I cannot smell is myself. I remember how Olesya smelt, subtle and intriguing.

I used to push my nose into the nape her neck and inhale for long moments.

I trained from the moment I finished breakfast. We had perhaps forty-five minutes for lunch, then more training, then forty-five minutes for dinner. Then more training. I was given biscuits at the end of the day but I asked for fish instead. My hunger is greater than I can remember, yet they feed me all the time. The drunk spetsnatz told me I had done well and to go to bed. I asked him when my father was coming. He did not answer, instead drinking from his bottle that does not contain mineral water. I am more tired than I have ever known, yet I do not feel sad or angry or scared. I must sleep now.

*   *   *

Day Ten

More training. So tired. Teeth have stopped aching. I still taste blood.

*   *   *

Day Twelve

I am missing Olesya very much. If I could just call her, even for a few minutes.

*   *   *

Day Thirteen

Today was a day of many changes and surprises. The first is that security guards met me at my cell first thing this morning. They carry sticks, metal sticks. They made a few jokes about giving me a shock but I turned to them and looked them in the eye. Even with all their body armour I could tell they feared me. They were quiet for the rest of the day. I think they are motherfuckers.

The second surprise was the other teenager. She is also a girl. I wonder if there are more of us, and if there are boys. I wanted to talk to her so badly, but they made us fight instead. I think she must be sick. Her kicks were weak, her punches all went wide. It was very strange. She looks terrible and is so pale she looks blue. At one point her skullcap fell off and I saw her scalp. Her hair has fallen out in clumps. I pulled my own skullcap down over my ears a little tighter. My head must look much the same. I began to cry and wondered what they have done to us. The other girl had trouble speaking. There is something wrong with her teeth I think. My own teeth are very sharp but I have stopped cutting my tongue on them.

The last surprise was being allowed to go outside.

Larisa told me to 'get some air'. I looked at the other girl who was sat cross-legged on the training room floor. She was hunched over, staring into the distance, too tired even to cry.

I left, running along gantries, glad to be away from the diesel stinking gloom of the oil rig. The wind was strong yet I felt no cold. The smell of the ocean makes me want to laugh and scream with joy. It was then I found the helipad. There is no helicopter, only crates with ragged plastic sheets tied to them. I would not know how to fly a helicopter even if one were waiting.

I am doomed to stay here. I simply want to leave and see my father again, but mostly I wish to see Olesya, if she is even real. I worry she is a figment I have conjured to keep myself company in this strange place.

When I returned to my cell the security guards were marching down the corridor with a black body bag. The guards looked guilty but kept their eyes locked straight ahead.

I asked Larisa who had died but she would not meet my eyes. 'You must be careful, little one. Do as they say, always.'

*　*　*

Day Fourteen

More training. The other girl did not join us. Larisa looked very tired and her eyes were red-rimmed. She did not speak to me. The drunk spetsnatz taught me how to use a knife. It was a practice one, of course, made of wood.

The security guards watch me closely as they escort me to and from the training chamber. I can sense their anxiety. I can almost taste it.

*　*　*

Day Fifteen

No training today. I heard shouting. I was allowed out of my cell in the afternoon. I went outside onto the gantries and let the wind scour away the diesel stink, breathing down lungfuls of ocean air. The salt wind makes me feel more awake than I have ever known.

I wandered on until I reached the helipad. The security guards were all there, metal sticks in hand. The male scientist stood before all of them. Two guards dragged Larisa to the edge of the platform, throwing her to her knees. I wanted to call out, but the words became stuck in my throat, silent behind my sharp teeth. The scientist raised his arm and for a second I was confused. Then the sound rang out.

He shot Larisa in the head.

She fell from the side of the oil rig into the seas below. I could smell blood, even at this distance, the coppery taste

33

strong on the wind. If the bullet did not kill her the sea will. It is freezing here. I could do nothing but stand and shake and blink my eyes. They meant for me to see this. I think Larisa was executed because she broke some rules. I too will be executed if I break their rules.

I went back to my cell and cried for my father. Then I cried for Larisa. I hugged myself and pretended the arms holding me were Olesya's, but they are not. I slept for a while and dreamed of being shot. I dreamed of falling into the dark blue swell of the ocean, my blood seeping out from the gunshot wound. I woke up crying. One of the guards was looking into my cell but he said nothing.

I must get away from this place.

*   *   *

Day Sixteen

My father arrived. He looks so different. His beard is neatly trimmed and his clothes are new. He looked less tired, he stands straighter. I tried to hug him but he stepped back, raising his hands with outstretched fingers. The security guards stayed outside the cell the whole time. The door remained open. My father looked at the bed. More of my hair falls out each night, the pillow is always a mess. I pulled my hat down over my ears and said nothing.

'Why have you sent me away? Was I in an accident?'

'You are an accident,' he replied. It was in that moment I remembered my last conversation with my father, forgotten for so long. He caught me in my room with Olesya. We had barely undressed and were only kissing but he became furious. Oleysa left the house after his raised his hand to her. I stepped between them and she slipped away, out of the back door. He locked me in my room for a week after that.

34

'You sold me to these scientists.' The words spilled from lips, incredulous. I folded at the waist, sitting on the edge of the bed, made low with shock. 'What have you done, father?'

'It was the only way.' He thrust out his chin and his voice was like a rusted hinge. 'You would not do as you were told and the Government does not tolerate what you do... What you are.'

'What have you done, father?'

'It is not my fault.'

I tried to speak again but cut my tongue on my teeth. The taste of blood made me angry. Who was this blue-eyed devil to sell me? What had he ever done except neglect me and spend our money on drink rather than food.

I went for his throat.

The security men came and shocked me with their batons. It took them three attempts. I snarled at my father and told him I was ashamed, even as I lay on the cell floor, twitching and bruised. I told him he was no father at all.

*   *   *

Day Seventeen

Nothing was said about my father. Nothing was said about Larisa. Training continues. I must be careful. Things are very serious. Even the spetsnatz has stopped drinking.

*   *   *

Day Twenty

I like the spetsnatz, even if he is drunk and says terrible things. He managed about two days without vodka. He will not tell me his name, so he remains 'drunk spetsnatz'. I even

35

call him that to his face. He laughs and says I have a lot of spirit.

*　*　*

Day Twenty-Four

There has been a lot of training. I do not speak unless I am spoken to. I eat when I am told to eat and shit and when I am told to shit. I am escorted from my cell by four security guards each morning and evening. It seems two are no longer sufficient.

*　*　*

Day Twenty-Five

They let me eat in the main canteen today. Strange to eat food with an escort standing watch but I was glad for the change.

Many things are changing, but today is when I noticed the most. I shower longer in the mornings but I hate hot water. I don't shiver anymore, even when naked. I have no mirror but I cannot feel hair anywhere on my head. There is no hair anywhere on my body. I feel like a little girl again. Dinner time is difficult, vegetables are disgusting, I prefer my meat rare, I prefer fish to everything else. I used to hate fish.

It was during dinner in the canteen that I could smell it. Blood. I stood up slowly with my hands raised so the guards did not strike me. I walked to the kitchens, past the serving counter. Three cooks crowded together in conversation; withered women, lined faces betraying their meagre existence. They look much like my mother did before she died. One of the cooks winced. She had slashed her hand while preparing food;

the silver length of the knife bore a long streak of crimson. The smell made me so hungry I could do nothing but stare at the wound. The cut woman saw me watching and began to cry. I was ushered back to my cell but each time I blinked I saw only bleeding flesh.

What is happening to me?

*   *   *

Day Twenty-Six

More training. All day we trained. Krav maga and knife. Running and climbing and jumping, over and over. It was just after dinner that the scientist in the surgical mask entered the training room. He had a gun in his hand, the same gun he had used to execute Larisa.

'You have learned well. Now is the time for you to prove how effective you are.'

I shrugged. I'd been doing that very thing all day.

'Kill him.' The scientist pointed at the drunk spetsnatz with the gun. He swore of course. Something about 'Godless motherfuckers'.

I tried to speak but my teeth made the words clumsy. All that came out was a snarl.

'Kill him,' said the scientist, 'or I will kill you.'

I did not know what to think. The drunk spetsnatz was the only person I spent any time with. They had executed Larisa, now I was to execute the spetsnatz. I folded my arms and did nothing. I would not become like them.

The scientist shot at my feet, missing by perhaps a metre. The gunshot was painfully loud in the confines of chamber. It was as the scientist fired at me that the spetsnatz made his move. The two men fell to the ground and the spetsnatz wrestled the gun loose, only to have his skull beaten in by two security guards who rushed in from the corridor. The scientist got to his feet and wiped his bloodied nose. Again the hunger rose within me. I resisted going to him and... I do not know what I would have done. He picked up the gun and shot the spetsnatz in the head.

'Pity,' the scientist looked at me with disgust, not so different from how my father had looked at me. 'You were so promising, but you are no use to anyone if you cannot obey.'

*   *   *

Day Twenty-Eight

No training today. Motherfuckers killed my teacher. They will not kill me I think. I will be the one to kill them.

*   *   *

Day Twenty-Nine

I did not sleep. All night my feet have shifted and stirred, not running or stepping. I do not fidget, rather it is a rocking motion. Perhaps if I had a tail I would have swum away on a tide of dreams.

But there are no dreams, just the realization they are coming down the hall to take me to the helipad. I will be shot. My body will fall into the water just like Larisa. This month-long reign of madness will be over.

I should be scared, but I feel only calm.

They are coming.

*   *   *

Later

We had almost reached the helipad when the klaxons began wailing. I was certain they would shoot me. Speakers announced the navy were en route and everyone should take cover.

They have thrown me back in my cell, I can smell smoke. I suspect they are burning papers. They are burning the proof we were ever here.

* * *

Later

I can hear loud hailers from outside yet I cannot decipher the words. There is crying coming from the corridor. I asked for the security guards to unlock the door but no one will speak to me. All I can do is wait.

* * *

Later

Gunshots. Not pistols but assault rifles. Very loud. I do not think the navy are interested in asking questions.

The security guards outside my door have gone. All night the sounds go on and on. Just as I think it is over there are more screams; people beg for their lives.

I write this under my bed. I have made up the blankets so the room looks unoccupied. Still I am not scared. The only thing I feel is hunger. There must be much spilled blood and I can almost taste it. It stops me sleeping.

* * *

Day Thirty

At least I think it is Day Thirty. I cannot tell that it is the next day. Certainly no one brings me buckwheat porridge, not that I am hungry for that.

A sailor unlocked the door and came in, searching the room. For a moment I thought I was safe under the bed. He reached the door then turned, dropping to his haunches. He had a big round stupid face with big round stupid ears sticking out from beneath his beret. He grinned at me and lit a cigarette, coughing a little and screwing up watery blue eyes. He was not so very much older than me I think. The smell of the smoke made me feel nauseous. It was as if I was smoking the cigarette myself.

'No hiding places for anyone,' he said.

I told him my age. I told him I had been a prisoner. The expression on his face changed, then it changed again as I emerged from under the bed. The sailor became very pale, the cigarette falling from his bottom lip as he stared at me open-mouthed.

'Hooy na ny!'

I asked him to help me, but instead he raised his assault rifle.

I had been trained for this.

I snapped my left hand out and knocked the barrel of the gun away, punching him in the throat with my right hand. Lucky for me he did not pull the trigger else I would have another ten sailors in here right now.

As it is I have one dead soldier in here. I have pressed him up against the wall so people do not see him. There is not much left. I bit his neck and face very badly. I did not realise my mouth was so very wide. My teeth rendered his flesh as if he had been stewed for many hours.

I dare not admit this even to myself, yet I must. It was the finest thing I have ever eaten.

*   *   *

Day Thirty-Two

The soldier's wristwatch told me it was midnight. That was when I took him outside. I expected him to be very heavy, but perhaps I am very strong. The sailor slipped over the edge into the depths below. Just like Larisa. I was sorry to see him go. He tasted so very good.

I looked up and saw the silhouette of the navy frigate in the darkness. There were less cannons and machine guns than I was expecting. More navy men were on the helipad and gantries, I could smell each one. I could almost feel them moving in the night, like hearing but not. A sensation I cannot name.

I ran back inside. Only luck prevented my discovery. I am back in my cell, not because I am imprisoned, but because there is nowhere else to go.

It strikes me I should feel something for killing the sailor with the stupid face. Regret perhaps. I only know that he would have killed me, if only he had been quicker.

*   *   *

Day Thirty-Three

The frigate is gone. The sailors are gone. The oil rig is full of bodies that are beginning to rot. I see faces of people I knew, people who kept me prisoner. I feel no joy that they are dead, I feel no sadness. Some are missing their heads, others shot in their faces. Most clutch gunshot wounds in their torsos. It matters not how they died, only that they are all dead.

I returned to my cell and wondered why the sailors did not take the bodies away, or why they did not stand guard over the oil rig. I cannot guess why. I am very alone.

I went to the kitchens for food but found something much worse. A tap had been left running, filling a deep sink with icy water. I turned the tap off and the water became still, showing a rippling reflection. I did not understand what I saw at first. A wide mouth, grotesque and full of protruding tips, sharp edges of triangular teeth. The lips were all but gone, the nose flat, like a dull stub. The eyebrows were gone, much like the hair beneath the hat.

I know the hair is gone because it is myself I saw in the water's reflection. I am seeing myself. This is what they have done to me.

Olesya will never want me now.

* * *

Later

I can hear aircraft crossing the horizon. They are sending bombers. Of this I am sure. This will be the last time I write in this book. I must go now. I must jump in the sea, fall into the dark waves like Larisa. I will swim away from here. I will swim away or I will die. I do not care. I must go now.

The plane engines grow louder. They will bomb the oil rig and everything that happened here will be forgotten, there will simply be a ruined oil rig. Ruins, and blood in the water.

THE LICKSPITTLE LEVIATHAN

DAVID LEE STONE

For Rhianna Pratchett

SUNLIGHT WASHED OVER the southern island of Lick, lending a terrible scene the sort of sharp contrast most of the observers could have done without.

It was like some sickening jigsaw of a man: all the pieces were there, they just didn't quite fit together in the right way. This was mainly because the edges were wrinkly and, in several places, enthusiastically chewed.

Hieronymus Blush, journeyman magician and newly initiated outreach merchant for the southern islands, stepped between the two grizzled fishermen in order to get a better look at the corpse.

He'd seen a lot of tragic accidents in his five years as an apprentice at the Magician's Proving Ground, but these mostly involved the victims disappearing without a trace. For some reason, the look of complete shock on the face of the corpse was particularly unsettling.

Nevertheless, Blush made a valiant attempt to pull himself together: something the poor native on the beach would never be able to do.

He focused on the sand, drawing a small circle distractedly with his big toe while pointing a thin finger at the body. 'I don't understand why he's...complete?'

All eyes turned to Ryerson, the slightly senior of the two elderly fishermen.

'He's all there because sharks don't like the taste of us,' the old man muttered, suppressing a burp.

Blush boggled at him. 'They don't?'

'No. Unfortunately, by the time they remember that, you're already in five different pieces.'

'Oh.'

Blush took several steps back and beckoned the tribal translator away from the scene. The young native wandered over, leaving the two fishermen to fill their pipes and argue over various aspects of the kill.

'New bad,' the translator growled. 'Not old bad. New bad.'

Blush glanced toward the tree line, and shook his head. He could see the vague outline of human shapes moving through the undergrowth, and had no doubt that the rest of the tribe were keenly observing the scene.

'I won't lie to you,' Blush said, when the tribal translator caught his eye. 'This is a bloody mess, and I'm not just talking about *him on the sand*. That special underground fruit your lot produce is in seriously short supply, and the merchants are up in arms. We can't wait another fortnight for the next batch.'

The native, who was possessed of far too much muscle for one so young, adjusted his loincloth and seemed to take a sudden and unnatural interest in the tip of his spear. Blush suspected, and not for the first time, that the translator was fearfully bright. He looked down at the curious fish anklet that adorned the boy's left leg, and wondered if he could be bribed.

'Do you understand what I'm saying? What's bad for us is bad for you. Unless-'

'No bloodfruit.'

'Are you deliberately *trying* to destroy this island's *only* solid trade? I don't think the chief would want-

44

'No Bloodfruit! People scared. Kill New Bad!'

'Can I speak to the chief? I know he doesn't speak plain tongue, but I was told that the witch doctor is quite fluent-'

'No. You speak *me*! Me alone.'

'Fine.' Blush held back the torrent of abuse he wanted to hurl forth, but something about the half smile on the translator's thick lips was giving him the creeps. 'They told me the translator was an old man, so you must be quite new here, yes? Just passed the big test or something, have you?'

The translator stared back at him, unblinking. 'You and men from your city kill New Bad.....if you can. Only then Bloodfruit.'

Blush opened and shut his mouth a few times before mooching over to the rejoin the fishermen.

'Well?' he snapped. 'It's a shark: I assume we can find the bastard and kill it easily enough?'

The younger of the pair, a sprightly octogenarian called Jed, knelt beside the head of the corpse and stared up at him myopically. 'We'll have a go,' he said, 'but there's something amiss with this as far as shark attacks go. Can't you see what's strange here?' He reached down, took hold of the head and pushed back a chewed fold of the upper lip. 'It's taken his teeth.'

* * *

THE FISH SLICER Kumatra, fourth son of a third nephew on his mother's side, sat on the rocks of Lickspittle Bay and performed the one task for which he held a great tribal responsibility. He sliced fish.

He sliced the fat ones.

He sliced the thin ones.

He sliced the ones that some of his more questionable cousins found strangely attractive.

Kumatra looked behind him at the generous pile of fish that constituted the morning's third haul.

Odd.

It was half the size it had been just a few seconds before.

Kumatra flipped onto his feet, tightened his grip on the filleting knife and padded over to the big flat rock he used as a base for his net.

There were two big holes in the side of the twine mesh, and a lot of the fish were splashing into the water: even the attractive ones.

Kumatra muttered under his breath, and crouched to snatch back the edge of the net.

He was just hauling part of the mesh over the base of the rock when a sleek green shark leaped out of the water and bit him in half.

A spray of blood fountained into the air, and Kumatra's legs remained standing for a few seconds while the rest of the fish flopped into the ocean.

The shark darted away.

*　　*　　*

THE BOAT SLOWLY circled the island, skulking through shallow waters as a series of inlet bays and ancient monuments drifted past.

Blush had never seen a giant statue in the shape of an octopus before, but the heathen tribes of the southern islands worshipped strange gods. There were rumours of underwater cities, subterranean caves dripping with the blood of human sacrifice and even the odd story about natives interbreeding with some of the more attractive fish.

I need to find this thing quickly, he reminded himself. *Otherwise, I'll be spending a night around the campfire with these filthy…Lickers.*

'I don't think much of the equipment,' he said aloud, folding his arms in a dissatisfied manner while attempting to avoid falling over the side of the boat. 'I take it you two are usually on a budget?'

Jed ignored the question and continued to the heave at the rudder lever, but Ryerson immediately stomped over to where the magician was standing.

'It's a decent enough cog,' he muttered. 'Square-rigger, strong rudder: a proper whaling craft. None of that stripped down wood rot you get from Breakers' Yard up in Dullitch.'

Blush heaved a sigh, and pointed towards the edge of the deck.

'I'm not talking about the boat, Ryerson: I'm talking about that load of old junk you've brought along! You're supposed to be expert shark hunters, for crying out loud.'

'And?'

'Well, it's hardly an arsenal, is it?' Blush gestured emphatically at the small and rather pathetic collection of weapons in the rolled out cloth bundle behind the elderly fisherman. There was a small lump-hammer, a hand axe, a kitchen knife and a small bottle of something that he fancied might have been brandy. 'It's a killer shark we're dealing with; not a bunch of rowdy market traders.'

Ryerson took a drag on the misshapen pipe that drooped from his lips. 'You need to understand that your best possible chance of taking down a predator in these islands is to engage the beast in close combat. All this running away scared and screaming nonsense just gives them a stronger sense of purpose. If they take the leg off a man and that man keeps on punching them in the face, often times they'll give the whole thing up as a bad job.

'Way back when I was a boy, I knew a man that got attacked by a shark out beyond the eastern reef. That shark took a hold of him and sunk its teeth into his very soul, but he

47

wasn't having any of it. You know what he did? He ran right out of the water with the beast still clinging to his right leg, and he stamped it to death on the sand. What do you think of that?'

'I think it's a completely ridiculous story, and I think that you just made it up. I also think that there's a good chance all three of us are going to die if you're genuinely intending to go into hand to fin combat with a shark that just made a *jigsaw* out of a man who, judging by his component body parts, was the size of a bloody ogre.'

Ryerson spat a hefty wad of phlegm at the magician's feet.

'Well, if 'un that's the case then it's a ver' good job we have a magic user to watch over us now, isn't it?'

Blush wrapped an arm around the mast before rolling up his opposing sleeve and displaying an open palm for the two fishermen to see. As he stared intently at the space in front his hand, a tiny glimmering ball of red light appeared within, swelling and swirling as it reached a higher level of intensity.

'I am a journeyman on the path of Fire Magic,' he commented. 'The burning intensity of my particular school of conjuration is feared by many, many creatures from all over Illmoor.' He leaned forward and gritted his teeth. 'I'm afraid that *fish* are not among them.'

* * *

THE TRIBE WAS out in force for the mid-afternoon ritual. This was a particularly important event, as it was well documented that the mid-afternoon gods often went off the deep end if they were given less whaling hymnals than the sunrise bunch.

If anything, the latest ritual was looking likely to be more dramatic than usual. It wasn't every day that the tribal witch doctor, Bodiker, made a personal appearance on the sand.

Dressed in a full garb of feathers and boasting curious

bark earrings and an angular fish mask, Bodiker was a sight to behold: preferably through a long range spyglass.

He danced, shimmied, sidestepped, convulsed and somersaulted in front of the tribe as they formed a sort of human snake on their journey to the water's edge....

....but he didn't quite make it to the water before an enormous ocean spray stopped him dead in his tracks.

The ocean swelled up and flumed a second time, exploding over the beach like an angry cobra darting for its prey.

This time, however, it spewed forth the rotted, half chewed and entirely toothless head of Kumatra, the fish slicer.

A series of frantic cries erupted from the conga-line as word spread among the tribe of this new horror that had been cast among them. Villagers ran in every direction as panic took hold of the natives' collective consciousness, dripping the poison of fear into each and every mind.

Only Bodiker stood firm on the sea-hammered sands of Lick, his expression firm and his eyes devoid of all wonder.

The old witch doctor looked out at the solitary, fast receding fin of the island's savage predator and thought: *I know who you are.*

He glanced back at his retreating horde, and tried to figure out which member of the tribe was missing.

* * *

IT WAS, BEYOND any shadow of a doubt, an elderly dog. Blush decided that to call the thing a bloodhound would have made the presumption that it had some measure of blood *in* it: a fact put in doubt by the pale jowls, rheumy eyes and lack of effort it seemed to exude with every movement.

'Are you sure this thing can track a shark?' he prompted, as Ryerson led the exhausting looking hound from the depths of the boat's ramshackle cabin. 'Only, it looks like it might not last the night.'

'Don't you worry about Dash,' shouted Jed from the back of the boat. 'He can smell a blood trail a mile away....even in water.'

'*Dash*?'

Ryerson glared at the magician as if daring him to challenge the validity of the dog's name. 'Yep.'

The senior fisherman unclasped the dog's wiry chain and whistled between his teeth. It was a shrill, pitchy note: the sort that made your teeth hurt.

To Blush's amazement, the dog immediately took a run up and vaulted over the side of the boat, hitting the water with a detonating splash.

Jed and Ryerson both dawdled to the starboard side of the boat and began to whoop and cheer in a most excited fashion while Blush worried about whether or not the craft would tip over if he crossed the deck to join them. After what seemed like a lifetime, however, he managed to crane his neck in order to get a good view of the dog that was now making a spirited effort to lead them in what had to be a completely random direction (as no disenchanted animal could possibly pick up any sort of trail at such speed). He started to wonder, once again, whether the two fisherman were possessed of a full ticket between them....or even half a ticket, come to that.

Jed quickly hobbled across the deck and took a firm grip on the rudder lever, swinging the wooden handle around and hauling on it with all his might.

The boat lurched and moved into a steep turn: they were now forging straight for a deserted reef a short distance from the main island.

'The natives call it Notmuch Atoll,' said Ryerson, squinting as he pointed a bony finger at the coral outcrop. 'It's a haven for sharks. I got this out on Notmuch in my youth.' He bunched one hand into a fist and knocked hard on his right leg: there was a hollow, wooden sound.

Blush just stared at him.

'What?' Ryerson demanded. 'Don't pity *me*, boy. Young Jed over there has two.'

'You're *not* serious.'

'Deadly.'

'You have *three* wooden legs between you? I'm so glad I went with the Fishermen's Guild for this job: there's absolutely no substitute for having confidence in the people you're working with.'

'He's got something! He's *got something*!' Jed was yelling and pointing ahead of the boat, where it seemed that Dash had paddled to the shore and trotted *out of the water*. 'I'm telling you: he's on the trail! We're going in!'

The dog had exploded from the lapping waves and was now beginning to pick up the pace. It sprang over the sands with an excitement bordering on lunacy, crossing the curved atoll like a demented racehorse.

Blush tripped and fell in an effort to scramble to the front of the boat.

'But he's heading onto the atoll! It's a lagoon island! For the love of all sanity, we're supposed to be chasing a shark! What did it do, dive out of the ocean and *run* onto dry land?'

Ryerson reached down and snatched a handful of Blush's hair, yanking his head to the right.

'You mean like *that*, Mister Magician?'

Blush stared out at the atoll, and swallowed. He was looking at a sight he wouldn't ever have believed was possible within the framework of the civilized world. He was looking at an image that would stay burned into his head until the day he boarded that mist-bound ship to Parts Unknown. He was looking….at a sleek green shark running across dry land on two incredible muscular human legs.

Blush opened and closed his mouth a few times, but no

sound came out.

The shark was complete: the head, midsection, fins and tail were all present. In that respect, it was very much a shark… with the slight difference that this *particular* member of the species could enter a marathon with a better than average chance of getting onto the podium.

It was just….*wrong*.

The legs were obviously jutting from the undercarriage in some hideous mutation that simply had to be the result of the sort of interbreeding Blush didn't even want to think about.

Surely, even as a native of Lick, *you had to draw the line somewhere*.

The thought persisted as the front of the boat thunked into the atoll's rocky outcropping.

Ryerson hurried over to the weapons, took the hammer and the knife for himself and tossed the miniature axe to Jed. When neither of them made a move for the whiskey, Blush scrambled over on his hands and knees to grab the bottle himself.

Despite their age and the fact that three quarters of their running appendages were wooden, the two fishermen moved with surprising alacrity. Blush had to use a minor fire conjuration on his ankles in an attempt to put in the kind of effort that didn't make him look pathetically unfit by comparison.

However, several factors quickly conspired to slow him down. Apart from the difficulty he'd always had wading through any body of water that went above the knee-line, and the fact that he was struggling to catch his breath, there was the moderately alarming scene now unfolding on the beach up ahead.

Dash had closed in on his prey, but the bloodhound had sensibly decided to slow to a soft pad as he drew near to the shark, which had - against everyone's expectations - suddenly turned around and was standing its ground. On the two legs that more than ably supported its frame, the Lickspittle Leviathan looked like a giant hovering wasp full of razor-sharp teeth…and the dog had evidently reached such a great age by quickly handing all prey over to the experts.

The experts in question were now staggering, limping and hobbling towards the killer beast, waving their respective weapons in a manner that did nothing for Blush's sense of confidence in them as highly trained whalers.

Jed reached the creature first, and took two mighty swings at it with the hand axe. The first one missed when the demonic, freakish thing hotfooted a speedy dodge, but the second one connected and stuck fast in its flank. Jed made a move to retrieve the axe, but the shark immediately went on the attack, kicking the old man swiftly between the legs and, when he doubled up, biting his head clean off. Blood volcanoed out of the opening in the newly ravaged neck and the rest of Jed's body collapsed in a heap.

Blush skidded to a halt, cried out in horror and, ripping the cork from the whiskey bottle, took several big gulps before emptying the remaining contents over his hands. Then, amid much coughing and spluttering, he began to mutter under his breath: the magic caught, spurred on and increased by the alcohol as the flames began to spring from his pores.

The shark and Ryerson were circling each other, looking for an opening. Ryerson was reaching back with the hammer, but had the knife twitching and turning in front of him, his hands moving quickly to suggest that they were capable of a lot of damage in only one or two strikes. The shark on the other hand, was just slowly pacing along, grinning manically: it had no choice.

Ryerson struck out, ducking under the great-headed torso to plunge the knife deep into the beast's underbelly. At the same time, he swung the hammer around and brought it into a rising trajectory, catching his prey with an uppercut that knocked it sideways.

Unfortunately, it was then that the old man made what turned out to be a cardinal mistake. He turned and ran.

The shark leaped after him, bowling him over and biting down hard on his wooden leg.

Ryerson screamed and clawed at the sand, trying to escape the prowling wrath of the mutant predator by kicking at it with his good foot…but even Blush could see that the next bite was going to be the last one.

Still mumbling cursed enchantments through trembling lips, Ryerson barely noticed as Dash, no stranger to danger and evidently a lot smarter than his owners, bulleted past in the opposite direction.

Ryerson had rolled onto his back and was frantically kicking and screaming, but the shark wasted no time, finishing him off by dropping onto its own ridiculous knees and biting him cleanly in two. It would have been the most horrific slaughter Blush had ever seen *had he actually seen it…* but the magician was halfway to another dimension, his eyes engorged with the magical fuel that now birthed a fireball the size of his chest.

The shark leaped onto its feet and bolted forward, running at the distant figure with a demonic intent so clear and purposeful that it almost created a scene of beauty to behold.

Blush shook himself from his reverie when the creature was still about fifty feet away from him. Then he simply released the ball of flame and watched it seer into the shark with an incredible explosion of heat and light.

The shark collapsed onto the sand and began to writhe around, one leg blazing merrily as it careered from side to side.

It was then that Blush noticed the familiar looking fish anklet on the burning leg.

Mother of all mercy, Blush thought. *It's the translator.*

This.....thing.....is the boy I was speaking to.

Blush felt a fleeting burst of pity for the terrible creature before it suddenly dawned on him firstly that the shark wasn't going to die and secondly that he needed time to prepare another attack. He backed away from the wretched creature that was desperately trying to flip, kick and scrape its way back into the water. Then he turned and ran for the safety of the jungle.

*   *   *

THE TRIBE WERE gathered around an ancient cooking pot when Blush arrived, puffing and panting, on the edge of the village. One by one, each of the villagers retreated inside their huts or hurried for the comparative protection of the main cave system. Only the tribal chief and Bodiker, the witch doctor, remained at the pot, both wearing the sort of sour, guilty expressions men always get when past wrongs return to plague the blissful ignorance of oblivious lives.

'Right. *Who is he*.....and don't give me any more heathen guff or else I'll report back to the merchant guilds and hiding the bloodfruit will be the least of your worries: you'll end up with an army on your doorstep.'

Bodiker and the chief exchanged glances, and a few words in the tribal dialect.

'Come on!' Blush prompted, gesturing towards the witch doctor. 'I know *you* speak plain tongue. *Who is he?*'

Bodiker removed his headdress and dipped a hand into the pot, fishing around distractedly for some delicacy that apparently eluded him.

'It's a shapechanger,' he said, his voice showing no signs of humour. 'I know of only one other creature that hungered for human teeth for its transformative powers....and it was the parent of this one.'

'But, listen – your translator…'

'…is the beast. Yes. What we feared has come to pass.'

'You *know*?'

'We can assume. I have lost two sons today, Mister Blush. You inspected the body of my oldest child this morning, and my other son went missing this afternoon while cutting fish for the tribe. This plague upon our people….is my own doing, and my own punishment.'

Blush straightened up, slightly mollified by the evidence of some apparent

honesty. 'I'm listening.'

Bodiker stepped away from the pot and fell onto his knees.

'Several years ago, a man was shipwrecked here on Lick. He claimed to be a fugitive from the mainland. We tended his wounds and restored him to health: he became one of us. He had – how do you people say it – a *talent*….for the teeth?'

'A dentist?'

'As you would say it, yes…but it was soon revealed that he did, in fact, hunger for the very ivories he claimed able to treat. He was discovered, caught red-handed and bloody-mouthed. When we confronted him, he changed his shape in order to evade capture, revealing a variety of diabolical talents. He was a curse, an abomination. He was cruel, and broken, and he liked to inflict pain: the tribe suffered terrible anguish as a result of his stay here.'

Blush nodded, noticing for the first time that both the chief *and* his witch doctor were fairly gummy.

'So what happened?'

'He was banished, and imprisoned in the sunken caves beneath the island, the world where only strange fish swim… but he committed an even greater crime while he was interred there. A forbidden pleasure: one of the great sacrificial sins.

He took a lover…from below.'

'To be honest, I'd prefer it if we could draw a discreet veil over that bit and take it as read. I'm assuming he was – what - executed?'

Bodiker bowed his head.

'Yes: a necessity. He was sacrificed to the sea gods, along with his forbidden fruit…but the child they had between them was spared and brought into the tribe.'

'You raised that lunatic's *son* as one of your own?'

'We felt we had no choice. The sacrifice provoked great anger among the gods, for we reaped neither fish nor bloodfruit in that terrible year. Besides, the boy was a perfect example of one of our own young, and showed no signs of his father's taint. He must have been biding his time. Now this evil comes among us. This nightmare. This terror. This…'

'…bastard son of a shark and a shapechanging dentist? Terrific news. Just tell me how to get into the caves. We need to end this. Now.'

*   *   *

THROUGH THE FOREST, into the undergrowth, beneath the giant vine tree, beyond the lowest tier of the tri-level cave system, behind an enormous heart-shaped rock, down the deepest slope leading to the longest, dankest tunnel lay a candlelit chamber containing a limpid pool of glimmering green water.

'Seriously – how much further is this place? I thought you imprisoned people here all the time: surely their sentence is served by the time you get them to the front door?'

Bodiker grimaced at the magician, and motioned to the pool.

'Swim below, and you shall find the sacrificial caves….

and much good may it do you.'

Blush took a moment to stare balefully at the witch doctor. Then he removed his robes and all but the most sacred of his undergarments, and dropped into the pool.

A vivid and boldly illuminated world of floating carcasses, severed heads, skeletal limbs and curiously misshapen fish turned slowly all around him as Blush swam through the emerald waters.

When one submerged tunnel bled quickly into another, he began to fear that his hastily gulped oxygen supply would give out before he could reach his destination, but a pool of light suddenly hovered above him and with two determined strokes he broke the surface of the water and clambered onto the rocks of a strikingly beautiful sunken grotto.

There were diametrically beautiful gems encrusted within the walls, two great stone altars wedged together in the centre....and an immediately recognizable tribesman standing at the grotto's only other exit.

The translator half stepped, half staggered forward, sporting two great wounds in his stomach and shoulder.

'You managed to change again then?' Blush smiled, patting his hands quickly on the altar and raising them to conjure a spark of flame. 'I suspect there were barely enough teeth in those two old timers for more than a few hours, though?'

The translator took another step, and flashed a mouthful of long, razor sharp teeth.

'I don't need a few hours to finish *you* off, *wizard*.'

Blush had begun to mutter with grim determination now: in such confined surroundings, he knew he had enough in the concentration tank to bring forth another dramatic burst of fire. Only, *this time* it had to be enough of a gout to get the job done.

'Your father made a terrible mistake down here,' Blush

warned, beginning to mutter the start of an incantation. 'You have suffered a cursed life as a result.'

'I agree, wizard….but we all make mistakes.'

The translator lunged forward, grabbing hold of Blush and heaving him into the air. The magician made no attempt to struggle against the attack, but continued to mumble as the heat built between his open palms. The translator charged Blush bodily against the wall, and snatched a rock from an open crevice beside the magician's head.

Raising it up with one arm, the tribesman was easily strong enough to hold Blush against the wall, pinioned helplessly as he aimed the rock directly between the magician's eyes.

The burst of flame was exactly that: a jet of fire that spewed over the translator's head, neck and shoulders, sending the young man staggering backwards with a blood curdling scream of pain. He hit the altar and somersaulted over it to land onto the rocks behind, burned horrifically and crawling with ponderous, painstaking effort to the grotto wall.

Blush picked up the rock that had been intended for his head and followed the shapechanger with it. Stalking him slowly and deliberately, he turned the wretched creature onto its back and lifted the rock high above his head.

'We do all make mistakes….but it falls to me to account for your father's.'

The translator looked up at him through sorrowful, bloodshot eyes. 'Then tell me, *wizard*, will you account for all of mine?'

Blush slowly turned to the darkened portal at the far end of the grotto, a portal that appeared so misshapen that it almost seemed to writhe and morph as he tried to focus on it. There, cloaked in shadow, something peered out at him, something *communal* that carried the weight of an entire congregation of tiny eyes. As the last light in the cave fizzled out, Blush discerned the patter of hundreds of tiny feet.

SHARKADELIC

IAN WHATES

REMARKABLY, NO SPECIFIC term has ever been coined for a shark expert. The closest Debra could find was 'ichthyologist', which simply means 'fish expert'. Apart from that there's 'marine biologist' and... ehm, shark expert.

Debra sighed, resolving to settle on a title for the piece later.

She hated that – going into an interview without a tagline in mind, a label. Oh, whatever she initially chose might well change later, once the interview had been concluded and she had the opportunity to hear the recording back with an analytical ear, deciding what to include and what to excise, which aspects merited emphasis and which should be reduced to mere passing mention, but winging it without at least *something* in place left her feeling exposed. Naked.

She hesitated before getting out of the car, studying the man's profile on her notebook one final time in the hope of last minute inspiration.

*   *   *

RYAN TURNER, 37 years old, born in Cambridge, UK. BSc Marine Biology and Oceanography, Plymouth University.

Following uni, Turner spent six months travelling: Thailand, Malaysia, Singapore, China, Hong Kong, and Australia. He clearly enjoyed the experience because soon after coming home he relocated to Oz, where he worked in conservation on the Great Barrier Reef – which was then in a far healthier state than it was reported to be these days – returning to the UK some eighteen months later. His reasons weren't specified. He landed a job in television, initially working behind the scenes on a number of wildlife and nature programmes, including several high profile series and an award-winning documentary. He subsequently moved from behind the camera to appearing in front of it, his craggy features and moderated tones becoming familiar to millions, as he gained the reputation of TV's resident shark expert.

Debra skimmed the list of programmes and the various books Turner was credited with writing. She couldn't escape the feeling that either she or the profile was missing something. This barely scratched the surface. The résumé detailed an impressive portfolio of work, but there was no indication here that Ryan Turner, marine biologist and TV presenter, was all the while nurturing unguessed-at talent as an artist.

She'd checked – of course she had – and Turner had never been to art school, never received *any* formal training in that direction – at least not that she could discover – nor had he shown any inclination or aptitude to paint. Yet two days ago she had stood in a major London gallery and been staggered by the scope, the sheer emotive power of his work.

She wasn't the only one. When Turner's expansive, almost psychedelic canvases first started to surface they took the international art world by storm. The fact that the artist's identity remained undisclosed didn't hurt, either; everyone loves a mystery. Each painting was signed 'Carcha' in the bottom right hand corner, but nobody was saying who stood behind that opaque pseudonym. Social media got hold of the story and helped fuel the flames of conjecture, with the intrigue soon spilling out beyond the rarefied stratosphere of the art world to capture the public imagination. It even made the national news, as a currently prominent pop starlet admitted to being 'flattered' to find her name linked to the enigmatic artist. Her denials did little to dampen speculation.

When it came, the inevitable reveal was perfectly stage managed, coinciding as it did with the announcement of Carcha's first ever exhibition.

Ryan Turner: *really*? Nobody had seen that one coming.

Of course, hindsight is a wonderful thing, and suddenly people made the connection. Marine biologist: sharks. *Carcha:* short for Carcharhiniformes; a taxonomical order that includes the hammerheads and the reef sharks. Add to that the titles he had chosen for his work, many of which could be construed as referencing the sea – 'Stormfront', 'Currency' (a play perhaps on 'Current Sea'?), 'The Net' (how foolish of them to assume this had anything to do with computers) – and it was obvious really.

Besides, when was the last time Ryan Turner had been seen on telly? A year ago, more than that…? No wonder he'd disappeared from the screen; concentrating on his paintings, no doubt.

News of Turner's first exhibition, to be staged at a prominent London gallery, sent a frisson of anticipation across the net. Invites to the preview became the hottest tickets in town, but, as a young freelance journalist not long out of college, Debra had little expectation of nabbing one. Despite a couple of notable articles already appearing under her byline, there were far more illustrious reporters in the queue ahead of her. But she had reckoned without Dominic. Sometime lover, constant friend, a dashing figure that flitted in and out of her life like a will-o'-the-wisp, forever treading that delicate line between scandal and acceptability: acerbically funny, handsome, dazzlingly intelligent, bisexual, unpredictable, and frighteningly well-connected Dominic.

"So, would you be interested in an invite to the Turner preview?" he had asked over coffee during the most recent of their irregular but always welcome catch-ups. The question came out of the blue, without preamble and unconnected to any previous topic of conversation. It said something for Carcha's status that Debra didn't stop to ask 'which Turner?' There was only one at this juncture.

"Are you kidding me?"

He grinned, clearly enjoying her delight. "What do I get as a 'thank you'?"

They ended up in bed; well, it was the least she could do.

*   *   *

DEBRA CHOSE HER outfit for preview night with care: a little black dress with a twist, veering towards the gothic without being brazen. Simple silver accessories – bracelet, belt buckle, decorative shoe buckles – though she did allow herself the luxury of white gold and diamond earrings and the shoes themselves were to die for. Jimmy Choo, with ridiculous four-inch heels that she would never normally dare attempt, but on a night like this they made her feel *good*. Predictably, most attendees were decked out from head to toe in designer, which was one of the reasons she wasn't; that and the cost.

She had seen Carcha's work online and in magazines, but that did little to prepare her for an actual physical encounter – and encounter was the word. Nothing else could convey the exhilaration of setting eyes on these broad, dazzling canvases for the first time. The hushed almost reverent tones of everyone else present assured her that she wasn't alone in being so affected.

Trial and error taught her not to stand too close; by all means dip in briefly to examine the finer detail or the brushwork if you felt so inclined, but in doing so you risked missing the point. Only by seeing the whole composition at a single glance could you appreciate the full emotional impact of a piece. She watched time and again as distinguished observers stepped forward to peer closely at a given picture, only to shuffle backwards almost immediately, as if compelled to do so.

"This isn't just a new way of painting," she heard one dapper gentleman – grey goatee beard and cravat – intone to a companion, "it's a whole new art form."

There was nothing traditional about the compositions – she could imagine her late granddad, who had fancied himself as something of an art lover, sniffing in disdain and dismissing the whole collection as 'ill-conceived abstracts' – yet they managed to reflect the world and the experience of living within it far more accurately than a painting that painstakingly strove for realism ever could.

Debra wandered around the gallery oblivious to the other guests, her attention riveted by first one canvas and then the next. No two affected her in quite the same way, though she sometimes detected parallels, a resonance of themes. 'Depth' and 'Horizons', for example. The former was an interweaving of dark shades: blues and grey-blacks and, on closer examination, purples and deepest greens; a combination that seemed to add texture beyond the two flat dimensions of the canvas. It drew the observer in, compelling you to strive to discern ever more detail, as if staring intently might somehow flake away the paint to uncover brooding secrets hidden beneath. Spend too long studying 'Depth' and you risked becoming disorientated upon looking away, left with a sense that while you were so absorbed reality had taken a surreptitious step sideways, leaving you behind.

'Horizons', with its subtle striations of pale blue and whites and silvers that drew the eye to the centre, where smouldered a heart of burnt umber and orange-red fire, had a similar effect, but whereas 'Depth' threatened to trap the viewer in a dark abyss with no escape, 'Horizons' held the promise of propelling you towards that distant sun, of sending you on a never-ending journey, a joyful dream that no one could possibly tire of.

Her favourite piece, though, or at least the one she found impossible to resist, was 'Sharkadelic': a vibrant chaos of clashing colours that, paradoxically, meshed into unexpected harmony; unlooked-for beauty arising from the ashes of spent discord. There was something disturbing about the painting, which proved fascinating precisely because she had no understanding of how it could possibly work. She spent long moments in contemplation, trying to decode its success and unable to tear herself away.

"Surprising, isn't it?" said a voice at her shoulder.

"Yes, yes it is, totally," she agreed, before realising that she recognised that voice. Her head whipped round.

Ryan Turner was a little shorter than she'd imagined, but otherwise met expectations in every regard. Handsome, with a lack of the usual celeb polish that still fell short of rugged; the real charm was generated by his smile and those pale blue eyes. In the split second it took her to face him, she did her best to convert her own expression from gawp to smile. Goodness only knew if she succeeded.

"Sorry, I didn't mean to interrupt," he said. "I saw you standing here, so still, so absorbed..."

"No, you're not, not at all." God, where was the journalist in her when she needed it? "But absorbed is the word. This is... remarkable."

"Thank you. 'Sharkadelic' is probably my favourite work in the whole show. Some of the others here are a little too... safe? But this one, I don't know, this seems to have a real edginess to it."

"Totally, but the others: safe, *really*?" She shook her head. "They're anything but safe, or only in comparison to this one.

Measure them against all the other stuff being painted today and they cut way beyond the furthest edge."

He laughed. "Thank you. For both your enthusiasm and for such heartfelt affirmation."

And then he was gone, reeled in by a smart-looking woman who hurried over to aim a perfunctory smile in Debra's direction and then whisk the Great Man away with a: "There you are. You simply must come and meet…" Agent or manager, Debra assumed, or both.

She could have kicked herself. That was her moment, her chance to ask Ryan Turner about his inspiration, his technique, his magic… And she'd blown it. There wouldn't be another. Already he was surrounded by sycophants and the great and the good. Somehow he'd escaped the circus for a brief moment and wound up standing beside her. And she had singularly failed to say anything meaningful. 'Stuff' indeed: brilliant.

The encounter took on an almost dreamlike quality. So sudden, so spontaneous and so brief; in its aftermath life resumed with no hint that anything out the ordinary had occurred, as if this had been a hiccup, a skipped frame in the reel of existence.

She wandered through the rest of the evening in something of a daze. The crushing disappointment of her own ineptitude acted as insulation against the full effect of the canvases, and she found herself unable to recapture her earlier mood. Turner made a brief speech, though the words slipped through her consciousness with little retained, like water seeping through sand. As suspected, no further opportunity to talk to him presented itself; until she was about to leave.

Having reclaimed her coat from the attendant, she turned towards the door to find him standing there, the smart-looking woman nowhere to be seen.

"I understand you're a journalist," he said.

"Yes, I am. Freelance."

"Would you like to interview me?"

"Yes, yes of course I would… Please!" No one had *ever* interviewed him, not since he was revealed as Carcha.

"Good; my place in Cornwall, day after tomorrow. Shall we say 8.00 pm?"

He hadn't given her the address but then he didn't need to. It was a matter of public record, and she was a journalist after all.

*　　*　　*

THE HOUSE WAS directly on the coast. Debra allowed plenty of time, not wanting to risk traffic jams or any other delay. The route was straightforward enough: M4 to Bristol, M5 to Exeter, and then the A30, skirting Dartmoor, to St Austell, where she'd booked a room for the night. She left North London in the morning, heading off as soon as the worst of rush hour had cleared, and arrived in St Austell mid-afternoon.

Then it was just a matter of killing time.

Despite the temptation, she hadn't tried to sell the interview in advance or even to gauge editors' interest. "There's no need, trust me," Dominic had said when she phoned to tell him of the unexpected opportunity. The realisation that, with both of her parents passed away, Dominic was the only person with whom she could share such thrilling news came as a sobering one. "Wait until you've done the interview before you start trying to hawk it around," Dominic advised. "Then you'll have actual sound bites to tempt editors with. An interview with Ryan Turner? They'll flock around this like gulls to a trawler, squabbling for the spoils. I'm so thrilled for you, pet." He was right, of course.

Even so, on the drive out to Turner's house she was

afflicted by doubts: what if he'd forgotten? What if he hadn't meant the invitation seriously, or was expecting her to phone ahead and confirm? She hadn't, reasoning that without a direct number she would only get through to an assistant or an agent – the smart-looking woman or her spiritual sister – and be deflected, put off. So she came here cold, relying on the tenuous thread of an unconfirmed invitation spoken in haste.

Turner's home stood on a rocky promontory, accessible via a narrow track that she missed at first in the fading light, hidden as it was between two cottages. They were the last two habitations she passed and the winding track proved an adventure in itself for someone more accustomed to urban roads, particularly where it skirted a perilously steep drop to the ocean on her right. There were no streetlights out here, of course, and Debra was grateful that she had again set out early and so was able to take this at a crawl.

Situated at the end of the peninsula, the property, when she finally arrived after a mile or more of hesitant progress, proved to be a wonder. She'd expected something traditional given the setting – tall white walls nestling among established trees, pantile roof and brick-built chimneys – but this was nothing of the sort.

Sensors triggered as she pulled up outside, bathing the house in light. The walls were all grey and glass – the grey looking as if it might have been hewn from local stone – and curved, as if to acknowledge the undulations of the surrounding countryside. The flat-roofed storeys were arranged one upon another in diminishing size like layers on a wedding cake, the whole seemingly embedded in the rock of the promontory itself, with grasses and plants spilling over the edge of the third and uppermost floor. A 'green' house, eco-friendly, one that seemed wholly appropriate despite its disdain of tradition.

After a final reassuring glance through Turner's profile,

Debra seized her courage, took a deep breath and climbed out the car. Halfway to the door a title finally popped into her head: *Carcha*; of course, the artist's name. No other label was necessary.

The door opened while she was still a few paces away, and Turner stood before her, all smiles and charm, just as he'd been at the gallery. "Please, call me Ryan," and she was ushered inside, to gaze around a spacious open-plan living room, minimalist and modern in furnishing and décor. The walls were dominated by ceiling-to-floor windows: vast expanses of glass that must have facilitated spectacular views in the daytime. Double glazed or maybe triple, because inside everything was warmth and calm despite the buffeting winds that were inevitable in such an exposed location.

They sat and sipped from elegant glasses; white wine that was chilled, crisp, and light. At first the conversation was relaxed, with Turner sharing anecdotes about his life as a biologist and within the world of TV. The reason she was here, his artwork, barely getting a mention.

At length he said, "Now, the interview; I presume you'll want to record it?"

"Please."

"That's fine, and you can ask me anything, anything at all."

"Thank you. There is one thing I'd like to know, before we start. Why me?"

"Ah, well." Again that smile, inviting trust and promising reassurance.

"You could have earned a fortune from one of the major glossies," she persisted, "had your pick of interviewers, and yet, you approached me."

"You intrigued me," he said, simply. "At the gallery, I mean. True, I could have gone to one of the magazines, negotiated a lucrative fee for an exclusive, but…" He gestured around the room, "I'm hardly in need of the money, to be frank. The books and TV work have paid well, and now that I've taken a break from them my paintings seem to be doing okay, for the moment at least."

She laughed, on cue.

"Given a choice between spending a few hours in the company of a crusty, cynical reporter who's seen it all before and is inclined to denigrate rather than investigate, or perhaps some gushing sycophant… Given a choice of *that* or an inquisitive and pretty young lady such as yourself…" He shrugged. "You're bright, fresh, hungry, and an opportunity like this might genuinely benefit you rather than becoming just another feather in an already crowded cap. I'm in the privileged position of being able to do whatever the hell I like, as opposed to what the bank balance dictates, and what I like is you."

"Thank you."

"Besides, Dominic vouched for you."

That last caught her by surprise. "*Dominic*? You know Dominic…? And he vouched for me how exactly?"

Turner laughed. "Nothing lascivious, I promise you. Yes, I know Dominic, who doesn't? He merely confirmed that you'd be ideal."

"For what?" And when had he spoken to Dominic – before or after the preview? Had their encounter two nights ago been something other than the fortuitous accident she'd supposed?

He sat forward, eager, excited, almost conspiratorial. "To share with the world what I do, what makes my work so different. You'd like to play a part in that, wouldn't you?"

"Yes, of course," she blurted, caught up in his enthusiasm.

"Good!" And he sprang to his feet. "Then I'll show you. I've a feeling we're both going to benefit from working closely together."

She smiled but didn't otherwise respond, having

concluded at the outset that the little black dress had as much to do with her being here as any altruism on Turner's part.

"Come, come…" He picked up the bottle of wine from the table and gestured for her to follow.

Still clutching her own glass, she scrambled to her feet and hurried in pursuit, as her host strode to a flight of chrome-banistered stairs that swept downwards in a great curve, too gentle and too brief to be considered a spiral. These led to another floor that was clearly beneath the level of the road.

Debra heard water before she saw it, and *smelled* it too: the sea. A great pool occupied fully two thirds of the expansive room they entered; the water level a foot or so below the floor. Rather than being flat and still like a swimming pool, the surface stirred restlessly. She realised too that this was simply a gallery or mezzanine. To one side, a far more modest flight of steps led down to a lower level still, and it was towards this that Turner headed. She hesitated, taking the opportunity to look around. Two easels of differing sizes rested against a wall; there was a long low work table which held a laptop at its centre and a unit of free-standing drawers stacked at one end – they might have housed anything: paints, pallets, brushes – and beside the table a tall cabinet. Dominating the wall above all this was a familiar image.

'Sharkadelic,' she murmured.

Turner paused and looked back. "Yes, this is where I painted it, where I do all my work."

She noticed then that there were windows on the far side of the pool, covered by blinds at this hour. Although the room might be below the road, those windows clearly looked out at something, perhaps granting a view of the sea. Yes, she could imagine that; Turner sitting here gazing out at the ocean with water sloshing directly beside him as he conjured his latest extraordinary composition.

"That's just a copy, of course, a print," he said, coming to

71

stand beside her. "Put up when the original was taken down for the exhibition in London, though that'll be back here soon enough, once the exhibition closes. This is one painting I won't part with, though I still have every intention of producing better."

"I'm sure you will," she said, her eyes lingering on the unsettling, compelling picture.

"I plan to start on a new piece shortly."

"Called...?

"Ah, that would be telling. You could even visit while I work on it, if you like. The first person to ever witness what I do, to be involved in the creative process. Do you think that might interest your readers?"

"Are you serious?"

"Of course."

He laughed and, putting the bottle of wine and his glass down on the table, took her hand, pulling her towards the next flight of steps. She didn't resist; wouldn't dream of resisting. This was another side of Ryan Turner, a gleeful, excited child that nothing in her research had prepared her for.

The steps hugged the side of the pool, which proved to be made of glass, reminding Debra of visits to the aquarium as a kid.

"This is much deeper than you'd imagine," Turner explained. "The tank is connected directly to the sea, though a simple system of airlocks, or waterlocks I suppose in this instance, ensures that the water level isn't dependent on the tides."

"Why go to all this trouble and expense, though?" she wanted to know.

Before he could answer, a great shadow shot past on the other side of the glass. Her mind grasped at familiar possibilities – sea lion, dolphin – rejecting each instantly. She knew at some instinctive level what this was. "Shark!" she blurted.

"Yes!" He laughed, clearly delighted at her reaction. "*Carcharodon carcharias* to be precise, the Great White Shark, King of the Sea – the mightiest, meanest fish in all the oceans."

She stared at him. "And you've brought one here?"

"I didn't bring it anywhere. The great white's been visiting these shores for decades, many a Cornish fisherman will tell you that. It was already here. I simply invited it in."

"But why?"

"For my work, of course. I'll show you."

He led an unresisting Debra back up to the room at the top of the pool.

"This is my secret." Releasing her hand, he went across to the table, opening up and switching on the laptop. "This is how I paint."

Images appeared of the screen, black and white footage that she quickly realised represented a view inside the pool. She watched, a little fearful but fascinated, as something crossed the screen.

"Sharks are remarkable creatures you know, much maligned," Turner said. "If I could erase one thing from the world's social consciousness it would be Spielberg's *Jaws*. That film did sharks a terrible disservice and embedded a fear of them into our cultural psyche, prejudicing us at every turn. *Galeophobia*, we call it. Might as well be *Jawsophobia*."

"You don't think the fear was already present then," Debra countered, "that *Jaws* and its sequels, and *The Reef*, and all the shark-themed schlock horrors that came after them, simply drew on an existing condition, exploiting what was already present for artistic and commercial effect? After all, sharks *do* kill people."

"Artistic?" He snorted. "Please…"

She was conscious of the risk – the last thing she wanted to do was provoke hostility and cause him to clam up – but she was a journalist: he'd presented her with an emotional button that just cried out to be pushed. No point in alienating him, though, so she smiled. "Fair comment. I've seen *Sharknado*."

"Sharks have been around for hundreds of millions of years," Turner said, ignoring her aside, "since long before anything we'd recognise as animals colonised the land. And in that time they've evolved. Slower than we have, perhaps, but they've been at it for a hell of a lot longer. The first examples of what we'd recognise as sharks appeared about 100 million years ago, did you know that? And since then they've diversified without really evolving much further, or so perceived wisdom would have us believe."

"You don't agree?"

"Not for the first time, perceived wisdom is flawed. The 'experts' have taken the broad view. There are some 470 species of shark in the world, each occupying a specific niche, varying in size from the lantern shark at less than twenty centimetres to the whale shark, the biggest fish in the seas, which can grow up to twelve metres or more. We still know very little about many of these species but assume that we do because we know so much about a few of them. In our arrogance, we extrapolate from our limited data to make assumptions about *all* sharks. Look at it this way. If you were to study in detail the evolution of most of the great apes – gorillas, chimpanzees, orang-utans etcetera – and assume this tells you everything you need to know about the evolution of all the apes, how wide of the mark would you be regarding one species in particular: humans? *That's* the trap we've fallen into. There's one species of shark that has developed intellectually far beyond its fellows and far beyond anything we've ever contemplated."

"The great white," she guessed.

"Exactly. All right, so the great white never built cities or cars or planes, or any of the trappings we associate with civilisation – that's not the direction in which its intellect lies and it has no capacity for such things: no feet, no hands, no jointed digits... But it doesn't need them. What a shark *does* need is the intelligence to remain apex hunter in a vast and ever evolving environment, to keep ahead of the game, and that it undoubtedly does possess.

"Are you aware that there's at least one pod of killer whales out there that specialises in hunting sharks, even preying on great whites?"

She shook her head.

"Orcas teach hunting skills to their young, passing specific techniques down through the generations, and this particular pod has developed specialised methods of preying on sharks, which aren't generally a staple of the killer's diet. Instances of them taking out a great white are rare, but here's the really exciting thing: whenever it does occur, every great white in the area vanishes, fleeing that part of the ocean for months, until the shark killers have moved on. You see what that means? Communication; intelligence. This has been known about for years, yet still none of the so-called experts have made the connection; still they fail to realise that here is the ocean's apex intelligence, just as we are the land's. People assume that dolphins are the bright ones, but they're playful, frivolous, capricious. If you want focused intellect then we're talking sharks, and great whites have taken that to a whole different level."

Debra hadn't known what to expect from the interview, but this definitely wasn't it. "And this realisation is what enables you to create your paintings?" she said, wanting to be entirely clear on the point.

"Yes, look." He turned to the laptop again, freezing the image as the shark passed in front of the lens.

She stared, trying to interpret the flat, ill-defined image. There was something odd... "What's that on its head?"

"A neural web." He bent over the keyboard again and the black and white image vanished to be replaced by a vivid scape of coalescing colours, resembling a crude representation of one of Carcha's paintings, an initial draft. "The shark wears the net quite willingly and is now, in effect, communing directly with the computer."

She stared at the screen as comprehension dawned.

"Sharks experience the world very differently from us," he continued. "They share our five senses – smell, taste, hearing, touch, and sight – but in the ocean light and sound move at different angles and speeds than they do through the air. Added to which, sharks have two further senses that we can barely comprehend; they can sense electrical pulses and pick up both vibrations and pressure changes. So a shark's perception of its environment is utterly different from ours; more refined, more complete, more complex."

"And that's what you paint," Debra whispered.

"Exactly!" From somewhere, presumably a drawer or the cupboard, Turner had produced a skullcap of fine gold wiring, which he now fitted over his head while continuing to explain. "The computer records each evolving image as the shark interprets its environment, and by wearing this I can share the patterns as they develop. I paint by a combination of direct organic feed and studying the stored images. Carcha's work represents the first ever collaboration between two different species: a human and a great white shark – the King of the Land and the King of the Sea. That's Carcha's true secret, but who would believe it?"

Debra shook her head. "I had no idea." And he'd chosen *her* to tell the world.

"Of course you didn't, no one does." He took her wine glass, still clutched in her right hand, all but forgotten, and refilled it from the bottle, picking up his own drink and raising it in salute. "A toast: to our new relationship and the work we will produce together."

She sipped, then gulped, reassured by the familiar action and taste.

Turner drifted away, to stand at the lip of the pool.

"There's a whole new world opening up, one that nobody's ever dreamed of before. The paintings are just the beginning. Soon I'll move into video art, interactive experiences…"

Presumably only once he had milked the paintings for all they were worth, and who could blame him? She strolled over to stand beside this man, this visionary, gazing at the water. She wondered what it must be like to wear that gold net, curious to know if it really helped him share a shark's worldview or if this was merely a touch of theatre, the recorded onscreen images providing all the inspiration he needed. One way or another, she determined to don that filigree cap herself and find out. She could hardly claim to be a reporter otherwise. Debra stifled a yawn, the long drive and the excitement of the evening catching up with her; best to go easy on the wine from now on.

Without speaking, Turner slowly put his arm around her. She tensed slightly despite herself but didn't pull away. This was it: the seduction they'd been skirting around since her arrival. She didn't mind and certainly had no intention of throwing away an opportunity like this by spurning him, so she tilted her head, meeting his lips with her own.

To her surprise the kiss was brief, over before it had properly begun. While she was still relaxing into the kiss, Turner pulled away and at the same time… pushed her. No gentle shove, this; caught completely off guard, she found herself flung forcefully out over the water, limbs flailing, wine glass flying from her hand as she fell towards the centre of the pool. Her shocked scream choked off as she hit and coldness enveloped her. She went down, sinking despite her best efforts not to, clawing at the water, dragging herself back towards the surface. Finally her face found air. "You bastard! Help me!"

He ignored her shouts, speaking in the same calm tones she'd heard emanate a hundred times from the TV screen. "The picture will be my masterpiece, the culmination of everything I've worked towards, and you will have made it possible. You asked what it's to be called. I can tell you now: 'Frenzy.'"

She struck out towards the side of the pool, kicking the water desperately, knowing that she wasn't alone in here. Overarm; front crawl, a stroke she hadn't used since uni. Sobs wracked her body but she refused to succumb to terror.

"I've shared the shark's perceptions in so many different moods," Turner continued, as if narrating his latest documentary. "But the most intense, the most glorious, is yet to come." He crouched down to pick up a pole from the lip of the pool. "Can you imagine the wonder of it, Debra? To share the emotions of the ocean's greatest killer as it tears into another sentient being, snuffing out a life with every sense heightened and enflamed by crazed blood lust. To paint *that*…"

He reached out with the pole, jabbing at her, pushing her down and away.

"You can't do this, you can't… For fuck's sake… *Help me!*"

She was forced to stop swimming in order to fend off the pole, but it only caused her head to bob beneath the surface again. The edge of the pool was so close and there was still no sign of the shark. Maybe… "You'll never get away with this!" she screamed as she came up and kicked desperately towards the sanctuary promised by the edge.

"Oh, but I will. The road back from here can be treacherous, especially at night and after a glass or two of wine. I'll be devastated, of course, when the police report hauling your car from the sea at the foot of the cliff. Such a tragedy…"

The pole struck her again, hard against the left shoulder. Prodding, pushing.

"Rejoice, Debra. You're about to be intimately involved in

my greatest work, just as I promised. You'll be immortalised. I'll even dedicate it to you."

Sound ceased as the water engulfed her once more, and a vast dark shape loomed out of the murk.

SHIRLEY

AMY & ANDY TAYLOR

REPORT BEGINS

Porbeagle arrived in good health, though clearly distressed. No existing facilities for sea animals – improvised tank was clearly too small. New blood-based network link-up seemed to take well; within minutes data-bearing corpuscles were sensed making the brain/heart loop. Dr Sands' insights into shark anatomy proved extremely useful in body segment assignment compliant with UN protocol TN4371. Twenty-nine distinct body segments were identified then equipped with required pain sensors, damage inflictors and wire connection points. Simulated activations showed all to be functional in pain delivery and flesh destruction. Animal-to-operator communication coded via new bloodstream uplink. Calibrated at the maximum permitted – one word per minute. Thought-reading and translation software all tested and functioned as normal. Transcript of initial animal to operator communication is shown below. COMMS indicates our message to shark. ANIMAL indicates animal's response.

COMMS	ANIMAL
Safe	Pain
Trust	Anger
Help	Attack

Minute 3 very encouraging. Natural attack instinct seems strong.

NOTE: At this point Dr Sands broke protocol, approached the tank and attempted to communicate with the animal. COMMS operatives left their posts to remove her, leading to one missed communication window. Area of contact between Dr Sands' hand and the shark's head was re-treated to avoid any human DNA contamination. COMMS transcript resumes:

COMMS	ANIMAL
Safe	Hunger
Food	Hunger
(At this point feed introduced via line)	
Trust	Pain
Help	Pain
Safe	Protect
Rest	Pain
(At this point, tranquilizer introduced via line)	
Rest	Sleep

After 3 hrs of tranquilizer-induced rest, first attack scenarios simulated. Response disappointing. No reaction to virtual competing predators (other sharks). No reaction to virtual food prey (smaller fish). Holding pattern of intermittent feeding, rest and repeat attack scenarios put on loop. No change to above results. Due to impending need, Porbeagle cleared for immediate use in transference scenarios."

REPORT ENDS

* * *

DR ROSE SANDS sighed as she bent forward in her chair and stared at the floor of the UK transference situation room. Being at war was distinctly un-warlike. It was more like the last fifteen minutes trading at the portside fish market back in her home town of St Just in Cornwall – a load of tired and irritable people trying to finish an unpleasant but necessary job whilst creating a whole lot of mess. The detritus of computer-based human endeavour lay scattered across the floor – coffee cups, McDonald's wrappers and empty plastic water bottles. And there were wires, loads of them, everywhere.

Up in the transference animation tank, Shirley the shark (Josh had told Rose that they all get nicknames eventually, and they're always alliterative, and always sound completely un-aggressive) was not looking good. Her muscle structure was mainly intact, but bits of flesh hung from her body at regular intervals. Through the gaps in the flesh Rose could just make out the remains of the damage inflictors which had ripped her apart – diode like orbs which would explode to replicate the results of an opponent's attack if it was deemed successful enough by the UN's central monitoring console.

The tiny wires which held them in place and provided the pathways for damage and pain communication, stuck out at odd angles like the bristles at the edge of Rose's kitchen broom. Rose could count at least eight, perhaps ten wires dangling from exploded damage inflictors and she knew Shirley only had twenty-nine in total, spread equally about her body.

How much longer could she last? Rose looked up to the tellcam feed from their opponent's situation room. The American grizzly bear stood tall and strong in its transference animation tank. The team of US operatives looked alert and orderly. Alert and orderly certainly did not describe the depressing scene surrounding Rose.

"You okay, Rose?" Josh whispered as he walked past, his hand brushing her shoulder. Rose looked up, nodded and tried to smile. It was enough reassurance for Josh to continue on his way. As he disappeared into the gloomy throng at the back of the room, Rose thought back to one of the few happy memories of the last few weeks, when Josh and her had found themselves the last two in the bar after post-work drinks, ended up going for dinner, more drinks and chatting for hours. It hadn't quite been a romantic experience, just comforting, a welcome glimpse of human warmth in an otherwise baffling and disturbing introduction to the world of the secret military.

"She could have killed you, you know?" Josh had said to her, a concerned look on his face. "When we'd fitted the sensors and we were trying out comms - one bite and you'd have been a goner. Why did you go up to her?"

The truth was Rose had no idea. She remembered being amazed that she was witnessing an animal's thoughts being flashed onto a screen in front of her. She had loved animals her whole life and chosen marine biologist as her career path. She felt she had understood some animals at fleeting moments but in that second, to actually *know* a shark's thought, and for that thought to be 'Attack'... She should have felt scared; instead she instinctively reached out.

"I don't know, I guess I felt sorry for her."

"But this is the same shark that killed your uncle! We assumed you had it in for her, that's why we dragged you off straight away. We thought you were going to kill her."

"I should never have let you talk me into going after her. Doing all those things to her. Getting involved in *this*."

"I didn't have a choice. Neither did you. Once they throw that line at you – 'Your country needs you' – you can't refuse, and in even talking to them you know too much for them to ever let you get back to your old life."

"Then maybe I should have killed that bloody shark instead of capturing it. Then none of this would have happened."

"Well you might not have saved her for long," Josh had said pointedly. "Britain hasn't won a transference scenario in thirty years. We've tried every native animal with even a hint of fight in it. And now we're pinning our hopes on 'that bloody shark' as you call her. I don't fancy her chances I'm afraid."

Rose could remember that particular conversation word for word. It floated to the top of all the other technical data, protocol and military process she had speed-learned in the last three weeks, with Josh's help. He was only a Transference Tech Op himself, barely two years in, but he knew what Rose needed to learn, he was a good teacher and, Rose suspected at least, a good person.

Sounds of thrashing and groaning snapped Rose out of her reminiscence. Every few seconds Shirley seemed to squirm or spasm in discomfort. She looked like a piñata that was one thwack away from spilling its sweets. To Rose, it seemed an odd way to fight a war, gambling the fate of entire nations on an individual fight to the death between two animals native to their respective countries. But then she'd seen, heard and learnt a lot of odd things in the last three and a half weeks. Just under a month ago, she'd been like every other global citizen, secure in the knowledge that the era of human conflict had passed. That ancient and barbaric concept of taking up arms against another country had withered thanks to over one hundred years of global peace and sustained economic growth.

Now she knew the ugly truth. War was still alive and well, it was just called 'transference' now – the theatre of conflict transferred from observable battlefields to secret situation rooms like the one she sat in, the pain and suffering transferred from humans to the animal kingdom. Every country took part in it, the UN refereed it, and not a single human soul in the world without top-level security clearance, knew a thing about it.

Rose cast her mind back twenty-five days to the moment her state of blissful ignorance had ended. The 12th of January, the day Uncle Frank had died, attacked by a usually docile

Porbeagle shark as he led a deep-sea fishing trip. She had identified the body, and spent barely a day in mourning before Josh had knocked at her door and told her that the next morning she would take him out to capture that same shark, the very same shark she was now looking at with a mixture of disgust and pity. And all because her country needed her.

What Rose needed was a time-out. She clicked her security card against the reader and swung the door open to go and claim her '6 minutes in every 60' break . As she left, Rose looked over her shoulder to glance at Shirley, convinced that it would all be over by the time she got back. As she stepped out of the room there was a mechanical groan as Shirley tensed against the wires holding her in place. It felt like the whole tank, and therefore the whole room, jerked. Rose walked out, head down, straight for the coffee machine.

On her return, a red glow of light seeped out into the corridor from under the situation room door, before receding again. The master alarm. Defeat must be close.

A burly man in khaki camouflage trousers and a green woollen sweater barged past. Ex-army, had to be, thought Rose. Since the disbanding of the armed forces thirty years ago it was now actually an offence to wear military clothing, but Rose suspected no-one was going to tell a man of his physical presence he was breaking a rule, and technically, if he wasn't carrying arms or displaying livery, he was well within his rights to wear green clothes if he wanted to.

Grant, the third transference shift manager (yes, Rose reminded herself, this had this been going on for nearly fifteen hours) swung round.

"Major Franks. I'm glad you're here. What's your strategic analysis?"

Franks sat down, brought his hands in front of his face in a way that could have been almost prayerful, and blew lightly on his first fingers.

"It doesn't look good." He glanced to the tell-cam in the top left camera. Rose's brain went back to Josh explaining this to her in one of their many late-night 'let's turn a marine biologist into a battle operative in little under a week' sessions: "The tell-cam is there to tell you what your opponent looks like. It's an un-hackable feed and a constant static shot. Your opponent has one exactly the same."

"The American bear looks strong. Her paws have sustained damage in defending herself, and her left torso is damaged from Shirley's last attack, but overall the impression is solid. I wish the same could be said of Shirley."

"She's fading, Franks," Grant concurred. "Life signs are fine, feed uptake still within expected boundaries. Technically she's got the strength to fight on, but she doesn't seem to want to. The last few minutes, it's like she's given up."

"What's she saying?"

Grant swung round and pointed to Goodson, on his third straight shift on comms. With a tap of a button, Goodson's personal screen came up on the team display, and the most recent one-word-per minute-instruction/response dialogue popped up:

COMMS	ANIMAL
Feed	Feed
Defend	Tired
Attack	Bite
Attack	Tired
Defend	Scared

"I wonder if the Aussies ever get 'Scared' from one of their Great Whites? It's bloody ridiculous. This is supposed to be a shark!" Major Franks' humour barely disguised his frustration.

"We didn't have long with her, Franks. And we only pulled one out. She might not be the fighting type."

The hotline rang. Another red light, to add to the master alarm. It was like some kind of 1990s Goth-rave, that Rose had vague memories of seeing a documentary about on the History Channel. Red lights, people in combats and industrial groaning sounds coming from the stage.

Poor old Shirley was on her knees, Rose thought to herself. Or at least she would have been had she had knees. It was a vaguely comical thought flashing through Rose's mind but almost as soon as she'd thought it, the wretched sight of the randomly spasming Porbeagle in front of her snapped her back to grim reality. Rose couldn't bear to watch. This wasn't the conservation work she'd always envisaged being her career, in fact this was the exact opposite – extermination.

She felt sick. Instead of helping preserve the life of many animals, she had aided and abetted the unnatural butchering and then long drawn-out slaughter of one specific individual. She felt like she'd failed.

It was time to go. There was nothing more she could do to help and no way she could undo what she and Josh had done.

He looked up and caught her eye. It was as if Josh had heard her think about him. How did he do that?

Rose tried to communicate in one look all the confusion, guilt and sadness within her. It must have worked in some way because Josh couldn't hold her gaze. Subconsciously he was acknowledging his complicity in their crime against the shark in the tank. He looked at the ground, shame-faced, and didn't see Rose turn and head for the door of the situation room.

Another groan echoed across the room. There was no way Shirley could have made that noise, it was a by-product of the beast shifting within its tank, the technical set-up attached to it scraping and tensing in response. Although explainable as a piece of audio, it still sounded sad.

Rose noticed the change of flooring as she crossed the threshold between situation room and corridor – hospital-style flecked lino to call centre-style carpet. Why had she never noticed it before? Perhaps because every other time she'd entered or exited it had been with a specific task, a sense of purpose or excitement. Right now her head hung in defeat.

The door clicked shut behind her. A split second of panicked shouting from inside the room stopped her dead. Then more groaning, first short, then a pause, then long, then short again, each burst building in intensity. More shouting and the sound of rubber soles on lino as the situation room operatives moved with urgency. What the hell had happened? Had the American bear finally got the kill?

Rose burst back into the room and ran back to her station barely five metres from the shark. She couldn't take her eyes off the fading but still beautiful animal in front of her. Shirley's tank sat on a circular mount, and only a few people had clearance to enter the two metre channel running around it. Being the marine expert gave Rose access and she stepped down into it, moving around the tank so that she could see Shirley head-on.

She faced the animal that had taken so much away from her. Her uncle. Her old way of life.

The American bear's attack had paused and there was a stillness and silence in the situation room. Shirley wasn't dead yet, but she was close. Rose looked straight at Shirley and was shocked to once again feel the urge to reach out.

Before she could, Shirley reared out of her tank, ripping out several wires and threatening to tip the whole thing over.

The movement within the room shifted. Rose personified it. She had tried to slip away and now she was back in the room, engaged. Support staff who had probably been looking for a reason to be somewhere else now weren't going anywhere. No one was leaving the room because Britain's shark was fighting back!

Rose positioned herself behind Matt Goodson, Comms Op. Matt's job was to conduct the one word per minute communication allowed between operating team and animal. It wasn't worth trying to manipulate the system; the transference situation rooms around the world were constantly open-uplinked to the UN. Rose wondered to herself if those unknown observers were seeing this.

Shirley arched her back and seemed to stand erect in her tank, primed. Muscles that looked wounded and useless sprung taught. The tightening of fibres pushed bloody fluids into the water of the tank, the seeping red dissolving into pink clouds.

The top of the minute came and Matt inputted his message to Shirley. It had been the same for hours, the same word repeated over and over.

Attack.

It had always been Matt's least favourite part of the process, forcing a dying animal to hasten its own demise on the off chance it might force a deadly mistake from its opponent. Resignation was not an option with this game. As Matt inputted the latest instruction, Rose could read the last few exchanges on his screen:

TIME	COMMS	ANIMAL
21:58	Attack	Tired
21:59	Attack	Tired
22:00	Attack	Pain
22:01	Attack	Pain
22:02	Attack	Threat
22:03	Attack	Defend

As Matt entered the 22:04 instruction it flashed up automatically on the master screen.

Total silence in the room. A pause that seemed too long, far too long. Rose walked towards Shirley's tank. For a moment she felt connected with the wired-up beast before her. Finally the response flashed up.

Attack.

A cheer erupted in the room. Rose looked up to her right and caught Josh's eye. He shook his head and began to smile. This was new territory. Shirley had already survived longer than they had expected and longer than any of the last few British animals to perish in this weird war-game, but this was something different. Shirley was attacking again.

It was unexpected and brilliant. But it made no sense at all. Where had Shirley found these reserves of strength? How had she suddenly developed an instinct to attack?

For the next ten minutes, Shirley unleashed a series of vicious attacks on the American animal. The live stats from the UN started to turn. The American bear's strength was ebbing, its attacks becoming more infrequent and less strategic. Barely believably, Shirley was winning. All the time Rose stood stock still, intermittently feeling that connection to Shirley again and willing her on.

A message flashed up on Rose's mobile: *Mum. Urgent.*

She didn't stop to think. Ever since Uncle Frank's death on the boat, Rose knew not to take any chances. But she couldn't call from the situation room.

She started towards the door. As she did, the latest communication popped up – it would be Shirley's eleventh consecutive attack:

90

TIME	COMMS	ANIMAL
22:15	*Attack*	*Rest*

A few uneasy looks around the room. It was understandable that Shirley would be tired after all these attacks, but there was disappointment that the attack run had ended.

Rose rushed through the door, eager to get her call over with so she could return to the action.

22:16	*Attack*	*Pain*

Josh slammed the desk in front of him. It had been going so well. "Why end your attack now Shirley, when you're finally ahead?"

The next few minutes were filled with regression. Five consecutive minutes without attack. Shirley had lost it again.

Rose walked back in, tucking her mobile back into her pocket as she looked around sheepishly. Her Mum had sobbed down the line to her. When was she coming home? Didn't she realise what she was going through with Frank's death? Rose had to blank out those unanswerable questions and get back to concentrating at the job in hand.

She looked round quickly, trying to assess the various screens to get an update. The comms link was still on the main screen.

22.21	*Attack*	*Attack*

Sighs of relief from around the room. Shirley was attacking again, but there was no discernible pattern to her erratic behaviour and every U-turn cranked up the tension. Josh sprang out of his seat and charged towards Rose. She was taken aback at his urgency, she couldn't remember there ever having been any physical contact between them whatsoever (though she'd often imagined it, but that was a different train of thought altogether). Now he had her by the shoulders and was staring straight into her eyes with conviction bordering on panic.

"It's you Rose, it's always been you!"

Now she really thought she was in one of her odd dreams, the ones that always seemed to have been written by Richard Curtis in full on rom-com mode.

All she could do was shake her head and implore Josh, with her facial expressions alone, to explain what the hell he was talking about. And there were a fair few other people in the room intrigued by this conversation now too. All eyes were on the two of them.

"Shirley's fighting. For you. I don't know why but it's you she's protecting, or it's you who is inspiring her to fight. Whichever way round it is, you're the reason."

Josh stepped back and appeared to calm down. A smirk spread across his face, his eyes flicking left and right as his brain sparked and crackled, and he strode back to his console with a new purpose. Two steps in he spun round and wagged his finger at Rose.

"Whatever you do, do not leave this room."

"Okay, Josh, okay," was all she could muster. From somewhere a chair had appeared behind her. She slumped into it, bemused.

The atmosphere within the room changed. Operatives were suddenly performing their routine tasks with more gusto, processing the information on their screens a millisecond earlier. Comms flashed up on master screen again:

Attack.

Attack.

"Okay, people, we might be on to something. Concentrate.

Do your work. Back her up!" Franks was barking the orders a little louder now. Then, under his breath, but in the silence of combined concentration, audible to everyone, "C'mon, Shirley... C'mon, girl!"

Attack.

Attack.

Shirley was perfectly still. Comms indicated she intended to follow the order to attack but she remained inactive. A few minutes ago it would have led to swearing and slammed down coffee cups. Now it was different. She was waiting. Ready, but waiting.

Then it came. And it was as fierce as it was sudden. Shirley launched forward, stretching her body taught and horizontal, and bit with all her might. Her head yanked from side to side, presumably as the American grizzly tried to stop the frenzied brutal attack. Rose tried to imagine what was going through Shirley's mind as she was fed a virtual image of her opponent direct into her cerebral cortex. Only the next set of comms interrupted Rose's train of thought.

Attack.

Rest.

Collective disbelief. Nothing from Shirley. Another minute passed. Looks started to move towards Rose. Had she moved, breathed, or changed how she was behaving in some subliminal way, and somehow stopped inspiring Shirley?

Comms was due. Now Matt, for the first time ever in a transference final phase, sought guidance. He looked sideways at his commanding officer.

"Franks–" He had hardly begun when the response arrowed back at him loud and direct.

"Order the attack and keep doing it!" Franks barked. "Now!"

Attack.

Attack.

Immediately Shirley sprang back into life. She attacked again. Now her body was almost vertical in the tank. Comms wires and feeding tubes pulled tight and looked like they might even break. Shirley wasn't supposed to physically be able to get into a body position like this, Rose thought to herself.

The freakish movements continued. In a bizarrely human way, she moved her body back and forth, like a heavyweight boxer softening up an opponent with body blows. Then she moved her tail back and brought it forward with such force that the glass tank shuddered and cracked under the impact. The whole room shook.

Technicians with security clearance rushed to the tank – a loss of structural integrity now would be disastrous.

All eyes were on the tellcam feed from America. The figure of a bloodied bear was swaying and staggering.

Franks wasn't whispering now.

"Attack, comms, attack! Finish him, Shirley, finish him!"

Attack.

Rest.

Shirley was still again. Rose started to feel like she could understand her. She was sure that, just like before, she was resting for just a short while before starting another vicious attack. She willed her on.

There was dull thud as Shirley hit the glass wall of her tank, but this time it was the back wall. A glance at the tell-cam showed the American bear lashing out with furious

94

power. Retaliation.

Again Shirley hit the wall, a huge lump of flesh falling off her dorsal fin. Rose could hardly bear to watch, but she had to.

Two, three, four more thuds followed. Shirley was now curled in the bottom left hand corner of her tank, cowering.

Another minute had passed.

Attack.

Pain.

All was silent in the room. Most stared at their screens intently, not wanting to be the operative whose system indicated a loss first. Some glanced at the tell-cam to see the ominous sight of the US bear gathering itself for a final, and likely decisive, attack. No one dared to look at Shirley.

Rose thought back to her Uncle Frank, lying there, peaceful, pale and entirely dead on the quayside at 6.37pm, the exact time she had positively identified him. Now she looked at this creature, this animal being that had savaged her human uncle, that had killed one so dear to her. Now, finally, and only now, it held her sympathy completely, at the moment before its own death.

She forgave Shirley. For whatever reason, she felt sure she had not meant pain on another being, had felt compelled to attack in a misplaced urge to defend. An honourable animal.

Rose got to her feet. Defeat was inevitable, but as her uncle had always said, "Better to die on your feet, than live on your knees."

Rose stood proudly upright but her head remained bowed. She took a great lungful of air, the action forcing her shoulders back and her head up high.

A massive thrashing whirl of noise came from the tank. Shirley sprang from her ball-like retreat and arced into a performing killer whale-style leap. She surged towards the top right corner of her tank. The moment before she reached the tank limit, she yanked her jaw open to its fullest extent then snapped it shut with awesome force. The ferocity threw Shirley forward with such momentum that for a moment it looked like she would escape the confines of her transference tank altogether.

As she hung there, limp from her final exhaustive efforts, the weight of her own body causing the sharp glass edge of her tank to pierce her flank, the live stats from the UN updated.

"Sir, it's a zero reading from America."

"Repeat, monitoring, repeat," Franks spoke calmly, even though the tension in the room was ready to explode.

"Zero reading, sir. It's a kill. Awaiting orange light confirmation only."

No one moved. Rose wanted to go to Shirley but the shared urge to remain perfectly still stopped her.

The orange beacon to the top left of the master-screen lit up. *The* orange beacon, the one that only the UN could trigger in the event of a confirmed kill of your opponent, a confirmed victory for you. The orange beacon that had never ever been lit in this situation room, a fact felt so keenly that the circuitry was checked before every transference, just to make sure that it would actually light up in the unlikely event that it ever needed to.

The room erupted.

Cheers, hugs, papers in the air, and the most incredible noise, far exceeding what forty-three people should be able to make. Josh fell to his knees, his fists shaking in victory, screaming "Yessss!" in a last minute World Cup Final winning goal style.

Franks sank to his haunches in relief.

At first Rose didn't move, then she slowly navigated her

way towards Shirley, stepping round, over and through the scene of raucous celebration.

She reached the tank and stretched her arms up above her head, trying to push Shirley back into the clouded water. Others saw what she was trying to do and helped until they managed to free the shark and Shirley slipped gracefully back into her tank, the fluid surrounding her now more blood and flesh than anything else. She was in a very bad way, but she was alive, and she had won. Britain's new animal had won.

Franks ran towards the tank, radio in hand.

"Vet team, get in here! Save this wonderful beast! Pain relief, now! Get to it!"

Men in white coats burst into the room and made their way towards the tank. Immediately one lobbed a cylinder into it and the whole structure and contents began to freeze. Rose was worried for a second but then relaxed when she saw the relief on Franks' face as he pressed his face against the tank and looked the now motionless Shirley in the eye.

"That's it. You're done, my beautiful girl, you're safe."

After a few seconds he moved away from the tank and climbed on top of the first row of Tech Op desks. Taking a deep breath, he turned to address the room.

"Ladies and gentlemen. Today, we have made history." He shook his head very slightly and gave an almost imperceptible chuckle. "Britain hasn't won a war in thirty years. Our standing in the world has slipped time and again. A once proud country brought to its knees and forced to assume third world geopolitical status. But no more. Because now, Britain has a new animal. Britain has a new hero. You have helped her; you have maintained her and you have supported her. And she's won! She. Has. Won!"

The whole room broke into cheers and applause once more. The hysteria and joy chilled Rose to the core. The limp, pain-ridden, gruesomely injured beast in the tank was a testament to the brutality of this new kind of war. A form of war kept secret by the world to maintain the economically crucial outward appearance of global peace.

Violence and deception. The transference of human aggression and hunger for power on to helpless animals. Rose wanted no part of it. She had reluctantly done her duty to her country, just like poor old Shirley. Now it was time to quit.

She wouldn't even stay for the debrief. She knew how and where Josh avoided the secure exit when he didn't want his absence recorded. She would sneak out while the situation room was still wallowing in this sick victory. Rose started to subtly manoeuvre herself towards the door.

"Please. Quiet, calm down," Franks raised his hands. "There is one person I want to thank especially!" Franks shouted over the hubbub, silencing the room at last.

"Where is she?" Franks scanned the room. "Ah, Dr Sands, there you are."

Rose froze. She looked back at Franks and the whole room looked at her.

"Dr Sands, I owe you an apology. I'd never heard of a British shark. And when I did, I thought it was impossible for a Porbeagle to fight at all, let alone win. But you made it possible. You found Shirley, and taught us how to get the best out of her. Thank you."

Rose smiled weakly and turned to walk away. She felt powerful hands on each arm stop her. The guards from the door had a hold of her. They were looking at Franks for their next instruction.

"You, young lady, are going nowhere. You've got a job for life. Shirley will fight many more battles. And you will be with her, and us, every step of the way. It won't be long until the Prime Minister will adjust our geopolitical strategy now that we have shown we can win. This changes everything."

Shirley, whose movements had slowed as the analgesic

set around her, let out one final haunting groan before she froze solid, ready to be transported, patched up, and re-programmed for the next battle.

Rose looked across the situation room, gazed straight in to Shirley's glassy, apparently soul-less eyes, and began to weep.

DEEP BLACK SPACE

TOBY FROST

"IT'S SUCH A SIMPLE mission that I'm surprised they gave it to us," Isambard Smith observed, leaning across the cockpit. Grimacing, he stretched towards the brass dials that measured distance from Earth in light years. His fingertips almost touched the small jar balanced on the instrument panel. "I mean," he added, "all we do is show up at the space station, receive a progress report from this computer and fly back to base. Easy."

Polly Carveth, pilot and ship's android, shook her head. She didn't look away from the windscreen, in case they hit an asteroid. "Boss, everywhere we go, there's always trouble. It's like we trod in it, and now we're walking it across the carpet. Except our carpet is the size of the galaxy. If it's not your girlfriend getting arrested for possession of stuff to enhance her alleged mental powers, or Suruk trying to collect the postman's skull for his collection -"

"Look," Smith replied, straining even harder towards the jar, "it's very simple. We fly to the research station, Calculus provides us with an explanation of why he's not been forwarding his data to the other logic engines, and then we go back home. I can't see what could go wrong." He lunged at the instruments. His fingertips brushed the jar, and it teetered backward, out of his grip. The glass container struck the floor with a wet crack. Yeast extract dripped out of the fragments. "Bollocks," Smith said. "We're fresh out of Marmite, I'm afraid."

"Hey, guys." Rhianna Mitchell entered the room in a swish

of tie-dyed fabric and unkempt hair, carrying the tea-tray. She was, technically, psychic. Occupying no formal position on the *John Pym*, she had appointed herself "wellbeing counsellor", which had irritated everyone.

"Careful," Smith said. "I just dropped my Marmite. You might want to put your sandals on."

"Oh, okay." She handed out the mugs.

"So," Carveth said, sipping her tea, "this computer - Calculus or whatever he's called. What exactly has he been researching, or is that a secret?"

"Void sharks," Smith replied.

Carveth almost stamped on the brake pedal. "Void sharks? Are you kidding? And we're going there?"

"Now, Polly." Rhianna sat down on one of the emergency seats and began to fuss with her skirt. "Void sharks are remarkable creatures. I've never seen one up close before."

"Now you can," Carveth replied. "So close we'll be able to inspect their tonsils just before they eat us."

"They don't eat people. They eat metal."

Carveth sighed. "Well, good thing we're not in a metal container, isn't it? Like, say, a spaceship?"

Smith blew across the top of his tea and watched the ripples. "The void sharks are getting in the way of the war effort. The damn thinks keep trying to chew up our supply craft – and if the supply ships don't get through, our chaps won't have enough kit to defend the Space Empire against Johnny Alien. If we can devise some way of keeping the sharks at bay, we'll have quite the advantage. The last thing any space captain wants is to discover a shark below his plimsoll line, chomping away at his bilge."

Smith peered at the windscreen. In the darkness of space, something tiny caught the light of the distant sun. "Check our targets, would you?"

Carveth reached up and rubbed at the speck with her

fingertip. It was still there. "That's it."

The space station turned slowly. It was grey, cylindrical, like a stone column with a satellite dish.

"Looks a bit dented," Carveth said.

"Meteor damage, I'd say. It seems to be coated in something, too. Maybe it's shark repellent."

"Yeah? Well, we could use some of that. Look."

The android pointed to the scanner: multiple small blips surrounded the station. Most just hung there, like junk, but the neat way that some of them weaved around, quick and graceful as fish...

"Void sharks," Smith said. He raised the binoculars.

The sharks lurked – waited – outside the station. They looked somewhat like the sharks of Earth, mixed in with eels, missiles and the huge rotary drills used to mine asteroids. At one end, banks of teeth designed to tear through rock and metal; at the other, a biological engine used to blast them through space in search of prey.

"Blimey." Smith glanced at the hunting rifle propped against the wall.

The speakers crackled above them.

"Hail and welcome, visitors," a metallic voice announced. "We shall open the docking bay. Enter, and behold the wonders of our realm!"

"Weird," Rhianna muttered, as the station's bay doors rolled apart.

"The whole place is automated," Smith replied. "Computers get a bit strange if you leave them on their own for too long. Cabinet fever, they call it."

Smith headed to his room. He was just loading the large revolver he carried when visiting the more obscure parts of the Space Empire – a Markham and Briggs Civiliser – when he heard a small cough behind him.

Turning, he saw Suruk the Slayer in the doorway. The alien lowered his hand from his mandibles and smiled. "Sharks and robots," he said. "It is not unlike my last birthday."

"I suppose so. But this time you're not supposed to be fighting any of them. Do you really need to bring that spear?"

"Of course. I would feel under-dressed without it. Just out of interest," Suruk added, "do void sharks have skulls?"

*   *   *

THE OUTER AIRLOCK closed behind the *John Pym*. Steam blasted from the inner airlock and two huge pistons drew the doors apart. Smith and his crew stepped into the foyer.

The hall was large and, for a space station, airy. Columns held up the vaulted ceiling. Pot plants stood against the walls, a sign of the quality of the processed air. But the hall ought to have been decorated in the colours of the Space Empire; polished brass and British racing green.

"It's been sprayed white," Carveth said.

"Perhaps they had the decorators in," Smith replied. He walked forwards, uneasy, suddenly aware of the gun at his side. "I'd have expected a welcoming committee, too."

"Look," Suruk said. He pointed with his spear.

A large banner hung from one of the pillars. It depicted four crossed lightning bolts on a purple background, zigzagging from the centre towards the corners. Beneath it were four letters: SRQC.

"What does that say?" Rhianna asked.

"Surquck, obviously," Smith replied. "Damned if I know what it means, though."

"Hands up!"

Smith whipped around. A robot stepped into view from behind a pillar, a Stanford sub-machine gun in its metal hands.

Suruk's spear flew out, hit the droid in the chest and clattered off its metal carapace. Smith went for his pistol.

"Freeze!" Something jabbed him in the back. A shadow fell over Smith's body. He stopped, grimaced, and slowly raised his hands.

The first robot walked forwards, covering them. Someone had given it a set of bizarre additions. It wore a kilt made of red material, and its chest-plate had been polished to a mirror-like shine. The machine bore the brush attachment from a vacuum cleaner soldered to the top of its head. The stripe of bristles looked like a Mohican.

"Well, well," the robot said. "Humans. What shall we do with you?"

"Bugger," Smith said.

"I shall process your suggestion."

"Arse," Smith muttered.

"Stop saying rude words!" Carveth snapped. "You're just making it worse!"

"Suggestion processed." The robot shook its crested head. "That does not compute. You must be taken to our leader for judgment."

"Your leader? Good," Smith said. "That's an excellent idea. Lead on, my good man."

The second robot prodded him in the back. "Walk."

*   *   *

THEY WALKED INTO the station, a robot in front of and behind them. The open hall gave way to a maze of corridors, all of them painted white. Jagged grey streaks had been drawn down several of the walls. For a moment, Smith thought that they were more lightning bolts, and then he realised that it was a crude attempt to imitate marble.

"You know," Polly Carveth said, "there must be somewhere

in the galaxy that isn't full of nutters. Surely, somewhere, something sane is going on."

"Really?" Suruk had been quiet, his shrewd eyes studying the machine walking in front of them. "I never seem to find it."

"That's because you *are* a nutter, Suruk."

Rhianna said, "That's not very kind, Polly. I'm sure we can sort this out. Maybe if we just focus on the positive aspects of our experience -"

"Like what?"

She frowned. "Well, I've not seen much litter."

"Silence, fleshlings!" the lead robot barked. Its crest was not very well-secured, Smith noticed; turning round nearly made the thing fall off. The funny thing was, he thought, that its bizarre outfit seemed oddly familiar, as if it was dressing up as something that he had seen before.

"Don't worry, crew," Smith said. "I'm sure there's a perfectly simple explanation for all this."

The lead guard stopped at a pair of doors. "Our master sits within," it said. "Behold."

It pressed the button, and the doors rolled apart.

They walked into a massive chamber. The walls were white, the floor chequered with tiles. The long side of the room was hidden by heavy drapes, apparently stitched together from a variety of laundry. On the far wall, somebody had spray-painted a mural, showing an eagle riding a void shark.

The logic engine stood in the centre of the room, facing the drapes. It looked like a matt-black, armoured loaf of bread slightly smaller than a railway carriage. That was to be expected. What Smith had not expected was the bedsheet pinned to the front of the casing and arranged to resemble a toga, or the hundred green data cartridges glued into a circlet and placed on top of the computer like a laurel wreath.

Slowly, the engine turned on tiny wheels to face the newcomers.

Speakers crackled into life on the front of the logic engine. "Visitors at my court! And who might you be, perchance?"

"Captain Isambard Smith and crew. We're here to speak to the logic engine Calculus about progress in the void-shark operation."

"Then I must disappoint you," the speaker said. "Calculus is dead. You stand in the glorious presence of Caligulator, divine Emperor of all space!"

"Er, what?"

"I am Caligulator. This is my throne room."

Smith swallowed hard and tugged his red jacket down. "Now look here! This is all terribly amusing, I'd sure, but the party's over, Calculus. You suffered asteroid damage while carrying out a research project about taming void sharks for military use. Your status report is six weeks overdue and, frankly, the chaps back at base are not impressed."

"Interesting," the computer replied. "That's more or less how I remember it too, except for a few details."

"Those being?"

"That my mother was a swan and my father was the god Zeus in the form of a talking bullock, and that I was set upon the world to usher in a new golden age. Otherwise, you're pretty much spot on."

Smith decided not to comment on talking bullocks. Instead he said, "Really."

"And, with the help of my guards and my Imperial Navy, I will purge space of barbarians."

"*Your* navy?"

The drapes rolled back, revealing a huge window. It looked straight out into space. In the distance, one of the system's suns flared. About a hundred yards from the glass, several dozen void sharks hung motionless, waiting.

"My navy," Caligulator declared. "Commanded by Admiral Sharkulus. Guard! Hail the admiral."

The robot guard stared out of the window. "I am experiencing difficulties executing that command, Emperor." It pointed. "Is that one Sharkulus?"

"No. See the one on the left – not that one – the other one. *He's* Sharkulus."

The guard waved. Sharkulus did not respond. Either Caligulator had got the wrong void shark, Smith thought, or Sharkulus lacked arms and the right sort of brain to respond, on account of being a shark.

Caligulator turned to face Smith. "The void sharks agreed to join my empire and fight for the cause of Empire, you see."

Rhianna put in, "You mean you can communicate with them?"

"Well," Caligulator replied, "they didn't say no."

Smith glanced over his shoulder at his crew. Rhianna was frowning, hand half-raised to her temple. He wondered whether she was attempting to use her psychic abilities. Carveth had started chewing her lower lip, and appeared to be trying to will herself to disappear. Suruk just came across as mildly entertained.

The doors through which they had entered were now firmly closed, and flanked by another pair of guards crudely decked-out as centurions. Smith saw that, across the metal, someone had painted the words Sharki Robotique Caligulator. *The sharks and robots of Caligulator*, he translated, noting that Caligulator had foolishly failed to put his name into the genitive case - conclusive proof that he had thoroughly malfunctioned. Smith turned back to the logic engine.

"So," Smith said, "let me recap. You have violated your programming and become convinced that you are a Roman emperor, which for some reason has inspired you to grant citizenship to the void sharks."

"Absolutely."

"Well then." Smith glanced at his crew. "You see, chaps? I

told you that there was a simple explanation. It just happens to be a demented one."

Caligulator said, "Oh, barbarians?"

"Yes?" Suruk replied.

"Don't admit it," Smith whispered. "You'll only encourage him. I'll deal with this. Diplomacy is required."

He took a step forward and put his hands on his hips. "Computer, shut up. You're got a damned cheek telling me what to do. I am an officer of the British Space Empire, and therefore incapable of being a barbarian. You, however, are not only a machine but, given your resistance to us, clearly some sort of villainous foreigner. I warn you, stop your nonsense right now, my good fellow, or you will live to regret it."

"An interesting point," Caligulator replied, "and validly made. On the other hand – guards, seize them!"

*　　*　　*

THE GUARDS DISARMED Smith and his crew, before leading them into a long chamber. It seemed to have been an observation room, long ago, but now it was full of old crates and broken machinery.

Smith looked out of the viewing window. The void sharks were motionless. Seen close up, they resembled nothing so much as torpedoes, but at this distance, they were more like a boxful of scattered cigars.

He wondered what they were thinking. Maybe Caligulator was right, somehow; perhaps they could be spoken to. But was it worth speaking to anyone who considered a loony like Caligulator to be a friend?

"Rhianna," he said, "could you make psychic contact with them?"

Rhianna nodded. Closing her eyes, she pushed her messy

hair out of the way and pressed her fingertips to her temples. She made a low humming noise, as if tuning up.

Smith, Suruk and Carveth leaned closer, like a family around a wireless set, to see what she might pick up.

"Got anything?" Smith asked.

"The signal's pretty dim," she replied, not opening her eyes. "But so are they."

"What are they thinking about?"

"Eating."

"Can you contact them? Maybe try to get them on our side?"

"Okay." She paused, frowned, moved her jaw as if chewing the cud, and said, "Cool. I've told them that we are here, and that we mean them no harm and come in peace."

Smith nodded. "So what're they thinking about now?"

"Eating us."

Carveth shook her head. "Oh, great. Couldn't you – I don't know – send them somewhere else? Tell them that there's some tasty metal at the heart of the sun. That sort of thing."

"I don't think they'd understand," Rhianna replied. "Too many syllables."

"Well, seeing how they appear to speak English, it's worth a try."

Suruk stood up and paced to the window. He stared out, his small, hard eyes and polished tusks reflecting against the glass. "To think of it," he mused. "All they do is fight, eat and destroy. What an existence." He sighed. "And I am cooped up in here. Most unfair."

Carveth looked at him. "You admire them, don't you?"

"I admire their purity," Suruk replied. "Survivors, unclouded by conscience, remorse or delusions of morality. They also have nice fins."

Smith leaned forward. "Look here, old chap, that's no way to talk. We're far better. Firstly, they're lower life forms.

Secondly, they've not got any legs. And thirdly, we're British, damn it!"

"True. They would make good prey, though."

Smith stared glumly at his boots. There had to be a way out of this mess. His face stared back from the polished toecaps, looking bewildered.

Something caught his eye, a twinkle of metal next to his heel. He bent down and found a screwdriver beside his foot. "Now this might come in handy," he said.

Carveth stared at him. "How? These are combat robots, not toasters. You can't just twiddle Caligulator's screws and hope his batteries fall out."

"That's as maybe" - Smith stood up - "but damn it, we have to try. I'll defeat this mad computer and his army of sharks if I have to stick my arm up his disk drive and unscrew his frontal lobes! Assuming computers have those."

* * *

CALIGULATOR WAS ADMIRING the void sharks when the guards brought Smith and his crew back to the throne room. At least, that was what Smith thought he was doing: since neither the computer nor the sharks had anything much like a face, it was hard to tell. At any rate, Smith was pretty sure that the end of Caligulator with the laurel wreath was his front: even Nero hadn't stooped low enough to garland his own arse, which would have required a fair amount of stooping. It was much easier to deal with the Empire's more powerful supercomputers, such as Thomas the Difference Engine, who at least had a large grey smiling face at one end.

Caligulator rotated slowly on his little wheels. "I have made my decision, barbarians. You are to be given such armaments as befit you, equipped with space suits – adorned with metal, naturally - and cast from the airlock into the arena, by which I mean space. There, you shall amuse us with your combat against my army of void sharks – for a while. Like a French cinema enthusiast, the last thing you see will be a great big 'Fin.'"

"Damn you," cried Smith. "You violate your programming, you turn against the Space Empire, and now you mention France? By God, sir, you will pay."

Suruk shrugged. "It could be worse, old friend. I believe it was Oscar Wilde who observed that if there is one thing worse than fighting sharks in space, it is not fighting sharks in space."

Carveth sighed. "I really hope you've got a good idea of where to put that screwdriver," she whispered. "Because if not, might I suggest a location?"

Slowly, Caligulator turned about five degrees on his castors, so that he addressed Carveth. "To you, however, I have decided to show mercy. As an android and hence the descendant of a machine, you have Roman blood, and hence must be regarded as a citizen instead of a barbarian."

"Great!"

"Which makes you a traitor. In the spirit of mercy, you will be married to the Emperor Caligulator. You will have the honour of feeding me grapes, or, in the event of a shortage, ball bearings. Lucky you, to sit beside someone as great as I! Perhaps I should copy my hard drive, just so I can experience that privilege myself."

*   *   *

"MOVE IT," THE centurion growled, as it nudged Smith into the airlock at gunpoint.

The three of them wore space suits. At the best of times, British Space Armour resembled a cross between a Victorian diving suit and a set of cricket pads. Caligulator's minions had welded crests to the helmets, giving them a reasonable resemblance to the armour of a Myrmillo gladiator. The look was completed with a makeshift trident, assembled from an aerial and a snooker cue.

Fat load of good that'll do, Smith thought.

He turned to the centurion. "Come on, this really isn't necessary, you know."

"You know, you're right," the robot replied. "Caligulator has gone completely mad. This shark-gladiator battle does not compute."

"Really?"

"Of course. Anyone sane would just shoot you instead."

Smith had a nasty feeling that, behind its metal faceplate, the robot was smirking at him.

The airlock slammed shut. Rhianna checked her helmet seal, and then Suruk's. A light flashed in the wall like a winking eye.

Suruk turned to Rhianna. "Your weapon, please – unless you have decided to take up the path of the warrior."

She passed him her makeshift trident. "There must be a way to do this without violence."

At the end of the corridor, the doors rolled apart. "I always thought that the end of my life would involve sharks," Suruk said. "But this is not quite what I had imagined."

"No?" Smith replied.

The alien shook his head. "I thought I would end up riding several of them into the sun. Oh well."

He pushed off, sliding through the vacuum towards the end of the airlock. Smith held out his arm, and Rhianna took his hand. Together, they followed Suruk into space.

Suruk caught the edge of the airlock and swung himself back onto the edge of the station. He held out his spear. Rhianna grabbed it and he pulled them back against the metal. Their boots were magnetic: although the outside of the station was coated in anti-shark paint, the magnets were strong enough to hold them in place.

Smith looked up at the side of the station. Caligulator was just behind the window, flanked by guards. At his wheels lay an array of mechanical objects – toasters, power tools, medical gear and what looked like a small oven. Carveth sat despondently among them, dressed in a sort of toga. Smith deduced that this array of junk constituted Caligulator's harem.

His radio crackled. "Friends," Suruk said, "we are not alone."

Flares of light in the depths of space winked out like little stars. They were the biological thrusters of the void sharks. "To battle!" Suruk growled.

"Wait," Smith replied. "I'm having an idea."

They waited. The sharks swung out on a wide angle, like a fighter wing moving into attack position.

"I've finished having my idea now," Smith said. "Listen, it's useless for Rhianna to contact them. But what if you were to relay Suruk's mind at them? He might be able to reach their level. After all, they're bloodthirsty carnivores, and he's a... noble warrior."

"Okay," Rhianna said, "think of something, Suruk."

"Hmm," Suruk replied.

Rhianna jerked violently, and she nearly floated off. "Could you think that a little less strongly? All those severed heads... It was kind of vivid."

"Well," Suruk said. "Perhaps I should be more subtle for our audience of ravenous space sharks. Which, incidentally, are closing in. It appears that we have attracted their attention."

Smith peered into space and saw that Suruk was right; the void sharks were closing. It was time to take command. He tried to give both members of his team a stern look, but his space helmet made that difficult. Instead, he slid the screwdriver out of his belt.

"Send them towards me," he said. "Suruk, think like they do. Tell them that we're sharks too."

The airlock door had been painted with the same thick repellent as the rest of the station, but the hinges had become chipped with use. He ducked down and drove the screwdriver into the gap, trying to push it under the paint.

His helmet speakers crackled. "I'm sending them your way," Rhianna said. "Yes, they're definitely coming towards you... right now!"

Smith's back prickled. He wanted to turn round, to see how close the void sharks were, but there wasn't time. The screwdriver slipped and slid free. He snatched it out of the vacuum before it could float away.

He stabbed again at the hinges. The screwdriver slid under the thick paint, up to the hilt. Smith levered it up and a chunk came away like a shard of glass; a black wedge of rubbery dried paint slowly spinning away from the station.

Metal gleamed underneath. Smith jabbed furiously as if he'd struck gold.

"Er, they're really close," Rhianna said.

"Just a second," he called back. More metal appeared. "I'm nearly -"

Rhianna cried out. Something hit Smith in the side, knocking him away. He flinched – saw that it was a pool cue – and a long grey body drove into the airlock door like a missile. The void shark thrashed. Sparks flickered around its mouth.

Rhianna bounced along the side of the station. She grabbed Smith's hand and pulled him close.

"They're ignoring us," Smith said.

She nodded inside her helmet. "I told them to go for the airlock instead."

Smith discovered that he was panting for breath. He was covered in sweat. "Suruk, did you throw a snooker cue at me?"

The alien shrugged. "Only in a friendly way."

* * *

"WELL, THIS IS most entertaining," Caligulator said. "Do we have any stuffed dormice?"

He squeaked around on his castors. "No? Oh well. I doubt the gladiators will last much longer anyhow. They'll probably plead for mercy any time now." He sighed. "It's at moments like these that I wish I had thumbs."

The sound of the void sharks hitting the wall rang through the throne room like a distant explosion. For a moment, there was silence. Carveth sat in Caligulator's shadow, frozen with anticipation.

And then the sound came; a drilling, scraping sound. Teeth grinding on metal. They were tearing their way inside. She looked up, suddenly cold.

"Emperor?" one of the bodyguard robots said. "Er, Caligulator? I have detected a class two threat." The scraping grew louder. "Make that class one."

"Well," Caligulator declared, "we can't have that! Lutebot, play a melody to sooth my audio pickups. My games must not be disturbed by the plebs!"

"You idiot," Carveth cried. "They're tearing their way inside! The void sharks are eating through the hull!"

"And who asked you?" Caligulator demanded. "I am an emperor. You are a dancing girl. Go on – dance, while I, er... emp."

"Right," Carveth said. "Great idea." The scraping grew louder. The lutebot turned its own volume up. Carveth bent down, pushed her way through the various objects and implements that Caligulator had married – among other things, he had a wife made entirely from forks – and came up with a thick cable. She heaved it across her shoulders.

"Oh-ho!" Caligulator cried. "A snake-dance!"

"No, it's your power lead," Carveth said. "And I'm going to bloody strangle you with it."

She leaped at him. It was only then that she realised the flaw in her plan. Not only was the lead too short, but Caligulator didn't have a neck.

* * *

SMITH TRIED TO direct the void sharks at the airlock controls, but there was no point: they simply tore straight through the metal. Acidic dribble weakened the steel, and rows of diamond-hard teeth finished it off. Half a dozen sharks thrashed at the airlock now, desperate to get in and feed on the metallic delicacies within.

"That's it!" Smith cried. "Bite down on that, Caligulator!"

A plume of air burst from the airlock. The void sharks had chewed through. It was decompressing. The hole widened, and one of the long, grey bodies slipped into it, wriggling into the inner airlock.

"Aha," Suruk said. "My turn." He grabbed the nearest shark, shoved it out of the way and clambered into the hole. He was lost from view for a moment, and a second later, the outer airlock slid apart. Air and scraps of broken metal shot out into the void.

"What now, friends?" Suruk called.

"Now? I'm going back inside," Smith said. "I'm going to find Caligulator and reboot his mad metal arse straight out into space."

"Hmm," Suruk replied. "With all these sharks around, I fear we are going to need a bigger boot."

"We'll see about that!" Smith replied, and he reached out

to the controls for the inner airlock.

"Er, guys?" Rhianna said.

Smith paused and looked round. "Yes?"

Rhianna frowned. She shook her helmeted head. "Sorry. I've forgotten."

"Not to worry. Let us know when you remember. Now, chaps – and void sharks – for the Empire!"

He pulled the airlock lever. The inner doors rolled apart, and the void sharks shot into the aperture.

As one, the sharks fell to the floor. Smith stood over them, bewildered. They lay on the linoleum of the entrance hall, wriggling but unable to move.

"I've remembered it now," Rhianna said. "I was going to say 'But what about the artificial gravity?'"

*   *   *

CARVETH REALISED THAT she was not going to be able to strangle Caligulator. Suddenly, she was painfully aware that she was standing up, surrounded by enemies, shouting abuse and holding a completely useless weapon.

"What's happening?" Caligulator demanded. "Why are the void sharks trying to get in?"

One of his guards looked round. "They, ah, want an audience with you, Emperor."

"Nonsense. Those plebeians? What is – wait, is my new handmaiden trying to escape?"

The guard said, "All data confirms that theory, great one."

"Well then, apprehend her!"

A robot centurion stepped closer. Carveth yanked the cable as hard as she could. It came away in her hand. An alarm sounded.

"Get her!" Caligulator cried. Clearly, Carveth had not found his power cable.

The centurion reached forward, and she bashed him with the plug end across his upturned bucket of a head.

"Yeah!" she cried. "I'm a newer model than you!"

The robot lunged at her. While strong, it was slow. She slipped aside, not quite falling over her own toga, and hit it on the head again. The robot stumbled and she shoved it away.

To her astonishment, it floated upwards. The guard rose lazily towards the ceiling, limbs flailing. Then she realised that other things in the room were no longer connected to the floor, herself included.

"Warning," a voice said over the intercom. "Warning. Artificial gravity system – unplugged."

*   *   *

THE VOID SHARKS rose from the ground. They plunged thrashing into the station's interior, and Smith, Suruk and Rhianna followed them. A robot guard floated into the corridor, raised its gun but was knocked back by half a dozen sharks before it could fire. In moments they devoured the guard, his weapon, and the floor he had been standing on.

"We have to find Polly!" Rhianna cried. "They're going to eat the whole station!"

"As long as they don't think we're part of it," Smith replied.

Emergency lighting came on, strobing red and green: Smith wondered how the hell that was meant to help anybody. A siren howled. Steam, for reasons unknown to him, vented loudly from the floor as they bounded towards Caligulator's throne room.

"Listen," Rhianna called. "Stop, guys. I heard something."

They halted. Smith twirled the dials on his suit's chestplate, which made him look as if he was trying to pick up a radio signal with his nipples. Faintly, he could hear a small, high-pitched voice: "Oh, bollocks, I can't stop! Get off my toga, you metal bastard – I can taste my breakfast!"

"I would recognise that whining anywhere," Suruk declared. "Carveth is near!"

They turned right, towards the sound. Grinding, creaking noises issued from deep below in the guts of the station.

Smith threw open a door and was confronted by a truly surreal sight. In front of a long window, like a mixture of drunken mermaid and foul-mouthed cherub, Carveth swirled in mid-air. Her makeshift toga fell apart around her, revealing her overalls. Weapons floated around her loose hair, and Smith recognised them as his own.

Suruk and Rhianna helped stabilise Carveth.

"Thank God you're here," she gasped. "I started spinning and couldn't stop. I thought I was going to puke – and in zero grav, that's not good. This place is coming apart," she said. "They're chewing through the blast doors as fast as they can close them. I thought I saw space suits further up."

"Suruk?" Smith said.

"Gladly," the alien replied. He bounced up the corridor, and out of sight.

At the edge of Smith's vision, a door swung on its hinges. A long grey wedge pushed it open, like the tip of a battering-ram. It was the nose of a void shark, striped with old scars and covered in dents.

"No you don't," Smith said. He raised his Civiliser, cocked the hammer, and fired.

The bullet tore a groove along its nose. The beast thrashed, and in a second it had disappeared.

Suruk bounded into the far end of the room. His right hand gripped his spear, and the left carried the severed head of a void shark. He looked like something from the deep ocean, some man-frog on the attack. There was a space suit under his arm.

"Time to depart," he said.

Carveth scrambled into the suit. Objects sailed out from the station; junk and torn metal. Bits of robot drifted away, whirling end over end.

"Good riddance!" Carveth cried as she fastened her helmet, and then the *John Pym* drifted past. "Bloody hell, that's our ship!"

"You're right," Smith said. "Men, this calls for desperate measures. We're going to have to engage in physical contact. Link arms, chaps."

They grabbed each other.

"Hold on tight," Smith said, raised his pistol, and shot the glass.

They flew out into space like a pip from a squashed lemon. The room behind them depressurised, sending a shower of glistening debris after them in their wake. For a moment, as they soared out, Smith was awed by the cold beauty of space, the vast desolation of the void. And then he smacked into the side of his spaceship.

* * *

"NO!" CRIED CALIGULATOR. "You cannot attack your emperor! I am a god! Can't you see how divine I am?"

The void sharks, tiring of stainless steel, tore into his casing, eager to get at the brasswork inside.

"I forbid it! Sharkulus, tell your minions to desist. Sharkulus? I'm talking to you. No, not you. Him. He's Sharkulus. No, wait, *he's* Sharkulus -"

As the void sharks tore open his casing, Caligulator did one final calculation. On the variables before him, he concluded, two statements of fact could be drawn: firstly, that he was still the god of space and, secondly, that the void sharks didn't give a toss.

* * *

THE *JOHN PYM*'s thrusters fired, and the ship left the ruins of the station to the sharks. The station hung in a twinkling cloud of torn metal, its steel skeleton dwindling by the minute.

The intercom squealed. "Get off!" Caligulator cried. "That's my memory bank – don't eat that – now, where was I?"

"Blimey," said Carveth.

"Yeah," Rhianna added. "That's like, really bad."

"Shark!" the intercom cried. "Everybody out of the water. I – I've got a lovely bunch of coconuts…."

"They're eating his brain," Carveth said.

"His brain went a long time ago," Smith said. He sighed and turned off the intercom. "A bad business, chaps. I think there's a lesson in this for all of us."

From the back of the cockpit, Suruk said, "Indeed. Even in space, there is always room for a spear."

Rhianna said, "I've learned that sharks have feelings too. Except that they're all angry feelings."

"How's about this for a moral?" Carveth replied. "It's called a void shark because you're meant to avoid it."

"Actually," Smith added, "I would say that the real lesson was, if you are a giant computer, don't go mad and try to take over the galaxy with an army of sharks. Not a very useful lesson, but a lesson nonetheless."

He shook his head sadly.

"Space is a harsh, dangerous place. Sometimes, in the cold darkness between the stars, the only certainty is death. *And* we've run out of Marmite."

The Shark in the Heart

DAVID TALLERMAN

"Is it a puppy?"

"It's not a puppy," his dad admitted.

"Oh." He'd been hoping for a puppy; a puppy had long been on the cards. But he wouldn't be disheartened. A new pet was still good news. It wouldn't be a cat, because his mum was allergic to cats. He was sure it wouldn't be a lizard or a snake. "Is it a rabbit?"

"It's not a rabbit. It's something better than a rabbit."

That just brought him back round to a puppy. "I give up," Noah said.

"Then come and look," his dad told him.

They trooped out through the patio doors and down the path towards the end of the garden. Noah's eyes roved for a hutch, a tank, a kennel (it wouldn't be a kennel), any indication of what his new pet might be. The garden was undisturbed - everything was where it had always been, except that now that he looked he noticed a wet patch near the rock garden where water had sloshed over the grass.

At that, his heart began to sink. By the time he had reached the pond, the enormous pond his dad had laboured over two years ago and then never got around to filling, he knew exactly what to expect. Moving his feet was like dragging two weights.

Fish were not better than a rabbit. He didn't understand how his father could imagine such a thing. Fish were the worst of pets, except maybe for snails. But he didn't want to be ungrateful. Perhaps if he took care of the fish then a puppy would come in time. Wasn't that how adults thought? If you could keep a fish alive then you could keep a rabbit alive and then maybe a cat (but not a cat) or a dog.

"That one looks different from the others," he said.

He had observed this fact without noticing it at first, but it was quite true. One of the six fish was unlike the other five.

"They're koi," his father said. "They come from Japan."

"Not *that* one."

Five of the fish were as long as the distance between Noah's hand and elbow, with red splashes like the skin of the girl in the year below whose house had burned down, and surprisingly ugly faces. The sixth was sleeker, larger, slate grey, with jaggedly protruding fins.

"That one *does* look different." His father looked puzzled for a moment. Then his doubts vanished into a grin. "Aren't they great?" he said.

*   *   *

IT TOOK THE sixth koi, the koi that was not a koi, less than a week to eliminate its pond-mates. They never found the bodies. Noah, who had been watching a lot of crime dramas on TV that week, suspected that maybe the sixth fish had buried them. He liked the idea. Now that he had only one fish, that one deserved the rank of pet, and he wanted his pet to be as ingenious as possible.

His dad, however, was less comfortable with the sudden

wave of violence that had engulfed their garden. "That was three hundred pounds of carp," he complained.

This seemed a lot of money to Noah, who had to bite his tongue not to point out that the dog rescue centre gave away puppies for free. "Maybe it's better to have one really awesome fish than six fish that are just okay," he pointed out instead.

The look his dad gave him said he didn't agree. "I didn't think koi are supposed to eat other koi."

"We should ask my sister," Noah's mum said. Noah's mum's sister had emigrated to Australia to get married, and now worked in a zoo.

"Doesn't she look after monkeys or something?" Noah's dad asked.

"It's a zoo. And they live near the coast. I think I heard somewhere that more people get attacked by sharks in Australia than die in car crashes."

"It's *not* a shark," Noah's dad said, and there was sharpness to his voice, as though it was something they'd already been discussing.

"A shark would be cool," Noah said, quietly and mostly to himself.

* * *

"HOLY *SHIT*," NOAH's mum's sister said, "I think that's a shark."

Then she looked guilty for having said 'shit' in front of Noah, although he was standing out of her view. Noah's mum had Skyped her sister and then they'd carried the laptop into the garden. Currently Noah's mum was holding it with the camera pointed at the murky water and the sleek creature knifing back and forth beneath its surface.

"It can't possibly be a shark," Noah's dad said, speaking loudly so that the microphone would pick up his voice. "The man who sold me it said it was a koi carp."

"I know what carp look like," Noah's mum's sister said, "and that isn't any carp."

"I don't think it could be a shark," Noah's dad said. But he didn't sound confident anymore.

"That would be the coolest thing ever," Noah suggested.

"Take some photos," Noah's mum's sister said. "I'm sure I can find someone here who knows more about it than I do."

* * *

LATER THAT DAY they got an e-mail from Noah's mum's sister. The title read simply: *URGENT!!!!!*

The e-mail read, "I asked Josh our marine expert and he says it absolutely definitely is a shark. You should call the police or something. Be really careful!"

"Oh my god!" Noah's mum said.

"It can't be a shark," his dad said, but without conviction.

"She's right," Noah's mum said, "we need to call the police."

"And tell them what? That I tried to buy koi carp and accidentally got a shark instead? They'll think I'm crazy. Or an idiot."

"Who *cares* what they think? We can't have that thing swimming about in our back garden. Maybe it's even illegal. We don't want to get into any trouble."

"You mean, more trouble than having a shark in our garden?"

As he'd listened to them talking Noah had felt something building inside of him, like a tiny storm brewing, and now he realised it was going to come out, whether he wanted it to or not. He hardly recognised his own voice as he sobbed, "Please, please, please don't call the police! Rover's my pet, you *can't*! They'll take him or away or shoot him in the head or..."

Noah's dad looked at him. "You called him Rover?"

"That's his name," Noah argued, trying not to snuffle. Fat tears were dripping down his cheeks, and he brushed them away with his sleeve, for his mother had told him frequently that tears did not win arguments.

"Look," Noah's dad said, in his most reasonable voice, "there's no reason it shouldn't be safe. We just all have to be careful not to fall in. Anyway, lots of species of sharks aren't dangerous to people. I read somewhere that most sharks are more scared of us than we are of them."

Noah's mum made the sighing sound she sometimes made then, the one that said she was tired of discussing something, and what was the use anyway when her husband was basically so unreasonable. "I think this is a very bad idea," she said. "Let's sleep on it."

* * *

WHEN A WEEK went by and they were still sleeping on it, Noah reasoned that somewhere along the way a decision had been made, and that it was a decision in his favour. That his father had begun buying fresh meat from the butcher's on the high street and throwing it hesitantly into the pond seemed to support this theory. Rover was staying.

Only then did Noah feel ready to announce his new pet at school. It would have been humiliating to tell everyone he had a shark, only for said shark to have vanished by the time he got home. The wait had given him time to plan his announcement for maximum effect. He started with his handful of close friends and let the rumours radiate out. He was careful not to exaggerate, trusting to the facts. By the end of the day, people he didn't know, even kids from the year above, were coming to him and asking about Rover. By lunchtime the day after, there was an eager crowd waiting in the playground, all of them wanting to hear the story of Rover's arrival and adoption.

Then, just as he got to the bit about when the e-mail from his mum's sister had arrived, a voice came from behind his shoulder, loud enough to drown out his own: "No fucking way do you have a pet shark. That's literally the most retarded thing I've ever heard."

Noah froze. The words he'd been about to speak gummed up his mouth.

It was Austin Tucker; inevitably it was Austin Tucker. There could be no good thing that Austin didn't try to destroy, no happiness he didn't instinctively want to sully, and his radar for opportunities to inflict hurt was infallible. Noah's moment of triumph would have drawn him as surely as a picnic drew wasps.

"Come on, shithead," Austin said. He was in Noah's face now; his breath smelled sugary, like he'd been eating sweets all day. "Tell everyone how you're a lying little prick."

Noah had never, ever stood up to Austin. He'd never conceived of such a thing. Even when he'd replayed their past run-ins in his mind he had never tried to recast himself in the role of hero. Such thoughts, he felt instinctively, were dangerous. Instead, he'd always imagined Austin as a force of nature; sometimes avoidable with care, but once encountered, irresistible.

Yet agreeing with Austin was something he would never be able to take back. To agree was to deny his pet. That was his only choice, and he couldn't do it. "Yeah?" he said. "If you don't believe me then come see."

For a moment Austin looked confused, as though Noah had spoken in a foreign language and he was struggling to translate. Then he said, "I'm not going to come and see it, you fucking moron, because there's nothing to see."

Noah was no less afraid; but courage was apparently like a snowball, and now the snowball was gathering speed. "You're just scared," he said, with contempt.

Austin's fists clenched. "We'll see how scared I am with my fist in your face," he said.

"If you're not scared then come and see."

There was silence around them now, a wall of it; the absence of sound produced by a whole crowd holding their breath. Had Noah pushed too far? The prospect of imminent pain was making his stomach feel soft and runny.

"Fine," said Austin, "I'll come and see your stupid bullshit imaginary shark."

* * *

NOAH SPENT THAT evening in his room, all but paralysed with fear. He was afraid that Austin would come. He was afraid he wouldn't. Perhaps he'd come and hurt Noah, or hurt Rover. Perhaps he wouldn't come and would say he had and that there'd been nothing to see.

The doorbell's chime was a shock like lightning. He actually jumped. Then came his mother's voice: "Someone to see you, Noah." She sounded uncertain. She knew all of Noah's friends and she would know Austin wasn't one of them, or even anything like them.

Noah almost ran, and then realised at the last moment how that would look and walked quickly instead, taking the stairs two at a time. Austin was standing on the doorstep. He didn't look quite the way he did at school. Without a crowd around him he seemed smaller somehow.

"Hi, Noah," Austin said, as though him being here was the most the natural thing in the world.

"Hi," Noah said. It was difficult to work the sound up through his throat.

Instead of inviting Austin in, Noah went out. He didn't like the thought of Austin walking through his house. He led the way through the side gate and across the patio and along

128

the garden path, his heart bloating in his chest all the while, threatening to rise up and choke him.

When they reached the pond, there was nothing there.

Rover was out of sight, perhaps beneath the cluster of pond lilies that bobbed at the far end. For one awful moment Noah was certain he wouldn't show himself, and an entire future played out in his mind, one that began with Austin punching him to a pulp and got worse from there.

Then a blade of grey broke the scummy surface: a sleek triangle that sent V-shaped ripples shivering to either bank.

"Holy shit," Austin said.

They could see Rover fully now. The pond was long and wide but not deep. Austin crouched at the edge, leaned over.

"Holy *shit*," he said again. There was awe in his voice.

Noah knelt beside him. He had never felt anything like what was taking hold of him then: it was as if someone else had occupied his body, someone stronger, less fearful, someone who didn't stop to think things through as he did. In a moment he had Austin's arm clamped with both of his hands and was holding it there, above the surface of the water, with a strength that couldn't possibly be his own.

Austin's fingertips broke the water, and immediately undulations spread, like the circles on a target board. Rover's direction changed.

"You're never going to pick on me again," Noah said. He had never heard himself sound so calm; so assured.

"Get off me!" Austin was trying to pull away; but for all his strength, Noah's was greater. Rover's fin was like an arrow, homing upon the centre of that spreading dartboard of ripples.

"Or pick on my friends," Noah said.

Austin's squirming had slowed - as though, now that he'd realised he couldn't escape, the fear was paralysing him bit by bit. Rover had covered half the distance to his dangling fingers and was closing fast.

"Or pick on *anyone*," Noah said.

"Okay. Okay! Just get off me! Please!"

Noah had never heard so much fear in anyone's voice before. Coming from Austin's mouth, it sounded beautiful. Exultation flooded through him.

He let go of Austin's wrist.

*   *   *

No one had ever been scared of Noah.

No one had ever respected him. He'd had friends and they liked him, but *respect*? He'd barely even understood the concept before now. He had never been the centre of attention. He'd never been the centre of anything. Now it felt as if he was the hub of his whole class, his whole year, his whole school.

Even Austin was his friend now. It was a side-effect he would never have guessed at. Nor had he had any say in it; it had just happened. Austin as a friend was better than Austin as an enemy. Not a day had passed when he hadn't suggested Noah come over to read some new comic book or play some new game. It was making it difficult to find time for his other friends, his old friends.

But that was okay. Everyone wanted to know him. Everyone wanted to visit. And if Noah understood dimly that it wasn't him they wanted to see but Rover, did it matter? After all, they were one and the same: a boy and his pet. He'd been concerned at first that their interest would die out after a few days, a week at most, but if anything it seemed to be growing.

There was only one problem. Being popular took up more time than he would have expected. When he wasn't talking about Rover or showing him to his now-regular visitors he was playing with his pet, which basically amounted to watching him swim up and down, because as amazing a pet as a shark was there wasn't a great deal you could actually *do* with it.

Sometimes Noah wished he could take Rover for a walk, on a skateboard maybe or in the stream that ran at the bottom of the road. But there were obvious problems with either plan, and in the meantime he had to settle for helping his dad feed Rover, watching as he tore the meat into scraps and turned the water briefly the colour of grape juice.

Anyway, none of that was the problem. The problem was that being popular and playing with Rover was taking up so much time that he couldn't do the things he'd used to do, and one of the things he found harder and harder to find time for was schoolwork. It just didn't interest him the way it had. What did spelling or multiplication or geography matter when you had a pet shark?

To Noah, not at all. But to his mum and dad, and to his teacher Mrs Higgins, they mattered a lot, he knew. His grades had dropped from As to Bs and Cs in the last month, and since Noah was now studying hardly at all, there was every likelihood they would drop further still.

Events came to a head one evening when Noah came down from his room to find Mrs Higgins waiting with his parents in the living room. For a moment he wanted to run back up the stairs and hide. But that, he knew, was the old Noah; boys with sharks for pets had no need to run or hide. He went into the living room and said, "Hello, Mrs Higgins."

"Hello, Noah," Mrs Higgins said.

"Mrs Higgins is here to talk about your grades," Noah's mum said, as if there was the possibility he hadn't worked that out.

"It isn't something I'd normally do," Mrs Higgins said, "but for you Noah, given what high hopes we all had of you, I thought it would be worth bending the rules."

It proved a one-sided conversation. Noah, who had expected nothing less, confined his answers to yes's and no's – mostly the former, for the majority of questions were along

131

the lines of, "You are going to try harder from now on, aren't you, Noah?"

"Yes," he said. Yes, yes, yes. And he tried to make the word sound suitably penitent. But his mind was only half on the conversation, or not even that; just enough to make sure he didn't say *yes* when a *no* was expected. For it had occurred to him almost immediately that it was perfectly possible to improve his grades without the need for any extra study at all.

He waited until the meeting was over and everyone was smiling and drinking tea. Then, when Mrs Higgins got up to leave, he said, "Maybe I could show Rover to Mrs Higgins?"

That's the shark, Noah's mum mouthed at Mrs Higgins. Rover had featured a lot in the conversation, though not by name.

"Of course I'd like to see Rover," Mrs Higgins said.

*   *   *

ONE OF THE reasons Mrs Higgins was a good teacher was that she seemed to find everything fascinating, no matter if it was or not. In his old life that had been something Noah liked about her. Topics that would have been boring coming from anyone else, like fractions and where Belgium was and why Henry VIII needed so many wives, became interesting purely through her enthusiasm.

Now Mrs Higgins was watching Rover with an artist's eye. "He's beautiful," she said. "You say he was just a baby when you got him? He's growing quite big."

She was kneeling on the edge of the pond, just as Austin had done. That was good, because Noah had planned to do to Mrs Higgins exactly what he'd done to Austin. But at the last moment he decided that it wouldn't work. Mrs Higgins was an adult and adults did get scared the same way that children, even mean children, even bullies, did. Probably lots of scary things had happened to her in her life; maybe even things worse than sharks.

"If you look closely," Noah said, "you can see his gills moving."

Mrs Higgins leaned still further. "Oh yes," she said, "I see what you..."

But by then Noah had hold of her head.

Her grey hair was fine and wispy. He had to bunch it and dig his fingers in to get a hold. Mrs Higgins was fine and wispy too, her wrists so thin that Noah was sure he could have encircled one with his own small hand. If she hadn't been bent over then perhaps she could have shaken him off; but curled as she was, any struggling on her part risked tipping her into the green-slicked water. It took little effort for Noah to hold her face just above its surface, and rather than fight, Mrs Higgins stayed perfectly still.

"Oh, Noah," she said. He was surprised by how softly she spoke, and how she sounded more sad than angry. For a moment - but only a moment - it almost put him off from doing what he had to do.

"Mrs Higgins," Noah said. "Thanks for coming here. You were right. We *do* need to talk about my grades."

*   *   *

AFTER MRS HIGGINS had gone, Noah found that he couldn't stop shaking. When his mum asked if he was okay he said that maybe he was getting a cold or something. It was hard to make the words. Noah's mum put a hand to first her own brow and then his and said that, no, he didn't have a temperature.

"My stomach feels funny," Noah said. It did. It felt like he'd been on a rollercoaster for hours, until his body no longer remembered what was up and what was down. "I think I'd like to go to my room."

133

Upstairs, sitting on the bed, the shaking got worse. He couldn't figure out if he was excited or scared or both. He couldn't forget the look in Mrs Higgins's eyes when he'd released her, the fear but also the disappointment. Back when he'd been getting good grades she had always looked proud to have him in her class; she'd smiled at him every time he got an answer right.

But she had never been afraid of him. He'd never seen her afraid.

After a while the shaking passed. Noah went downstairs. His mum looked worried. "Are you feeling better now?" she asked.

"I'm fine," Noah said. And he was.

*　　*　　*

HE HAD IMAGINED that would be the end of it. With the threat of more bad grades out of the picture, with Austin on his side and almost everyone in the school either his friend or wanting to be, he could imagine no further impediments. He and Rover would be friends for the rest of their lives, and nothing could stand between them. He had read somewhere that sharks could live for more than thirty years - an almost unimaginable age for a nine year-old. They would hang out together, go to college and then university together. And then Noah would get a job, like a pool attendant maybe; one where they could be together all day long...

"Noah," Noah's mum said, "your father and I have been talking and we think that Rover is becoming bad for you."

She had come into his room and found him unprepared. Unlike with the meeting with Mrs Higgins, he'd had no time to plan a defence. "What?" he said.

"We're all going to discuss it together when your dad gets

134

back from work, but I wanted to talk to you on my own first."

"Rover's the best thing that's ever happened to me," Noah said, with feeling. "The only really good thing, ever."

"That's not true," his mother said, sounding hurt. "And even if it is, good things can sometimes harm you in the long run. That's something you learn as you grow up."

"Rover would *never* harm me," Noah said.

"Perhaps not deliberately," his mother agreed, though she didn't sound convinced. "But since you got him, you've been changing. Your grades are down. You don't spend time with your old friends. There are people coming round all the time that I don't recognise. Sometimes I'm not sure I recognise *you*, Noah."

He wanted to say, *My grades are down because I don't care about them and I'm not spending time with my old friends because my old friends were losers and there are people coming round that you don't recognise because I'm popular now and everybody wants to be my friend and maybe that's why you don't recognise me either.*

But he said none of those things. Instead he said, "I understand."

"I'm glad," his mum said, and she really did sound glad. "Your dad was afraid you wouldn't, but I know you're still my clever boy. And we'll make it up to you, I promise."

"Maybe we could go and say goodbye?" Noah asked. "I mean, before ... you know..." It was easy to let a tremble into his voice. There was a part of him that was ready to cry at even the possibility of losing Rover.

"Oh," Noah's mum said, caught by surprise. "Well, I didn't mean it had to be right away."

"I think it would hurt less if we did it quickly," Noah said. "You know, like with a plaster."

"That's sensible," his mother agreed. "You're right, there's no point putting hurtful things off."

It's true, Noah thought. He hadn't had much experience in causing hurt before this last month, but he was a quick learner.

* * *

"WILL THEY KILL him?" Noah asked.

"Of course not," his mum said. "We'd never allow it. They'll take him somewhere safe."

Noah took a step closer to the pond's bricked edge, gazing down at the dark water. "But he won't have any friends."

"He'll have shark friends," his mum said. She was eyeing his feet nervously.

Noah edged further. The tips of his trainers overhung the water now. He knew why his mum was scared. She was imagining him falling in. That was how fear worked. Fear was something else he'd come to understand well since Rover entered his life.

What he'd learned was: people aren't afraid of what's happening to them right now, they're scared of what *might* happen. The worse the bad thing that might happen is, the longer they stay scared. If the bad thing was bad enough, maybe someone would stay scared forever. But he didn't need forever, only a few weeks, just long enough for his mum to think things through. Noah figured that what he had in mind would be scary enough for that.

"I think he knows what's happening," Noah said. "I think he looks sad."

"That's just how sharks look," Noah's mum told him. "Noah, don't stand so close."

It was tricky, but he managed to shuffle a fraction nearer. Now only his heels were on the brick. "He was the best pet ever," he said, "the best anyone's ever had." He leaned forward.

"Noah!" His mum moved quickly; all at once she stepped forward and grasped for the hood of his coat. But Noah was even faster. He was already stepping back, and her fingers brushed past him without gaining purchase. Now his mother was nearer the edge than he was, and Noah flung out his own hand, caught her arm and pushed. Her balance already lost, she teetered forward.

Just a moment ... a moment with Rover drifting implacably towards her, slicing the water into two neat halves, that was all it would take. Then he'd grab her hand, help her out, and maybe he could even pretend it had all been an accident. But she'd know, she would know, and she'd know too what happened to anyone that tried to get between Noah and his best friend.

At the last instant, his mother's head turned. Her whole body was turning; without balance, parts of her were falling in different directions. Yet it all seemed to be happening slowly, like on TV. He couldn't tell if she was trying to look at him or if that was just the way her head happened to be plummeting. But whatever the reason, her eyes caught his. Noah saw fear. Just as he had expected, her eyes were brimming over with fear.

But it wasn't fear for herself.

It should have been too late to pull his mum back. He wasn't big enough, and she was too far gone. The strength he found was the same strength he'd pinned Austin with, that had let him hold Mrs Higgins – but now it clenched his fingers on his mother's arm and defied gravity and equilibrium and swung her like a pendulum and hauled her to the safety of the pond side.

Then the strength poured every drop of itself into his legs and he was running, through the garden, down the path, into the street, and on and on and on.

* * *

IT SEEMED LIKE he'd been wandering the streets for hours. He was hungry and his legs ached. Yet when he got home his dad was still at work, and only a single hour had gone by.

His mum was waiting in the living room, sat on the settee with her knees pulled up, a pose she only adopted in the worst of crises. He could see that she'd been crying; her eye makeup was streaked and she hadn't tried to wipe it. "I've been worried sick about you," she said.

She didn't sound angry. He had almost hoped she would be. "I'm sorry," Noah said. "I'm sorry about what I did." *Or what I nearly did*, he thought. *What I got so close to doing.* "I'm sorry I ran off. I'm sorry I'm an awful person."

"You're not an awful person. The only people who are awful people are the people who never stop to realise what awful people they're turning into." His mum smiled. It was a small, sad smile that nevertheless made Noah feel a little better. "But you know," she said, "that Rover has to go."

Noah nodded. Yes, he knew that Rover had to go. He had known it from the moment he ran away. Because there was a second shark now, a shadow-shark in his heart, and it was eating it piece by piece. Soon there would be nothing left and the boy called Noah would be gone, replaced by someone with his name and his face and his parents who would nevertheless not be *him*.

"I'm going to take the day off tomorrow," his mum said, "and sort it all out. I'm going to ask your dad to take the day off too. I promise we won't let anyone hurt Rover and that we'll make sure he can go somewhere he can be happy."

"I'm not sure sharks get happy and sad like people do," Noah said.

*　　*　　*

THIS TIME, NOW that it was for real, Noah went to say his

138

goodbyes on his own. He didn't go so close to the water; just near enough that he could make out Rover's sleek shape spearing at the green-tinged depths.

He felt he should make some sort of speech, maybe try and make sense of the time they'd spent together or thank Rover, reassure him, promise to visit him in his new home. Yet Noah didn't feel like saying any of those things. Down there in the darkness, Rover didn't look like his friend anymore. He just looked like a really big, scary fish.

"Goodbye, Rover," Noah said.

But if Rover even knew Noah was there, he gave no indication. He just swam back and forth near the bottom, like he always did.

Maybe, Noah thought, sharks don't care that much about people at all.

*　*　*

WHEN HE GOT back from school the next day, Noah went straight to the garden. He wasn't ready yet to go inside.

A girl in the next year up had asked him about Rover and he'd stammered out an answer and then burst out crying. After that the girl had laughed at Noah and soon other people were laughing, and afterwards nobody wanted to talk to him, although they sniggered when he went by. Once again he was the Noah of old, as though the last few months had never happened.

Noah was planning to sit beside the pond for a while, pondering its emptiness until he hurt a little less. But when he got out there, his father was waiting.

"In a way," his dad said, "I feel like what happened with you and Rover was my fault. For not getting you a puppy like you wanted and buying koi carp instead, and not realising that one of them was in fact a shark, and then for convincing your mother that a shark was a suitable pet for a nine year old. So after the police and the people from the Sea Life Centre had left, I made a little trip. Noah, say hello to your new dog."

Noah looked at the leash in his dad's hand and followed it all the way to the animal straining at its other end.

"Dad," he said, "I'm pretty sure that isn't a dog."

DEEP RED BELLS

JOSH REYNOLDS

"Isn't it magnificent, Ms. Gallowglass?" Charles St. Cyprian said, as the black Crossley 20/25 came to a stop on the crest of the hill, overlooking the Dorset coastline. The motor car's engine clicked rhythmically for a moment, before falling silent. It had pulled up in a bare depression in the curve of the hill, just down the slope from a large coastguard cottage. The cottage was surrounded by a dry stone wall, which extended part way down the slope. A chill winter wind curled in from the sea. In the water below, bands of rock ran parallel to the shoreline. Among the steeply dipping formations of rock was a large, curiously kinked arch of limestone that rose above its fellows and looked for all the world like a door.

St. Cyprian got out and spread his arms, encompassing the landscape below. "Look at that! Like a folded corner on a page in the Book of Ages, that is," he said enthusiastically. "The Thirly Dor - lovely."

"It's a rock, innit?" Ebe Gallowglass said, chewing on the end of an unlit cigarette. She leaned over the windshield of the Crossley, her pointed chin resting on her crossed forearms. She was short and dark, with black hair cut in a razor-edged bob, and a battered flat cap resting high on her head. She was dressed, with louche aplomb, in a man's suit tailored for a woman of her small stature, beneath a convoy coat.

In contrast to Gallowglass, St. Cyprian was tall and rangy. He had an olive cast to his skin and hair a touch too long to be properly fashionable. All of this, combined with a suit straight from Gieves and Hawkes under his battered army greatcoat, made for a dashing, if trifle exotic, presentation. He spun on his heel, frowning. "A rock, she says. Philistine, says I. Have you no appreciation for the natural wonders of the world? That, my good woman, is the Thirly Dor. A derivation of the Old English, 'thirl' meaning to drill or bore -"

"Like you're doing to me now?"

"Quiet, you," St. Cyprian said. "Likely a derivation of 'thyrel', meaning hole. And 'dor', of course, means door." He jabbed at the distant rock formation. "The question, of course, is what exactly it's a doorway *to*." He looked at her expectantly.

Gallowglass squinted. "It's a pretty rock," she said.

St. Cyprian threw up his hands. "Why do I bother?"

"I thought we came out here to look into a case of whatchamacallit, not look at rocks," she said. "I can see rocks at home." 'Home' was London, and the Cheyne Walk flat that came with the offices of His Majesty's Royal Occultist.

Formed during the reign of Elizabeth the First, the office of Royal Occultist (or the Queen's Conjurer, as it had been known) started with the diligent amateur Dr. John Dee, and had passed through a succession of hands since. The list was a long one, weaving in and out of the margins of British history, and culminating, in the Year of Our Lord 1920, in one Charles St. Cyprian and his erstwhile apprentice, Ebe Gallowglass.

Their responsibilities included the investigation, organization and occasional suppression of That Which Man Was Not Meant to Know—including ghosts, werewolves, ogres, fairies, boggarts and the occasional worm of unusual size—by order of the King (or Queen), for the good of the British Empire.

"Those aren't rocks; you're thinking of pavement. And yes," St. Cyprian said. "Get my Gladstone out of the boot, there's a good apprentice." He snapped his fingers at her.

Gallowglass gave him a rude gesture in reply and slid out of the Crossley.

"Assistant," she said, as she pulled his black Gladstone bag out of the boot of the motor car.

"What?"

She smacked the bag into his belly, doubling him over. "I'm your assistant, ain't I?" she said. He wheezed and nodded.

"Right, yes, my apologies," he said as he straightened, arms clutched protectively about the bag. "Do be careful. There are breakables in here." Gallowglass shrugged. St. Cyprian rolled his eyes. "To answer your, quite impertinent, question, we're here because - delightful seaside geological formations aside - we've been asked to come. And the word you were thinking of was 'possession', by the way. We- Ah! Here's our host now," he said, as a young woman came into view, following the dry stone wall down from the cottage.

"Charles!" the woman called out, as she drew close. "Is that you?"

"You tell me," he said, as he met her halfway. He glanced at Gallowglass. "Ms. Gallowglass, meet Dahlia Fitzgrace. Dahlia Fitzgrace, my assistant, Ebe Gallowglass."

Fitzgrace looked Gallowglass up and down. "Is that what you're calling it now?" she asked St. Cyprian. "For shame, Charles - she's dressed like a tramp."

Gallowglass blinked. Before she could reply, St. Cyprian hurriedly said, "Tut, Dahlia."

"What did you say?" Fitzgrace fixed him with a look.

"I said tut," he replied.

"Say that again, Charles, and I'll biff you one right in the honker. I have endured quite enough these past few days without being tutted at by a perfect ass." Fitzgrace lifted a fist warningly. "You took your time getting here. I sent that telegram two days ago!"

"Well, we did come from London, Dahlia. Not exactly a

trip to the corner shop, you know," St. Cyprian said, and then, after a moment's hesitation, "How's Gussie?"

Dahlia's face crumpled. The anger went out of her eyes, replaced by something else; sadness, St. Cyprian thought, or perhaps fear. She glanced back towards the cottage, as if afraid someone might be watching them. "He's... not well," Fitzgrace said softly.

"No change, then?"

"I... You'd best come and see for yourself. I put the kettle on as soon as I saw you pull up." Turning back towards the cottage, she led them up the slope and into the cottage, which was neither as neat nor as tidy as it could have been. "I apologize for the state of things. Gussie's man gave notice two days in," Dahlia said, as she swept a stack of papers out of a chair. "Those SPR chums of Gussie's were here for three, but that ass McDougal got into a huff when I sent for you, and the lot of them buggered off to go play with crystals or look for spooks, or whatever it is they do." She hesitated. "To tell the truth, I think they were glad to get out of here."

"Ah, yes, well, the Society for Psychical Research and I are rarely on the same page. And McDougal is a frightful ass, but I would expect better of him than to encourage Gussie in this foolishness," St. Cyprian said, as he took a seat. In truth, he had a tremendous amount of respect for the Society, engendered in him by his own mentor, Thomas Carnacki. When Carnacki had held the position of Royal Occultist, he had often worked with the Society to investigate strange phenomena.

"It wouldn't take much," Dahlia said. A kettle began to whistle somewhere and she darted off. Gallowglass lifted a bound stack of papers and showed it to St. Cyprian.

"*Malevolent Maisie*," she said, reading the typed title. She flipped through it and whistled tunelessly. "Cor, that's a lot of ripped bodices."

"Yes, Dahlia is this year's answer to Rosie M. Banks,

producing widely read and inevitably maudlin tripe with a speed that would astound the messenger of the gods himself." He took the manuscript from her, flipping through it himself. "A distraught critic once came at her with a shrimp fork in the dining room of the Savoy."

"It was a meat skewer, and it was at the Regent Palace Hotel," Dahlia said as she re-entered the sitting room, a tray balanced in her hands. "And really... Tripe?"

"I did say it was widely read," St. Cyprian said.

"Some of us have to work for a living, Charles. We can't all luck into a government stipend," Dahlia said, pouring tea into a trio of cups. "This beastly business has utterly put paid to my schedule. My editor is screaming for my scalp as we speak."

"I'd hardly call it luck," he murmured. "More like a lifetime's worth of screaming nightmares." As if on cue, a low, insistent sound dribbled down from somewhere above. It wasn't quite a moan, so much as an animal noise that jabbed at the listener's hindbrain. Dahlia didn't look up. Her cup shook in her hands, and tea slopped onto the table. St. Cyprian caught the cup as it fell, and set it down.

"Has he been doing that often?"

"Since he... Since that day," she said.

"Maybe you'd best explain, then."

Dahlia closed her eyes and nodded. "The cottage is mine. I come here to work. The quiet, the relative isolation, it helps me to bang through a manuscript in record time. No distractions, you see." She smiled bitterly. "Gussie's been badgering me to allow him to stay. He's potty about fossils, you know."

"Yes, I do recall an incident with an ichthyosaur skeleton in the Drones billiards room," St. Cyprian said. "And he was forever tramping the coast, looking for bits of bone and loose teeth. I read his monograph on ancient survivals in Britain – it was quite thought provoking."

"It's a waste of time, is what it is," Dahlia said harshly. "I

145

thought when he joined the Society for Psychical Research, he'd found a new hobby. Instead he combined his obsessions in the most ludicrous ways." She looked at St. Cyprian. "Do you recall that business with the crystal egg? Or the time he joined the Esoteric Order of Thoth-Ra?"

"Unfortunately," St. Cyprian said. "I was never very clear on what he was looking for, though perhaps I should have asked him before he attempted...whatever it was he attempted." St. Cyprian cocked an eye towards the ceiling. Another drift of noise slithered down from the first floor of the cottage. This one was louder, and put him in mind of something hungry or angry, or both.

"He was obsessed with the past. And the Thirly Dor," Dahlia said. "He said it was a 'psychical beacon' or somesuch tommyrot. 'History has weight, Dahlia,' he said, 'and it weighs more heavily in some places than others." She shook her head. "He thought it was a… A sort of marker…"

"Like a folded corner on a page in the Book of Ages, say?" Gallowglass interjected. St. Cyprian shot her a warning look and she smirked and settled back in her seat.

Dahlia shook her head. "Something like that, I suppose. When he found that tooth, he was ecstatic. Happy as a pig in muck."

"Tooth?" St. Cyprian asked.

Dahlia nodded. Upstairs, wood squeaked. She hunched forward, clasping her mug of tea in both hands. "A bloody big shark's tooth. He found it somewhere down amongst those rocks, lodged in some nook or other."

"Big?"

"Big." She gestured. "People find the like all the time up and down these coasts. Big teeth, little teeth, it's a wonder sharks manage to bite anyone at all, if you want my opinion." She frowned. "It was after that things turned rotten."

There was a thump from upstairs. She started. Then she

shivered and pulled her jumper tighter about herself. "It was those idiot chums of his that put it into his head to try and make a – a psychosomething..."

"Psychometric reading, " St. Cyprian supplied. "Some people believe that certain objects, particularly those once in close proximity to a living thing, can transfer knowledge of their history to one with psychical ability. To see what it saw, experience what it experienced, somehow." He was beginning to get a picture of what had occurred, and it wasn't pleasant. "What happened after this reading?"

Dahlia's eyes welled up, and she snatched up a sheet of paper and used it to blot her eyes. "Nothing at first. They thought he'd failed. But he started having nightmares...about the sea, and the dark and – and blood, and he grew moody, and distant...and then, he tried to – to drown himself."

St. Cyprian sat back. "What do you mean, tried to drown himself?"

"I mean, Charles, he ran down to the beach and tried to fling himself into the ruddy ocean! It took McDougall and two of those other idiots to restrain him. They hauled him upstairs and strapped him down – they tried to bring him back with their dratted crystals, but Gussie – he –" She broke down then, and began to weep silently, her shoulders heaving. St. Cyprian reached for her, and she pushed his hand away. "I don't need your sympathy, Charles. I need my brother back," she said, her voice a harsh rasp.

St. Cyprian retracted his hand and stood. He looked at Gallowglass. "I rather think it's time to examine the patient, don't you, Ms. Gallowglass?"

"Past time," Gallowglass said, shooting to her feet.

"Second door on the left at the top of the landing," Dahlia said, but didn't move. She stared at the dregs of tea in her cup, as if trying to read her future.

St. Cyprian waved Gallowglass on ahead and bent over

Dahlia. "I'll do what I can, Dahlia. Stay down here, no matter what."

She didn't look at him, but grabbed his hand instead. "Be careful, Charles."

"Always am, dear heart," he said, with faux levity. "Back in a tick."

He took the stairs quickly. Gallowglass was waiting on the landing. She gestured to the door in question. She tapped her nose silently, and he sniffed. There was a distinctly unpleasant odour hanging on the air.

St. Cyprian hefted his bag and went to the door. He had witnessed cases of possession before. It wasn't as rare as all that, unfortunately. The human mind was like a sponge, absorbing whatever foul essence happened to be wafting through the aether. But some sponges were more absorbent than others, and that was where the real trouble started. If Gussie had been locked out of his own mind by something unpleasant, it wasn't going to be easy to get him back. He took a breath and opened the door.

The room smelled of standing water and seaweed rotting in the sun. It looked as if a schoolboy had decorated it – books lay in piles everywhere, and tottery piles of copies of the *Journal of the Society of Psychical Research* occupied the corners. Display boxes of fossils of various shapes, sizes and colours occupied the walls and the top of the writing desk. Across the bed, a large window looked out towards the sea, and St. Cyprian could see that the weather had taken a turn for the nasty. Rain spattered the windows, and made interesting shapes on the glass.

Gussie had been strapped to the bed. His clothes were stained with food and blood. His eyes were closed and his teeth were bared in a grimace so tight that St. Cyprian feared that the corners of his mouth might tear at any moment. He made a low, gabbling noise in his throat, like the sound a fish might make as it flopped in the bottom of a boat, and wriggled in his straps.

St. Cyprian pulled a stool over to the bed and sat down. Gussie was thinner than he remembered, and he smelled a good deal worse. Then, Gussie had long been a proponent of the school of natural odour, despite the complaints of various flatmates and paramours. This, however, wasn't merely 'eau de Gussie' but something more pervasive and unpleasant. "By their smell can men sometimes know them near," he muttered. He glanced at Gallowglass. "Can you smell that?"

"Foul, innit?" she said, waving a hand in front of her face. "Like dead fish."

"It's rather more than that, I should say." St. Cyprian frowned. "Did I, or did I not, give you Harzan's monograph on the detection of abhuman manifestations?"

"Was that what that was?"

He sighed and shook his head. "Sometimes I despair of you, Ms. Gallowglass." He bent over Gussie. "Hand me the obsidian mirror, would you?" He held out his hand as Gallowglass rummaged in the Gladstone. She handed him a flat, polished, black disc, which he held under Gussie's nostrils. He peered at the fogged surface for a moment before tossing it back to her.

"Reality, if you will, is a coral reef," he said. "We are the fish that inhabit said reef. And while there are predators which lurk within the reef, they are neither numerous nor particularly hard to avoid, if you're careful. But outside the reef, well... that's a different matter entirely. Forces and presences born in the darkness, eternally hungering for the light of our fair world, donchaknow?" he said, prising open Gussie's eyelids to peer into his eyes.

"So he is possessed, then?" Gallowglass said, placing the mirror back in the bag.

"Yes, but only God knows by what," St. Cyprian said.

"No two Saaitii manifestations are alike. Some are rather like psychic fungus, while others are a good deal more...ambitious." He stepped back. "Let's find out which one this is, shall we?"

Without waiting for Gallowglass's reply, he traced the sacred shape of the Voorish Sign in the air with a finger and let his inner eye flicker open. The spirit-eye, Carnacki had called it, though Fitzgrace and St. Cyprian's other acquaintances in the Society for Psychical Research insisted that it was merely a very focused form of extrasensory perception.

Whatever it was, it had taken him several years to learn how to utilize it safely. Humans were, by and large, as sensitive to the paranormal as animals were to earthquakes. They simply couldn't process it as well. Humans needed reasons for things which animals took on instinct.

The inability of the human mind to correlate all of its perceptions was one of humanity's built-in defences against the many, *many* predatory malignancies that swam through the outer void. But sometimes you were forced to shuck those evolutionary blinders first thing, otherwise you risked being snapped up unawares.

Augustus Fitzgrace, unfortunately, had possessed neither the training nor the ability to avoid being taken by whatever had come upon him from out of the abyss. It had smashed its way into his undefended mind, and now lurked there, like an unwelcome tenant. And it was up to St. Cyprian to try and roust the intruder out.

But first, he had to find out what he was dealing with. As he concentrated, the world became soft at the edges and yet more vibrant as his senses expanded to fill the void left by his thoughts and physical sight. He heard a rushing and a roaring, as if he were caught in a storm-tossed surf, and he felt, rather than saw, the shadow of some unseen shape pass over him. His eardrums began to throb painfully with a strange pressure. The throbbing sensation grew louder, and became distinct. He felt as if he were in a bell tower at vespers, and he clapped his hands to his ears unconsciously.

Then, out of nowhere, a snapping maw came at him, all triangular teeth and bloody froth. Startled, his third eye slammed shut hard enough to send a wave of pain rippling through his mind as he was abruptly wrenched back to reality. He staggered back against the occasional table, flailing, trying to brace himself. He expelled a shaky breath.

Gallowglass stretched a hand towards him and snapped her fingers. "Focus," she said.

"Quiet, I'm ratiocinating," he said, batting vainly at her hand.

"What's that mean when it's at home?" she asked.

"I mean, I'm trying to figure out what I just saw," he said.

"Which was?"

"Teeth," he said. "Lots of teeth."

"What sort of teeth?" Gallowglass asked.

"I don't really see how that's relevant at this juncture..." St. Cyprian began. He trailed off as he looked around the room, and saw the boxes mounted on the walls, filled with triangular shapes. "Hang on a tick." He looked at her. "Ms. Gallowglass, you are a wonder and a treasure. Has anyone ever told you that?"

"Sure. Lots of people," Gallowglass said, with a shrug.

St. Cyprian shook his head. "Yes, well I actually mean it." He gestured to one of the boxes. "Shark's teeth. What did Dahlia say? This all started when he tried to do a reading on a shark's tooth..."

Gallowglass's eyes widened slightly as she looked at the box and then back at the figure strapped to the bed. She was about to speak, when Gussie made a gurgling moan, and began to thrash with more vigor than before. The air was thick with the smell of brine, and the wallpaper began to bubble and sweat. Condensation beaded on the window panes as the frames buckled and split at the corners as if something heavy were pressing against them. Gallowglass reached beneath her coat for the Webley-Fosbery revolver holstered under her arm. St. Cyprian caught her hand. "Won't do any good, I shouldn't think," he said.

"What is it?" Gallowglass hissed.

"Well, it's not a Saaitii manifestation, which is good. But it's something just as dangerous, which is bad. And I'm afraid I've rather done the equivalent of tossing chum into the water. Help me hold him down, before –"

The sound of the strap popping was loud in the close confines of the room. Gussie bucked, and the straps tore, one by one. He was up in a moment, his mouth wide, and his eyes like polished black stones. He hurled himself off the bed and at his saviours. St. Cyprian shoved Gallowglass aside. Gussie's fingers snagged the lapels of his coat and St. Cyprian found himself swung about forcefully, so that his back smashed into the window. There was a sound like the din of vast bells in his ears, punctuated by the cracking of glass. He grabbed for Gussie's wrists, but he was already moving backwards, through the shattered window, and into the storm outside.

St. Cyprian's fingers dug into the frame of the window. Splinters slid beneath his fingernails and rain stung his eyes as he scrabbled at the wood for purchase. His stomach roiled queasily as the world spun about him, and his ears were full of the clangour of the bells. He felt his grip weakening. Then Gallowglass was there, her slim hands snapping out to catch his wrists. Before he knew it, she had hauled him back into the room and slung him onto the bed. As he tried to articulate his gratitude, she sprang past him, drawing her pistol as she went.

"You're welcome. He scarpered downstairs," she said. She darted through the door and he staggered after her, pausing only to snag a teakwood case from the Gladstone. As he pursued Gallowglass, he tore the case open and snatched at the object within – a disc of beaten silver. On its surface were engraved the signs of the Saaamaaa Ritual, crafted by the hands of the last of the ab-human priests of Raaee sometime in the 1600s, and then confiscated by Dr. John Dee. Like the obsidian mirror, it was a tool of the trade, and it had proven itself useful in similar situations. He'd brought it on the off-chance that something other than a Sumerian demon was squatting in Gussie's *corpus*.

Even as he descended the stairs, he heard a scream, and then Gallowglass's Webley roared. He slid into the sitting room and saw Gallowglass struggling with Dahlia, both women cursing with equal virulence. "Charles, your tramp tried to shoot Gussie!" Dahlia wailed. Gallowglass stomped down on the other woman's instep, and Dahlia gave a yelp.

"She stopped me from shooting him!" Gallowglass snarled, gesticulating with her smoking revolver.

"Who told you to shoot him?"

"He tried to kill you!" she shouted at his back, as St. Cyprian made for the door. It had been torn from its hinges in a display of distinctly un-Gussie-like strength. Rain pattered the paving stones outside.

"Who hasn't?" he shot back as he darted out into the rain, the Saaamaaa amulet clutched in one hand, the words of the incantation of Raaee running through his head. If he could get close enough to Gussie, he might be able to drive out his unwelcome tenant. "Come on, he'll be heading for the water!"

"How do you know?" Gallowglass called out as she hurried after him. They found the stairs cut into the seaward cliff, leading to the shore, and began to climb down as quickly as they could, given the rain.

"Weren't you listening before? Dahlia said he'd tried to drown himself. If it had been a bee, it would have stung me," he said, shaking his head. "I thought something foul had caught a ride back into our world when he sent his mind out, something from Outside. But it wasn't from Outside, though it's just as alien, in its way. And like a perfect perisher, I stirred it up and put the scent of blood in its metaphorical nostrils."

"What is it?" Gallowglass demanded.

"It's obvious isn't it? It's a ruddy shark! Or the ghost of one, at any rate," St. Cyprian said. He caught sight of Gussie's pale form, shrouded in sodden pyjamas, staggering awkwardly into the waters around the Thirly Dor, his arms flailing helplessly. He ducked his head and charged across the shore. Gallowglass shouted something, but her words were lost in the crash of the surf.

He plunged into the waves after Gussie, who bobbed out towards the limestone arch like a ginger cork. St. Cyprian shed his coat as he splashed after the other man, and then dived under the water, swimming for all he was worth. The thing which had control of Gussie's form was all appetite and no mind; it wouldn't understand that Gussie couldn't breathe underwater.

Gussie's head vanished beneath the water in the shadow of the Dor, and St. Cyprian dived after him. Gussie sank down, his limbs moving out of synch. St. Cyprian caught at the back of his pyjamas, and got an elbow in the cheek for his troubles. He tried to hook Gussie and drag him upwards, but the latter was having none of it. He seemed determined to drown himself. He fought St. Cyprian's rescue attempt, turning viciously on his would-be saviour, his teeth snapping together in a burst of bubbles. He flailed at St. Cyprian, biting at him. Blackness began to creep in at the edges of St. Cyprian's vision, and his lungs ached with a growing need.

With a final burst of desperate strength, he pressed the silver amulet to Gussie's brow and spat the words of the Raaee incantation. Seawater filled his mouth and poured down his throat as he forced the words out in a gargling mumble. There was a flash of light, achingly pure and painfully bright, and

Gussie went limp. As St. Cyprian dragged him to the surface, he felt a vast pressure leave Gussie and shoot downwards into the dark. He didn't look back.

St. Cyprian's head burst through the roiling waters and he sucked in a heaving lungful of air. Holding tight to Gussie, he dragged the barely conscious man towards the shore, which seemed agonizingly far away. He saw Gallowglass at the sea's edge, waving her arms and gesturing wildly. Between the storm, the tide, and the thunder of his own heartbeat in his ears, he couldn't hear whatever it was she was saying.

Gussie began to splutter and cough. St. Cyprian paused in his swimming to check on him, and he caught sight of something huge and dark inside of an oncoming wave.

The water about him felt as if it were growing colder as the thing drew closer. He couldn't make out its shape, besides an impression of size and hunger. Fear filled him as he once more began to haul the semi-conscious Gussie towards the shore.

He could feel it gaining on them. He saw Gallowglass splashing towards him, her Webley in hand, her mouth open in a shout. St. Cyprian dragged Gussie around and shoved him towards Gallowglass. Then, his heart hammering fit to split his chest, he whirled, brandishing the Saaamaaa sigil like a weapon. The wave rose up over him and he saw hundreds of sharp, triangular teeth, and he screamed the words he'd used to banish the presence from Gussie's mind even as the wave bore him under.

Teeth tore at him, and he choked on seawater. Something rough scraped against him.

And then he was rolling onto shore. Large, hard things clattered across the rocks around him, spat out by the water. The thunder in his mind receded, and he rolled over onto his back as the water retreated. He looked up as Gallowglass waded towards him through the surf. "Still alive?" she said.

"Barely," he croaked, extending a hand for her to help him to his feet. "How's Gussie?"

"Alive. Water-logged, but alive." She ignored his hand and bent to pick up one of the things the wave had left behind. She tossed it onto his chest. "Looks like your pal has all of the teeth he could want, now," she said.

St. Cyprian looked down at the object and saw that it was a shark's tooth, black with age. He picked it up and pushed himself to his feet. "Somehow, I think Gussie might be over that particular obsession." He weighed the tooth in his hand, and then hurled as far out into the water as he could. "If he's smart, at any rate."

SHARKCOP 2: FEEDING FRENZY

ALEC WORLEY

DETECTIVE DALE CARDIGAN squinted through his night-vision binoculars at the jetty below. Amid a haze of green and black, he could see at least six guys unloading plastic crates from a beat-up old fishing boat and piling them into a trailer-truck parked nearby. The bigger of the two men standing to one side matched the description Dale had received from a snitch earlier that day. Blue baseball cap, grey mutton chops, and skin cured to leather by a lifetime of fishing beneath the Hawaiian sun. It was Chuck Hardladder all right, the toughest fisherman in Kahlua Bay. He was swigging at a can of beer and enthusing to a smaller man in a hooded top – his buyer, no doubt – while the goons struggled with the thirty-foot crates.

The men appeared relaxed, but Dale couldn't shake the feeling that these guys knew they were being watched. Maybe Dale had made one too many surveillance sweeps. Maybe the buyers were experienced enough to recognise an unmarked Department-issue Ford when they saw one. Or maybe it was the fact that Dale's partner was dancing on the roof of the car.

Dale tossed the binoculars on the dash and heaved himself out of the passenger seat, wincing at the ache in his joints. He looked up at his partner who was stamping his feet, slapping his arms and thighs, and glaring down at the men on the distant jetty as though every one of them had just spilt his drink. Dale guessed he was attempting some kind of Maori war dance, although he looked more like a mime angry at being given a parking ticket.

"George?" said Dale. "Didn't we talk about this?"

Detective George Chum slapped his chest with both hands and hooted like a gibbon. He was topless save for his shoulder-holster, and exposed the kind of body rarely seen outside of TV commercials that want to terrify people into buying a gym membership. The moonlight traced his enormous, crescent-shaped scar, which curved from chest to waist.

"I'm sorry, Dale," he said, pausing to waggle his tongue as though someone were strangling him, a common sight in the offices of the Kahlua Bay Police Department. "I know you're a man of science, but I follow a different path. The gods of the hunt will reveal our prey, but first they demand tribute."

He began gyrating his hips, as though trying to unscrew something with his buttocks.

From the moment the captain introduced Dale to his latest partner, Dale's gut had told him George would be different. Then again Dale's guts told him a lot of things. They usually told him, 'You're gonna need a toilet in the next two minutes', or, 'I'm in spasm. I think you forgot to take your pills'. But Dale's innards mostly just grumbled, 'Cardigan, you're too old for this shit... Seriously, you're 92.'

Dale had once dreamed of spending his autumn years sipping margaritas on a yacht, leaving the criminals of Kahlua Bay far behind. But he knew only too well that in his line of work such dreams had an almost supernatural tendency to be snatched away shortly before retirement. Old Hunk Murphy – God rest his soul – had been a week from retirement when the captain decided to partner him with a wild-eyed maniac who believed the best way to solve crimes was to shoot anything vaguely human-shaped. Then there was Patch Kennedy, who had been tracking some arms dealer back in '83. Patch had got so drunk at his retirement party that he failed to notice his farewell cake had been replaced with a pile of land mines covered in frosting.

Dale had never considered himself a superstitious man. As a cop he was known for his practicality and caution; he rarely went by anything unless he'd read several books about it first. But Dale had seen too many cops screaming 'Noooooooooo!' over the bullet-riddled body of an older partner to believe that nearing retirement equalled anything other than imminent death. The day after Patch Kennedy's explosive demise, Dale marched into the captain's office and filed a request to postpone his retirement indefinitely. Since then he had survived several high-speed car crashes, countless explosions and more suicidal hotshot partners than he could count. Dale had once joked that the captain was only partnering him with guys he wanted to get rid of. The captain had shrugged off this suggestion with an overzealous laugh and an introduction to the cocky young detective who was dating his daughter.

"They say," said George, attempting a moon-walk, "that the knights of Camelot would perform this dance before riding into battle. As did the samurai before them."

Yelling at George only ever seemed to encourage him. Fortunately Dale was blessed with the sort of wise and world-worn voice that people couldn't help wanting to listen to in case they missed something profound.

"George," said Dale, in a voice like warm marmalade. "The hot dog shack by the station closes in twenty minutes…"

George paused in the middle of a bongo solo.

"And there's a species down there that's pretty endangered right now."

"The only endangered species out there tonight," said George, staring into the middle distance, "is crime."

"Attaboy, George," said Dale. "But can you open the trunk first? I need my Zimmer frame."

* * *

DALE AND GEORGE ducked behind a pile of fishing nets as they crept towards the suspects on the jetty. Having insisted on wearing his shades, George had walked into every mooring post on the way there. He clutched his dented nose and winced as Dale peered over at the men nearby. The goons rolled down the shutter on the back of the truck and nodded to the buyer in the hoodie.

"We're done, holmes," said the buyer. "We be back next Tuesday."

"Now you hold on there," said Hardladder, crushing another beer can in his fist and tossing it into the water. "I said you owe me another two crates of beer. Perhaps you couldn't hear me on account of that hobo that was playing the bongos."

"We already been through this shit, man," said the buyer. "You got twenty-four bottles of mutton chop shampoo, a replacement liver, and two-hundred crates of beer. Minus the two crates you drank while we was unloading."

Hardladder sneered, revealing a set of teeth like a karate-chopped picket fence.

"Don't you lecture me 'bout drinkin', college boy," he warned a nearby seagull. "I drink to forget my navy days. Sharks ate every one of my buddies when our boat got torpedoed."

The buyer left Hardladder to crack open another beer.

"Course, it was me that torpedoed it," he recalled. "I was so drunk I loaded the thing the wrong way round." He cackled to himself and took a swig. "Ah, good times."

"Kahlua Bay Police Department," announced Dale, resting his 1958 service revolver on the rim of his Zimmer frame. "I'm afraid you boys are under arrest for the fishing and sale of a protected species. Time to say something cool,

George... George?"

George's pistol slipped from his hand and bounced into the water. Dale glanced round to see his partner staring at his fingers. They were smeared with blood and George's battered nose was dripping onto the wooden planks of the jetty. He sniffed and his eyes darkened as a strange smile crept across his face.

"Please tell me you remembered your nose plugs, George."

The buyer and his cronies had bolted for the truck the second Dale looked away. The detective shuffled after them on his Zimmer, taking a trembling aim at the tyres while George groaned and swayed, fighting to control himself.

Meanwhile, Hardladder regaled himself with another anecdote.

"Then there was this time I arm-wrestled a 29-footer off the coast of Martha's Vinyard..."

The truck's wheels screamed as they spun, flinging a cloud of dirt in George's face. He reeled backwards into Dale as the elderly detective fired, his shot missing the truck and passing instead through Hardladder's thigh. The fisherman peered down at the blood now squirting from his femoral artery. He tutted as though the pipes under his sink had sprung a leak. Dale recovered and looked up at George.

His eyes had turned jet black and the lower half of his face bristled with more triangular teeth than his mouth could contain. Dale had seen George's 'gift' in action before: at several crime scenes, the autopsy room, and a kid's birthday party. Hardladder seemed to finally remember which plain of reality he inhabited when he saw George's body expand grotesquely, ripping apart his shirt and pants, his entire head swelling into a huge conical snout. It was as though someone had pulled a rip-cord and George had inflated into a 5,000lb Great White Shark.

Hardladder dropped his beer and lurched down the

jetty towards his boat, the wound in his leg decorating the planks behind him with a trail of blood. The huge fish flopped after him, its thrashing bulk rattling the boards and beams. Hardladder leaped aboard the stern of his boat, swiping through the mooring ropes with a machete as the shark closed in. He ran to the wheelhouse and twisted the ignition key, hearing the shark's fins slapping the planks behind him, its jaws clashing with a rhythmic, hollow clunk. The boat finally surged away, churning the water in its wake as the shark dived in after it.

"No, George!" cried Dale, helpless. "He's our only lead."

He saw Hardladder fling a spent beer can at the triangular fin that sliced through the water towards him then sank below the surface. Hardladder levered the accelerator just as the shark burst from the water like a stripper from a cake, its tail clearing the surface for an instant. It belly-flopped onto the stern, catapulting the fisherman into the sky.

The huge animal rolled itself upright and opened its cavernous jaws as Hardladder plummeted screaming towards them. Dale winced, not at the monumental clash of teeth that echoed across the glittering waters, but at the thought of the paperwork that now awaited him back at the office.

*　*　*

"CHUM, GET IN MY OFFICE! NOW!"

Captain Rosenbloom's face was a deeper shade of crimson than usual. George did his best to look casual as he grabbed a brown paper lunch bag from his desk and swaggered into the Captain's office. His colleagues averted their eyes out of habit, so used were they to the sight of him striding into the office dripping wet, naked and demanding someone lend him a tie.

"Unless you got a guide dog you better take those shades

off when I'm talking to you, detective," said the Captain as he lowered himself into his seat. His desk was flanked in one corner by a startled-looking Grizzly that the Captain and shot and stuffed for no other reason than he felt particularly angry that day. George removed his sunglasses and tossed the lunch bag onto the desk.

"Our next lead, Captain," he said.

The Captain stared at George's offering.

"Is this another bag of faeces, detective?"

George nodded. "I figure there's enough of that fisherman guy in there for forensics to extract some DNA or whatever and find out who he was."

"We know who he was, you idiot!" screamed Rosenbloom. "It's his buyers we want!"

"You could give that bag to Goldstein," said George. "Isn't he the guy who can tell where stuff has been just by poking his finger in it?"

"You're thinking of Henrickson," said Rosenbloom with a sigh. "Goldstein is the hypnotist with OCD."

"Cool," said George. "And don't we have a guy who can start fires with his mind?"

The Captain's eyelid twitched.

"Yes," he said slowly. "We also have a woman who remembers everything, a guy who remembers nothing, and a bestselling novelist who clearly has nothing better to do."

He rose from his chair, a vein pulsing in his neck as he planted his immense fists on the desk. "We also got a ventriloquist, a cannibal, and a guy from Mars."

George braced himself as the Captain drew a breath that made his suspenders creak.

"AND NOW I GOT AN IDIOT WHO GOT BIT BY A SHARK ON HALLOWEEN OR SOME SHIT AND NOW TURNS INTO ONE EVERY TIME HE SMELLS BLOOD!"

He swung round and punched the head off his stuffed bear.

"WHY IS EVERY DETECTIVE ON MY FORCE A SIDESHOW FREAK?"

"Human Resources said you need to call me a 'normality-alternative.'"

Rosenbloom's immense shoulders slumped in defeat.

"I'm sorry, George," he said. "You're off the case."

"What's that, Captain?" said George, leaning back in his chair and speaking loudly enough for the rest of the office to hear. "You're saying my methods are just too badass for this department? Now you want me to hand in my badge and go lone wolf?"

"No," said Rosenbloom patiently. "I just need you behind a desk for a while where no one's gonna bleed near you."

George shouted at Rosenbloom's startled secretary. "I know I'm hardcore, but I get results, dammit!"

"NO YOU DON'T, GEORGE!" The Captain spun around, his fury reignited. "THAT'S THE GODDAMN POINT! SOMEONE'S STEALING OUR SHARKS AND I NEED SOMEONE WHO CAN FIND OUT WHO!"

"Sir, please calm down," said George, shrinking into his chair. "I'm frightened and I don't have another sandwich bag."

Having realised his hands were nearing George's throat, Rosenbloom withdrew behind his desk.

"I know you're new around here, Chum," he said, straining every single word through his teeth. "So let me explain. We got every species of shark known to man swimming around Kahlua Bay, which is why we got every tourist, marine biologist and big-shot movie producer circling for a piece of our action. Surfers come from all over the world just to get eaten by our sharks and people pay us a fortune to let them film it. Around here, every week is goddamn Shark Week!"

The Captain's phone rang. He grabbed the receiver,

screamed into it, then hurled the entire device through the nearest window. He stood before George panting, his eyes wild.

"And now I got the DA, the mayor's office and the Discovery Channel busting my ass over this case. Have you seen the state of my ass right now?"

"Sir, please pull up your pants."

Rosenbloom ignored him and clutched his face with both hands.

"Why in God's name did I ever transfer here? Last week I was yelling at a guy who solves cases with his dead grandmother. This week it's a guy who can turn into a fish."

"Actually," interjected George. "Unlike fish, sharks have skeletons made of cartilage rather than bone, which reduces their weight and saves them energy. It's really a miracle of natural engineering..."

The Captain drew another enormous breath, then clutched his chest and sank back into his chair, his face turning from volcanic red to a soothing blue.

"It gets me right there too, sir," said George. "It's like nature just can't stop coming up with cool stuff, right? The other night I saw this documentary about these scientists who were using shark brains to cure Alzheimer's..."

"Someone call a paramedic!" screamed the secretary as she rushed to Rosenbloom's side. "The Captain's had a heart attack."

The other detectives surged into the cramped cubicle as the secretary began frantically pumping the Captain's chest with both hands.

George went to edge towards the door, but found himself trapped amid a crowd of angry faces.

"What the hell did you say to him this time, George?" someone said.

"Nothing," replied George. "He was just really excited

about me definitely still being on the case."

He edged towards the door.

"We swapped stories about Vietnam and stuff and he told me I was one of the finest detectives in this department. And he's so gonna fire whoever put shaving foam in my boots that time."

A gnarled hand caught George's arm and yanked him out of the Captain's office.

"I got us another lead," said Dale, his eyes looking even more weary than usual. "I found fragments of hay in the tyre tracks from the harbour last night. So I sweet-talked the gals in the lab who said it's a special sort of processed animal feed. Then I spent six hours visiting every farm, zoo and veterinarian in this city until I finally found a match."

"See what you get when you honour the gods, Dale?" laughed George. "You and your 'police work.'"

George grabbed his tassled leather jacket and hurried out the door as Dale turned to search for something on his desk.

"Has anyone seen my lunch?"

* * *

"JUST A PET store, huh?" said Dale to the clerk. "Then how do you explain that?"

He pointed the feet of his Zimmer frame at the floor-to-ceiling shark tank that covered an entire wall of the warehouse. Dozens of sharks of various species circled behind the glass, eyeing the visitors moodily. The clerk was one of those muscle heads who hung out at the gym on the beach. His arms swelled impressively as he folded them across a chest the size of a dining table.

"It's our executive range," said the clerk. "Nothing says 'I'm king of the castle' like a tank full of killing machines, right? Buy three or more and we throw in a 'Minion-B-Gone' system. That's a push-button employee-disposal unit that comes in your choice of trapdoor, collapsing footbridge, or a chair that tips backwards."

"C'mon, sport," said George, cracking his knuckles then wincing, "who're the buyers?"

The clerk counted them off on his fingers. "Bill Gates, Donald Trump, Cher…" He paused and smirked at George. "Though on your salary, detective, I might be able to do you a deal on a few piranhas."

Dale restrained George before he could square up to the clerk.

"You know what I smell here, kid?" said Dale.

"Adult diapers?" said the clerk.

"Shark-laundering," said Dale. "Kahlua Bay's shark population has nearly halved this last month and I see a lotta sharks in there."

"Hey, we breed them right here on the premises, old man," said the clerk. "You want me to go get the papers? 'Cos I got another twenty minutes before I open."

George pushed Dale aside and looked up at the clerk, making a weird strangled sigh as he realised the guy looked a lot smaller from across the room.

"I'm your worst nightmare, punk," he growled into the clerk's nipples. "I can smell something fishy on you and I'm the guy who's about to swim up your ass."

George turned and kicked over a cloth-covered bucket, spilling a quantity of bloody fish meat across the floor. The clerk laughed as George recoiled from the mess.

"What's the matter, detective?" he said, shoving past. "You scared of a little blood?"

He scooped up a handful of entrails and dangled them in George's face.

"You really, REALLY don't wanna do that," George

stammered, taking another step back.

A sound like that of a golf club striking a coconut echoed through the store and the clerk slumped to the floor.

"What did you do that for?" said George. "I'm wearing my nose plugs."

"You mind telling me next time?" said Dale, lowering his Zimmer frame as he regarded the unconscious clerk bubbling into a puddle of pureed fish. "And why are you taking his pants off?"

"I got an idea," said George, still tugging at the clerk's jeans. "Me and this guy are pretty much the same body type, right? I'll borrow his clothes, take his place here for a few days and wait for the buyers to call."

"I got a better idea," said Dale, looking from the shark tank to the puddle of blood at George's feet. "Take out your nose plugs."

*   *   *

THE CLERK AWOKE, his head ringing almost as loudly as the phone on the wall. He clambered to his feet, wondering why his pants were around his ankles, and picked up the receiver, pausing first to blow rancid fish meat from his lips.

"I need another five portions," said a malevolent English voice.

The clerk looked around. The store was still closed and there was no sign of the two detectives.

"Sure," he whispered. "It's just that…"

"Right away, please. Or will I be forced to find a new storage facility?"

The voice hung up. The clerk winced as he felt the lump on the back of his head, then moped off to find a Band-Aid.

*   *   *

George took another gill-full of water, savouring its warmth and saltiness. He had dived to the floor of the tank to avoid most of the blood Dale had poured in after him. It was easier to control himself the further away from the source he got, but he could still smell it from down here, its delicious tang tickling his senses. He caught his grey and white reflection in the glass wall of the tank, his fathomless black eyes gazing back at him. He glided past, enjoying the feel of the water cradling his bulk as he lost himself in the churning roar of his surroundings.

When George was in shark-form, his world was simple and immediate. No one yelled at him for eating suspects or pleaded with him to put some clothes on. He often felt the urge to abandon dry land, but the persistent call of duty always shouted at those feelings to get back in line. An old-timer like Dale needed an apex predator like himself to keep him on point. Plus, George could never tell Rosenbloom he was quitting. It would break the Captain's heart.

George lifted his conical snout to see a halo of sharks circling above him, and a familiar yearning filled his heart.

He snatched away his tail as a hulking Great White went to bite it off. It was the shark's way of saying, 'I'm terribly sorry, but your name escapes me.'

During his first few transformations in the wild, George had discovered that sharks liked to cultivate a reputation for being the coolest of all sea creatures, a status they strove to maintain because it not only kept them in fish but also really annoyed those asshole dolphins. But sharks' devotion to their social standing meant that they were terrified of embarrassment, and so the etiquette of the hunt had to be adhered to at all times. Approaching a potential prey item without first assessing its correct identity was considered the greatest of social blunders. Every shark knew that attacking a piece of driftwood, having mistaken it for a seal, likened you less to a highly evolved hunter and more to a randy yet myopic turtle attempting to mount a sea urchin.

As George had found to his cost during several bloody encounters, the problem was that sharks are chronically short-sighted, and use their teeth to distinguish the world around them in much the same way blind people use their fingers to read braille. So when a shark enquires of a human whether or not they are a seal, the conversation usually ends abruptly with lots of screaming and blood, while the shark makes a hurried exit and hopes that no one was watching.

A shovel-nosed Tiger Shark chomped the Great White's tail as if to say, 'Ripp, my dear fellow. What seems to be the trouble?'

Ripp bit the other shark in half as if to say, 'Who said that?' then chomped down on his remains in a manner that thanked whoever it was for asking.

Ripp swam through the billowing cloud of blood and curved his bulk around to face George again, glaring at him with eyes that looked like they had been hole-punched into his head.

Besides biting things, sharks' primary method of communication with other sharks was body language, a medium with which George had always struggled when in shark form as he kept forgetting he was composed of fins and teeth rather than arms and legs. Turning to face Ripp, George whipped his tail and lowered his head in what he hoped was a show of dominance, cocking his fins in a sequence that he was pretty sure spelled out, 'I'm Detective George Chum. You can all relax now.'

Ripp apologised for not having the faintest idea how to get to the post office.

The other sharks started circling George, keeping a safe

distance from Ripp in case he was feeling especially polite. A Hammerhead wondered whether George were some kind of decoy with a camera inside him, and everyone agreed that someone should bite him and find out.

George's snout thudded into the glass wall of the tank as he dodged another inquisitive bite from Ripp. He shook his head and saw that the pet store clerk had returned and was opening a panel in the side of the tank. George tried to swim further down for a closer look, but Ripp blocked his path as he prepared to make another potentially lethal query. George swam back to the other sharks, wriggling frantically in an attempt to indicate the clerk and articulate a warning.

The other sharks looked appalled and assured him that Ripp's mother was most certainly not a dolphin.

Ripp rocketed towards him, about to give George a severe rebuke, just as the clerk flipped a switch and a deep mechanical groan reverberated through the water. George went to swim towards the surface, but something dragged him backwards. He circled around and saw Ripp straining behind him, his huge tail sweeping uselessly against the quickening current. Behind the Great White, in the floor of the tank, a circular drain had opened, a whirlpool trailing into its centre. Ripp and a dozen other sharks were sucked into the vortex, spinning into a blur before vanishing into the drain with a sound like a walrus sucking milkshake through a hosepipe. The other sharks fought their way free as the hole began to iris shut and the suction subsided.

Dale had told George that they needed a man on the inside if they were going to find out who had been stealing the town's sharks. It was time for Dale to discover the inside of what. He aimed his snout at the centre of the shrinking hole and dived.

* * *

GEORGE HURTLED THROUGH what felt like the world's longest, darkest and most uncomfortable water-slide before crashing head-first into freezing, bloodless water. He went to right himself with a swirl of his tail and was disappointed to find that his fins had now split into a familiar pair of human legs. His head broke the surface with what he hoped was a manly yell, before wiping his eyes and taking a look around. The possibility of freezing to death or drowning became less of a concern when he realised he was surrounded by gliding grey fins, their owners no doubt admiring the chandelier of succulent limbs thrashing below the surface.

As the largest of the fins curved towards him, George felt himself hooked under each arm and scooped from the water, as though he were a stray hair someone had found in their soup. Two men in black aprons and bandanas strained at the end of a metal pole as they lowered him towards the floor. He had apparently fallen into another shark tank, although one much smaller than in the pet store. Ripp and his fellow sharks looked even bigger as they swirled behind the magnifying glass wall.

George shrieked as cold metal kissed his buttocks. He had been lowered onto a steel trolley surrounded by several more men all wearing black aprons and bandanas. They pinned his arms and legs as they tied his wrists and ankles to the trolley with towels. George's protestations were quickly silenced by the sound of a knife being scraped down the length of a sharpener. He found himself desperately trying to cross his legs.

His captors made room for a man in a black chef's jacket and twirling a kitchen knife the size of a samurai sword. He was so fat he looked as though he had been baked into existence. The chef laid aside his sharpening tool and peered at the crescent-shaped scar on George's torso. George tried to flex his abs.

"I had no idea *homo carcharodon* was on the menu," the chef said, his voice so deep and imposing it sounded as though he were speaking into a tuba. Like the other men, the chef was entirely bald, his head so smooth and rounded that it looked as though his features had been felt-tipped onto a balloon.

"You no doubt recognise me from television," he said.

George shook his head.

"Sushi Central...?" the chef prompted. "The biggest sushi restaurant in the state of Hawaii...?"

George stared blankly.

"I have my own cooking show. I'm on billboards and magazines all over town."

George shrugged and made a face.

"I'm Chef Oruka, for Neptune's sake! There's a statue of me on top of this building. It's the biggest landmark in Kahlua Bay. You can see it from space."

"I thought that was a lighthouse to stop the cars from crashing into the buildings."

Chef Oruka snorted and twirled his sword as he turned to regard the shark tank.

"Detective Chum," he began.

"My name gets around, huh?"

"Indeed," said Oruka. "The clerk at the pet store found your underwear and it had your name sewn inside it."

"Dammit, I wish Dale would stop doing that!"

"Is it possible that you are as brainless as these mindless savages you so admire?" said Oruka, indicating the sharks circling inside the tank.

"'Mindless'?" said George. "Well, that's a pretty racist attitude, pal. Sharks're actually..."

"However," said Oruka, cutting him off. "As a human – a part-time one at least – I would have thought you'd know that it takes a great deal more than brawn to make it to the top of the food chain."

Oruka threw back his head, as far as his apparent lack

173

of a neck would allow, and squeaked like a balloon being forced through a letterbox. His kitchen staff answered him with a chorus of high-pitched squeals and clicks. Their fingers fused and lengthened into sleek grey flippers, their mouths stretched into cackling beaks, and blowholes dimpled the tops of their heads.

"Seals," gasped George. "I knew it."

"*Homo odontoceti*," said Oruka, still in human form. "That's 'were-dolphin' to you."

The chef shoved the trolley through a nearby door and into a kitchen filled with dolphins wearing black aprons and bandanas. Poised on their tails like ballet dancers, they squealed orders at one another as they packed and sliced wads of rice and pink fish-meat with their flippers, arranging them on brightly coloured dishes with the flawless concentration of bomb-disposal experts. They barely noticed their boss wheeling a naked human on a trolley through their midst.

"Unlike you, detective," said Oruka. "My pod and I began life not as humans, but as creatures of the sea, our natural, superior intellect wasted beneath the waves. Have you ever tried discussing Polish literature with a walrus?"

George stared at a dolphin placing carefully arranged dishes on a seemingly endless conveyer belt that snaked through the kitchen.

"Desperate for intelligent conversation we approached a group of tourists off the coast of Provence," said Oruka. "But the poor devils had been stranded in their boat for several days and tried to eat us. We managed to swim to safety, nursing our gnawed flukes beneath the moon of All Hallow's Eve…"

Oruka wheeled George before a huge window overlooking a cavernous amphitheatre open to the afternoon sun. The conveyor belt of food spiralled around the tiers of tables that surrounded a huge swimming pool in which dolphins frolicked for the amusement of the human diners.

"We wandered the earth as men on a quest to find an intelligence that equalled our own. A quest that we knew was doomed to frustration when we learned of man's bewildering reverence for shark-kind. How fitting that humans venerate a creature that matches their own mindless pursuit of consumption."

George stared in horror at a procession of shark fins, each standing in a long dish of rice streaked with sauce. The dishes proceeded along the conveyor belt and down into the amphitheatre below.

"Soon," sneered Oruka. "The entire shark population of Kahlua Bay will be extinct and I will have a Sushi Central on every beach in the world. Then we'll see who's the dominant species."

One of the dolphin chefs squeaked at Oruka in such a way that if subtitles had materialised across his chest they would almost certainly have read, 'What would you like us to do with the body, boss?'

"I think we'll get quite a few boxes of temaki out of this one," said Oruka patting George's stomach. "I have to check in with the diners now, but have a sample ready for me when I return."

With a bow, he handed his sushi-sword to the dolphin and left the kitchen, still honking with laughter. The dolphin rolled the sword between his flippers. George closed his eyes and braced himself, then heard the familiar sound of Zimmer frame on skull.

"Dale?"

The dolphin fell to one side, revealing the elderly detective wearing a busboy uniform. Every dolphin in the kitchen froze.

"K.B.P.D," said Dale, drawing his gun. "Any of you boys move and you'll feel my foot up your blowhole. You 'kay there, partner?"

The nearest dolphin slapped Dale's gun aside, then back-flippered his face, slamming the dentures from his mouth and launching a single bead of blood from his whiskered nostrils. George watched the trembling red globule fly towards him as the dolphins swarmed over Dale like he was a bucket of sardines. The blood splashed George's lips, melting into his tongue and igniting the primal core of his brain. As Dale disappeared under a pile of furious dolphins, each trying to slap the elderly detective into unconsciousness, George felt his body inflate. His arms flattened into fins that tore through his bonds. His legs fused into a huge tail that smacked the dolphins aside like rubber skittles. Dale scrambled for cover as George flopped onto his rippling white belly.

George felt a frenzy coming on at the thought of the many sharks that had journeyed down that conveyor belt, wrapped in a blanket of vinegar-soaked rice and coated with sesame seeds, perhaps even seasoned with crab or a dab of spicy wasabi. George wondered for a moment if they came with bacon. He was slapped out of his reverie by a dolphin that roundhoused him with its tail. George reeled for a moment then the rage was on him. He caterpillared into the mob of dolphins, snapping at anything grey and squeaky.

* * *

DALE RETRIEVED HIS hat and dentures and struggled to his feet. In a kitchen filled with a rampaging shark and a pod of dolphins wearing aprons and armed with sushi knives, Dale knew he was the last thing to which anyone would pay attention. He picked his way through the welters of blood, flying dolphin heads, and squealed expletives as calmly as if he were moseying through a cornfield in June with a stalk of hay between his teeth. Entering the supply room, he shuffled over to the shark tank. The great fish prowled behind the glass, excited by the presence of blood in the next room.

"Hang on now, fellas," said Dale. "This may take a while."

He lifted his Zimmer frame and swung it at the inch-thick glass.

*   *   *

"Chef Oruka, we've had a couple of complaints," said the floor manager, tugging at his collar, whether from nervousness or the discomfort of his clothed human form it was difficult to tell.

"Oh?"

"The diners seem a little bored by the floor show."

The manager indicated the dolphins in the pool at the centre of the amphitheatre.

Oruka looked confused.

"They're solving Fermat's last theorem on a giant chalkboard," he said. "That's impressive isn't it? Look, that one's just questioned the theory of modularity using binary coefficients."

One of the diners bounced a crab cake off the back of a dolphin's head, knocking its glasses into the water.

"Fine," seethed Oruka. "Bring out a few hoops and the dolphin-cannon. Give these brainless bipeds what they want, so long as they're paying for it."

"Also," said the manager. "There have been a few complaints about entrails in the food. I think there may be a problem in the kitchen."

A thunderous boom shook the building. Above them, the kitchen window exploded as a shark and dolphin-infested waterfall tumbled into the amphitheatre. One of the diners looked up at the incoming avalanche and was relieved to have a good excuse for not leaving a tip.

*   *   *

GEORGE AWOKE FROM what had felt like a deep and pleasant dream. He couldn't recall any specifics, but the dominant colour had definitely been red. He found himself airborne and naked, carried aloft by an irresistible wave of water, before landing with about as much dignity as one can expect in an ornamental palm tree. The ornament toppled over and deposited him on a podium beside the pool where the floor manager had been due to introduce an all-dolphin rendition of Euripides' *Medea*.

Sharks rained about him, as Ripp and his fellow inmates crashed onto the tables, snapping at the legs of diners as they fled or dodged the assortment of dismembered dolphin parts that were showering the area like soggy meteorites. The pool at the centre of the amphitheatre overflowed, washing the chalkboard clean and infuriating the dolphins who were about to present a revolutionary argument against the use of linear algebra in mapping vector spaces.

The drenched diners recovered as the initial deluge subsided to a steady trickle and the occasional crash of falling debris. George grabbed a dessert plate and covered his modesty, although everyone would have agreed that there were far more offensive parts of him that needed covering.

"Kahlua Bay Police Department!" he cried, producing his badge, although no one dared consider where from. "This is Detective George Chum and you…"

He pointed at Oruka. The chef was struggling to heave his bulk from the swimming pool, despite the efforts of several dolphins helpfully prodding him from behind.

"You're under arrest for the receipt and sale of a protected and frankly awesome species sourced from the proud waters of this great town."

The diners gasped.

"That's right, folks," said George, "you've been tricked

into eating some of the greatest treasures of Kahlua Bay: her sharks. You see..."

He grabbed the dripping microphone with the nonchalance of a man both warming to his subject and oblivious to the threat of electrocution. He pointed again at Oruka, who glared back at him.

"What this man – if I can even call him a man – doesn't understand is that nature isn't a battle. The natural world isn't a war. It's about harmony. It's about friendship. It's about..."

The cannon beside the pool roared and George ducked as a dolphin flew over his head and crashed into the salad bar.

"What the hell, man?" yelled George.

The surviving dolphins jeered at him, making obscene gestures with their flippers.

Barging past George, Ripp wriggled towards the edge of the pool, baring his teeth as if to say, 'Who said that? If you don't tell me I shall be forced to approach and ask in person, and damn the social consequences if you turn out to be a surfboard or something.'

The dolphins squeaked with laughter. One of them squealed back at him, his subtitles saying something along the lines of, 'Go chomp on an oxygen tank, you intellectual guppy.'

Ripp and the other sharks dived into the pool as the dolphins raised themselves on their tails and surged backwards, beckoning with their flippers. Within seconds the pool was a riot of slapping fins and snapping jaws.

Chef Oruka wobbled towards the exit as George scampered after him, brandishing his badge at the astonished diners while struggling to keep a grip on his loin-plate. Oruka's escape route was blocked by a pile of washed-up furniture and he turned to face his naked pursuer.

"You're going to state pen, big guy," said George. "Now tell me who's at the bottom of the food-chain."

Oruka closed his eyes and took a deep breath that seemed

to last forever. To George's astonishment, the chef's body began to expand, bursting out of his clothes, as he toppled onto his belly and swelled into something resembling a black and white submarine with beady brown eyes and a mouth studded with sharp teeth.

"You're a...?"

"*Orcinus orca.*"

George shrugged. "Help me out here, man."

"A killer whale, you moron!"

"I thought you said you were a dolphin?"

"I'm a type of dolphin, you ignoramus!" bellowed Oruka as he charged, rowing his flukes like oars, his belly slamming the floor as he thundered after George. George turned and fled past what had once been the dolphin pool but which now resembled a serial killer's washing machine. He wasn't entirely sure where he was running to, but felt convinced that if he screamed loudly enough an opportunity would present itself.

The pounding behind him ceased and George looked over his shoulder to see Oruka slam a black flipper at a pile of debris. A discarded sushi sword somersaulted into the air. With the same dexterity the chef had displayed in his human form, Oruka caught the hilt of the weapon in his blowhole, bowed his head and fired the sword at George with a vast exhale.

The world seemed to slow to a crawl, as it often did at times like these. George tried to fling himself out of the way as the razor-sharp missile drilled through the air towards his heart. Just as the sword neared George's chest, someone launched themselves in front of him with a long, low groan that made the feat appear even more spectacular. The sword skewered Dale's chest and he flopped into George's arms like a sack of potatoes wearing a tweed jacket with a sword-hilt broach.

George cradled his partner as he threw back his head and

went to scream something into the sky.

"Please don't," coughed Dale.

The old man's eyes twinkled with tears as he pressed a gnarled, liver-spotted hand against George's cheek. George tried not to recoil.

"Just do one thing for me," said Dale.

George nodded. "Anything, pal. It's just that…"

Oruka was galumphing towards the dolphin-cannon at the far end of the pool. The creep had found his getaway.

"Pay attention, George," said Dale. "I'm about to say something profound."

"Okay, okay. Just make it fast."

"Be…" he said, "yourself…"

"I will," George nodded and smiled, then went to leave, but Dale caught his arm.

"What you are doesn't make you *who* you are…"

"Got it."

By now Oruka had managed to stuff himself tail-first into the cannon.

Dale squeezed George's arm.

"It's who you want to be…"

George nodded furiously, as a pair of wounded dolphins aimed the barrel up over the highest tier of the amphitheatre and out to sea.

"That makes you…" gasped Dale, "yourself…"

"Sleep well, old friend," said George as the dolphins lit the cannon's fuse.

"Dammit, George. Get your fingers out've my eyes. I'm not finished…"

But George had already unsheathed the sword from Dale's body and was racing up the stairs of the amphitheatre.

Dale clutched the wound in his chest and cried out after him.

"You forgot your plate!"

The fuse sizzled into the barrel, igniting the cannon with a roar, and launching Chef Oruka into the air like the world's fattest torpedo.

George sprinted towards the balcony and leaped into space, holding the sword above his head as Oruka soared towards him.

"Free this, Willy!" he cried.

Oruka rolled his eyes before the sword sheared him in two, showering George with blood and internal organs as the two halves of the killer whale flopped to the floor either side of him. George plunged, bright red and naked, into the crimson water of the pool below. The soup of blood and dolphin chunks bubbled for a moment before George leapt several feet into the air, his gills rippling, teeth glittering, fins spread wide, accompanied by his victorious brother sharks. As Dale squinted against the sun, he could have sworn they gave George a high-five.

* * *

HAVING DISMISSED HIMSELF from hospital on the grounds that screaming at his employees always made him feel better, Captain Rosenbloom entered the ruined amphitheatre with a horde of uniformed cops. He found Dale doing his best to dab the blood out of his tie with a napkin.

"You might wanna get that chest wound looked at, Cardigan," he said.

"Oh, I've seen worse," shrugged Dale. "By the way, your perp's over there."

He indicated the two halves of Chef Oruka laid out on the floor nearby like two oversized and exotic steaks draped across a barbeque. Another boom echoed across the wrecked amphitheatre. Dale and Rosenbloom looked up to see the last of the sharks sail over the wall and out to sea.

"So long, George," Dale murmured. "Have a surfer on me, pal."

He could see Rosenbloom was gearing up for another rant about the DA's interest in his ass, but Dale was not in the mood.

"Take it easy, Captain. I'll do the paperwork in the morning."

"And make sure you finish it before next week," said the Captain.

"What's the rush?"

"The commissioner rejected your last request to defer retirement," said the Captain. "This time next week you'll have officially retired."

He slapped Dale on the back and stalked away in search of someone else to shout at.

"Time to buy that yacht you been saving for," the Captain called out.

Dale heard a slapping sound above him. He looked up to see a twelve-foot Tiger Shark, a straggler from the busted tank, slithering towards the edge of the broken window directly above his head. The fish see-sawed on the ledge for a moment, gnashing its razor-sharp teeth.

Dale sighed.

"I get seasick anyway."

SHARKBAIT

RICHARD SALTER

IT WAS PERHAPS the slowest getaway in history, but at last they had drifted far enough away from the yacht to fire up the engine. The noise was loud, but not so loud as to wake the slumbering occupants of *Le Merchant*, the luxury yacht belonging to the infamous Madame Yvette Beaumier.

Laurel Wright took off her mask and gloves and tossed them into the sea. Her partner, Jacob, gently steered them further away from the scene of the crime.

Before long, the yacht was out of sight as they approached the rocky coast of Malta. There were a number of caves in the cliff face in this area, which is why they had waited for three days before executing the heist, waiting until Beaumier moored her boat here.

Laurel took over the rudder so that Jacob could get out of his black ops clothing and put on his wetsuit. Laurel slowed the engine as they approached the entrance to a particular cave, guiding the boat into the narrow entrance with skill and care.

It was, of course, much darker inside, but Laurel could see enough to bring the boat to rest partially up on a sandy patch of land at the back of the cave. A second boat was moored next to them, tied to a post driven into the ground. The second vessel was purple, in stark contrast to their current white boat.

Jacob stayed in the boat while Laurel jumped out. In a few hours this cave would be visited by the first of the day's tourist boats, so it was vital they didn't leave any evidence of their visit. The first rays of dawn didn't reach this far in yet, so Laurel lit a flare. She took an oxygen tank and mask from the purple boat and handed them to Jacob. She then stripped off her black jumpsuit to reveal a bikini underneath. She noticed Jacob had paused to watch her but she didn't care. She loaded their balaclavas, voice changers, clothes, her phone and their guns into a sealable bag, which she clipped on to the inside of the white boat. Then she clipped a smaller bag to Jacob's belt. She checked the zipper was closed and that the bag was secure. Inside was the diamond. If Jacob lost it, all this would have been for nothing.

They were ready. Laurel climbed aboard the purple motorboat. She made a final check of the ground to ensure they had not left anything behind, then she untied both craft. She started the engine of the purple boat and, a moment later, Jacob started the engine of the white. One after the other, they steered towards the cave entrance. Laurel dropped the flare into the water on the way out and it quickly went out. She watched it sink into the crystal clear water and come to rest on the bottom. They would need to head out to much deeper waters to safely dispose of the evidence of their crime.

She headed away from *Le Merchant*, with Jacob following behind at a distance. Laurel wondered if anyone had woken up and discovered the robbery yet. They passed a few other boats, but by now Laurel looked like a tourist in a bathing suit, and Jacob was just another early morning diver.

Soon they were far enough out that there were no boats close enough to observe them and the soaring rock cliffs of Malta were a fair distance away.

"You ready?" she called back to Jacob as he pulled up behind her.

"Sure, I just hope the sharks don't take bites out of me along the way."

"You'll be moving too fast for them," Laurel assured him. "Just hold on tight."

Jacob nodded. He reached down and unlatched a series of bolts in the floor of the white boat. As he lifted the specially installed trapdoor, water immediately flooded into the boat. Jacob pulled on his goggles and put the regulator in his mouth, then waited patiently for the boat to sink. Laurel watched until he was fully submerged and then she waited. She had to give him time to swim underneath her boat and grab on to the handles he had attached there yesterday. She was tempted to leave him, but of course he had the diamond. So far she'd not seen any sharks, but that didn't mean they weren't out here. She was damn glad Jacob was the diving expert. She'd dived many times but he had insisted he be the one to go under the boat, and Laurel hadn't been inclined to argue.

Three sharp raps on the hull told her that Jacob was in position. She opened the throttle and moved off, gently at first, circling a couple of times to ensure there was no trace of the other craft from the surface. By now it would be on the bottom of the Mediterranean. She steered towards the main island of Malta, heading towards the marina at Grand Harbour and the safety of tourists.

Just in time too. The police had scrambled multiple boats now. Someone on Beaumier's boat must have called for help. With luck, none of the conscious passengers could give any kind of description of the robbers or of their boat, but Laurel was taking no chances. As she drew closer to the island, she passed more and more boats, including fishing vessels with their distinctive eyes painted on the prow, as well as two police dinghies. It wasn't long before the *pulizija* approached Laurel. She decreased her speed and then turned off the engine as they neared, noticing that she was drifting close to a marker buoy.

An officer leaned out as they passed.

"Excuse me, you speak English?" Laurel nodded. "Have you seen a white speed boat with two people aboard, both dressed all in black? They would have been moving fast."

Laurel felt relief. Somebody on the yacht *had* seen them leave, yet all of Laurel's planning had paid off.

"I didn't notice anyone unusual, officer," Laurel replied, adopting an American accent.

The officer looked over into Laurel's boat but obviously saw nothing suspicious. A lifejacket, snorkel, camera. Laurel had been careful not to leave anything of interest on display.

"No need. They're armed and dangerous so we're asking everyone to head back to land for the time being."

"Thank you, officer. I'll go back in right away."

There was a loud thump against the hull of Laurel's boat. She jumped in surprise. At first she thought she'd run into the buoy, but it wasn't close enough.

"Oh my, what was that?" she said, remembering to maintain her accent.

"Might be a great white," the officer said. "They're pretty active today so be careful. I suggest you wear your lifejacket at all times too."

"Of course," Laurel replied. She picked up the jacket and pulled it on. "I hope you catch your bad guys!"

The officer nodded and motioned to the driver to move away. The *pulizija* powered off towards the next tourist boat.

Laurel was worried. Something must have happened to her passenger. She had visions of dragging a shark onto the shore and cutting its belly open to get the diamond back. If Jacob had got himself eaten she would be mad as hell.

The big lug was still in one piece thankfully. While Laurel steered along the fairway to the wharf reserved for smaller boats, she caught a glimpse of Jacob swimming over to nearby rocks where a group of tourists were practising diving. Laurel glanced over as the instructor helped him from the water. By the time Laurel had docked, Jacob had removed his mask, flippers and tank and was limping towards her.

"What happened?" Laurel asked as she secured the boat to its mooring.

"You dragged me through a bunch of fucking mauve stingers, you bitch!"

"Well I didn't see them. Besides how did they get you through your wetsuit?"

"One of the fuckers got tangled around my leg. When you stopped I got my knife out to try and cut it away but it stung my ankle. I banged my head on the hull."

"What happened to the bag?" Laurel asked.

"What bag?"

"The bag with the fucking diamond in it."

Jacob held up the tattered remains of the empty bag.

"I must have shredded it when I put the knife away."

"You absolute fucking moron!"

"The sting hurt! I hit my head! I wasn't thinking straight."

"Oh my God. We're going to be crucified! How could you be so stupid?"

"Seriously, you want to try getting stung by a jellyfish."

Laurel ignored him. Her mind was racing. She tried to focus on a solution rather than the thought of what her employer might do to her, or what she was going to do to Jacob. "We need to get out there again. It must be at the bottom of the sea. Oh Christ, we are so dead if we don't deliver."

"Maybe we should have this conversation somewhere else?"

Laurel nodded. She knew they'd have to wait until police activity died down anyway. The chances of someone else finding the diamond were remote, and to be honest they were safer without it right now. Still, this was not going according to plan. And how were they going to find a single diamond at the bottom of the sea? The marker buoy would help, assuming they found the right one. But as they walked from the marina, Jacob threw another wrench in the machine.

"I'm not diving down to look for it."

"Yes you fucking are," Laurel said.

"No way. You should have seen how many great whites were down there."

"They won't hurt you. Right now you're more likely to die from me shooting you than being eaten by a shark, believe me."

Jacob's limp was more pronounced now. He was clearly in pain, which helped lighten Laurel's mood somewhat.

"I'm not going down there," he said. He ducked into a small corner shop and Laurel followed him, keeping her voice down so the owner wouldn't hear them.

"Then you can tell our employer that you screwed up our mission."

Jacob stopped and turned. He leant in close. His bad breath was almost overpowering.

"Oh no. This is your mission, you're in charge. Your plan went wrong. I'll call him up right now and tell him if you like."

Maybe Jacob wasn't as stupid as Laurel had pegged him. She held up her hands.

"Okay, fine. No problem. I'll text him and tell him the diamond's safe and we're waiting for the heat to die down. That should give us a couple of days to retrieve it."

Laurel needed to think. She went outside while Jacob searched the shelves of the shop.

She couldn't ask for more cash without arousing her employer's suspicion that something was wrong. The chalet was on their employer's tab so she couldn't divert those funds. She could try to sell the rental car, but she doubted anyone would pay her enough for it to hire a professional salvaging team. And what would she tell them anyway? Jacob was by far the most qualified to go searching on the seabed, so what they needed was something to keep the sharks away. How much would a cage cost, she wondered, and a boat capable of lowering it? No good, the cage would limit Jacob's search range. She couldn't afford to pay for an experienced scavenger to go after it. She needed a shark expert to go down with Jacob long enough for him to find the diamond without shitting his wetsuit.

The other option was for Laurel to go down instead. Mentally, she stuck a label on that thought: *last resort.*

Jacob emerged from the shop carrying a small bottle of vinegar. He rolled up the wetsuit leg and poured the liquid over an angry red rash on his ankle.

"Oh fuck, that feels better."

"Shhhh!" Laurel hissed. A policeman was approaching. He wasn't looking at them yet but it was only a matter of time. Laurel reached out and grabbed Jacob, pulling him in close, and locked lips with him.

He seemed stunned at first but either he realized what she was doing, or he really thought she was kissing him. Either way, his breath made Laurel feel like throwing up in his mouth. At least then he'd know how she really felt about him. The policeman passed by into the shop. Laurel pushed Jacob away from her.

"Come on, time to go."

*   *   *

"This is nuts."

Jacob was right, it *was* nuts. But it didn't bother Laurel. All she had to do was convince *him* that this was going to work. She didn't need to convince herself.

"They said she has a gift."

"A what? A gift? Are you taking the piss?"

"No, Jacob. Sharks love her. She's like a good luck charm. You can't go wrong."

Laurel knew full well that her plan wouldn't make any difference as to whether Jacob got eaten or not. That was just fine. She'd spent the day talking with many divers, telling them that she had lost her engagement ring in the sea and wanted to go retrieve it, but she needed someone to keep her 'husband' safe while he went down to look for it.

Some of them turned her down flat, others said they were too busy or wanted a fortune to help. But some of them gave her similar advice.

She needed Sharkbait.

At first she thought they meant a particular brand of marine food. Then she thought they meant dropping hunks of meat out of the boat to distract the sharks from Jacob while he dived. One woman laughed at that suggestion.

"Sure," she said. "Whip 'em up into a feeding frenzy while your husband searches underneath them."

She had a point.

No, Sharkbait was something quite different.

She was a girl with magical powers, so the legend went. And it was almost a legend. One guy told Laurel that this young islander single-handedly fought off three great whites with her bare hands to rescue a drowning surfer. An older lady swore blind she'd seen a shark bow to the sea nymph as she strolled across the waves. Slightly less fanciful tales revolved around tourists requesting her help to keep the sharks at bay while they searched for missing items in the waters, or of a young girl helping to rescue folks stranded at sea before they were eaten. Whatever the story, one common theme stayed more or less consistent: Sharkbait had a way with sharks.

In reality she was nine years old, pretty, with long curly hair and a wide smile. She was taller than the two friends she played skip-rope with, and held herself with a confidence that belied her age. For a moment, Laurel couldn't help but think of her own little girl, a bit older but with the same glow about her.

Penny was Laurel's reason for taking this job and risking another stretch in Holloway. Her no-good, layabout ex-husband had an iron-clad case for keeping Laurel away from her daughter, so it didn't matter to her whether she was behind bars or out in the Mediterranean sunshine, she still felt locked up. As soon as this job paid out, she would snatch her daughter away from his crummy, rundown flat in Islington and take her to somewhere as beautiful as she was.

It was quite easy to find Sharkbait. Everyone seemed to know about her. Apparently, people would come to her regularly asking for help. Her parents were quite willing to let her do so, for worthy causes. Laurel wondered what kind of parent would be okay with sending their young daughter out to swim with sharks.

"Her father will want to come with you," one man had warned Laurel, "but he's a nice man with lots of amazing stories to tell about his incredible daughter."

Laurel guessed Sharkbait's father might take a dim view of his little girl helping two criminals find a lost diamond, especially with the substantial reward announced on the news for anyone who could find the missing gem. The report said details on the two criminals were sketchy and the police were appealing for information. The pair was still being careful to avoid the police, but for now nobody knew what they looked like.

"What are we going to do?" Jacob asked.

"We're going to lure her out and kidnap her," Laurel replied.

"How do you propose we do that?"

"How much money are you carrying?"

* * *

"Sharkbait! Sharkbait! Come quickly!"

The daylight was fading when the boy approached Sharkbait and her friends.

"You must come quickly!" he cried. "A boat has capsized! The tourists are surrounded by sharks! They need you!"

"Let me tell my father," the girl replied.

"There isn't time!"

"Okay. Ester, Liena – tell my dad where I have gone."

Sharkbait's two friends hurried away while she ran after the boy. Laurel and Jacob watched her progress. As instructed, the boy led her straight to their position. Laurel quickly steered the boy out of sight of Sharkbait and paid him the remainder of what they had promised.

"What are you going to do with her?" he asked.

"We just need to talk to her, that's all. Remember if you say anything, we'll find you."

The boy looked terrified but took the money and ran off. When Laurel returned to Jacob, he was holding Sharkbait's arm. They were hidden in an alcove. Laurel was keenly aware that Sharkbait's father was probably close behind by now. The girl was strangely quiet, and Laurel was surprised Jacob hadn't needed to put a hand over her mouth.

Moments later, Sharkbait's father and her two friends ran past, heading for the beach. Now Jacob did place his hand over the girl's face, but she made no move to resist or call out.

The immediate danger passed, Jacob released her. Laurel stared into the girl's eyes. She saw no resistance there, but neither was the stare vacant. There was an unfazed confidence to her that was unnerving.

"Listen up, love, we don't want to hurt you. We need your help, okay? We couldn't ask you nicely so we're sorry for

193

snatching you, but I promise you won't get hurt as long as you do everything we tell you to. Do you understand?"

Sharkbait nodded. The girl was smart, she didn't make any move or any sound. Maybe this wasn't her first time as a kidnap victim. Or perhaps after you stare down great whites, the company of crooks doesn't seem so scary.

Jacob placed a hand on Sharkbait's shoulder and the three of them moved off.

After a ten minute car ride they reached their little chalet. The tiny holiday home was part of a complex of various sized chalets, sharing a swimming pool and tennis courts. Everyone staying here was a tourist, so none of them saw anything special in Sharkbait as the trio walked to their unit. Indeed her Mediterranean skin tone was almost half way between Jacob and Laurel's, so she could almost pass for their daughter.

While Jacob took a shower, Laurel ordered food and put the television on for the girl. She sat and watched in silence. When the food arrived she barely touched it. When Jacob returned to the room, she didn't acknowledge him. She showed no fear or apprehension at all.

Laurel left Jacob to watch her and eat *klamari mimlija*, while she took her turn in the shower. She wanted to stand under the hot water forever, but she didn't think leaving her idiot partner alone with an underage girl for any length of time was wise, so reluctantly she had to step out.

The child was asleep, so Laurel switched the TV over to the news. She wanted to see if Sharkbait's kidnapping was common knowledge yet, but there was nothing about it on the broadcast bulletin.

"Is she supposed to protect me from the great whites?" he scoffed, indicating the sleeping girl.

"*She* is a local legend. You saw how she dropped everything to run to help those tourists."

"What tourists?"

"The ones we paid the kid to tell her about."

"Oh, them."

"She didn't hesitate. She ran after him to help. What use do you think she'd be if the legends *aren't* true?"

Laurel was almost convincing herself. She highly doubted the girl was a sea nymph. So what was her secret? What talent did she have that might save a boatload of tourists from ravenous killers of the sea? Where did her confidence come from?

"I've heard a lot of talk today, but so far nothing to stop me being eaten."

Laurel wanted to scream at Jacob. Great white sharks hadn't killed anyone in Maltese waters for over half a century. The big lug would be fine. He was the fucking diving expert. Laurel had been warned he wasn't the smartest fish in the sea, but nobody mentioned anything about irrational cowardice.

"Fine," she said. "There'll be too much heat to dive tomorrow anyway. Let's get up early and maybe we can find some way to put her to the test."

Jacob didn't ask her what she had in mind, which was a relief because she had no idea. It had been a long day and Laurel was bone tired. She handcuffed Sharkbait to the bedframe and turned in for the night.

*   *   *

WHEN LAUREL AWOKE, Sharkbait was standing at the foot of the bed, staring at her. Laurel punched Jacob awake.

"Did you let her out?" Laurel hissed.

Jacob stared groggily at the girl. "What the...?"

Laurel got up, checking the girl's unshackled wrist and then the open handcuffs still attached to the bedframe.

Incredulous, Laurel asked, "How did you do that?"

Sharkbait didn't answer the question.

195

"I'll make you a deal," she said.

Jacob advanced on her. "You're in no position to–"

"Shut up, Jacob!" Laurel snapped. "What's the deal?"

Sharkbait spoke to Laurel only, clearly marking her as the brains of the operation.

"I'll help you get your diamond. I know you stole it and I know that's what you've lost. I won't fight, I won't try to get away, and I won't tell anyone."

"And what do you want in return?"

"I want you to get me into the new shark attraction in Sliema. I've been trying to get in since they brought two tiger sharks in but they won't let me. I want to talk to them."

"You want to talk to the owners?" Laurel clarified.

"No." She stared at Laurel like she'd said something crazy.

Jacob was about to protest again but Laurel waved him into silence.

"Deal."

Sharkbait smiled and went back to the television. She opened a leftover container of food and started eating.

"Have you lost your mind?" Jacob whispered at Laurel.

"Far from it. We do this for her and we get her complete cooperation. You saw how she got out of the handcuffs. She could cause real problems for us if she wants to. Besides, this might be a chance to see what she's capable of."

*   *   *

IT WAS STILL early enough that there was little traffic on the roads. It took about twenty minutes to get to the new Shark Conservation Centre. The parking area was closed but Laurel wouldn't have left the rental there anyway. Instead they parked on a nearby side street.

Laurel had no problem breaking in. It wasn't exactly a maximum security facility. Disabling the security cameras without alerting anyone took longer than getting the door open. Once inside, the two security guards provided little resistance. One was already asleep. The other found Jacob's knife pressed against his neck before he could reach the alarm button.

"Her again," said one of the two guards. His name badge identified him as Dwardu. He scowled at Sharkbait. "Always hanging around the doors, trying to get in. You've been banned from here, remember? Got some help this time, did you?"

"Take us to the tiger sharks," the girl said.

The access point to the tank was past the observation tunnel, an enclosure surrounded on all sides by marine life behind glass. The tank itself was huge and contained at least two tiger sharks that Laurel could see, as well as several smaller sharks and all manner of other aquatic life. At the end of the tunnel the guards led them through a concealed door in the wall and up a flight of stairs to the open top of the tank. Jacob still held the other man at knifepoint while Laurel told Dwardu to comply or be responsible for the death of his colleague.

Sharkbait was fascinated by the creatures in the tank. Laurel could see them from above now, distorted by the water but no less deadly.

"What are you going to do?" Dwardu asked.

Sharkbait answered. "We need to set them free. They're not happy here."

"That wasn't part of the deal, love," Laurel said. "We got you in here but we don't have the resources to rescue sharks. It will be opening time before long and a lot more people are coming, so talk to your sharks and let's go."

"Resources," Sharkbait repeated, lost in thought. "Money."

"Exactly. You'd need to hire a specialist crew even if you

197

could convince the people that run this place to give them up."

Laurel decided to try something. She nodded towards the tank. "Have they been fed yet?" she asked Dwardu.

"The sharks? No. It's too early."

"Good. In you get."

"Are you crazy? I'm not getting in there!"

"You'll be taking her with you." Laurel nodded to Sharkbait. Dwardu clearly didn't know who the girl was, and had no wish to dip even a toe in the tank.

Laurel nodded. Jacob stepped forward and sliced a deep gash in Dwardu's forearm. The guard cried out, clutching the wound.

"What did you do that for?"

"To prove a point. Jump in or your friend here gets fed to the sharks in pieces." She nodded towards the second guard, still held fast by Jacob with a knife to his throat.

Reluctantly, Dwardu sat on the edge of the tank, cradling his injured arm. Before he could change his mind, Laurel planted a foot in the middle of his back and pushed.

Dwardu fell into the shark tank with a splash, the water around him turned red, blood spreading slowly in every direction. It didn't take long before the sharks were circling. Dwardu came up for air, starting to panic. "How long do I have to stay in here?" he gasped, his eyes fixed on the closer of the two sharks. Another joined its fellows from the far side of the tank. So now there were three.

Laurel turned to Sharkbait. "You'd better do your thing if you want to save–"

The girl jumped in before Laurel finished her sentence.

Something astonishing happened. The sharks' behaviour altered almost immediately. Sharkbait swam to Dwardu and put a hand on his shoulder. The tiger sharks seemed to grow anxious, if it were possible for fish to experience anxiety. They became skittish, wanting to come nearer but seemingly unable to. After a few more seconds, all three of them had moved away until they disappeared from view.

Laurel helped Dwardu and Sharkbait out of the water.

The four adults couldn't believe what had happened. Laurel was in shock. She had assumed it was all make believe. She expected to have to pull Sharkbait out before Dwardu got eaten.

Sharkbait sat quietly on the side of the tank, not shivering, but completely calm.

"You convinced now?" Laurel asked Jacob.

"Those aren't Great Whites," Jacob replied. But Laurel could hear the edge of surprise in his voice.

The guard Jacob had been holding saw his chance and grabbed the knife. He plunged it into Jacob's shoulder and took off down the steps.

"You idiot!" Laurel screamed, picking up the knife and going after him.

Behind her, she heard Dwardu's skull slam into the side of the tank. She didn't look back. If the other one made it to the front desk and raised the alarm, they'd be in serious trouble. The guard was nearly at the end of the corridor. Laurel was just steps away, but instead of pursuing further she stopped, aimed, and hurled the knife.

It thudded between the guard's shoulder blades and he pitched forward to the shiny floor. He didn't move again.

Laurel collapsed against the wall, breathing hard. Goddamn Jacob, letting go of him like that. Nearly ruined the whole operation. She glanced at her watch. It was seven AM. There would be people on the streets now, and the usual morning traffic would be building. Before long, more folks would come to tend to the animals. They had to leave now.

Jacob arrived with Sharkbait. She wasn't resisting. If the dead guard bothered her as they stepped over him, she didn't show it. Strong girl, Laurel mused. Jacob recovered his knife as he passed over the corpse.

"Fuck, Jacob. I didn't want to kill them."

"I need stitches," Jacob said, ignoring her. "Let's go."

Laurel found a first aid kit at the security desk and bandaged the wound hastily, enough to prevent the dumb lunk from leaving a trail of blood for the police to follow. While she did so, Sharkbait used the towel Laurel had brought to dry herself off. Then she tied back her damp hair as they left the aquarium together, being careful not to be seen.

The urge to run once they hit the street was overwhelming, but instead Laurel kept their speed to a walk as they passed early morning joggers. Sharkbait could easily have made things very difficult for them at that moment by making a fuss. Instead she moved along quietly, keeping her end of the bargain. At last they reached their car.

The journey back to the chalet took a lot longer than the drive out. Traffic was starting to snarl up the roads and the usual cacophony of horns filled the air.

Back at the chalet, Jacob stripped off his shirt and sat down on the bed. Laurel couldn't give a shit if he bled to death just so long as he found the diamond first. But even as she threaded the needle and plunged it into his flesh, almost relishing the pain she was inflicting, she knew full well that he wasn't going diving anytime soon. His arm hung limp at his side. He might recover full use of it given time, but they needed to be out of here tonight at the latest. Adding murders to the diamond heist and the kidnapping of a minor, the authorities would lock down the airport and send every officer they had to look for them.

Laurel wasn't planning to leave Malta by air, her employer had a different plan to get them away, but still it was going to be next to impossible to get Sharkbait to the marina, head out into open water and have enough time to find the diamond.

She briefly considered leaving Sharkbait at the chalet, since Laurel wasn't as bothered by the sharks as Jacob was. But, she decided, it was safer to bring her along in case she was found before they got the diamond. She knew their plan, she knew what they looked like; she could ruin everything.

"I'll dive," Laurel said. "We need to get out there today."

* * *

IT TURNED OUT that the one advantage of killing the guards had been to divert Malta's limited police presence to searching for the killers instead of patrolling the waters, looking for the diamond thieves. Malta was not huge, and as such the police would no doubt not take long to connect the diamond theft to the Aquarium murders, but given no obvious link between them, it gave Laurel a little more time.

As they traversed the narrow streets and reached the wide expanse of the marina, they didn't encounter any police activity. Laurel spotted no police boats in the bay. So far they'd managed to keep Sharkbait out of sight. Now, though, they needed to cross the marina to the wharf where their boat was moored, and they'd be in plain view of everyone.

Laurel grabbed Sharkbait's arm. "Listen to me. You're going to walk ahead of Jacob and me, okay? We will be right behind you. If you try to alert anyone, I'll put a knife in them. If you try to warn anyone, I swear I will go back to your home and slaughter your mum and dad. Do you understand?"

"My mum's already dead," Sharkbait said.

This surprised Laurel. A flood of sympathy filled her and she wanted to give this poor girl a hug. But she had to see this through.

"Just your dad then. He won't see the knife coming."

"You don't have to threaten my family," the girl said. "I'll keep my end of the deal."

Laurel nodded. She genuinely believed the girl would play along. "You see the purple boat tied up at the end of the last wharf? That's our boat. Now move."

Sharkbait walked confidently out of the side street into the open, striding past the cafes and restaurants and gift shops towards the water. It was nearly noon and the sun was blazing down on the tourists seated on patios, milling around or heading to or from their boats. Laurel and Jacob followed, trying very hard to look touristy. Word must have got around by now that Sharkbait had gone missing. Given her local fame, it was only a matter of time before someone recognized her.

The first to do so was a woman, maybe Laurel's age. She looked like a waitress, and she had just climbed out of a water taxi to head for her place of work. When she reached Sharkbait, she stopped her and put her hands on the girl's shoulders. She spoke in Maltese. By the concerned look on her face, she was asking if Sharkbait was okay.

Sharkbait, to her credit, replied in English, clearly enough for Laurel to hear.

"I am fine, sorry for scaring everyone. My father already knows I am safe."

The woman seemed confused. Laurel hung back with Jacob, pretending to search for something in her bag while he looked on, feigning impatience. Sharkbait's friend spoke again in Maltese.

"Oh, I am just practising my English. Mr Scordato says we should speak English at every opportunity."

The waitress seemed okay with this. She spoke some more and then hurried off. Sharkbait carried on walking. Laurel started breathing again. She waited until the waitress had passed by and then set off after the girl again.

Was this going to work? Laurel almost found herself believing it would. Truth be told, before she'd seen Sharkbait in action at the aquarium, she would have been okay to dive for the diamond without the girl's protection. Now it was as if she was on their side, working hard to help them get what they needed. Perhaps she just wanted them gone from her life. Perhaps she was enjoying it. She was impossible to read.

They reached the purple boat without any more interruptions. Laurel untethered it, they jumped in and headed out of the marina.

Jacob took over the steering with his good arm. Meanwhile, Laurel struggled into her wetsuit. She wasn't looking forward to this but, oddly, diving with Sharkbait made the prospect more appealing. She had offered to buy the girl her own wetsuit and mask but she had refused. Laurel intended to force the girl to use the spare demand valve on her tank. There was no way she was going to waste time surfacing every minute to let the girl get some air.

They had reached the marker buoy now. Laurel indicated that Jacob should be on the other side of it, nearer to the island. He dutifully moved the boat. It was of course impossible to tell if they were in exactly the right place. It looked right, relative to the island and the buoy, but Laurel knew the search was unlikely to be quick.

She handcuffed Sharkbait's wrist and then her own so they were connected. Then she put on her mask and regulator, and indicated to Sharkbait that she could use the yellow coloured emergency tube when she needed to breathe. Sharkbait didn't seem concerned. She must have dived a million times out here without any bulky equipment to slow her down. She made Laurel feel much calmer, despite her growing dread that they would never find the diamond before the police caught up with them.

Laurel flipped them both over the edge of the boat and into the water.

She saw the sharks almost immediately. They were significantly bigger than the tigers. Laurel gazed down at the grey backs of the magnificent creatures moving below. This was what Jacob had seen while clinging on the underside of the boat. No wonder he was so concerned.

There was a tugging on her tank. She turned to see Sharkbait taking oxygen from the spare regulator. Then the girl dived deeper. Laurel had no choice but to follow. She was surprisingly strong, pulling Laurel down at speed. Laurel felt slightly panicked. She had not expected the girl to be in control of their descent. As they passed at eye level with the gliding sharks, Laurel's heart pounded. But the miracle happened again. As soon as they saw the girl, they turned sharply, urgently swimming out of her way. Magic.

The seabed was thankfully not too far at this point and their feet touched down just moments later. Sharkbait took another shot of oxygen and then moved off, combing the sea floor. Laurel followed beside her with little choice in the matter. She tried to ignore the dazzling array of wildlife on display and concentrated instead on spotting the diamond. She intended to search strategically to make sure all the territory was covered and she didn't repeat herself. It was hard to get her bearings long enough to even begin breaking down the area into searchable zones. And it didn't help that once again Sharkbait was taking the lead and moving very fast.

Somehow, impossibly, Sharkbait led Laurel straight to it. Nestled next to a rock, partially buried by sand, the diamond lay waiting for her to pick it up. Laurel's relief was overwhelming.

She turned to Sharkbait to give her the thumbs up, but the girl wasn't there.

Confused, Laurel felt a sharp tugging at her wrist. She raised her arm to her field of vision, guessing that once again Sharkbait had inexplicably slipped the handcuffs. Instead she cried out, regulator dropping from her mouth as she struggled to understand what she was seeing.

Her hand was gone. A jet of blood under pressure squirted from her ruined wrist out into the water.

She didn't feel any pain. Sharkbait still had the cuffs attached to one wrist, but she was far away from Laurel now, swimming gracefully through the water. She didn't seem to need to come back for oxygen.

Still there was no pain. With her remaining hand Laurel managed to shove the regulator back into her mouth and she cleared it of water. She was breathing in ragged gasps and she forced herself to calm down. She tried to swim upwards but she wasn't getting very far. Blood was still pumping from her wrist. Through the mask it seemed surreal, like the damaged arm belonged to someone else.

Then Sharkbait swam by. How had she got free? Did she order a shark to come bite Laurel's hand off?

The loss of blood was making it hard to focus. Laurel thought she saw Sharkbait soar past her again, swimming effortlessly. Laurel must have hallucinated the girl's mouth opening impossibly wide to reveal rows and rows of razor-sharp teeth. Somewhere in Laurel's mind it occurred to her that perhaps the sharks weren't repelled from the girl by some magical power, but instead kept away out of *fear*.

Laurel's eyes closed as she drifted back to the seabed. She forced them open, wanting to see again this girl's impossible transformation. There she was, swimming away now. She held the diamond in one hand as she headed back to the boat. Laurel struggled to remain conscious as she watched. There was some commotion in the boat, Laurel saw it rocking back and forth as beside it, Sharkbait's legs could still be seen treading water. Then Jacob crashed into view, blood staining the water around him.

Sharkbait took a moment to glance in Laurel's direction for the last time. Instead of the beautiful Maltese girl, Laurel saw her own daughter, Penny. She felt calm, even as the sharks circled her, no longer afraid to approach now that Sharkbait wasn't close.

Laurel waved to her daughter with her good hand. *Go,* she whispered silently, the regulator falling from her lips. *Go take the diamond and claim the reward, you clever girl. Go free those tiger sharks.*

Mummy loves you.

Goblin

KIM LAKIN-SMITH

THE ENGINE FAN buffeted overhead, its huge silver fins slicing through the air just a metre above him.. It was difficult to focus – concussion? Had to be a definite yes after the speed of the impact. Was that blood on the blades? His blood?

Lieutenant Whates went through a mental checklist. His fingers moved, all ten. Toes too. There was an issue with his right leg – the pain was pretty acute – and he had a weird numbness on the right side of his head. He felt around with his opposite hand.

The blood had already begun to crust at the open wound where his ear should have been. A hollow wind blew on the right side of his brain, switching timbre from high to low as he shuffled around in the debris.

Light filtered in through the revolving blades – too white, too harsh. Whates cringed against its insistence, sheltered his eyes and turned his attention to his leg. A hunk of fuselage material had sliced into his skin like a knife into a birthday cake.

"Shit, Whates. You stupid bastard." His words echoed back to him in the dusty remains of the hull. The bodies of Lulan and Cheddar George hung lank in their harnesses. On re-entry, the corporals had been exposed to the worst of the radiation from the hole in the hull. Whates had no time to save them; in the seconds between life and death, he'd tucked in behind the panel separating the hull from the engine – a sheet of depleted uranium. Speeding towards Arcadia's surface, he'd listened to the screams of the others and soaked his pants in anticipation of impact.

"I let Saul pilot, despite his lack of experience," he admonished himself, and got lost in supercilious regrets – 'I never got to go with a Rubanese girl', 'I'll never see El Terine, or the southern star-beds twinkle over Du Ham beach', and 'I didn't get home after all.'

But here he was, sliced into and debilitated but very much alive next to the two bodies of his men hanging in their harnesses.

"Come on, Whates. Get with it," he said aloud, his cadet training kicking in all these years later. *Talk to stay alive.*

"Now, what are you going to do about this fucker?" He crooked his damaged leg, resting his ankle on the opposite knee. The shrapnel stuck out of his shin like a fragment of exoskeleton. "You've got two choices here. Move with it in or risk pulling it out." Whates snorted. "No kind of choice." Gritting his teeth, he got hold of the shard.

"Ah, you bastard!" He yanked, felt a pure rip of pain and hurried to tourniquet the wound with his belt.

Arcadia's rabid sun was already heating up the hold. Whates knew he hadn't long before he was baked alive in that tin can. Struggling to his feet, he ricocheted off the upturned cargo and thumbed the print pad alongside the suit locker.

"Good, good." The locker door slid aside; he stepped in and bonded himself into the 4400 factor weft, making it extra snug at the right shin to hold his flesh together in place of the belt. Tearing a square of duct wadding, he forced it tight against the clot spot where his ear used to be. The helmet was slipskin; it bonded directly onto his face, turning his brown skin black.

*   *   *

208

THE LAGOON WAS very still and very dark. Way overhead, the rock canopy was speckled with icy blue stars. Except, these stars crawled on thread-fine legs and it was their abdomens which pulsed with cobalt light. The fatter spiders lived up in the crevices; smash them and their innards burnt a hole in the floor. Scar had learnt to live with them instead.

"Don't bother me none," she'd told Scratch after a while. Because it was true, and because the real threat lay in the womb of the water. She'd glimpsed the fin once or twice, just occupying its bit of surface.

Scratch sniffed the water's edge on occasion. Mostly though, he stayed back while she filled the canteen – a battered old thing with her mother's initials on it. Her Daddy Uncle hated her venturing so far down into the cave system, but Scar couldn't help it. There was something that affected her down there amongst the glowing. She could have sworn she heard its heartbeat. A slow tug and ebb of blood through dense muscle meat.

"I hear you," she would whisper to the creature in the water. "I hear the boom of your wickedness." Listening in, she'd press one hand to her chest and the other to Scratch's bowed ribs. "Hear that, Scratch?" she'd say, and the dog would eye her mournfully and turn away his muzzle.

Today there was another heartbeat though. Scratch sniffed it out too; he pricked up his raggedy ears.

"Yep. What's that, huh?" Scar mussed the backwards forwards fur on the dog's back. Scratch stared out into the gloom and bared his fangs. "No need, boy. No need," she soothed.

The heartbeat was a stutter. It reminded her of Old Sire Wan and his velveteen drum. Wan's crusted fingers would puck, puck, puck against the drum, and sometimes Newlean, the inn keeper, would take down her pipes from the nail in the wall and make her lips buzz with eerie notes.

But today's beat was unaccompanied.

"Come on, Scratch," she said to the mutt. "Our monster ain't going anywhere." With a swift glance back at the still black water, girl and dog set off into the labyrinthine cave system.

*　*　*

EVEN INSIDE HIS suit, Whates pumped out sweat. Arcadia's salt flats were white as angel wings. The heat baked at the edges of his view. Smoke billowed overhead; it surprised him to see the hull relatively intact except for the hole in one side where the asteroid had struck.

"Bastard Saul," he whispered – and then regretted it. The pilot deck had caved in on impact. Whates didn't care to inspect the exposed guts of the deck; he suspected Saul would be spread pretty thinly over what was left of the console. But he did need to take action. The skin suit would hold out for a few hours but he was losing blood, added to which no one was coming to rescue him. Neither he nor the crew had wanted to trigger the ship's Retrieval Beacon. Bad enough they had been sent to overhaul the theonite cells in the weapons' rig. "No fucker wants that job," he'd told Saul when the allocation came through. But who were they to question orders? Just a gear squad who kept things greased.

He was on his own then, and bleeding out inside a skin suit. Arcadia swelled around him. The water tab he'd popped inside one cheek subdued his thirst. Now the question was how far to the nearest burrow and could he reach it before the Bethzine arrived and put a chisel to his skin to make a senseless golem of him? Either that or brew up his meat and make trinkets from his bones. Regardless, out on the salt skim, he was a commodity. His only hope was to get out of the sun.

"Remember Mother Em," he told himself, forcing one

foot in front of the other. "'No matter what trouble you find yourself in, keep your eye on the horizon and swim into that blue.'" It had been a favourite saying of hers and he repeated it over now she was dust in the wind and him not long to follow.

"Swim into the blue. Swim into the blue." He tried to keep the horizon in view, his eyes gone weepy against the glare. Salt left its layer on him. It was a taste of death in that whited out world.

"Swim out into the blue. Swim out into the blue." Mother Em's mantra and common sense kept him stepping on. Sooner or later, he would come across the bunker hatch leading down into one of the inhabited burrows under Arcadia. He hadn't cause previously to attempt entry to the dark zones below.

"Never wanted to step foot on this rancid crust." He said the words aloud because he wanted to voice his complaint. It was a lousy lieutenant who would lose his squad, worse still one who couldn't guide a new pilot through Arcadia's predatory stratosphere. And all this to fix the weapons' rig supposed to detect and destroy the very space debris which had brought his craft down.

"Very fucking poetic," he told the universe, sensing it home in like a carnivore scenting blood.

*   *   *

"Now, Scratch, ain't that always the way of things? Just a short time earlier and we'd have got to him first," whispered Scar from their hidey hole at the entrance to the burrow. She'd chosen one of the camouflaged exits as opposed to the larger, more obvious bunker hatches so she could observe the man a while. But she was too late. There was blood on him – she could smell that on the air. So too had the Bethzine. They swarmed around him while riding on the backs of giant scorpios. The man didn't like that.

"Don't like it one bit, hmm, Scratch. See how he fights them? Got a good hook on him. Wearing a skin suit too. You think he's naked under there?" Scar's Father Uncle had recently explained about the making of people, and while Scar knew she was made a little differently, it didn't stop her marvelling at the crude biology of it all.

It made her sorry to see how they baited him, these Bethzine with their hair so long and silvery, and their bodies fine as whipwood and decorated in beads and chakra oil and scorpio carapaces. To the rear, the elderly and the youngsters went about setting up camp. Poles were righted up and knotted tight to one another, great swathes of woven stuff thrown over to make tents and carpets unrolled on the ground. All this while the sun sank overhead and the man fought tooth and nail. At last though, the stutter heart hurt his chest and she watched him collapse.

"The poor soldier. He can't take them all," she told the tatty dog nuzzling her leg. "What's he coming down here for anyways? No business for a soldier man like that. And what would he have the Bethzine do? Ride on by? Offer him a tug on a water bladder? Not likely. Not when he's half-dead already."

Her nose wrinkled and she sighed crossly. The stupid soldier had brought her up to the surface when she was far happier sloshing around in the dark of the burrows. And what was she to do now that he was pinned under the weight of a Bethzine chieftain, his hands forced behind his back and trussed to his ankles?

The Bethzine hoisted him up and moved him near the latrine which one boy had dug and parted his buttocks over. Tying him to a peg, they pawed over the skin suit, trying to work their way under – or check their prey for belongings. Empty-handed, they abandoned him for the shade of the newly erected tents. Soon smoke rose from a camp fire. The scent of burning was weak out in the open, Scar being used to the throat-catching billowing off the fire pits lit below. Her stomach rumbled.

"Yep, it's getting near Eatings. You know it too, Scratch." The dog snapped at the air a couple of times, as if there was sustenance to be had.

Scar crossed her arms and tucked her hands up under her armpits. She frowned, puckering the stitch line down her forehead. It didn't exactly make sense to her but she didn't want to leave the soldier tied to that peg – and not because the Bethzine would treat him like any other wounded livestock. She just liked the flutter of his heartbeat, if that's what she was hearing. That, and now she had seen him, there was something so beautiful about the texture of his synthetic skin. Black as the ink water of the lagoon and so very smooth and solid looking over his bones.

But what was to be done? The Bethzine would never give the soldier to her and she had nothing to trade. With their ornate costume and bone-white faces, they had always unsettled Scar. On the rare occasions the Bethzine ventured down the burrows, silence would fall like a shadow. They would move between the caverns, tall as night, white as salt, making their purchases from the underground market before slipping back out into the light. 'Ghosts' her Daddy Uncle called them

"I can't leave the soldier man though. He'll end up stew or scorpio feed."

Scratch eyed her ruefully and chased an itch behind an ear with a back paw.

"Yeah, I don't know why I'm wasting time here either." Scar pulled at the root stock of her floppy, leather hair. "We'll sneak over when the light goes out. Unpluck that chain from its anchor and hurry the soldier man back below with us." She squinted at the horizon where the huge white sun was making its descent. In a very short space of time, the glare of sunlight would give way to the absolute darkness of night. She just hoped the soldier's life didn't get snuffed out first.

*   *   *

"STOP BEING A lazy bastard!" Mother Em had told him all that time ago. "Get up out of bed and be something." And so he had, signing up to the Terra Guard back when he still had baby fat and no notion of ending up marooned on the bur star, Arcadia.

"I have no eyes," he said softly, because it seemed to be true. Everywhere was blue-black where once it had been blinding. But then he became aware of the sack over his head and, shifting his limbs, heard the chink of a chain. Pain gnawed at his leg and the side of his head. There had been Bethzine, appearing in the hot distance of the day like coral grown up from the salt flats. With nowhere to run to, he'd tried to fight them off with his fists. But the scorpios – hell, how he hated those creepy-crawlies, all slobber-tailed and chittery – had guaranteed his surrender.

"Now what, Whates?" he said into the bag. "Is this the ending for you? Is this how you go out?" He liked the idea of being clever enough to get loose and evade his slaughter. But then it occurred to him that he had neither the energy nor the survival skills to escape the tribesfolk. He could run all he liked; they'd just mount up and chase his scent.

"I'm not lazy. I'm dying, Mother Em," he told the nagging voice in his head.

Blinking in the pitch black, he thought he glimpsed hundreds of tiny dots of effervescent colour – luminous, like the fish shoals back on SanAd. He wanted to swim with them, far out beyond the sweet dark of pain, into the drift of nothingness. So convinced was he by the light flow that he snarled instinctually as his hood was tugged off.

"Still now, soldier man. You'll bring the Bethzine running out their tents otherwise and then we'll all be done in – you and Scratch as fodder, me as an Unthinky." The voice belonged to a young girl. Whates struggled to process what was happening. The vivid day had given way to night. A short distance away, the tents of the Bethzine were lit from within.

A second creature was alongside the girl. Whates heard it snuffling at his head wound. He could see very little but he had an impression of four legs and a muzzle. Like the girl, the creature – was it a dog? She had called it Scratch – smelt strongly of brine. He thought it might be the scent of a UV balm; skin suits were expensive, the reserve of military personnel and business-funded scientists.

"Help me," he croaked.

"One who likes to state the obvious, huh?" She fiddled with the chain; he was surprised to feel it slack as, ever so slowly, she eased it free. "Going to have to walk some on that leg you got torn up. Yeah, I saw you hopping about on it. But maybe your second skin will keep you put together long enough. We only got to get as far as my Daddy Uncle and he can fix you up. Good as he fixed me."

She hesitated a moment, her silhouette picked out against the light from the tents. Then she reached down and fed an arm though his, tugging like the child she was. "Come on now, soldier man. Don't want me to set Scratch biting at your heels now."

He managed to get to his knees and, despite the agonising pulse at his shin, got to his feet. Only then did he notice how small she was – just a bitty thing who pulled on his arm, leading him away from the tents and into the blackness.

"I can't hardly see a thing." He put his hands out in front, cutting a breaststroke through the denseness.

"Don't worry. I can see enough for both of us." The girl was staring up at him; Whates understood that much from the opalescent eyes that shone out at him. He stumbled back a moment, but she led him on, muttering quietly about the gift of sight in the burrows and how her Daddy Uncle – as she referred to someone – had enabled her to peer through the gloom. "Scratch'll help lead you too," she added.

Whates was glad not to see a second pair of eerie eyes just floating in the dark. Then again, knowing the dog was there and not being able to see it was unsettling in itself. He was willing to trade death at the hands of the Bethzine for a walk in the wilderness with the girl and her dog though, no matter how strangely they might have evolved.

"Who are you?" he whispered. But before the girl could answer, a figure reared up in the blackness ahead.

Whates clutched his sides instinctively, feeling for a weapon which wasn't there. The girl and her dog went to ground; he saw her eyes shining out and something new. Burnished white fangs, lots of them, all crowded into a child's mouth.

The golem staggered towards them, a great lolloping thing that had once been a man but was now mindless other than in serving the needs of its masters.

"Ol ark! Ol ark!" it cried as it ran. A Bethzine cry apparently, designed to bring the camp to life. In the distance, Whates saw the flaps on the tents going back and the tribesfolk emerging, torches in hand or buckling on sword belts. Already the scorpios were being brought around from their sandnest and harnessed in readiness.

"Oh, Father Uncle will curse my ashes for this one!" The girl tugged on Whates's arm and rolled her fingers into a fist. "Smack the golem down, soldier man, or it'll never stop yelping."

Whates was used to acting on orders. He stood no chance against the Bethzine and their scorpios, but the golem was bred for servitude not violence. The shape of it suggested a large man-once-was, reduced by a knock from a chisel into a sluggish lump made for carrying, animal husbandry and emergency meat.

Whates pushed against the pain and crushed his fist into the golem's jaw. A second time and a third, he drove his fist into the thing. Crumpling over, it howled with a cloudy misunderstanding of its suffering. At his side, the girl tugged on him again and the dog started snarling.

"Enough, soldier man. This way, this way."

He followed after, fighting against the sensation of weightlessness in the dark. At their back, the Bethzine offered up yowls to the night and rode out in all directions.

Whates felt a huge tug of hopelessness. There was nowhere to go in the darkness of the desert.

Except then the girl must have dropped to ground; certainly he couldn't sense her next to him. "Where are you?" he hissed. But then he felt the dog weave between his legs and a hand grabbed his.

"Down now, soldier man. Into the burrows."

Stepping towards the girl's voice, he found a dip in the ground which gave way to a sudden slope and rocky descent. The night cut out overhead and he was bathed in silence.

* * *

SCAR'S HEART BEAT very fast. Two anterior chambers drove the blood around the cartilage bonded to her skeleton, keeping the muscles lively.

She'd done it. The soldier man was safe in the burrow and neither she nor Scratch were any worse the wear for helping him. She pictured the Bethzine running in zigzags, back out on top, trying to locate their lost quarry, and she smiled at the thought. It didn't please her to deprive the tribesfolk of a meal, but the soldier man had sent his weak pulse out into the world and her skin had prickled.

"No doubt Daddy Uncle will say why I had to find you like I did. He's a knower, about all sorts of things and situations." Scar got hold of the man's wrist and pulled him after her as they descended. She liked the texture of his skin suit – smooth in one direction, faintly barbed if she ran her hand the other way. "There'll be light up ahead. There now. You see it?"

She let go, pointing at the subtle glow off the marsh lamps in the next corridor. "You can see the tide marks here where Arcadia's water left the surface and went underground all those years back. My Daddy Uncle, he says water brought with it all the creatures of the deep, all the sea vegetables too, and the moss slime we use as fuel. And that's gotta be true about the creatures because here they all are, slopping about in the rivers below us."

She saw the soldier squinting. He hobbled after her, but kept his distance. Scar had a feeling it came of him seeing her and Scratch in the light, and she felt a little sorry and a little angry. It wasn't her fault that she'd been stitched so, just as it wasn't her Daddy Uncle's fault that he'd been forced to save her with the materials to hand.

"Where are we going?" said the soldier. He was panting heavily. Blood was coming fresh at his leg wound again; Scar smelt its ripeness in the air. She understood why it excited her – there was a time she'd been bleeding too and felt so lousy with sickness that she longed for the Nothingness. But then Daddy Uncle worked his magic on her and raised her up, close enough as from the dead. Scratch had come next, when he got smashed under a boulder. Difference was her Daddy Uncle used his best supplies for her while Scratch got the scraps.

"He did you alright though, didn't he, boy?" she said, explaining her history to the soldier man. "My Daddy Uncle, he's an apothecary. A fine one too. Works out of his store in the catacombs. Oh, don't look on so. It's just a name for a part of the burrows. Ain't no soul buried there. If there had been we'd have used those old bones for some practical purpose by now."

"So you are made up mostly of fish?" Sarcasm poured off the soldier and he scrubbed a finger under his nostrils as he walked. "Of course you are." He shook his head. "Fucking Arcadia."

*　　*　　*

DOWN AMONG THE spiders, she would sit at the edge of the lagoon and try to catch a glimpse of her kin. No one knew about the lagoon. In their twilight existence, there were more than enough tales of monsters without tracking down the real ones.

"Stay in the light and the suckers can't get you," Old San Wan would say, putting down his drum a while and puffing on his moss pipe.

But Scar liked the dark. She'd the eyes to see with and skin peppered with pulse receptors. To her, motion had a taste as distinctive as the smell of blood; it tickled her nostrils and agitated her gills.

"I'm thinking a soldier man like you is new to the burrows," she said, leading him through the entrance tunnels to the market. The man nodded. She wasn't sure he really heard her though. Every so often his eyes would roll back into his head and he'd stumble. She'd grab his arm and do her best to support him.

"Well, so you know, here's a place to live like any other. Air's pumped from above." She pointed out the fat leather hosing that was buckled to the rock face. "We grow the crops that like the least light and we trade, amongst ourselves and the survivors up top." She stabbed a finger towards the craggy ceiling.

"My name is Whates," the man muttered as she pushed him on. "Lieutenant Whates."

"I'm Scar. And this is Scratch." She nodded at the cavern that opened up in front of them, lit with thousands of moss torches and echoing the noise of industry and voices. "And this is the marketplace."

She had rather hoped to show the place off, but the soldier – this Lieutenant Whates – was all but crawling on his knees now. The fibrillating heartbeat was slowing and it was all she could do to get him to move between the stalls, which were set into the rock and packed with wares. Smells of metalworking, tanneries, spice sacks, moss mulching and steamy stew crocks imprinted her nose like a map. She negotiated the pathways without needing to take in her surroundings. Instead, she concentrated on the soldier while Scratch ran on ahead and barked a warning to others to clear the way.

*　*　*

HE CAME TO as a cup of salty froth was pressed to his lips.

"What's that?" he managed, choking against the fluid as his head swam.

"Drink now, Lieutenant Whates," said the old man stooped over him. The cup came back and Whates did as instructed, didn't have the capacity to do otherwise.

He struggled to focus. "The child calls you Daddy Uncle?" The old man had a grey face, whiskers, and his breath smelt of herbals. A scar of stitches ran down one cheek. "You are a doctor?"

"An apothecary. I know the uses for the stuff we can grow here and the minerals we can mine." He tutted. "The skin suit

220

has held the leg together well but now what, Scar? Would you have me slice it open when I have no means to clot the blood?"

"In this whole store, Daddy Uncle? Gotta be something. Gua-gum? Limepaste?"

"Only thing that'll guarantee the knit is the same cartilage I stitched into you. The radiation has set against his bones. You can tell so by the yellow in his eyes." The old man lent back, dabbing some potent plant stuff on Whates's brow. "Same as you when your daddy's ship crashed."

"Use that then."

"There ain't no way. The last of it is gone." There was a clattering of pots and an unscrewing of jars. "Best I can do is patch up his head and wait for the fever to take it." Quieter, like it was meant for the girl's ears alone. "Why'd you bring him down, Scar? Haven't I given you company enough with Scratch here?"

Whates heard the girl give a snort and say "I liked the sound of him!", the shadows of her arms thrashing about.

"The sound?" The old man didn't understand any more than Whates did in his state of sickness.

"The beat of him. Bo-boom." She mimicked his heartbeat softly, a hand against her chest. "Bo-boom. Bo-boom."

"His heartbeat? Well, okay. I can't question it, Scar. We both know you are much altered since I had to remake you. Maybe you did hear him – liked what you heard too. Doesn't alter the fact I can't mend him. Not without the shark fin. The cartilage is regenerative. I've nothing else like it."

"Inside this whole stinking place?"

Whates heard the girl's anger. He swung his head to one side and tried to process the view of shelves stacked high with witch jars and little spice sacks, vases filled with blousy cotton flowers and all manner of dried animal parts strung about.

"Got to be something to draw the fever out," he mumbled,

and tasted salt on his lips and the sour broth in his mouth.

"Got to be, Daddy Uncle. Got to be."

A sigh of exasperation escaped the old man's lips. "Scar. Do you have any idea how much shark fin is worth? Even the smallest piece of it? A small fortune, that's what. Got another value too in the way it adapts to our cells. There's not many were taught the right way to administer it. Folk have been known to sell a body part to buy a sliver but it won't do nada without the knowhow. Now…" Again with the clatter of jars and rustle of leaf matter. "Are you going to let me make your soldier man as comfortable as I can or keep yacking at me about a lack of medicine I can't fix?"

* * *

IT WAS A short time after Eatings that Scar made up her mind. Tearing the last hunk of black bread in two, and feeding half to Scratch, she got a wobble in her belly and knew she had to do it. Daddy Uncle ministered to the soldier man in-between weighing out goods and offering his sage advice to customers. Every now and then he'd tense his shoulders up around his ears and give a hefty sigh; nothing hurt Daddy Uncle more than failing to save a soul. Scar knew as much from bitter experience the day he pulled her and her daddy out from the wreckage of their craft and only managed to save one. Radiation had turned her daddy's skin a filthy shade of yellow and crisped his eyes. The apothecary couldn't save him, only the daughter with the broken spine.

Now it was Scar's turn to play rescuer. "I'm going out a while," she told Daddy Uncle, who grunted and carried on cutting up a scorpio tail, fat as one of the stalactites in the lower caves. Leaning in by the soldier's one good ear, she whispered, "I go get your medicine now. Don't you die now, or I'll have gone swimming with that monster for nothing."

She'd an idea that Lieutenant Whates didn't like the sound of her place. He moaned incoherently, locked between consciousness and death – an ugly dream state she remembered from her own crash landing on Arcadia. It was a savage sort of world where folk scraped out a living and tried to avoid being baked alive. But it was better to have a chance to keep on living and she was grateful for her Daddy Uncle's intervention. She meant to offer the soldier man the same hope.

With Scratch gambolling ahead, nosing the dank air and stopping regularly to cock a leg, she headed off into the market. She waved to those who knew her and shouted out. Stopping for a drink from the well, she strode out of the cavern and into the warren of tunnels, moving from the newer, inhabited sections to the narrower routes which were the first to be cut all that time ago. Some of the walls were daubed with red crosses, indicating a tunnel in danger of collapse. Scar took no notice, just climbed deep down, ducking under the scaffolding carved from sun-hardened mosscake.

"I guess there's only one way I'm going to get to keep the soldier man, hmm, Scratch? I've got to go after the monster"

Scratch might have understood, but it seemed unlikely. Instead he was focused on the salt lick on the briny walls as they came closer to where the waterways ran. Running his tongue along the slick surface, he gave a tight sneeze and looked surprised by it.

They came at last into the great hole with the spider-lit canopy. Ahead lay the lagoon. So very still and melancholy in its blackness. Somewhere inside lived her monster – or, as her Daddy Uncle would have called such a thing, goblin. He had told his stories – and Old San Wan and Newlean sang their stories – about the creatures that made it underground when the water sank. Among the fairy-tales and folklore were the Tall Truths – stories which had a grain of truth to them. Talk of goblins was popular – terrible creatures with mottled,

223

rubbery skin and finials of teeth – a great, curved jaw full. Luckily the goblins kept to their realm, deep down below where the water was lightless.

But Scar knew where the monsters lived.

"You stay on the shore now, Scratch." She pulled something out of her pocket – a paring blade that reflected prettily under the blue insect glow.

It might have been nice if Scratch could have turned to her and said, 'Okay'. She missed having friends. The other children in the burrows stared at her seams and kept clear. So it was just her and her dumb, beloved dog. He panted at her, eyes expectant, and she gave his head a pat. "Stay here," she said sternly and that he understood, sniffing at the floor and lying down.

"I'm telling you now, Scratch. I'm not awful keen to wade out there. But what's the use in rescuing the soldier man if I'm just going to let him choke out on Daddy Uncle's bed? No." She dragged a hand back through her floppy leather hair and pursed her lips. "This has got to be the way of it." Glancing down at her rag-dog, she gave him a crooked smile. "See ya later."

Kicking off her sandals, she edged her toes into the water. It was just as she had expected, searingly cold – at least until she waded in past her knees and up to her waist. Either she adapted to the chill or warmer currents ran beneath the still surface.

A few steps more and she lost her balance, the rock beneath her feet disappearing suddenly. Fighting a tremendous crush of panic in her chest, she flailed her arms and regained her footing.

"Come on now, stupid. There's no use stopping now when the monster already knows you are here." Suppressing the instinctual agoraphobia she felt at the idea of so much open space beneath her, she stepped off the drop and swam out.

Overhead, the spiders swam in their own black element, weaving and clambering and twinkling bluely. Using the breaststroke she remembered from her childhood, she pressed on through the water, knife in hand. Back on shore, Scratch began to bark. 'Yes, I sense the monster too,' she wanted to shout back, and also to shush the dog before he spooked the fish. But then she saw the fin rise up in the distant water and slide towards her like a hand parting salt.

'So here comes my monster,' she thought, and sank down under the water. Blinking, the gloom cleared in front of her as she got used to it. Plankton danced, millions of them, in tiny, jerky zigzags of movement. She got a sense of so much hidden life out there in the lagoon and, beyond it, the seas at the core of Arcadia. Her lungs tugged at her, needing to draw fresh breath. She regretted that she hadn't sprouted gills which functioned fully, only the abilities to home in on sound – like the soldier's heartbeat – and being agitated by coagulating wounds. Her monthly spill of blood had begun recently; that had agitated her too, forcing the child in her to start evolving into a new and uncommon shape.

Ahead, the dark shape of the shark flick-flacked side to side, coming towards her. She fought the ache in her lungs while treading water and gripping the knife. The monster swam hard, aiming its great snout at her – only to veer off to one side and around her. Slowing, the creature circled her.

The eyes were small and dull, almost lifeless. It was indeed monstrous, head squashed horizontally, the 'nose' protruding grotesquely. The body was long, sleek and muscular with small fins and the thin slits of gills.

Scar struggled to stay submerged as the goblin continued to circle her. The filarial sensors on shark and girl picked up on one another and rebounded back. She found herself questioning the knife in her hand. Was she better suited to a life beneath the water? Would her throat sprout functioning gills if she just stayed below long enough? And what use was a soldier man in a skin suit next to the magnificent predator making its lazy circuits around her?

'Maybe I'll let my knife go and just watch it fall away into the darkness,' she thought.

If Scar had doubted her extraordinary metamorphosis in anyway before, she was forced to acknowledge her swift reaction when the shark attacked. Drifting just an arm's length from Scar, the shark's response was both grotesque and extraordinary. The whole of its lower jaw unhinged and extended, its new mouth parts reforming. Stretching unfeasibly wide to expose many curved and needle-like teeth, the creature drove towards her head.

Scarlet reacted on instinct and respected in kind. The burning in her lungs evaporated. Her jaw unlatched and craned wide – wider – disjointing and extending out from her face. The curves of her teeth bore down on the shark and the two open jaws smashed into one another. Girl and shark ricocheted back. The shark drove in again, its lantern jaw slicing through water and plankton. The creature snared Scar's shoulder; Scar kicked out against the bite, forcing the shark to surface with her. She wheezed, dredging air deep into her lungs as she and the shark thrashed about, sending great licks of froth across the glassy surface. Back on the shore, Scratch barked incessantly.

The fish broke free of her and Scar saw the foam turn red.

"You have a piece of me. Now it's my turn."

In seconds, the whip of the goblin jaw broke through the water again; Scar countered with her own distended snarl. At the same time, she slammed her hand around to grip the top fin, cupped the tip and sliced it clean away. A second wave of blood joined the first. Diving down again, she drove her foot against the wound. The shark skimmed past her shoulder and weaved away into the sequinned black of deeper water.

When Scar emerged onto the rocky shore, Scratch was on her in an instant. His yapping demanded to know where she had been, what had caused all the noise and why Scar was hurt. She sat down on the ground, sending spiders scuttling. He sniffed at her shoulder as she picked out the teeth.

"Monster's real," she told him, gasping for breath and holding up the glistening hunk of fin.

*   *   *

THE OLD MAN had propped him up with a number of hard pillows. The pain shots into one of his arms had helped the fever to temporarily abate. Whates took sips from the salty tea when it was offered and tried to be thankful that he was destined to die in that twilit underworld and not in some stock pot or hanging from a harness. "Well, Mother Em. Guess I did get off my ass after all," he murmured, and bared his teeth as a tight wire of pain passed up his leg. The pain subsided and he relaxed his jaw.

"I'm sorry not to be more use to you," said the old man. "I never would have thought it possible to reengineer a living thing, but sometimes what I do here is less method than experiment. Scar and that yapper of hers worked out the best." He tugged on his beard and stared up at the hock wreaths and body parts. "Others, not so well."

It occurred to Whates that he might yet end up in a stock pot and he wasn't entirely sorry. Wasn't it better to go ahead and be useful in death than tucked away in a brown box in the ground? Like Mother Em back on SanAd, where the shoals of fish swam and the southern star beds twinkled.

"On Du Ham beach." Whates snorted. So he was back there again so soon, reminiscing over the sights he had never seen and the women he would never know! Life, death…it was all gravy on Arcadia.

"Hang in there, Lieutenant. At least until Scar gets back from wherever she's sulking. She's done her best by you, headstrong little savage that she is!" The old man smiled and chuckled to himself.

It was the shadows appearing in the doorway which stripped the apothecary of his humour. "Oh, Scar," was all he managed, reaching for the long thin knife he had been using to cut soap blocks and staying behind his stone counter.

Propped upright, Whates saw the Bethzine warriors fill the doorway. Two of their number stepped inside – the chieftain who had brought him down on the salt flats and a woman with her white hair in a braid down her back and many obsidian rings extending her neck.

"The skin snake. We have come for it. We want it back," said the woman. She spoke very well, like someone who has studied a language and taken pride in perfecting the accent.

"By skin snake, I take it you mean me." Whates choked against the back of a hand. It took too much breath to speak. His vision grew red and he had to fight to stay conscious.

"The skin snake is a man, a soldier." The old man kept his knife raised and his voice steady. "Lieutenant Whates he says his name is. Sent here to repair the weapons rig out at Far Point. It ain't like we got military personnel clamouring to come down here to this white rock and help us out any. Besides" – he nodded his head in the direction of the bed – "man's dying anyway from the radiation. Can't we give him rest as he goes into the Nothingness?"

The woman translated all of this into the toc-tongued language of the Bethzine, the chieftain listening patiently as she spoke. The tribesfolk in the doorway were more vocal; they clanked the tips of their swords off the rock floor and gestured expressively towards the old man and to Whates.

When the chieftain spoke, he did so in a whisper of a

voice. His skin shone fantastically white against his beaded clothing and the gloom below ground.

"The girl is known to you?" the woman translated.

"She is. But she's not here. Just a young 'un too. Doesn't mean no harm." Knife at the ready, the old man was ready to defend his point.

"She watches us sometimes. Peeps out from the hollows with her demon eyes. But there is a difference between watching and stealing."

"Can you steal a man you do not own?" Whates got the words out between strangled breaths.

"We own everything that crawls in the white world," said the translator, focusing on him with a look of elegant contempt.

"And when the sky goes black?" Whates remembered the density of the Arcadian night. Surely the girl with her spectral eyes owned that aspect?

"Then we tell our tales of demons," said the woman without waiting on the chieftain's word. "And we take our swords to every beast and goblin."

"Guess me and the soldier man got lucky then." Scar squeezed between the tall Bethzine crowding the doorway. She looked up as she passed them, a child tempted to stick out her tongue. Scratch came tip-toeing after.

The chieftain patted the girl's head as she went by. He smiled and said something to his fellow Bethzine that made them laugh.

"Your daughter is a lively spirit. She will make someone a fine wife." The translator nodded towards the tribesfolk in explanation of the joke.

Scar was less amused. "What's the people eaters doing down here?" she said, glaring at her Daddy Uncle.

"They smelt you out." Resting his knife against the counter, the old man took a seat on a stool. He scratched his neck. "So, now what? I take it you want to take the lieutenant with you?" He stared over at the bed, sorry if resigned to the way things had panned out.

"We must recover what is ours." The translator listened while the chieftain spoke. She looked at Scar. "And the girl must be punished for stealing."

"Wait up there! We don't need to be so reactive." The old man was worried now and holding out his hands to his wares. "All this has done is speed up your next trip down to the market. Surely we can make a trade – you leave things be and I provide goods you find of use." He waited expectantly.

Scar slapped the wet hunk of fin down on the counter

Daddy Uncle was immediately on his feet and backing away. "A fin? How'd you find a fin, girl?" He looked back and forth between Whates and Scar. "Where'd she get such a thing?"

"From my monster." Scar reached for the old man's knife. She drew the blade cleanly through the centre of the fin and held one half out to the chieftain. "I'm sorry I stole the soldier man but I had to have him. And now my Daddy Uncle is going to make him better with this. It is shark fin. Very precious. Very expensive." She emphasised this last word and the translator followed suit when relaying the information to the chieftain.

"Only half mind. I need the rest to heal the soldier man." Scar glared at Whates, who saw the peculiar light in her eyes and felt a weird, undulating shift between hope and mistrust of the girl and her strange biology.

* * *

THE FIRST TIME the blood came was a shock. No one to ask except Daddy Uncle, who looked her straight in the eye and said, "It's straightforward enough and messy at the same time." He explained the straightforwardness of her cycle and the messiness of sex. She'd wrinkled her nose and the stitches had stood out on her forehead as if dividing her thoughts about the whole thing.

But that was some time ago and she was grown enough to face the chieftain head on. Scar held up the half a fin; although she was the one who had taken it, now she was back amongst civilisation she felt a wave of nausea. There was something too familiar about the shine of the shark fin. She thrust it towards the Bethzine.

"It is very valuable, for medicine or for trade," said Daddy Uncle, stood behind her.

The chieftain let his translator finish. He peered past Scar at the bed where the soldier sweated. Opinions were offered from the doorway. He raised a hand and the voices fell silent.

Approaching the counter, he took the piece of fin from Scar. He went to turn away, stopped, stared at the girl hard and ran the bloody flesh down her cheek. He smiled, gently still, and walked away.

Passing the fin to one of the warriors by the door, he cleared his throat and spoke quietly to the woman. Without reaction she said, "The soldier is yours. The girl is sharp and is to be allowed to keep her demon eyes. But there must be punishment."

Before Scar could scream or her soldier draw ragged breath, a Bethzine warrior put his sword to Scratch's throat and tugged. The dog fell off to one side, legs jerking as the blood spilt. In his final agonies, Scratch looked to Scar with such miscomprehension and need for reassurance that she wanted to tear off her own skin.

Scar opened her mouth to speak but what came out was a guttural roar – rage so absolute that her mind went black. The new and secret part of her unleashed. Gasps went around the room. She saw fresh miscomprehension and fear on the faces of the Bethzine.

Her large and powerful jaw unhinged and she snapped at the air. The Bethzine gabbled in alarm.

"Scar. What have I made you?" said Daddy Uncle at her back, his voice regretful and wavering.

Scar had no comprehension. She craned her disjointed jaw wide, wide open. Scratch's killer was striding away; she flew at him, leapt on his back and sunk her angled teeth into his neck. The blood beneath her lips made her eyes glisten and she gulped at it, clenching down even as the man bucked and slammed his back against the cave wall. She was surrounded by noise, all those voices raised in horror at the predator she had become. Scar kept biting down, forcing the flesh between her teeth as the warrior slumped and finally collapsed.

Releasing him, she leapt aside and squatted beside his body. His juices clung to her chin. She wiped them away with a forearm as her jaw locked back in and the Bethzine deserted their dead and fled back to the surface.

* * *

THE FEVER FOLDED back over Whates, thick and white. Where the pulse had once been restricted to the wound in his leg, now it spread through all of his nerve fibres. He wanted to sweat it all out – the radiation poisoning, as well as the guilt for bad decisions which had cost his men their lives. Most of all, he wanted to lose the memory of a strange little girl made monster.

He'd a sense of the old man's movements at the counter – stitching the girl's wounded shoulder then slicing and heating the shark fin, rubbing it into a shot cylinder and tapping out the bubbles. The girl cleared away the dog's carcass. He'd seen her shoulders heave with the effort. When she returned, she seemed unburdened. Her eyes shone even in the light.

"What are you going to do to me?" he wanted to ask the old man. "What kind of horror will you make of me?" But his words evaporated in the heat of his fever.

"Would it not be kinder to let him die?" said the old man.

The girl peered in at Whates from his inner darkness. "I need a new friend," she said, and then, "And soon I will need a mate."

The old man approached, blocking out the light.

"Okay then," he said, and to Whates, "Grit your teeth now, fella."

The shot cylinder punched in at the Lieutenant's spine.

BLOOD RELATIONS

ANDREW LANE

THORPE WAS IN LOCK-up when they came for him.

Conditions in the jail were filthy and dangerous. Predatory gang-members lurked around corners, in doorways and even in the roof space, waiting to drop onto passing prisoners and mug them for whatever they were carrying, or often just for the fun of it. Bacteria multiplied so fast in the dirt filling every corner that you could almost see the sticky film of potentially fatal infection spreading as you watched. The constant heat made the gang-members twitchy and the bacteria virulent.

"Don't make eye-contact with anyone or skin-contact with anything" – that's what Thorpe had been told when he'd been sent there, a year before. It was the judge who had said it, which had worried him straight away. In all that time he wasn't sure he could remember looking into a face or touching anything that hadn't been disinfected with bleach wipes first. Most of the small allowance he was given by the prison authorities went on the wipes – that and the multiple overlapping protection rackets run by the gangs and the prison guards. Those inmates who preferred to spend their allowance on cigarettes, porn or drugs, rather than protection, were easily spotted – they were usually missing a couple of fingers, and maybe had an oozing rash across their cheeks. The missing fingers could have been caused either by infection or by violence, but the oozing rashes were a give-away sign that some virulent bacterium had gotten a foothold in their immune systems and wasn't going to let go.

Only thirty per cent of prisoners made it to the end of their sentences. That was a chilling statistic. The judge had warned him about that as well. Thorpe had promised himself that he would be one of the minority, but now, a full year on, he wasn't feeling optimistic. The odds were stacked against him.

The door to his cell slid open at three o'clock in the morning. Before he was fully awake, two guards in ceramic body-armour, gloves, face-masks and helmets had picked him up and carried him out onto the corridor. A third guard was standing there ready, holding a neural stunner like a club. Despite the lateness and the darkness, voices were floating from cell to cell – a threatening soup of conversations, threats, screams, bad dreams and hallucinations.

He was deposited in a metal chair in front of a metal desk in a metal room. There were stains on the desk. His bleach wipes were back in the cell, so he kept his hands folded carefully on his lap.

The two guards stood in the corners nearest the door. They stared at him with curiosity in what he could see of their eyes through the face-masks. This was obviously something out of the ordinary for them. Thorpe wondered with a sick sensation in his stomach what was going on. He couldn't see any path out of this situation that worked to his advantage. His appeal had already failed, and nobody cared enough that he was in here to try and get him out. Nobody cared enough to visit, or even write.

The door opened and a man walked in. He was wearing an expensive business suit and gloves. A facemask covered his mouth. He looked to be in his fifties – a touch of grey at the temples, a rash of broken veins in his nose. A waft of aftershave came with him. It had been so long since Thorpe had smelled anything that hadn't made him recoil that, to him, it was the sweetest odour he had ever experienced.

He remained silent. His tendency towards smart-alec remarks had been beaten out of him early on in his sentence. Someone would tell him what was going on eventually.

"I apologise for the lateness of the hour," the man said. At least, that's what Thorpe thought he said. The facemask muffled the words to near-indecipherability.

The man shook his head in annoyance, reached up and pulled the mask off. "I've had all the shots," he said. "I know most antibiotics are useless now, but there are still one or two that work, if you can afford them."

"And you can afford them," Thorpe said, surprising himself. He had honestly intended to keep quiet until he knew what was going on.

"I can," the man said. "My name is Jensen. William Jensen. Have you heard of me?" When Thorpe shook his head, Jensen continued: "No matter. I do try to keep my name out of the media as much as possible. Suffice it to say that I have considerable influence in this city, both politically and financially. Anything I need, I can buy, and I don't have to worry about the price."

"Not everything," Thorpe said, "or you wouldn't be here."

Jensen grimaced – a quick twist of the lips, over almost as quickly as it had begun. "Very perceptive, Mr Thorpe. Yes, you're right – I have discovered that some things are beyond my means. It's not a comfortable discovery."

"And somehow I can help."

"That's why I am here," Jensen confirmed.

"And the Governor is happy with that, I suppose?"

"The Governor and I play golf. I asked him for a favour and he granted it. I may have to lose the next couple of matches in exchange, but it will be worth it – I hope."

"What do I have," Thorpe asked with a flicker of genuine

236

interest, "that a man like you could possibly want?"

"You have good genes," Jensen replied. He smiled at Thorpe's obvious confusion. "Let me explain. I have a daughter – aged eighteen. She is very precious to me, and I spoil her horribly. She went missing a week ago. I need someone to get her back for me."

"I'm not a mercenary, or a hostage negotiator," Thorpe said. The momentary hope that had flared within him was guttering out now. This was some kind of mistake. Jensen had got the wrong man, and whatever leverage Thorpe might have had was just an illusion.

"She hasn't been kidnapped," Jensen replied, surprising Thorpe. "If she had, I might have been able to do something to get her back – pay a ransom, perhaps, or fund a hostage rescue mission. No, she has gone missing of her own accord. She has run away, and I can't find her." He glanced away, towards one of the metal walls. "I think she has fallen in with what men like me quaintly call 'the wrong crowd'," he said quietly. "Drugs are involved, undoubtedly. It's a teenage rebellion, of course, and one I expected – but I didn't expect her to go this far. I always thought that whatever happened I would be able to get her back. Now... now I'm not sure. Anything could have happened to her. I've paid money to law enforcement, private detectives, mercenaries and criminals, but nobody can find her for me. There are too many places in this city that are in shadow, and nobody can see what's hiding there."

"I'm not a social worker or counsellor either." Thorpe shrugged: just an awkward hunching of his shoulders while his hands were still in his lap. "I really don't see what I can do. Maybe you think I've got some information, some intelligence about the people she's fallen in with that I've picked up while I've been here, but as far as I know I don't. I was never part of what you call 'the wrong crowd' when I was out there, in the real world, and I'm not part of it in here either. I just want to

serve my time and keep my nose – and everything else – clean."
He paused, and sighed. "I suppose I could make something
up: tell you that there's been talk in here about some rich bitch
who's left her well-off family because she's fallen desperately
in love with some drug baron, and I'll only tell you his name
if you get me released, or at least get me a cell with a window
and a dose of those expensive antibiotics, but I presume you'd
have me truth-scanned so there's no point. I don't want to get
your hopes up."

"Honest," Jensen said, nodding. "Your file indicates as
much. Thank you for not wasting my time. The thing is, it's
not what you know that I care about – it's what you are."

"I'm a small-time data thief," Thorpe said. "That's all there
is. Not even a page-worth of information."

Jensen smiled the smile of a man who knows something
that the people he's negotiating with don't. "Your file is
bulked out with a full genetic scan," he pointed out. "Do you
remember having a skin sample taken from your arm when
you were incarcerated? All prisoners have one. Their genes
are catalogued and the information is shared between law
enforcement agencies across the world, in case you reoffend
somewhere when you release, and the top five international
healthcare providers. It goes into an anonymised data library
of DNA cross-referenced with medical history. The healthcare
providers use the data to look for new gene-therapies that
might be able to cure a range of medical conditions – for
people like me." He paused. "I own one of those healthcare
providers, which is how I got access to your data."

"Anonymised?" Thorpe said. He raised an eyebrow, trying
to look calm and confident, but inside him a small cold spot
of fear had begun to blossom. He'd heard rumours about
this kind of thing happening. "You're telling me that if some
billionaire somewhere needs a replacement liver or a heart
then he could find a match somewhere in one of the country's

prisons with just a couple of clicks of a button? Is that why I'm here? Does someone have designs on my internal organs, or my eyes, or my bone marrow? Do you?"

Jensen shook his head, smiling. "I won't insult your intelligence by denying that there is some… oh, informal trade in organic material from the prison community, but no, that's not the case in your case. After all, if I wanted some biological tissue from you I'd hardly arrange to interview you first." He paused, frowning. "Unless it was your tongue I wanted, of course. That would be different. I would need to know that it was in good working order. But no – I'm more interested in what I can put into you, rather than what I can take out of you."

Thorpe leaned forward, intrigued, but worried. He could feel sweat trickling down his ribs and prickling on his forehead. He was just about to place his hands on the metal table that separated him from Jensen when he suddenly realised what he was doing, and pulled back. 'What you can put into me?' he parroted.

"Have you heard of gene-splicing, Mr Thorpe?"

He had – vaguely – but he wasn't going to admit it. "Can't say I have."

"It's a process where genes from one creature are introduced into the DNA of another, or so I am informed. It started off many years ago with mice being given genes from a species of jellyfish that glowed in the dark. The resulting mice also glowed in the dark. Very pretty, but there's not much of a commercial market for glowing mice, given that cats have no spending money." He smiled, to indicate that he was joking. "Since then the process has become very common in plants – disease and insect predation in crops like wheat and rice have more or less been wiped out thanks to genes transplanted from other species. It's so common that it's hardly ever talked about any more, when it comes to plants. With animals, and certainly with humans, there are barriers. There's what they call the 'Euch!' factor, in the public mind. If you talk about taking genes from a fish and putting them into a pig, for whatever reason, people automatically go 'Euch!' And then there's the ethics committees as well." He sighed. "So much paperwork. So many people to bribe. It's far easier just to do it in secret."

The little bud of cold fear, which had begun to wither while Jensen was speaking, flared up again. Thorpe felt a tremble running through his hands. "I take it from what you've said that you want to experiment on me. Do I get any choice in the matter?"

Jensen stared into his eyes for a long moment. "What I need you to do, Mr Thorpe, requires your willing co-operation. I have a list of twenty three names of prisoners whose genetic make-up is suitable for what I have in mind."

"And I'm the most compatible?"

"No, you're just the nearest to where I live. If you say no, then I'll just move to the next name on the list. I am hoping, however, that you will say yes."

"Forgive the obvious question, but what's in it for me?"

"Freedom."

That took him aback. No 'if's, or 'but's, or 'we'll put in a good word to the authorities'. Just 'freedom'.

The question was: at what cost?

"Who do I have to kill?"

Jensen laughed. "I like you, Mr Thorpe. You get straight to the point. No, you don't have to kill anyone. You just have to undergo a little operation, and then lead a group of mercenaries to the place where my daughter is located. They will take it from there, including any necessary killing."

"But you don't know where your daughter is located." His brain whirled, putting the jigsaw pieces together. "An operation? Gene-splicing? You're going to put something in me that will help find your daughter!"

Instead of answering directly, Jensen stared at Thorpe for a while. The silence between them lengthened, grew taut to the point of snapping. It seemed to Thorpe that Jensen's gaze was roving across his face, his scalp, his temples, as if looking for something.

"Sharks are amazing creatures," he said eventually, as if casually continuing the previous conversation, "They have remain almost unchanged, unevolved, for millions of years. They are perfectly designed for what they do – there's no reason for them to evolve because it's almost impossible to improve on them. Brainless, yes, but they don't need brains. What most people focus on is their teeth, of course, but their sensory organs are…" – he shook his head – "…much, much better than any machine we can build. A Great White Shark, for instance, can detect a single drop of blood in a volume of water the size of an Olympic swimming pool. Not only that, but it can work out which direction the blood has come from based on the minute difference in the time of arrival of a scent between one nostril and the other. A Great White can detect and locate prey over miles of ocean. Once they've done that, they become a missile of flesh and teeth, aimed straight at that prey."

"I'm not a shark," Thorpe whispered. His hands were shaking.

"Ah, but you can be. I'm assured by my experts that we can splice the olfactory bulb of a Great White Shark's brain into your brain, implant its olfactory epithelium inside your sinus cavity and bathe the neurons in a solution of stem cells that will allow them to connect up – man with shark, shark with man. A little gene therapy as well – some shark genetic material introduced into your bloodstream, encased in a viral carrier – and within a few weeks your body will have incorporated that genetic material into your own DNA. It's a remarkably simple process. You'll need to get used to the new sensations, of course, but it's not as if we'd be introducing something completely new, like radar, or the ability to detect radio waves. Your brain can already make sense of odours – we're just boosting its ability several thousand-fold."

"So that I can find your daughter?" His voice was rising, becoming hysterical, but he couldn't help himself. "So that I can, what, sniff her out wherever she is in the city? What are you going to do – drive me around in a limousine with the window down and my head hanging out like a dog, sniffing at everything that goes past until I detect her?' He slammed his hands on the metal table, regardless of the stains. The guards twitched forwards, but Jensen waved them back with a minute gesture. 'Do you really expect me to go along with this... this lunacy?"

"That depends," Jensen said calmly. "How much do you want to be free?"

"Why can't you just use a dog, for God's sake?" Thorpe asked. "It's not like this kind of thing has never been done before! People have tracked animals for ages!"

"We've tried." Jensen shrugged, a pained expression crossing his face, as if he was mourning the time that had been lost. "A dog's olfactory system may be a thousand times as complex as a human's, but it isn't as complex as that of a shark, and a dog can only indicate direction very crudely, by pointing its nose or its paw in the right direction. We need someone who can detect my daughter at a long distance, who can distinguish between where she is now and where she has been. We need someone who can tell us which streets we need to go down, which buildings to enter, which corridors to take, what height she is at. We need you, Mr Thorpe." He made a gesture with his hand. "Believe me, I would have preferred to make this offer to someone else, but not everyone has a genetic makeup which is compatible with what we need to do.

You do. You should be proud." His mouth twitched. "It's about the only thing that distinguishes you from the sub-norm."

"And afterwards?" Thorpe asked, pulling back from the table and looking at his hands. Whatever stain was on the table had transferred to his palms: a rusty, reddish dust.

"We can remove the brain tissue and the olfactory epithelium fairly easily. The genetic material cannot be removed, but it can be deactivated chemically – rendered into junk DNA like so much of the human genome."

"This brain surgery – is it risky?"

Jensen shrugged. "Apparently it's hardly even brain surgery. The olfactory bulb is right at the front of the brain. The nerves from the olfactory epithelium just plug right into it." He smiled. He probably meant it to be reassuring, but to Thorpe it looked like the rictus of a predator exposing its teeth just before taking a bite out of its prey.

"The surgery will take several hours," Jensen continued, "but there's no need to go in through the skull. My surgeons will cut upwards between your upper lip and your front teeth, then drill upwards through your sinuses. Once they've made a hole large enough they can use miniature cameras and remote manipulators to do the work. Keyhole surgery, apparently. The material they need to implant is no bigger than a pea. When they've finished they'll plug the hole with flesh taken from your upper thigh, and then introduce the extra olfactory epithelium into your sinuses on the way out. All you'll be left with is some stitches inside your upper lip which will dissolve away within a week. There'll be some discomfort, but there's nothing to worry about. Nothing life-threatening." He paused. "Are you in, or are you out? If you have any reservations, don't waste my time. I have other people to see if you say no."

Thorpe didn't say no, of course. He had reservations, of course – enough to fill his brain with thoughts that flashed and whirled like a shoal of fish frightened by a predator –

243

but he needed to get out of the prison, and this was his only chance. So he said yes, and damn the consequences.

He was taken from the interview room to a garage where a limousine was parked. No paperwork, no goodbyes, no returning of his meagre possessions – just a quick removal, as if the system wanted to forget about him as quickly as it could. The limousine's windows were darkened, and there was a glass barrier between the back seats and the chauffeur's area. It was only when the car started off that Thorpe realised he had traded one cell for another. The only thing that had changed was his level of comfort.

Jensen leaned back in his seat, closed his eyes and slept. Thorpe couldn't sleep. The thought of someone cutting through his upper lip and peeling it back, then drilling up through his sinuses until they reached his brain, kept looming up in his thoughts, obscuring whatever else he tried to think about.

The journey took under an hour. Judging by the sounds outside they had driven into a city, but when the limousine stopped they were in an underground car park. Jensen led the way to a lift on the far side. The chauffeur accompanied them, probably to make sure that Thorpe didn't try to run off. Freedom, it seemed, only went so far.

They operated that night.

Lots of blood tests, X-rays and MRI scans were done first. They didn't feed him. Apparently he had to have an empty stomach for the operation. He'd been hoping for something different from the standard prison slop, but even the freedom to have a good meal was denied him. A nurse injected him with a pre-op anaesthetic in his thigh without even asking him, or warning him. He was just a piece of meat to them.

The last thing he remembered was looking up into the circular lights as the anaesthetist placed a face-mask across his nose and mouth and asked him to count backwards from ten.

He got to six before he floated away into black waters, borne away by the tide.

*   *   *

THAT SAME TIDE deposited him on the shores of consciousness again some unquantifiable time later. He remembered momentary fragments of memories from the interim – wrenching off the face-mask and throwing up as they wheeled him out of the operation, watching as blurred figures put needles into both arms and strapped him down to a bed, hearing the regular bleep…bleep…bleep of a heart monitor – but when he awoke properly he was in a darkened room, surrounded by machines. A nurse was standing over him. She smiled reassuringly, but there was something in her gaze that told Thorpe she was scared. Scared of what? He was strapped down!

His nose felt like it was the size of a small puppy. Bandages crossed his face, and there was something like a pillow pressing up against his nostrils from below. He could only breathe through his mouth, and his mouth was as dry as sand.

He was like that for three days before they took the bandages off. "There'll be some discomfort," Jensen had said, but he hadn't mentioned to Thorpe the fact that the surgeons had packed what remained of his sinuses with absorbent surgical dressings to soak up all the blood from their handiwork until the flesh healed. The pain when they pulled the dressings out was worse than anything he had ever experienced – like someone had poked a pair of pliers inside his nose and was trying to pull his entire brain out through his nostrils.

And all this time, he couldn't smell a thing.

That began to change on the fourth day. He woke salivating, smelling food. It wasn't just that he could *smell* food, though – he could smell each individual part – the chicken, the broccoli, the rice, even the salt. The saliva spilled out of his mouth and down his chin, and he had to swallow repeatedly before he could take a breath. He could tell, thirty seconds before a nurse entered the room, that someone was coming. After a few hours he could tell which nurse it was – not by their perfume, because they didn't wear any, but by the distinctive smell that each nurse had – their own personal human pheromones. He could smell traffic outside, and he could even tell the difference between night and day, buses and cars, petrol and diesel, additives and additive-free. It was as if smells were colours, and he could identify an entire spectrum of a million hues. He knew whenever an operation started or finished elsewhere in the hospital because he could smell the blood and the other bodily fluids as they leaked out. He knew when anyone died in the hospital, because that too had its own distinctive smell.

He couldn't smell himself. Absolutely nothing. For a while that had puzzled him, but then he had realised that sharks either didn't know or didn't care where they were. It was everything else they were interested in.

When Jensen entered the hospital, on the fifth day, Thorpe knew he was coming from the moment he got out of his limousine. His aftershave was that distinctive. It got more and more distinctive until he entered the hospital room, seemingly wafted on an invisible cloud of the stuff. There were other scents on him as well – the leather upholstery of the car, the crab salad he'd eaten for lunch, the cheaper aftershave and deodorant of his chauffeur, and something else. Something flowery, but dry, like old petals.

Jensen stared down at him in the bed. The needles and the tubes had been removed by now, and all he had was a blood pressure cuff on his arm that inflated every thirty minutes and an oxygen sensor pinching his right forefinger.

"Time moves on," Jensen said. "No 'How are you feeling?' or 'I hope everything is okay' – just straight to the point. "Are you ready to go?"

Thorpe nodded gently. Despite all the reassurances of the nurses that everything had healed up nicely, he still expected a waterfall of blood to come out of his nose every time he leaned forward. "I think so," he said.

Jensen frowned, and leaned his head to one side. His lips pursed. "What is it like?" he asked quietly.

Thorpe shrugged. "It's like… it's like I can see colours with my nose," he said quietly. "It's like every draft and every breeze is an arpeggio of smells."

"I don't understand," Jensen said.

"Then I can't explain. The words don't exist."

Jensen looked away, disappointed. "I have arranged some initial testing," he said. Reaching into his pocket he pulled out a handkerchief, and suddenly the floral smell became a lot more intense. "This is my wife's," he said. "Can you smell it?"

"Yes. Obviously."

"Then let's see if you can find my wife. She is somewhere in this hospital, sitting reading a magazine. If you can find her within, oh, ten minutes then I think you are ready to find my daughter."

A nurse removed the blood pressure cuff and oxygen sensor, and helped him out of bed. He was unsteady on his legs, but they had a wheelchair for him. The nurse wheeled him out of the room and into the corridor.

The nearest that Thorpe could come to understanding the sensations that washed over him was that it was as if every smell was a different hue of coloured light, and there were a thousand lights all shining at him from every direction, some pulsing and some steady, some blindingly bright and some dim. But it was more than that – colours didn't provoke emotions, or reactions, but different odours made him feel

247

happy, sad, angry, disgusted and aroused, all at the same time. He was swamped in emotions, drowning in them. He couldn't cope!

He felt a sharp scratch in his elbow.

"A mild sedative," Jensen said from behind him. "It will help you distance yourself from what you are experiencing."

Within moments a swimmy feeling washed over him, and he found himself floating backwards in his own head, observing what was happening but distanced from it. Not caring about it – at least, not as much. Rather than being overwhelmed by a million different smells, all clashing and all provoking him to some emotion, it was more like he was seeing a world in which messages had been left on every surface, every piece of material.

It was like there were many years' worth of Post-It notes stuck wherever he looked – the ones on top being the freshest, the ones on the bottom the oldest. Each Post-It note held a message – "I am scared", "I am pregnant", "I am dying", or just, "I am here".

With an effort of will he found he could push the messages themselves into the background – aware of them but not reading them - and search for a particular handwriting. That was the closest metaphor he could find to understand intellectually what he was doing instinctively. As he had said to Jensen, there were no words to explain it, and without words his mind kept switching between different comparisons.

A train of messages written by the same person – Jensen's wife - led down the corridor. He gestured to the nurse to push him in that direction. As she did so, his head swung around, getting a feeling for where the scent of that particular person got bigger or smaller. He closed his eyes to minimise the distraction of sight, but he was still seeing – just in a different way, a way that had so much more depth to it, so many more dimensions.

A concentration of odour now, a whole set of piled-up messages saying, "This way!", and the chime of an elevator door opening. He gestured to the nurse to wheel him inside one of the lifts. A backdrop of ozone and grease, and in front of that backdrop there were piles of Post-It Notes from everyone who had been in that lift over the past few years. Too many to read.

"Which floor are we on?" he asked hoarsely, but he already knew. The smell of people and disinfectant and food was down; the smell of pollen and aircraft fuel was up. He was on the top floor. "Go down, one floor at a time. Make sure the doors open on each floor."

Different floors, different sets of messages. One was obviously paediatrics – he could smell babies, children, vomit and faeces. One was oncology, suffused with the bitter smell of impending or suspended death. One was for of surgical theatres: open wounds, concentration and anaesthetic. And then…

"Here," he said as soon as the doors started opening. The old flowers smell of Jensen's wife's perfume was suddenly blooming in his nostrils.

The nurse went right, but he waved his left hand. "No - that way."

A junction of corridors caused more and different odours to bloom. He chose to go right, where the floral scent still underpinned all of the others. Left at another junction, then straight across a hallway and –

"Here," he said. He opened his eyes, knowing already that they were in a cafeteria. The smell of ground coffee and lasagne that had been kept warm for several hours was unmistakable. He could tell that the meat had been past its use-by date before it had been cooked. He could smell the sadness of family and friends sitting at various tables, thinking about the happy past and the uncertain future.

Thorpe opened his eyes. Jensen's wife was sitting over in a corner, looking uncomfortable. She had a cup in front of her – Earl Grey tea, with one sugar. No – one and a half. Her perfume surrounded her like a blaze of light, nearly blinding Thorpe. She had cancer as well – something growing in her lungs. It was just a still, small voice at the moment, but it would get louder with time. There was no smell of fear in her, or in Jensen. Neither of them knew.

"Well done," Jensen said. "Would you like some water?"

"I'd like some food. Something better than here – a pizza, maybe. There's an Italian restaurant over in that direction" – he pointed to the nearest window – "where they're using fresh garlic and authentic Italian tomatoes. I want that pizza."

"We don't have time for that. My daughter –"

"Pizza, now, or you can take me back to my room." When Jensen hesitated, Thorpe added, "Think of it as keeping me fuelled, if you like. Just get me that pizza."

Eating took on a whole new intensity, with the tastes of the various herbs and spices filling his nostrils even before he bit into the slices themselves. He tore at them, filling his stomach. The cheese – four different cheeses, in fact, including pecorino and parmesan – was an incredible melange of subtle strands of flavour. Somewhere in there he could even taste the grass that the cows that eaten to make the milk which made the cheese.

"Now," Jensen said after a while. Thorpe felt like arguing, but there would be all the time in the world for pizza, and burgers, and the whole world of food, after he had done his work.

They took him down in the lift to the limousine. There were two people-carriers parked behind it. Thorpe could smell five… no, seven men sitting inside them. They had been there for a while. They were sending unconscious messages of barely controlled violence. He could smell something else as well – something smoky but sharp. It took a few moments before he realised that it was the smell of the propellant in the cartridges which packed their guns.

A periscope-like device had been fitted into the roof of the limousine. When he slid inside he saw what it was for. Handles on the inside could be used to rotate it, but instead of eyepieces there was a flexible hose that led to a mask that would fit over his nose, secured with elastic. It was a periscope for scent rather than sight.

The limousine's engine purred into life, surrounding the car with a cloud of hydrocarbons and the tang of hot metal. Somewhere in there was a sharp, sweet overtone of petrol that hadn't been burned up. The engine could do with servicing, Thorpe thought, as the car slid smoothly up the ramp of the hospital cark park and into the street. The people-carriers followed. The realisation that he could diagnose engine trouble just from the smell of the exhaust, and cancer from the smell of the sufferers' breath and sweat, made Thorpe think. He suddenly had a vision of a future in which he could make a lot of money from his new gift. Previously he'd been counting the days until the shark-flesh inside him could be taken away, and the genetic material switched off, but now he was thinking that there was an upside beyond his freedom. He needed to talk to Jensen about that – or maybe after he'd found Jensen's daughter he could just fade away and lose himself in the city. After all, he'd always know a few minutes in advance if someone was coming for him – time enough to run.

There was a metal case in the back of the limousine. Jensen opened it, and took out a pillow wrapped in polythene. The artificial smell of the plastic made Thorpe feel dizzy. Jensen removed the pillow and handed it to Thorpe.

"My daughter's pillow," he said quietly. "It should have her pheromones on it. If not, there are other things we can try."

"Can you put the polythene back into the case?" Thorpe asked. "It's swamping everything else."

Jensen frowned, but complied with the request. As the metal lid of the case closed, and Thorpe held the pillow to his face - breathing in deeply - he was surrounded by and infused with a cloud of complex smells: sweat, perfume, shampoo, natural oils, even tears and saliva. It all added together to form a picture of a girl - her hopes and dreams, her loves and fears. Thorpe could almost see her face in his mind, the picture was that strong. He could also smell in her the distinctive human essence of her father and her mother, along with something that was purely her.

"I've got it," he said, handing the pillow back. "Now put that thing away so it doesn't confuse me."

Sitting in the back seat, the rubber mask over his nose and a black cloth mask over his eyes, with Jensen on one side of him and the nurse on the other, Thorpe leaned back and took in the smells of the city.

If leaving his room and entering the hospital corridor had led to a thousand-fold expansion in what he was smelling, then moving from the hospital to the street expanded it a million-fold. In his mind he could see thin or thick scarves of scent leading in all directions. People – hundreds and hundreds of them – animals, uncooked food, cooked food, sewage, wine and beer and fizzy drinks and water, plants and machines and oil – everything was there, layer upon layer of information. Somewhere over to the right he thought he could smell the prison, a faraway stench of desperation, fear and violence. Nearer, on the left, an old girlfriend's perfume drifted through the periscope and into the nose-mask. The unexpected scent immediately flashed up memories of their time together in his mind, but the scent was suddenly gone, overwritten with the smell of water polluted with garbage, oil and complex chemicals – the main river that ran through the city. Behind that was sweeter water – the various tributaries that fed it. And everywhere there was the smell of bacteria, disease and infection.

Seeking one particular scent against that background was like trying to see a lit match next to a searchlight.

They cruised for half an hour before Thorpe detected a trace of something similar to the scent on the pillow. He tensed, and felt Jensen shift beside him. He turned the periscope left, and then right. The smell was stronger to the right.

"Turn right," he said.

The car turned a few seconds later. The scent grew stronger, then weaker.

"Turn around. Go back."

It took twenty minutes of jerky driving before he was happy that they were heading in the right direction. The smell grew stronger and stronger. Despite the other distractions he could clearly distinguish it, and focus on it.

They were driving through a rough area. He could tell just by what was coming through the periscope to the mask. Poverty, disease and hopelessness had their own distinct odour. There were more people packed into this area as well, each one distinct to his nostrils. Each one an individual, unique compared to all the others.

Eventually he asked Jensen to stop the car. She was close now. Very close.

He pulled the mask from his nose and opened the car door. Jensen reached out a hand to restrain him, but he got out and stood in the middle of the street. The black mask was still over his eyes, blocking out the light, but he didn't need it. He could visualise the entire street just by the way it smelled. More than that, he could visualise what was behind the walls and the windows – an olfactory form of X-ray vision.

He turned until he was facing the direction that the girl's

pheromones were wafting from, and tilted his head to one side. With his nostrils vertical rather than horizontal he could sense what height the odours were coming from.

Up. Thirty degrees.

He pointed. "She's up there," he said. "In a room with a broken window. She's asleep. There are five other people there – four men and a woman. I can smell take-out food, some of it weeks old, and what I think is heroin. Unwashed clothes, and unwashed bed sheets. Oh, and there are guns. Several guns."

"Thank you," Jensen said from behind him. "More than I can say. We can take it from here."

Car doors opened and slammed. Seven men smelling of tension, anticipation and gun oil walked past Thorpe, each one telling his own story with the chemicals that drifted from his body.

Silence for a long while, then the sudden sound of gunfire matched, moments later, by the odour of burned propellant. The coppery smell of blood. Sharp urine, as bladders gave way in terror.

"What's going on?" Jensen whispered. "Dear God, have they got her? Is she still alive?"

"They've got her," Thorpe confirmed. He could smell that she was awake and confused. Her odour faded as she was moved out of the room and into the corridor, then brightened again as the breeze down the stairwell caught it and took it out of the building towards Thorpe.

He knew that he should have felt something – pride, pleasure, anticipation of his freedom – but Thorpe just stood there, mask over his eyes, experiencing what was happening without having any emotions about it. He didn't care, and he didn't care that he didn't care. He was living purely in the moment.

At Jensen's murmured instruction the chauffeur took Thorpe by the arm and led him back to the car. Thorpe went meekly with him. Nothing seemed to matter.

The girl was weeping hysterically when she emerged from the building. A private ambulance arrived – Thorpe could smell the antiseptic and the wound dressings inside. The girl was put inside, and Jensen went with her. The armed men returned to their people carriers and drove away.

The limousine moved away, heading back to the hospital. All the way Thorpe had the mask over his nostrils and the periscope revolving, experiencing all the stories that were going on around him, swimming through the sea of scents. He supposed that he should be worried that the surgeons were going to take the shark olfactory bulb and olfactory epithelium straight out again, despite the fact that he'd already decided that he wanted to keep them, but he couldn't feel any concern. Whatever happened, happened. He wouldn't plan to avoid it, but just react to circumstances.

When they got to the hospital car park the chauffeur held the door open for him. "Mr Jensen has asked that you join him and his family upstairs, in their private suite. He wants to thank you personally, and introduce you to his daughter."

The lift took them straight up to the same floor where Thorpe had been operated on. The chauffeur led him a different way down the corridor, to a room with many people in, all talking happily at the same time. Some were relatives of the girl, judging by the chemicals exuded by their sweat glands. Others were friends, legal advisors, consultants. But mainly they were family: other daughters, a son, two grandparents and Jensen's wife as well as a bunch of cousins.

That was the problem. With just Jensen's pheromones, or his daughter's, to deal with, Thorpe had been able to remain in control. With all those related bodies in the room sweating out pheromones that had the same rough mix of chemical components, Thorpe couldn't help himself. He lost it. The scents overcame him, triggering some primal reflex. A red mist of hunger engulfed him.

A woman turned to look at him, and screamed at whatever she saw in his face.

That was the last thing he remembered until he awoke in his hospital bed again.

*　*　*

HE WAS STRUNG up with monitors and drips. His head ached. He tried to raise a hand to his face, to see if there were any dressings there, any evidence of another operation, but his wrist was fastened to the metal bed frame with cuffs. Both hands, both legs were restrained. A strap across his chest prevented him from even sitting up. He should have felt fear then, but there was nothing there. No emotion.

He could smell blood. A lot of it: even for a hospital.

It was only when he overheard two nurses whispering in the corridor that he understood what had happened. He had managed to kill fifteen people before hospital security stopped him, mainly ripping their throats out with his fingernails and his teeth, but also using various bits of cutlery that were on a buffet table. When they pumped his stomach out they got flesh from each of those fifteen people. He'd eaten his fill, and was still eating when they restrained him with a massive dose of sedative.

They would put him back in prison, of course, but that didn't worry him.

He was the predator now.

Feast of the Shark God

C L WERNER

A COLD WIND rushed across the waves, reeking of the briny deep. Shintaro Oba could feel his skin prickle beneath the loose material of his kimono as the breeze swept past him. At the stern of the little fishing smack, he could hear his companion's teeth chattering. The boy struggled to keep the boat steady, trying to prevent his shivering from throwing them off course. The boy wasn't a samurai; he hadn't been exposed to the rigours of a warrior's life. Oba trusted him just the same. Denkou knew what failure would mean.

Oba risked only his own life, but Denkou had much more at stake. From the corner of his eye, the samurai caught the boy looking back towards the shore. The village of Ogashima was back there, nestled between the cliffs. Mikiko was there too, tied to the altar at the base of those cliffs. Denkou had thrown everything away for her sake, casting aside his family and his home – even his god – on the chance that she could be saved.

"Watch the waves," Oba warned Denkou. "Four eyes are better than two for this kind of business."

"I'm sorry," Denkou said. "It won't happen again. I will stay alert."

The samurai tightened his hold on the bone grip of his uchigatana. The sword was a massive weapon, over two feet in length, designed to cut down enemy warriors with ease. Many hideous foes, both mortal and demon, had perished upon Koumakiri's steel. Deep within himself, Oba couldn't fight back the feeling that even this famed blade wasn't enough for the task he'd set himself. What weapon, after all, was enough to destroy a god?

Oba endured the fear inside him with the same acceptance he did the cold wind. Fear was nothing shameful – so long as he didn't let himself become afraid. There was a difference between acknowledging the emotion and allowing it to take control. The bold samurai was the one who used his fear, harnessed it to drive him to still greater effort. Only by failing to make that effort would he dishonour himself.

Wanikira, the shark god of Ogashima. What effort could a mortal make that could overcome a god?

Oba drew a deep breath, feeling the sting of the cold air in his lungs. Perhaps it was impossible, but he wouldn't turn from the path he'd set himself upon. Even in death, a man could keep his honour.

The dark waters of the bay rolled under the fishing smack, making the tiny boat tilt upwards as each wave struck. Oba shifted his foot around the bottom of the boat, feeling for the heavy burden they'd brought with them. A sharp pain shot up his leg as his shin struck against the bulky object. He felt reassured to know it was still there. In his long years hunting demons across the provinces of Mu-Thulan, he'd observed that even these supernatural horrors had to obey many of the limitations suffered by mortal creatures. He prayed to his ancestors that the same was true of gods when they deigned to manifest in the material world.

"Sir Oba," Denkou whispered, his voice quaking not from

cold but from fright. The smack lurched to one side as the boy pointed a shaking finger towards the starboard.

The samurai cast his gaze where Denkou directed. At first he could detect nothing, only the same swaying blackness of water that had surrounded them ever since their escape from Ogashima. Then he saw it, a grey shape slicing through the waves. The fisherman had recognized it at once, but it took Oba a moment to appreciate that it was the tip of a fin.

"Wanikira," Denkou hissed in a tone that somehow managed to mix reverence and loathing.

Oba braced himself up in the bow of the boat. "Get us closer," he ordered Denkou. "Put us right beside it."

The boat creaked and groaned as Denkou rowed frantically, trying to steer the smack closer. The fin continued to knife its way shoreward, but unless they could close the distance between them, the shark god would sweep right past on its way to Ogashima. The samurai clenched his fist in silent frustration. Whatever his intentions, however sincere his determination to confront Wanikira, there was nothing he could do now to force that contest. He had to stay in the bow, ready to act the moment an opportunity presented itself. Getting that chance was Denkou's trial. Everything depended now upon the fisherman and his own strength and determination. Only the boy could bring them where they needed to be.

The grey fin continued its speedy advance towards the shore. Oba felt his heart cracking with despair. They wouldn't reach it in time. They wouldn't be able to intercept Wanikira. The shark god would claim its prey.

Denkou realized the same thing. Oba heard the boy moan, then was nearly knocked off his feet as the little boat surged onwards. The fisherman was plying his oar like an incarnate fiend, forcing the smack through the driving waves.

The samurai's clothes became drenched by the water crashing against the prow.

Closer now, near enough that Oba could see more clearly the great grey fin. Moonlight revealed the deep notches and scars that peppered the scaly grey hide. The fin was triangular in shape, arcing back at a depressed slant, little rivulets of water dripping down its sides as it slashed a course through the waves.

Closer! Still closer! A nauseous smell of rot and brine slammed into Oba's nose, nearly choking him. The samurai had to blink back tears as he focused upon the approaching dorsal fin.

Closer! Oba reared back with his sword, holding it outstretched behind him.

Closer, and the uchigatana flashed outward, chopping into the scaly hide as the fin knifed its way starboard of the little boat. Oba felt the impact shudder through his bones, the force almost causing him to lose his footing and pitch down into the churning waves. Thin, treacly blood oozed from the savage cut, a six-inch flap of flesh dangling by ribbons of meat slapped against the side of the truncated fin.

Denkou gasped in amazement as he watched Oba strike Wanikira, then his amazement sank into horror as the fin continued onward, the shark god seemingly oblivious to the wound visited against it.

Oba slid Koumakiri back into its sheath and scrambled to snatch up the barbed fishing spear from the bottom of the boat. "Follow it!" he snarled at Denkou, already knowing they'd never catch up to their quarry. Even as the thought came to him, there was a sudden thrashing in the waves ahead. A gigantic tail, split into two blade-like lobes, erupted from the water and flailed from side to side. The stricken dorsal fin submerged a moment later, drawing the lashing tail after it.

"It can be hurt," Oba called out, wondering if he was

trying to reassure Denkou or himself.

Denkou released the tiller, pointing at the sea. "Wanikira has turned! He is coming for us now!"

Oba spotted what Denkou had seen, the ripple surging through the sea, breaking the waves as it swept towards them. A dull, shadowy mass was swimming just below the surface, speeding forwards with great flicks of its immense tail. The samurai lifted the fishing spear high, bracing himself for the shark god's charge.

The great beast lunged up from the sea, flinging itself into the darkened sky like an arrow loosed from a bow. In the moonlight, Oba could see the sleek streamlined shape of the creature, its long pointed snout and massive jaws, the scaly body with its broad pectoral fins and their bony flanges. Wanikira's giant tail whipped about ferociously as the shark god leapt through the air, the blade-like lobes staving in the side of the boat.

"We're sinking!" Denkou's scream of horror broke the ghastly fascination that had seized Oba. The samurai had made the mistake of staring into the black depths of Wanikira's eyes and found himself gripped by the awful power of that inhuman gaze. Too late he recovered himself; too late he made to cast the spear into the plunging monster. As quickly as it had breached the waves, Wanikira came smashing back down, speeding back into the depths.

"Try to keep us afloat!" Oba shouted. He stared at the sea, watching as the dark shadow of Wanikira circled them just below the surface. If the beast would only show itself once more, if it would only rush to the surface before their boat went to the bottom!

Behind him, Denkou muttered the few sutras he knew and frantically tried to bail water from the boat. "We can't stay afloat!" the boy cried. "The next big wave will sink us!"

Oba kept his eyes on the sea, fixed on the black shape that was Wanikira. He could feel the water spilling into the boat, rising steadily around him. First it rushed around his ankles, and then it surged up to his knees.

"It's hopeless!" Denkou raged, abandoning his futile efforts to save the boat.

The water had risen to Oba's waist now. The gunwales were barely above the sea. Any moment the boat would sink away beneath them, plunging down to the bottom of the bay. Unmoving, the samurai maintained his focus, watching as the shark god circled them. "A man is not beaten until he draws his last breath," Oba said, fire gleaming in his eyes as he saw the shadow streak up towards the surface.

Wanikira's jaws snapped against the side of the fishing smack, rows of serrated teeth ripping through the wood. With a shake of its head, the shark god reduced it to splinters. The beast pushed forwards, its maw opening to snatch meatier prey from the doomed boat.

Even as the monster threw itself forwards, Oba stabbed the spear into its side, sinking it deep into the scaly hide and transfixing two of the beast's gills. Wanikira twisted about, snapping at the samurai. He felt the tip of the creature's snout rake across his leg as he jumped back. Before the beast could bite at him again, he took hold of the object they'd brought from Ogashima. Completely submerged now, the bulky mass refused to budge at first. Then Denkou was there beside him, straining and shoving, knowing that this was their last chance.

Wanikira's first attack now aided the two men. They were able to push their burden through the boards the shark god's tail had splintered. Freed from what buoyancy the boat yet possessed, the anchor-stone plummeted towards the bottom of the bay. The heavy rope fastened to the stone snapped taught. At the other end of the line, the spear embedded in the beast's hide shivered. For a horrible moment, Oba thought it would tear itself loose. But the samurai's thrust had lodged the barbed tip deep in the monster's body. Instead of being ripped free, the spear now pulled at Wanikira.

Oba and Denkou threw themselves into the sea as the shark god flailed and thrashed. The fishing smack was obliterated by the monster's violence, but however fierce its struggles, Wanikira could not dislodge the spear or defy the weight of the anchor stone. Whipping its mighty tail, gnashing its great jaws, the shark god was dragged down, plummeting to the seabed, far fathoms below.

Oba watched the shadowy shape vanish into the depths. With the burden of the anchor stone dragging at it, there was no chance that the creature could swim. It was trapped at the bottom of the bay.

"Is it dead?" Denkou wondered. The fisherman was paddling towards Oba through the waves, his expression one of dread.

Oba swam to Denkou, catching hold of the boy's arm so that they wouldn't be separated by the rolling sea. "Dead or not, it won't trouble Ogashima again," the samurai said. "The anchor stone will keep it from being able to swim. Its stuck at the bottom where it can't prey on your people anymore."

The dread evaporated from Denkou's visage. His expression became one of joyous relief. "Then you've saved Mikiko!"

"*We've* saved Mikiko," Oba corrected the boy. He wasn't so proud that he couldn't acknowledge the invaluable role Denkou had played. Peasant or warrior, Denkou had been his comrade in arms, and had proven himself a man of courage and determination.

"It's a long swim back to the village," Denkou observed, glancing back towards the shore and the faint lights of Ogashima.

"Then we had better start," Oba told him. "It would be a sorry thing to vanquish a god and then drown on the way back."

As they made their way back towards Ogashima, Oba turned his thoughts back to the events of the past day and the strange turn his journey to the village had taken.

*   *   *

A FILE OF simple wooden huts, their thatched roofs slowly yellowing beneath the bright sun, climbed up the defile. Between them, the houses left a track wide enough for a half-dozen men to walk abreast. Behind them there were only the jagged cliffs rising up to the sky. Made of black volcanic rock, the cliffs were coated in heavy clumps of moss and weed, stubborn stands of grass maintaining a precarious hold wherever a few inches of dirt had gathered among the rocks. Below the line of huts, at the end of the village, was a narrow strip of beach, a motley collection of fishing smacks drawn up onto the sands. Further along the beach, heavy nets of rope were staked out upon timber frames so that the sun might dry them. Gulls circled about the nets, swooping in to tear at some stray fin or tail that had been left behind by the fishermen.

"So this is Ogashima." The samurai scratched his chin as he stared down at the village from the top of the defile. The remoteness of the place had given him pause when he'd first heard the rumours about it. Evil things, after all, preferred to work their malignance in the shadowy corners of the world. Ogashima, nestled in a little crack along Shinanno's shore, certainly seemed isolated enough for a demon to make its home. Yet as he looked down at it, the scene seemed far too placid and tranquil to support the old legends he'd heard.

Shintaro Oba's gaze hardened. He knew only too well the perfidy of demons. The Sekigehara clan had been destroyed by a demon's deceit, abolished by the Shogun and annihilated by his armies. Only Oba had escaped, charged by his late lord to wander the lands of Mu-Thulan until he found the hiding place of the monster and reclaimed the clan's honour. The samurai had spent many years seeking out demons, hoping that the next fiend he challenged would be the one he was hunting. Some of his foes had been crude beasts, others had been sly tricksters and a few had even masked themselves in the shapes of men.

When it came to demons, it was a fool who put too much trust in appearances. Oba hadn't survived as long as he had by indulging foolishness.

The samurai's armour was tied in a bundle slung over his back, but both his swords were within easy reach – the jewelled washizaki and the long-bladed uchigatana with its bone-hilt and guard. The short sword was a mundane heirloom of Oba's family, but the uchigatana was a sacred relic of the Sekigehara clan. Its name was Koumakiri and it had been forged especially to destroy demons. Many of the fiends had been sent beyond the Kimon Gate by the sword, yet always the devil he hunted eluded him. Maybe Ogashima would finally bring an end to his search.

With a warrior's swagger, Oba marched down the village road. Faces peeped out at him from doorways, sullen weathered countenances that were too timid to allow the discontent in their eyes manifest in their expressions. The daimyo of Shinanno was known for his harsh taxes and draconian policies. Lord Tsugimoto had aspirations for his favourite son to become heir to the still childless Shogun. Such aspirations demanded expensive gifts and bribes – things the peasants of his fief were expected to pay for. Oba had found little affection for samurai among the farmers of Shinanno, now he found the same resentment among the fisherfolk. If Tsugimoto wasn't careful, he might see all his ambitions go up in the flames of a peasant revolt. No bribe was enough to make the Shogun forgive civil unrest.

As he moved deeper into the village, Oba noticed the wooden sign of an inn hanging from a post set before one of the huts. Marginally larger than its neighbours, the inn sported a tile roof and a small stone icon upon the lintel. At first Oba thought the crouching statue was that of a shisa, one of the guardian dogs adopted by many islanders to protect their homes from evil spirits. A closer look revealed the figure to be fishlike rather than the amalgam of canine and feline aspects usual in a shisa. A fanned tail coiled around a scaly body that sported sharp fins and a piscine head with a fanged maw that grinned down at the street below.

Oba returned the statue's stony gaze. If the rumours he'd heard bore true, then he might meet the inspiration for the monstrous fetish soon. He studied the image a moment more, trying to decide how much of the figure might be reality and how much was artistic imagination. With a shrug, he dismissed the effort. Speculation only served to make monsters bigger than they were.

The room inside the inn was partitioned by a few inner walls, but overall much of the space was given to a single common area. There were no mats upon the floor, only the bare wood of its boards. A timber counter and a handful of tables were the only furnishings. There were no benches or stools, only a few cushions to accommodate the comfort of patrons. Many of the fishermen clustered about the low tables shunned the cushions anyway, preferring to squat on their haunches in a crouch as they drained their cups.

The samurai lingered in the doorway just long enough to kick off his sandals. When he turned to climb the few steps from street to room, Oba found every eye in the place turned towards him. The same unspoken resentment he'd seen in the street was there, the same smouldering hostility.

"Innkeeper!" Oba called out. "Sake for a traveller from Akagi!" His eyes canvassed the room, finally picking out the proprietor, a thin-faced man with squinty eyes and a bulbous nose. The innkeeper sketched a bow and gestured for Oba to follow him to a table away from his other customers.

Oba set down his bundled armour and sat on the threadbare cushion. As soon as he was seated, he laid Koumakiri beside him on the floor – within easy reach should he have need of the sword. The innkeeper blinked nervously at the uchigatana, but managed a smile when he faced the samurai himself.

"I fear the sake of our humble village may not suit your distinguished taste, sir," the innkeeper apologized. "Please do not take insult."

"So long as it is wet," Oba told the man. "After such a long journey, I would take a drink from a kappa's skull!" He glanced past the innkeeper, watching as several of the fishermen rose from their tables and walked out to the street.

The innkeeper noticed the turn of Oba's gaze. "I must apologize, sir, but we of Ogashima are a simple folk, unaccustomed to the company of samurai… and ronin."

Oba's eyes took on a steely glint. "Be wary of who you call ronin," he advised. "There is no insult in weak sake, but there is much in discourtesy."

"I beg your forgiveness, sir," the man said, bowing before turning and hurrying away to fetch a bottle for the warrior.

True to the innkeeper's warning, Oba found the sake to be of poor quality. If the man had brought back a jar of seawater Oba doubted it could have been any less palatable. Even so, his thirst needed sating and he soon had the first bottle drained and called for a second to be brought to him.

It was when he'd nearly emptied the second bottle that a new group of men entered the inn. There were five of them, two the samurai recognized as being among the fishermen who'd left in such haste earlier. Two of the others were fishermen as well, one young and the other older, their features bearing such similarity to one another that Oba judged they must be son and father. Both of them sported a finer quality about their clothing than the other fishermen he'd seen. The fifth man was dressed in a long robe of silk embroidered with stylized waves and leaping fish. An iron rod was thrust beneath the wide sash that circled his waist and upon his head he wore the tall cap of a priest. There was a wizened quality to his face and his black beard was grizzled with flecks of grey. The priest's eyes, however, were possessed of a youthful intensity and there was no mistaking the broad shoulders and powerful build bundled beneath his silken mantle.

"Forgive the disruption," the older fisherman said as he approached Oba's table and bowed. "I am Jiro Nikata, headman of Ogashima. This is my son, Denkou, and Priest Seizaburo." The village chief's face spread in an embarrassed smile. "You have come from Lord Tsugimoto? We have already paid our taxes. His lordship should know that. Ogashima is a loyal village. We wouldn't try to cheat on our obligations to Shinanno." He waved his hand at the cup Oba was holding. "You can tell for yourself that we live humbly on what our magistrate leaves us. Millet and rice, all the fish we catch go to fulfil our obligations to his lordship!"

Oba drained his cup, turning it over as he set it back down. "I am from Akagi, not Shinanno. I have no connection to Lord Tsugimoto. My name is Shintaro Oba and I am a samurai of Sekigehara."

"It is a strange path that leads a warrior from Akagi to Ogashima," Seizaburo said. "You have lost your way perhaps?"

Oba met the priest's icy stare. "Perhaps," he said. "Only hindsight can say what is accident and what is fate."

Seizaburo nodded and turned to Jiro. "Surely this man is not from Tsugimoto. You should extend to him a better measure of Ogashima's hospitality."

"Toshio!" Jiro called out to the innkeeper. "Bring the samurai your best sake. Something befitting of his rank and station!"

While the innkeeper hurried away to attend the headman's orders, Oba exchanged pleasantries with Jiro and the priest. It was natural enough for the villagers to ask for whatever news the samurai might have brought with him, isolated as they were from the outside world. For his part, Oba started to hint at the rumours that had led him to Ogashima, but a warning look from Jiro's son Denkou put him on his guard and he hastily dropped that line of conversation.

When the sake arrived, Oba saw Denkou shake his head. The youth closed his eyes and tilted his head, for just an instant taking on the aspect of a man asleep on his feet. After the warning, Oba contrived to drink far less than he appeared to, pouring only a tiny amount into his cup and spilling much of that as he clumsily raised the vessel to his lips. Warily he studied Jiro and Seizaburo to see if his pretence was passing their scrutiny. When he judged he had them convinced by his deception, the samurai feigned the sudden onset of a debilitating fatigue.

"I fear I'll need... accommodation," the samurai mumbled, blinking from Jiro to the priest. "My... travel... has tired me more... than... I thought." With fumbling fingers, Oba grabbed Koumakiri's guard and the strap binding his bundled armour. He started to rise to his feet, then slumped to the floor. Shaking his head in confusion, he repeated the effort, then slid onto his side in apparent slumber.

The villagers waited a few minutes before they started speaking among themselves.

"You aren't going to leave him here?" Toshiro's worried voice whined.

"We will move him to Jiro's house," Seizaburo said. "He will be safe enough there."

It was Jiro's turn to feel anxious. "How long will he sleep? If he awakens…"

Seizaburo's words snapped at the headman like a whip. "He will sleep well into next afternoon. With all of the adderfish venom he drank, he might not stir for a few days. By then there will be no danger of his interfering." The priest barked out a bitter laugh. "He spoke of fate, but the sutras teach that fate is the province of gods, not mortals.

"Not even a samurai may change what has already been written."

*   *   *

SHINTARO OBA WAS carried by the fishermen to Jiro's house, and laid in a small room at the rear of the hut. The samurai was as careful to maintain his pretence of sleep as he was to maintain his hold on Koumakiri. It was as well that the fishermen didn't try to pry the sword from his grip. Oba suspected they knew better than to touch a samurai's sword – even that of a sleeping warrior. Many a man had been slain for dealing such an offence, a dishonour that could be forgiven only with blood.

Keeping his eyes closed, Oba focused his other senses on his surroundings. He felt the passing of the hours by the gradual cooling of the room as the fierce sun retreated towards the horizon. He judged that it was nearly twilight before he heard furtive footsteps in the hallway outside his room. Firming his grip on Koumakiri, letting one of his eyes open by the slightest sliver so he could watch the door, Oba braced himself for whatever was coming next.

The door slid open and a man slipped inside. Oba was ready to draw his sword in case Seizaburo had reconsidered the wisdom of letting the samurai sleep and had taken it in mind to employ firmer measures. But the man who turned to face him wasn't the priest. It was Denkou, the headman's son. The youth's face was drawn with worry, his expression almost frantic as he moved towards the samurai.

"Sir Oba, are you awake?" Denkou whispered.

"Thanks to you," Oba replied, rolling onto his side. He let Koumakiri rest across his leg, one hand still closed about the blade's grip. "Why did your father and the priest want to drug me?"

Denkou knelt before the samurai. "It was because you came to Ogashima," he said. "Seizaburo was worried and wanted you out of the way."

"Why?" Oba asked.

"You have heard the rumours about our village," Denkou said. "You have heard that a sea-demon haunts our waters and has caused our catch to dwindle."

Oba nodded. "Yes, and you were afraid I would ask questions about the demon?"

"I have heard stories about you," Denkou said. "When we brought last year's catch to the magistrate in Hitane, I heard about a lone samurai who killed the spider-demon of Shizo. They said he was a samurai of Sekigehara who carried an uchigatana. You are him, aren't you?"

There was no mistaking the desperate entreaty in the question. "That was me," Oba confessed. "Since my lord's death, I have hunted demons wherever they hide. I came to Ogashima to destroy the fiend that has preyed upon your village."

"Seizaburo would have had you killed instead of drugged if he heard you say that," Denkou told Oba. "You see, it was the priest who brought the demon to Ogashima. It is called Wanikira, a shark-god. Instead of driving away our catch, the god drives the fish into our waters. My father has been smuggling most of our catch to Boss Jinbei in Torodani."

"Then your village is prospering from Wanikira?" Oba asked.

"As long as we worship the shark-god, Seizaburo promises us a good catch every season," Denkou said. "But a part of that worship is that we must make an offering to the shark-god once each moon. A sacrifice chosen by him from among the village maidens." An anguished moan threatened to crack the youth's voice. "This month the sacrifice is to be Mikiko! She'll be taken down to the beach and tied to the altar, left there as an offering to Wanikira!"

"The shark-god will take no more offerings," Oba vowed. He set his hand on Denkou's shoulder. "You aren't alone now. There are two of us to fight for Mikiko's life."

Denkou shook his head. "We can't fight the whole village," he groaned. "They cannot see beyond the profit Wanikira brings them. Not even Mikiko's father loves her enough to defy the shark-god."

The samurai stared hard at the boy, judging the depth of the determination he saw in Denkou's eyes. "But you do," Oba told him. "Let that be your strength. Because if we don't fight the village, then we have to fight the demon itself."

"I have a boat," Denkou said. "I was going to row out to the cliff and stay with Mikiko when the shark-god came for her."

"Now we will use your boat to meet the shark-god before it gets there," Oba said. "A few other things and we'll be ready to meet Wanikira on its own terms."

*　*　*

GREAT BONFIRES DOTTED the beach as Oba and Denkou swam towards shore. The whole of the village appeared to be gathered on the beach, their voices raised in plaintive wails to Wanikira. The priest Seizaburo could be seen engaged in heated conference with Jiro and the rest of the village elders.

It didn't need Denkou to tell Oba that something unusual was going on. Wanikira was late coming for the sacrifice and Seizaburo was trying to calm the agitated villagers. From the tone of the elders, it seemed the priest was having a difficult time placating them. His threats about the wrath of the shark god were nothing beside Jiro's fear that without the monster to drive fish into the bay the prosperity of Ogashima would wither away. Divine curses were nothing beside the idea of poverty.

Denkou gave scant notice to the villagers. His eyes were turned towards the cliff and the bamboo altar that had been raised at its base. Lashed to the altar was a slender shape garbed in white, her long dark hair hanging loose about her head. Mikiko's face was almost as pale as her kimono, giving her a ghostly aspect. The hours of waiting for the shark god to appear and visit upon her a hideous death had drained her of all energy. She lay against the bamboo frame, eyes clenched shut so that she might not see the beast when it came for her.

From the first, Oba had warned Denkou that the village might not be appreciative of Wanikira's destruction. Certainly Seizaburo and the elders wouldn't thank them. He'd cautioned that they would need to steal ashore unobserved and then try to rescue Mikiko before anyone saw them. If it came to a fight, it could very well be them against the entire village. Even for a samurai, those were forbidding odds.

The two men managed to reach the beach before they were finally spotted. The villagers gazing out to sea were looking for the huge dorsal fin of their god, not a pair of swimmers. One fisherman, Mikiko's father Takata, wasn't looking out to sea or watching for Wanikira. His eyes were drawn to the figure of his doomed daughter. So it was that when Oba and Denkou emerged from the surf near the cliff, Takata saw them.

For just an instant, Takata locked eyes with the two men. Fatherly instinct urged him to keep quiet, to let the men free his daughter and escape. Parental affection, however, was unequal to the prosperity the shark god had brought him. Leaping to his feet, the fisherman raised the alarm. "Denkou and the samurai! They are after Mikiko!"

The alarm brought the wailing villagers away from their prayers. They stared in confusion at the two men; uncertain what was going on or what to do. Seizaburo solved the question for them. Waving his arms overhead, the priest shook his iron rod at the rescuers. "They profane the shark god! They are why Wanikira shuns us! Destroy the infidels! Prove your devotion to Wanikira!"

Given a focus for their anxiety, the villagers surged towards the cliff in a shouting mob, fetching up fishing spears and boat-hooks as they charged past their boats and nets. Oba called out to them, trying to stem their fury. "This Wanikira is no god!" he shouted. "It isn't even a demon, just a beast from the depths of the sea! A thing of flesh and blood even as you!" The samurai's words fell on deaf ears. The mob continued its furious charge.

Oba seized Denkou, pushing the boy towards the wooden walkway that led to the small ledge on which the altar had been placed. "Go!" he ordered the boy. "Help the girl! I'll keep these vultures at bay!" Denkou hesitated only a moment, torn between the thought of Oba using his sword against his neighbours and his appreciation that it was the only way to save Mikiko. Love outweighed any sense of community and the boy dashed across the narrow bridge.

Oba sprang up onto the span a moment later. Drawing Koumakiri from its sheath, he stood at the edge of the bridge and glared at the oncoming mob. His kimono soaked and torn, his skin bleeding where splinters from the boat had ripped into him, the samurai presented a grim sight, like some avenging wraith conjured from its tomb. The rush of villagers faltered when they came near, their fury unequal to the ferocity they found in Oba's gaze.

The standoff might have held had Seizaburo not thrust his way to the front of the mob. The priest raised his iron rod and berated the villagers for their timidity. "Is your faith in Wanikira so feeble that you will let a single man break your courage? This is a test, a trial set to you by the great shark god! Prove yourself truly devoted to Wanikira and you will be guarded against any ronin's sword!"

Goaded by the priest, the fishermen surged forwards. There was neither pity nor mercy as Oba met their attack. The time for doubt and sympathy had been before the fighting started. Once the fray began, a samurai couldn't allow anything to stay him from his purpose. There was room in his mind for only one thought: to kill. All else was but distraction, something to defile the purity of his warrior code.

A wiry youth was the first to challenge Oba's steel. Thrusting at the samurai with a barbed fishing spear, the peasant collapsed back among his swarming neighbours, his weapon and the arms that gripped it sliced in half by the sword's razored edge. A black-bearded tough was the next to feel the warrior's blade, his shoulder torn open as Koumakiri clove through flesh and bone and sent the foe pitching into the surf.

Behind him, Oba could hear Denkou shouting at the villagers, begging them to stop fighting. Wracked by despair and fear, a feminine voice joined the boy in his frantic pleas. Even after being abandoned to the hunger of the shark god, Mikiko was horrified by the carnage Oba was visiting upon her kinsmen. Whenever the fishermen started to pull back, the lashing tones of Seizaburo sent them surging back with threats of divine wrath and the loss of their god's favour.

Drawing back from the reach of Oba's sword, the mob parted, making way for Jiro and four other fishermen to come rushing forwards. Between them they held a heavy net, rocks tied among the ropes to weigh it down. With a fierce cry, the men flung their burden at the samurai, hoping to catch him in its coils and render him helpless.

Instead of recoiling before the attack, Oba leapt down from the bamboo platform. His sword flashed, the blade cutting through the net as it came hurtling towards him. His lunge continued through the debris of severed ropes, carrying him onto the shore. Before his attackers could retreat, he was among them, lashing out with his blade, cutting down men with every sweep of Koumakiri.

An anguished scream rang out from near the altar. Oba spun about as Denkou came dashing past him. The boy's face was pale with horror, tears gleaming in his eyes. He fell to the bloodied sand at Oba's feet, staring at the mangled body of one of the men the samurai had cut down. Oba stared at the body. In the red havoc of battle, he hadn't even been aware that he'd killed Jiro.

The grim tableau of son mourning father brought silence to the mob. They faltered in their purpose, drawing away from the tragic scene. Again, it was Seizaburo who rallied the villagers to violence.

"The son has brought death to his father!" the priest shrieked. "His faithlessness has killed your headman! To regain the favour of Wanikira this evil must be purified! Kill! Kill the treacherous son! Kill this murdering ronin! Purge them from Ogashima!" Seizaburo turned, snatching a burning brand from one of the bonfires. "Cleanse them in the flame of purity!"

Oba could feel the obscene power within Seizaburo's voice. As he met the priest's gaze, he felt the same hypnotic lethargy that he'd encountered when he looked into Wanikira's eyes. It took a supreme effort of will to tear away from the priest's mesmerizing stare. When he did, the villagers were already rushing back to the attack, trading clubs and spears for torches.

"Back to the cliff!" Oba snarled, seizing Denkou and pulling the boy back to his feet. As he shoved Denkou towards the bridge, Mikiko rushed down to catch her faltering lover. Leaving the boy in her charge, Oba spun back around to confront the enraged mob. The villagers drew back from his threatening sword, and then Takata ran forward and hurled his torch at the samurai. The warrior retreated before the flying brand. Soon the other villagers were following Takata's example, darting forward to cast blazing torches at Oba, then racing back to the bonfires to snatch new weapons from the flames.

"The bridge is on fire!" Mikiko's shout struck Oba like a physical blow. He turned away from the mob, saw that the bindings holding the bamboo together had been set alright by the torches thrown at him. He looked again at the enraged village and the crazed priest whipping up their fury with his frenzied cries. There was just a chance he could fight his way clear of the peasants and escape, but that would mean abandoning Denkou and Mikiko.

It was no choice at all for a samurai of the Sekigehara clan. Gritting his teeth, Oba leapt up onto the bridge and drove himself through the raging flames. Clear of the fire, he caught hold of Denkou's arm and helped Mikiko carry him towards the platform. "Back to the altar!" he shouted. He glanced at the spray being cast about the cliff by the rolling waves. Would it be enough to keep the fire at bay?

The dim hope that the spray might save them from the flames was shattered when Oba looked back towards the beach. Under the exhortations of Seizaburo the villagers were pushing several fishing smacks into the surf. Their intention was clear. They'd come at the altar from the seaward side and cast their torches onto the platform. They'd leave their enemies with the terrible choice of being burned alive or throwing themselves into the sea to be dashed against the rocks by the waves.

Mikiko offered another choice. Rising from where Denkou lay prone beside the altar, she pointed up at the cliff above them. "We used to climb the rocks as children. There are many handholds. You can escape!"

Oba scowled as the first of the boats began to row out from the beach. "I will not leave you behind," he told her.

"And I will not leave Denkou," the girl replied. Oba grabbed Mikiko and pushed her towards the cliff.

"Start climbing," he ordered. "I'll see that Denkou is right behind you." Oba's eyes took on a steely glint when he saw the defiance lingering in Mikiko's expression. "He risked everything to save you," he snapped at her. "Don't make it all for nothing."

The samurai's stern words drove Mikiko back to the cliff face. Her pale hands and tiny feet scrabbled for purchase on the rocks. Slowly, her white-clad form began to ascend. Oba turned from her and knelt beside Denkou. Pulling the stunned boy upright, he struck him across the face, trying to shock him back to his senses.

Denkou's eyes fluttered, some coherence returning to his gaze. The initial horror of seeing his father killed seemed to be retreating. Yet the boy was oblivious to Oba, staring instead out to sea. When Oba turned his head to follow Denkou's gaze, he understood that the tragedy of Jiro's death had lessened only because a greater horror had supplanted it.

"Wanikira!" Denkou gasped in a terrified whisper.

The notched dorsal fin of the shark god was stabbing upwards from the waves. It lingered there a moment, then surged towards the shore in a strange, undulating lunge.

278

Oba could see the shadowy bulk of Wanikira beneath the water. While he watched, the immense beast propelled itself forwards once more in a powerful thrust. Too late, the boat of villagers saw their god. Right in the path of the beast, their boat was smashed to kindling by the scaly bulk.

The villagers on shore cried out when they heard the screams of the doomed fishermen. They watched in horrified fascination as Wanikira emerged from the surf, its immense mass lumbering not towards the cliff and the altar but out onto the beach. The creature didn't swim through the surf, but instead pushed itself along the bottom with its clawed pectoral fins. Behind it, the shark god dragged the ponderous anchor stone Oba had fastened to it.

Vast and hideous, a grotesque hybrid of fish and lizard, Wanikira gnashed its jaws as it emerged from the bay. A flick of its powerful tail smashed one of the bonfires, scattering burning brands all across the beach. Screaming villagers saw the monster recoil from the flames and turned to try and drive it back into the water with their torches.

Seeing himself losing control over the villagers, Seizaburo ran towards Wanikira, trying to put himself between the shark god and the terrified peasants. Waving his arms, shrieking a sutra at the top of his voice, the priest tried to wrest command of the chaos around him. He locked eyes with the monster, fixing his hypnotic gaze upon those black inhuman orbs.

For an instant, Wanikira was still, submitting to the priest's mesmeric power. Oba wondered if this was how Seizaburo had called the monster up from the deeps and kept it lingering along Shinanno's shore, controlling the creature and through it controlling Ogashima.

Whatever control Seizaburo had, it was broken in a matter of heartbeats. One of the burning logs Wanikira had scattered with its tail had landed beside it, smouldering against the behemoth's scaly hide. Its sluggish mind finally reacted to the pain of its scorched flesh. In its pain, the beast slipped free of the priest's power. Striking forwards, its giant jaws snapped shut about Seizaburo, serrated teeth ripping through his torso and leaving the lower half of his body bleeding in the sand.

Shocked by the priest's death, the villagers retreated before Wanikira as the monster dragged itself further onto the beach. Its lashing tail smashed another bonfire, throwing burning logs inland to land among the thatched roofs and paper walls of Ogashima's huts.

"Come on," Oba growled at Denkou, turning away from the havoc unfolding on the beach. He led the boy to the cliff, pushing him up onto the rocks. Denkou had regained enough of his wits to make his ascent, climbing with a dazed, unthinking skill born of long familiarity.

Oba was right behind the boy, following him up the rocks, ready to help should Denkou slip or falter. Only once did he risk a glance back towards Ogashima. The buildings were aflame now, great fingers of orange fire and plumes of black smoke rising into the sky. Caught between their burning homes and the raging shark monster, the fishermen threw themselves at Wanikira, trying to drive it back. The beast's jaws were stained with their blood, its path marked by the mangled bodies of its victims. All the attacks managed was to encourage the behemoth, provoking it into pursuing the peasants further into their burning village.

Mikiko awaited them at the top of the cliff. She helped Denkou as the boy appeared at the edge, lending her strength to her lover's waning endurance. As she came back to help Oba, the samurai waved her back. It was a matter of pride to him that any task he set for himself was one that he finished on his own. Though his own muscles ached from the many ordeals he had put himself through during the night he wouldn't submit to his fatigue. With a final effort, he pulled himself up onto the rocky shelf.

"Ogashima is gone." The words were Denkou's. Oba looked up to see the boy and Mikiko staring back down into the defile. Tears rolled down their cheeks as they watched their village burn. Through the smoke and flame, Oba could see the great bulk of Wanikira still thrusting itself further into the conflagration, still pursuing the remaining villagers. Its primitive brain was too simple to equate the fire with the pain wracking it, so instead the beast lashed out at the peasants. Wanikira couldn't understand that it was dragging itself into a trap from which there would be no escape.

"Do not mourn your village. Ogashima died a long time ago," Oba told his companions. "It died when your people listened to Seizaburo, when they started feeding their daughters to a monster just to satisfy their own greed."

Down below, the burning façade of the inn spilled into Ogashima's street, burying the smouldering hulk of Wanikira beneath an avalanche of fiery debris. The shark god writhed, gnashing its jaws in spasms of silent agony. The three survivors on the cliff watched as the beast burned in the same pyre as those it had destroyed.

"There was only one thing Seizaburo said that I can agree with," Oba told Denkou and Mikiko. Firelight glistened from the jewelled hilt of his short sword and reflected off the gold adornment of Koumakiri's scabbard.

"Fire is the best way to purge a place of evil."

Le Shark

LAUREL SILLS

"Well Leslie, I'm not sure you could really say I *laugh* in the face of Death. No, it's more like I *smile* at him. I'm like, 'Hey! Death my friend, we know each other, ay?'" Carlos looks deep into the presenter's eyes, giving a slow wink. He thickens his accent a bit, low, husky, Mexican. "You have to understand Leslie, we see each other so often, we must become friends." Leslie nods earnestly, her eyes widening. Leaning forward, he places his hand conspiratorially on her knee, "You know, Leslie, before I get ready to do a stunt, I kneel down, and I pray." Leslie makes an empathetic sound in her throat and leans in closer. "Yes, I make my peace with God." His eyes flicker briefly to the camera, "People are always saying, 'Carlos, you are too brave, let the poor stunt man have a turn!'"

It is Leslie's cue to laugh. She obliges, flicking sleek black hair over her shoulder in just the right way to avoid the flytrap of her lip-gloss.

"Well, Carlos, no one could say you aren't brave! And so generous! Tell me, where *did* you find the time amidst jumping out of helicopters and surviving the red carpet to open *The Carlos Academy*?" Leslie turns to the camera, "For those of you that don't already know, Carlos has dedicated his spare time to setting up a stunt school for inner-city underprivileged children." Her eyes are dewy with emotion, "Tell us Carlos, how *do* you do it?"

Carlos pauses to think, "As you know, Leslie, I grew up on the mean streets of Mexico City. I know what it's like to dream, to want more from life. I had to claw myself out of the dust, the… well, Leslie, the *turmoil*." He pauses again, eyes looking searchingly into the distance, "I want to give these dear children the helping hand I wish I had been given. Not everyone has the willpower, the *passion*," his eyes move to Leslie, "that I do."

Leslie seems lost for words; she is shaking her head in disbelief. A voice in her earpiece brings her back to herself, "Well, I'm *so* sorry to have to say this but that is all we have time for. Thank you, so much, for coming down to talk to us today."

"Oh no Leslie, thank you."

"And that's a wrap, people!"

Carlos and Leslie remain seated, lingering as people start to disassemble the lights. Leslie smoothes a crease out of her skirt. "Wow. That was a wonderful interview, thank you for being so open with me."

"You know, it is strange; I just can't help it. I feel like around you, I can't be anything but honest."

Leslie looks light-headed, "Oh, Carlos, that's…"

"Would you go to dinner with me tonight, Leslie?" Leslie takes in quick gasps of air, worrying that she will hyperventilate, "Oh, yes, that would be so —"

"Good. It is settled. I will have my assistant take your number." Carlos turns and swiftly exits the room. Leslie looks at the door for a few moments before sitting down again. Glancing around the emptying studio, she covers her face with a pillow, and lets out a hysterical squeal.

Carlos's assistant Marco meets him in the hall, towel and Evian at the ready. "Good one Carlos, you nailed it!" he forces enthusiasm into the statement.

"You think so? I thought I might have laid it on a bit thick with the *dear children*?" Carlos flops onto the chaise longue in his dressing room, stuffing a handful of roasted soybeans into his mouth.

"People lap that crap up," Marco says, picking up a discarded towel.

Smoothly pouring the water into a chilled glass, Marco lays out a more casual outfit, then exits in search of Carlos's obligatory 12pm cosmopolitan.

Carlos moves to the dressing table, admires his reflection for a moment, begins to rack up a line.

Carl

Carlos stiffens at this misnaming, but does not deign to face the perpetrator of the error.

"If you're not a cosmopolitan I don't want to see you."

Ah but Carl, you don't really have a choice.

He is reclining on the chaise longue, wearing a pinstriped suit, the collar unbuttoned around his huge, impossible neck. As before, Carlos is mesmerised by The Shark's mouth, currently hanging open to reveal his teeth cushioned in thick red gums. A smouldering cigar is secured on the savage point of a tooth. His bare feet rest on the gleaming glass coffee table.

Carlos looks at him, speechless, face white beneath his tan, hands shaking.

"How—" He swallows and starts again, all trace of a Mexican accent gone. "Who let you in here?"

Calm, Carl, please. You know that I need no permission. Sit.

Carlos sits.

The Shark looks around the room, removes his cigar from its pinioned position and ashes into the soybeans. *This is a nice place, Carl. Much nicer than where you were when last we met.*

"It—It's *Carlos* now." This point seems important somehow.

The Shark tips its pointed head towards him to offer Carlos the full force of its black, emotionless eyes.

Carlos looks away. "I've dreamt of you—"

Carl, you make me blush.

"I had half convinced myself that you were not real, that I had been mad, that it had been a drug-induced hallucination – God knows I've had enough of those – but—"

The Shark lets the silence ring, letting Carlos listen to his own words.

"But I always knew that I was lying to myself. I always knew you'd come back."

Look around you, Carl. We need not dispute the past. He closes his gaping mouth to drag at the cigar, then lets it hang open again. Smoke issues from the gills, drifting out from his collar.

It's time to pay me back.

Carlos grips the edge of his chair. He forces himself to hold the open, unblinking gaze. "I have no daughters, no wife. I made sure—" His voice is shaking. Stealing himself he adds, "I can't pay you if they don't exist."

The Shark crosses his muscular legs that strain the seams of his suit.

This means nothing. Any woman that is yours, I will have. I start tonight.

An elegant business card appears in Carlos's hand.

"*This* place? This place is *yours*?"

The Shark's teeth snap together. Carlos flinches back as The Shark lunges towards him, the rough tip of his nose inches from Carlos's own. Carlos holds his breath, trying to stay completely still despite his trembling.

This place has pushed its luck. It is time it made a sacrifice to me in return for its effrontery. I will destroy this place. And you will be my tool, Carl Adams. If you do not do this thing for me, I will take you in her place.

The Shark opens its jaws wide, so that Carlos is peering past rows of serrated teeth into the black mouth of Hell. The

285

immensity of The Shark's mouth mesmerises Carlos for a moment, the teeth poised above his forehead and beneath his chin. A thick, stagnant vapour rises from the maw, the stench of fish and salt and rancid meat. One bite. That would be all that was needed.

I start tonight.

* * *

MARCO ENTERS THE room to find Carlos staring at the empty chaise longue with abject terror. He looks up, glassy-eyed, then quickly down at his hand. He jumps, apparently shocked to find himself holding what appears to be a business card.

"Carlos?" Real concern colours Marco's tone. "What is it, Carlos? I have your cosmopolitan. Is it the coke? Should I call an ambulance?" Marco is constantly worrying that he will find Carlos face down in a cloud of white powder.

Carlos reaches for the cocktail and knocks it back in one. He doesn't look up. "No. What are you fussing about? I'm fine!"

The pallor is leaving his cheeks as Carlos reflects on how relieved he is that his mother is already dead.

"I have arranged for the presenter to come to your room at eight o'clock sharp." Marco hopes this will please. He is disappointed.

Carlos flashes pale once more, leaning back suddenly on the dressing table.

"I start tonight," he says, his voice vague and small.

This isn't like Carlos at all.

"You start what tonight?"

Carlos blinks, shakes himself and looks up at Marco for the first time since he entered the room.

"That's good." He clears his throat then passes Marco the card. "Make us a reservation here."

Marco narrows his eyes, as Carlos bends down for another line, before inspecting the card.

Le Shark. A unique dining experience. Reservations essential.

Marco has heard of Le Shark. It is renowned for its A-listers and eccentric menu, where shark meat features in every dish. The diners also have the dubious pleasure of being able to look through the Perspex floor into a huge shark tank at live examples of their meal. It seems a bit morbid to Marco, but it is exactly the type of place Carlos would take a girl, if he ever bothered with dinner. It is a step that Carlos normally skips with his dates.

*   *   *

LESLIE IS STANDING in the lobby. She is wearing a tight-fitting mint green dress with matching stilettos, her dark fall of hair a perfect contrast. She is dressed more delicately than when he saw her that morning. The makeup she wears now is artfully applied to make her deep brown skin glow, without the heavy foundation and deep red blusher required in front of the cameras. Replacing the thick Chanel chain is a delicate gold one, with her name, *Leslie,* glistening at its end against her dark skin. A pang of guilt stabs through Carlos as he observes her. She is nervously licking her teeth, taking quick surreptitious glances at herself in the huge gilt mirror behind reception.

But there is no time for such feelings.

"Hola, chica," he says.

"Hola," she spins to give him her sparkling, live-TV-audience-wowing smile.

He puts his hand on her waist, leaning in to set a lingering kiss on her cheek, before pulling back to look deep into her eyes.

"You look beautiful tonight, Leslie."

She daintily shrugs one shoulder, clearly aware of this fact already, and he guides her outside to the waiting limo.

The paparazzi are waiting, as they always are, and cameras flash as he opens the door for her. About to duck in behind her, the reflection of one of the journalists in the polished panels of the car catches his eye. He twitches to look over his shoulder but is blinded as the wall of flickering lights take this opportunity to get a clearer shot. In the strobe vision created he sees The Shark, standing amongst the men elbowing each other. He nods at Carlos – in greeting or approval, Carlos cannot be sure – and in the next instant is gone.

His stomach turns as he finally takes his place beside Leslie and a valet closes the door. These pictures will be splashed all over the news in the morning no doubt, but they will not be merely speculating on the nature of their relationship.

Carlos looks at Leslie, who is sitting rather primly on the far side of the seat, her hands folded in her lap. The streetlights flash their yellow glow as they pass the car window, creating a pulse in which Leslie is clear, then in shadow, clear, then in shadow.

"Is everything alright, Carlos?" Leslie asks.

He realises he has been staring at her, and God knows what expression she has seen flitting across his features in the flickering light. He shakes his head, laughs, flashes a smile.

"My apologies, Leslie, I was far away, thinking of the poor children. You look so beautiful, I cannot think what I have done to deserve this night, when I know there are some who are cold and hungry."

"Oh," she says simply.

"I am sorry, you do not need to hear such things, this is *our* night. Let us enjoy it."

"No, I— it's just that, I agree." She looks down at her dress, her perfectly shining red nails. "Why *should* we indulge in such decadence, when there are people in this city that can't even afford healthcare?"

Carlos shifts uncomfortably, which contrasts with his wise nod. Leslie believes it is because he is struggling with his own guilt.

"I have always been so impressed, Carlos, by people like you. Who have really lived that life, you know?"

He looks out of his window, but doesn't respond.

"I mean, what do I know? I had a pretty nice childhood. We didn't have a lot of money but my folks really cared about me. I was never hungry, always felt loved. I just can't imagine what it was like—"

"Please," Carlos interrupts, "I cannot bare to hear the sadness in your voice." He leans over and softly takes hold of her chin. "Let us enjoy our time together—"

"Oh Carlos –" Leslie wraps her fingers over his. "Why don't we go get a burger instead? We don't need fancy restaurants and cameras and all of that – *nonsense* – just to enjoy each other's company. We could donate the money we would have spent at Le Shark to a children's home. What do you say?"

Now Carlos is the one who is lost for words, considering this kind, generous, beautiful woman. What was he thinking? His heart swells suddenly, with longing and with something else – is it fear? Whenever he has felt this feeling in the past, he has used it as a good indicator that it is time to stand up and run the other way, quickly, before anyone can think of belonging to anyone. But it is too late for all of that now, isn't it?

"That is a wonderful idea, Leslie," Carlos finds himself saying breathlessly. He leans forward and taps on the dividing window.

"Driver, to the nearest diner, if you please!"

*   *   *

THEY CAUSE QUITE a stir. The limo pulls up beside a battered

Cadillac, the long back protruding half a car's length into the lot. Carlos walks around to open Leslie's door. She steps a long leg out, takes his hand, and together they enter the busy diner, full of families, workmen and milkshake-slurping teenagers. At first it is their glamorous attire that draws attention, but soon there is an audible murmur of excitement as people recognise him. Snatches of "*That's Carlos!*" follow them as they take a window booth. The waitress that attends them is wide-eyed with amazement as she holds her notepad, the novelty perking her up out of her weary exhaustion. She tucks a strand of lank, grease-damp hair behind a pointed ear.

"My name is Mindy and I'll be your server tonight," she says, eyes glued to Carlos, taking two laminated menus from beneath her arm.

"Can I get you some drinks while you're looking at the menu?"

"Well let's see," Leslie says, eyeing the plethora of fried choices, "I think I can order now. I'll have a Coke-float, and a cheeseburger."

"And I'll have the steak, rare if you will. And a ginger beer."

Mindy does a strange movement in between a bob, a curtsy and a bow, before rushing back to the open kitchen, where every other member of staff can be seen crowding around her.

"I think we're a little overdressed," Leslie says, glancing over the room full of people openly staring and taking pictures on their phones.

It isn't long before a small line forms to get Carlos's signature – and sometimes Leslie's too – on everything from napkins to baseball caps. When Mindy elbows her way through with their order, the crowd respectfully disperses to let them eat. Carlos is strangely touched by that.

Leslie closes her eyes as she bites into her burger, savouring the moment.

"When was the last time you did this?" she asks.

"So long ago that it seems a different life."

The steak is not rare, but Carlos enjoys it anyway, as Leslie tells him more about her childhood, about college, her internship, and her road to success.

Carlos doesn't talk about his own. Everyone knows about it, that right-place-at-the-right-time sensation, that wondrous discovery from which he has never looked back. A real, modern-day miracle.

The paps have picked up on their unusual dining choice from Twitter and Facebook, and have started to crowd around their window. They smile, wave, hold up the menu and give a thumbs up. This diner will never be the same again.

Some of the photographers notice Carlos' face change at one point; the glossy grin falls to be replaced by a clear, stark horror. They look over their shoulders, trying to see what it is that he sees. But there is nothing there.

*   *   *

CARLOS EXCUSES HIMSELF and walks swiftly through the diner, manoeuvring around tables and outstretched, pen-wielding arms. Carlos finds the toilet empty, and locks himself into a cubicle. There is no seat, so he merely leans against the wall, wiping the sweat from his brow with a trembling hand and catching his breath.

He presses his palms to his closed eyes, experiencing again and again that still, drawn-out moment, when the steak is metallic in his mouth, and The Shark is there, not looking at him but at Leslie. And in that moment it is like he is The Shark, anticipating the taste of Leslie's hot, thick, beautiful blood. The feel of her soft, buttery flesh parting luxuriously from her bones as he rends it with his teeth.

Swallowing that mouthful of steak had been unpleasant.

Carl.

He straightens, pressing himself between the toilet bowl and the cubicle wall. Soft footsteps come to a halt outside his door.

Carlos clamps his jaw tight to stop a whimper escaping his throat. Slowly, he crouches down, until he can look underneath the cubicle door.

Smart, pin-stripe suit trousers, matched with a pair of bare feet, the skin a dusky, mottled grey.

They stay there, as Carlos looks at them, thinking of the body, the *head,* that they are connected to.

Carlos straightens, carefully pulls back the lock, and opens the door.

"Why—" Carlos clears his throat. "Why tonight?"

Because our time together is over. I need my payment, and I need it now.

"What if I don't?"

The Shark opens his jaw and a strange, hacking, gagging sound grates from the tiles. Carlos realises The Shark is laughing.

Let me show you.

Carlos is hovering above a tank full of writhing, thrashing, hungry sharks. He is leaning forwards at an impossible angle. As he gets closer to the surface, the inhabitants smell his blood, smell his rising panic, and are stirred to a frenzy of snapping and leaping. And then he is falling, hitting the cold water, and the hard, muscular bodies of the sharks. In moments the water has gone from brown to a deep, deep red—

Carlos is cowering on the cracked and dirty lino of the toilet floor. He is alone.

Pulling himself up, he staggers to the mirror, holding onto the basin to keep standing. He looks bad. His oiled hair is dishevelled, his eyes wild and white, his skin paler. His dark brown hair suddenly stands out to him as obviously dyed. His tanned skin becomes ruddy before his very eyes.

Is The Shark taking back his gift? Or is it that Carlos is simply seeing through his own sham?

Leslie is looking a little uncomfortable by the time he returns, with concern apparent in her amber eyes.

"That was my agent," he lies. "It seems our little stunt has already spread far and wide. He tells me that even though we have eaten here, we must at least make an appearance at Le Shark. I think he had to pull some strings to get us the table, if you understand."

"Why not?" She beams, "I'm *dying* for a drink."

*　*　*

LE SHARK IS full of sleekly-dressed, glittering customers. Leslie is smiling and nodding as they walk the transparent floor, basking in the radiance of entering and being noticed by these important people. It is different from the welcome they received at the diner, and, to Carlos, does not compare favourably. Beneath, dark shapes stir and follow their movement as they pass. Carlos is aware that they are gathering below them, following their progress, and wonders if Leslie has noticed this strange phenomenon.

"Welcome to Le Shark," the hostess greets them with a frozen smile, her young face already paralyzed with Botox. "We have a private room prepared for you, if you will follow me?"

She leads them up a narrow, curling stair at the back of the room, along an open, upper dining area lined with tall tables. Uncomfortable patrons perch on spindly stools picking at various shark-based dishes. The room they are ushered into is small with a table for two. It is little more than a balcony really, open to the floor below. They are on display.

Below them the floor is cut out, so that here the shark pool is open to them, with only a steel railing to stop careless celebrities from stumbling in. If you were to jump, fall, or be *pushed*, from this height, you would plunge into the tank.

A stony-faced waitress brings them two frosted cocktails, each with a small shark tooth floating in them, attached to the glass with a silver chain. You can un-clasp them and take them as a souvenir. Carlos removes his and discreetly drops it on the floor.

Leslie sits and leans on the railing, peering at the vista, as those below peer surreptitiously back. She raises her glass.

"To a wonderful evening."

He raises his own, and takes a much less dainty sip than she does.

"It seems almost a shame," she says, gazing at the water that has begun to churn with menace. "Such magnificent hunters. They should have the freedom of the ocean. Except here they are, for our amusement, ready to become *our* meal. When in nature it is the other way around."

"They keep them hungry," Carlos says, before wondering where the thought has come from. How did he know that?

He almost chokes on his cocktail when he looks back at Leslie. The Shark is standing behind her.

"Carlos? What is it?"

She looks around, but in the time it takes her to turn, The Shark is gone.

"Why don't we take a closer look?" he says.

Leslie thinks his voice is strange, vague, as if being drawn up from unplumbed depths. As if the words are not his own.

"You mean, go down there? To the tank? Is that allowed?"

"Anything for you, Leslie."

*　　*　　*

AFTER SOME CONSULTATION with the manager, they are guided to a back stair, with a door that must be unlocked, and down a steeper, much less glamorous stairwell.

The tank room is vast. It stretches the entire breadth of the restaurant, illuminated by bright blue underwater lights, with a narrow steel walkway traversing the centre of the pool.

"Can I walk along it?" Leslie asks the waitress excitedly.

"Um, I don't know—"

"Come now," Carlos says, "it is perfectly safe, is it not? There is a railing, and we are perfectly sober, I can assure you."

"Well, I guess—"

She is clearly uncomfortable. She has not been briefed for this situation, but has been instructed to pamper to Carlos's every whim.

Leslie's heels clang on the bridge as she walks slowly along it, gazing at the sharks. Carlos looks up at the blurred shapes of feet and legs.

He leans in to the waitress.

"I wonder my dear, could you perhaps bring us some champagne? The best in the house?"

He slips a fifty-dollar bill into her hand.

She nods, obligingly, and they are alone.

Carlos strolls along the walkway, to where Leslie is now leaning on the rail, a smile quirking her beautiful mouth.

"This has been the most *magical* evening, Carlos. Do you treat all of your women this way?"

"My women? Are you *mine*, Leslie?"

They are close, breathing each other's breath, lips tantalisingly near.

"I'm yours," she whispers, and he kisses her.

The kiss is soft, and sweet, and not what Leslie was expecting.

Then he breaks it with a gasp that sounds very much like a sob.

"Carlos?"

He turns his back, shaking his head, then looks at her. Tears are filling his brown eyes, his bottom lip trembling, his hands bunched into fists.

"No," he says.

"No? What did I do?"

But he is not looking at her; he is looking just over her shoulder, shaking his head in despair.

This time when she turns, she sees it.

"What the—?"

Give her to me.

"What is this Carlos? Some sort of joke? Are you filming this? Why is he wearing a mask?"

"Oh – Leslie—"

And now his face crumples as the tears spill out over his cheeks.

Leslie can see that it is no mask.

"What are you? What do you want?"

My children are hungry.

Leslie is aware of splashing below as the water is stirred to froth.

"No!" Carlos takes hold of Leslie and pushes her behind him. "You cannot have her, take me instead."

"What are you saying, Carlos? What the hell is going on?"

She grips his shoulders and feels his whole body trembling.

"I made a promise, Leslie."

Carlos's accent has changed. It is no longer husky with the dusty deserts of Mexico. It is now a tremulous, bland, middle-American.

"A – A deal, with this – this monster."

Monster, Carl? I am hurt.

"He – he made me what I am, everything I have, the fame, the money, everything. I'm a fake, Leslie. I'm not Mexican, I'm from Wisconsin; my name isn't even *Carlos*. It's all just a mask, a fake to glamour people, to make me interesting. To make me a *star*. And in return—"

Such a simple trade. Just some women belonging to him. Fame cheaply bought.

"So you were going to… to *feed* me to him?"

She takes a step back, clasping the railing, white-knuckled. Carlos nods pathetically.

"But I couldn't do it." He straightens, turns to The Shark, "I told you. Take me instead."

He puts a shaking foot onto the railing.

"Wait!" Leslie takes hold of the back of his shirt.

"It's the only way, Leslie."

He jerks away from her.

The Shark stands silent, enjoying the exchange.

She tightens her hold.

"You'll have to come and take him from me." Leslie lifts her chin, hoping The Shark can't see the tremor in it.

That is not how it works. It must be an offering, freely given. Otherwise it is just meat.

"So, what happens if he doesn't?"

The Shark shifts on his weird, thick-skinned feet.

She pulls Carlos back – he is blubbering now in bleating whimpers – and shields him with her body.

"Come over here, if you can, and *take him*."

The Shark does not move.

Carlos, if you do not come to me now—

"Then what? *What?*"

She reaches down and takes off a shoe. Raising it, she throws it at his grotesque, gaping head. The aim is good. It cuts through the air, the moment slowed, the spiralling heel going straight for the pointed nose. The Shark does not move to avoid it. The shoe passes through him, and continues its journey to slap into the water, where hundreds of teeth furiously fight over the dead leather.

"You can't make him, can you?"

Carlos stands up behind her.

"He can't?"

If you do not sacrifice yourself to me now, it will be another time, another place. I may not be able to touch you, but I can alter things. It is remarkable how little we consider the delicate balance we are living in. For instance, the way the slightest imbalance in a plane engine can send it crashing into the sea. Cliff roads are supported by such subtle complexities of stone and earth. A shift in the shingle can cause cars to plummet to the sea-washed rocks below. A single screw in a metal bridge—

Leslie throws herself backwards as the walkway begins to vibrate, shoving Carlos behind her.

You will live with this fear for the rest of your ridiculous, pathetic life, which you are living on borrowed *time.*

The metal creaks, pitches, and buckles at the centre, as the whole structure shudders closer to the agitated sharks. But they are near the end now, using the anchored end of the railing to haul themselves back up.

"Funny thing about America," Leslie says as they reach the safety of the concrete floor. "It's pretty damn big."

They back up until they meet solid wall.

"Carlos, you got a problem with moving in country? Never going overseas again? Generally avoiding shark-infested water?"

Carlos does not have a problem with that.

"You can call me Carl, if you like."

The Shark watches them leave – the woman walking lopsidedly in one shoe, ushering Carl ahead of her up the stairs – and gnashes his teeth with annoyance.

Just stay out of the water...

He hates it when people figure that out.

THE SERIAL KILLER WHO THOUGHT SHE WAS A SHARK

JENNI HILL

SHARKS. TIGERS. CROCODILES. Polar bears. Man-eaters, all of them, given the opportunity and the incentive.

These days they're protected. Tagged. We kept them in zoos before the twenty-second century – now they're carefully watched in their natural environment.

> *Tyger Tyger, burning bright,*
> *In the forests of the night;*
> *What immortal hand or eye,*
> *Could frame thy fearful symmetry?*

You think that's a mosquito buzzing around that Bengal tiger and her cubs? That's a drone camera. Solar-powered. Autonomous. They're not even top of the range anymore. A twenty dollar donation to the World Wildlife Fund will buy ten of them, or so the ads claim.

All these man-eaters. All in their natural environment. There are hardly ever accidents anymore. Hardly ever.

But humankind has little tolerance for things that are out

to kill them. So why do we protect these man-eaters? Why do we coddle them?

There's the biodiversity angle; the idea that the more species there are, the more robust life on Earth is. That's the pragmatist's view –whether you're hoping that when a fungal plague hits the rainforest just one or two species of tree will have the defences to resist, or whether you're hoping that when a plague hits humanity, we'll be able to dissect just the right kind of monkey and find the antibodies we need to survive it. All very practical.

The romantics say we're conserving these creatures for future generations. The number of species that were wiped out before our time is alarming, and our children – *won't somebody think of the children*? – will never get to meet them. The cloned animals just weren't the same.

Learning from them is another reason to keep these man-eaters around. There's a whole industry that's grown up around their study. We phased out zoos partly because all you can learn from a killer whale trapped in a tank instead of a thousand miles of ocean is how exactly a killer whale reacts when it is trapped inside a tank instead of a thousand miles of ocean. Hint: the uses for that kind of data are limited. As surveillance technology got better, we just didn't need cages anymore.

And then there's the fact we keep these man-eaters alive because we're absolutely fascinated by them.

The lesser spotted tree frog is close to extinction? Humanity doesn't give a shit. The graceful, beautiful, sharp-toothed, bloody-mawed polar bear is on the verge of destruction? That's a different matter.

They're beautiful, these creatures. They fascinate us. And they're deadly. They're all the more beautiful and fascinating because of how deadly they are – or should that be the other way around?

We feel the same way about serial killers.

Don't believe it? For every documentary about man-eating beasts, there's one about serial killers. There's a whole genre of novels built up around them, not to mention your films, dramas, docu-dramas, cult-docu-drama-interactive-ebook-fanfiction-webseries-diarycomics – you name it, they've got it.

Sure, you wouldn't want a serial killer living in your neighbourhood, no more than you'd want a great white in your backyard pool, but it doesn't mean you won't log in to the W.N.F. webcam channel every week to see what your favourite killers have been up to. You're fascinated by them.

The Worldwide Neuraldiversity Fund doesn't keep killers in cages anymore. Not when you can learn so much more about them by studying them in their natural environment.

* * *

SHE WATCHED THE waters, scanning for prey. Sunlight glinted tantalisingly from the waves and from the golden skin of surfers further along the beach.

"How are you feeling today, Courtney?"

The blonde on the beachlounger turned over and pulled her sunglasses down to glare at the speaker.

"I'm fine. Why are you looking so chirpy?"

"I've got some good news!"

Courtney's gaze took in Tom Chen from his sandaled feet to his bespectacled nose, to the dark hair spilling out from underneath his unfashionable baseball cap. "Do tell."

"The W.N.F. approved our travel application. We're leaving tomorrow!"

"Well, that certainly is good news." She fingered her shark tooth pendant thoughtfully. "I should go home and pack.

What do they wear in Sydney?"

"These days? A lot of sunscreen. Although I guess you don't need it, do you, as sharks don't get cancer?"

"Don't be ridiculous. That's an urban legend. One perpetuated by conmen with sharkmeat to sell." She picked up her rattan beach bag. "Come on, then, if you're coming."

They left the beach, with Tom following behind, explaining that he was only joking, of course he knew that sharks did get cancer (Courtney did remember his doctorate in zoology, didn't she?) and Courtney half listening, half planning her vacation wardrobe.

As she left the beach, several tanned, gorgeous young men in surf shorts all had the information beeped to the W.N.F. app on their phones, glasses or other personal devices: the waters were safe again.

* * *

A BLACK SUNDRESS hit the top of the pile in the chic black leather suitcase. Several tiny cameras, some of them airborne, some of them installed in the walls of Courtney's beachside apartment, tracked its movement.

A biker jacket made of soft grey suede and a shark tooth necklace joined the dress in the case.

The necklace had been a gift from the man who had been Courtney's handler before Tom Chen. He'd given it to her on the night they'd fallen into bed together after a particularly good bottle of Cabernet Sauvignon, an act which had seen him fired for gross misconduct.

The W.N.F. had *some* standards.

In an office elsewhere, two W.N.F. interns watched the camera screens and took bets on whether Courtney would pack the black lace Wonderbra or the blood red one. She packed both.

Heading for the bathroom, Courtney pulled her bikini top over her head and dropped it on the floor. Then she stepped out of her bikini shorts and stepped into the gleaming white shower cubicle. Several cameras tracked the Miami sand and sea salt as the hot water rinsed it from her tanned breasts and gracefully long legs.

It had been mentioned by concerned souls at the W.N.F. that filming serial killers in their own bathrooms was a violation of their privacy beyond even that committed every day by the established system of handlers and subjects. Others at the W.N.F., with louder voices, had pointed out that bathrooms, with their wipe-clean walls and handily accessible drain outlets, would be a dangerous place to let serial killers enjoy any privacy. Visitors to the residence could be chopped up and disappearing down the plughole before a W.N.F. tactical ops team had even broken down the door.

Thus, any killer enjoying the privilege of entertaining guests in their own homes had to endure cameras in every part of their lives.

Courtney enjoyed lots of privileges. She had been a very good girl lately, and such privileges were dispensed as rewards for good behaviour.

Privileges such as trips out of the country. Courtney had been working towards Sydney for quite some time.

* * *

DESPITE THE FACT that it was arrogantly named the Worldwide Neuraldiversity Fund, the W.N.F. did not hold an entirely global jurisdiction. There were still some nations in the world that kept their killers in such backward institutions as prisons, that treated their killers and their violent citizens as criminals, humans gone wrong, rather than cases to be studied.

Some such places, such as Courtney and Tom's

destination of Australia, also objected to the ubiquitous camera surveillance employed by the W.N.F. This Australian phobia of surveillance technology was one of several lasting effects from a particularly nasty dictatorship in the late 2090s which demonstrated a love of airborne surveillance cameras and a penchant for state executions. Thankfully the dictator had been deposed, but some countries have long memories.

Therefore, as Courtney and Tom had their boarding passes checked, paid their exorbitant carbon off-set fee, (nearly the price of the flight, these days) and passed through the airport gates at Miami International, the small airborne cameras that were Courtney's constant companions ceased to follow her, all seven of them stopping in mid-air as if hitting an invisible wall.

"Goodbye, darlings, goodbye!" Courtney blew them sarcastic air-kisses. She'd done the same to the cameras in the walls of her apartment, when Tom had picked her up in the cab.

Tom glanced back over his shoulder as he walked towards the gate with Courtney. The cameras still hung in the air, waiting for further instructions, their blank eyes staring.

Courtney didn't call them 'cameras' she called them her 'remoras', because she liked the way it sounded.

The cameras did remind Tom now of remora fish, detaching themselves from some great predator, but he dared not take that thought too far. For what perils could such a predator be swimming into, for the parasites to abandon her now?

*　*　*

As THEIR FLIGHT reached the North Australian coastline, Tom woke up to find Courtney still working on the same slides as when he'd drifted off to sleep, hours earlier. Her brow furrowed in concentration, she was studying the tablet on the fold-out table in front of her. Many used their glasses, contact lenses or other private devices for such work, but private browsing was not allowed for killers under the W.N.F.'s jurisdiction.

Tom was travelling to Sydney's *Earth Life* conference to present his research to an audience of W.N.F. and non-W.N.F. alike. Courtney accompanied him not only because of the difficulties involved in assigning her a substitute handler, but also because she was due to present some of his work alongside him on stage. In fact, it might be more honest to say that she *was* some of the work he was presenting.

Tom would be interviewing her onstage and, to make her more comfortable with the idea he had given her the questions in advance. It was these she studied now, mouthing the words to herself in between sips of gin and tonic.

"Courtney, you've been doing that for a long while. Don't you think you should take a break?"

"Don't be ridiculous, Tom. When sharks stop swimming, they die."

A non-sequitur in any other conversation, but Tom understood Courtney's outlook on the world. In fact, he encouraged it. The links between the W.N.F.'s work and the animal conservation done by similar organisations such as the W.W.F. were many, (although the animal charities resented the comparison) – surveillance, conservation, study – and it was Tom's theory that Courtney's tendency to view herself as a predator, as an endangered animal being studied, was what allowed her to adapt to the handler/subject relationship without many of the usual adverse side effects. All subjects were routinely psych-tested, and Courtney was scoring highest in the programme to date. She identified with sharks in particular.

"That may be true for sharks, Courtney," some species of them, at any rate, "but you need rest, and leisure time. Did you bring anything with you other than work?"

"Nothing of interest."

"Here." Tom bought up the conference programme on his glasses, and with a swift eye movement sent it to Courtney's device. The five day *Earth Life* programme covered lectures on the latest research in biology, zoology, anthropology and psychology, among other disciplines; the brochure on Courtney's tablet covered not only the lecture material, but also featured pages on the conference's notable guests.

"I don't like that photo of me." A gif of Courtney flicked her hair for the camera – Tom knew it had been taken by her previous handler.

"Sorry, they took it off the W.N.F.'s site. I'll ask them to swap it for another, if you like."

Courtney shrugged, suddenly distracted. She'd seen the lecture promoted on the page next to theirs. *The Ethics and Politics of Shark Fishing.*

While endangered species were protected far more carefully in this century than any before it, there were still a few shark species that could be fished legally, their fins highly prized for the making of shark fin soup.

Traditionally a Chinese dish served at weddings and other special occasions, rumoured to have been invented by an emperor of the Sung dynasty, the soup had nearly gone out of fashion due to several high profile campaigns by Chinese activists in the early twenty-first century. Recently, however, it was seeing a worldwide rise in popularity, despite concerns about cruel fishing methods, and the fact that protected species were just as likely to turn up in the dish as the unprotected ones. World Wildlife Fund sharkcams had thrown up a plethora of evidence against the corporate fisheries, but somehow the transgressions were always blamed on individual boats, individual fisherman, rather than any particular company.

One of the speakers on the panel was Brad Starland, the head of a chain of Australian restaurants now famous for the dish. His promise of a soup 'fit for an emperor' was tempting diners all over the world, and his business partners at Hashimoto-Smith Fisheries had put enough funding behind the advertising campaign to turn Brad's recipe into a brand in itself. Tom hated him, as did many conservationists. He hated the man's blatant disregard for ecology, and he hated the outdated notion of his home country that Brad was making money from.

Inscrutable Chinese emperors full of Eastern wisdom, he thought to himself. *What was next, Fu Manchu?*

He watched Courtney studying Brad's animated profile photo, which grinned back at her again and again from the deck of a yacht, blond hair and white teeth shining in the sun.

Tom drifted back to sleep, although later he thought he remembered Courtney waking him up to tell him, in shocked, urgent tones, "Do you know how they harvest the fins? They cut them off at sea and throw the sharks back in the water, because the fin is the most valuable part of the animal and they say it's too expensive to bring them into land. They're still alive, but they can't swim, so they sink to the bottom and suffocate, or get eaten by other sharks. Look, there's a video..."

But he wasn't sure whether he'd dreamed it.

*　　*　　*

THE FIVE-STAR FITZ-FIELDING hotel sat on a pier jutting out into the glistening blue waters of Sydney Harbour. It featured fine dining, an outdoor pool, extensive conference facilities, and guests could even enjoy taking speedboats or jetskis from the end of the pier.

No cameras observed Courtney and Tom's arrival at the

Fitz-Fielding. Neither was their entrance to the Earth Life Welcome dinner, later in the evening, recorded for webcam or CCTV, although many pairs of eyes covetously observed the young man in the tuxedo escorting the tall blonde in the figure-hugging grey suede dress.

Tom did, Courtney had to admit, scrub up quite nicely. She had helped him pick out the tuxedo, of course.

A mix up with the tickets left Courtney and Tom separated at dinner – something for which he apologised profusely, although he soon cheered up when introduced to his dining partners. Courtney watched him jealously from behind her menu. She had been left sitting between a fossil fuels enthusiast and the C.E.O. of a wind power company, who had a lot to disagree about.

The two women didn't ask Courtney what her interest was in the *Earth Life* conference, and she didn't let on. She imagined explaining that she was attending as Tom Chen's science project, and kept her mouth shut.

When the main courses arrived, Courtney was just slicing into her rare tuna steak, while the fossil fuels nut told everyone how much more authentic coal power was, how good it felt just to get back to one's roots, when the handsome blond man sitting opposite Courtney leaned across the wide table and introduced himself.

"I'm Brad. Brad Starland. I feel like I should recognise you from somewhere, Miss-?"

"Charlesworth. I'm Courtney Charlesworth. I think I just have one of those faces?" Courtney recognised the man now, presumably from the same place he recognised her. Brad Starland was the chef whose photo she'd seen in the conference program. She smiled without showing her teeth. "Pleased to meet you."

"How's your meal?"

She considered. "Good. Bloody. How's yours?"

"Terrible. I can't believe we lost this contract." He held up a piece of tuna steak on his fork. "It's too pink. They haven't even tried to hide the fact this was grown in a vat."

"It tastes fine to me. I think –"

"There's no muscle texture." Brad interjected. "You can stretch and restretch the vat-grown muscle fibres all you like on the machines, but there's no substitute for a real fish that's been swimming around in the ocean all its life." As Brad interrupted her Courtney wondered what his muscle texture would taste like. "Eat this, and you'll be hungry again a few hours later."

"That's fascinating. But isn't dolphin-friendly tuna fishing kind of difficult these days?"

Brad smiled. "Have you ever eaten dolphin?"

A bearded man with a similarly gym-toned build reached for the bread basket in front of Courtney. "Brad, I couldn't help overhearing, but it sounded like you were boring this beautiful young woman with our business matters."

Brad's companion was introduced as David Hashimoto-Smith, heir to the corporate fisheries of the same name and one of the chief investors in Brad's chain of restaurants. David seemed concerned that his business partner had let something slip, dolphins being illegal to hunt, but Courtney assured them that (a) she did not give a damn about dolphins (true), and (b) that she was too much of a harmless airhead to know what was illegal and what wasn't (false – but a predatory behaviour that came to her as instinctively as a hunting tiger crouching in the grass).

She didn't care about dolphins – they'd always struck her as sort of smug – but part of her wondered how poor, conservation-minded Tom Chen would feel if he overheard this conversation.

Brad and David were handsome, educated and extremely privileged. Courtney knew the type; she'd grown up around them. Men used to wealth and used to being the focus of any conversation.

In short, they were the type of men who'd receive W.N.F. danger alerts from Courtney's cameras, if they were in the area.

After dinner, Tom Chen uncharacteristically did not seem keen to seek out Courtney's attention. From what she could overhear it sounded as though he'd been sat next to old colleagues from his university days. Wasn't he neglecting his duties as her handler? Did his W.N.F. jurisdiction even apply here?

She sat on the edge of the hotel's indoor fountain, watching koi carp swim lazily round and round, and wondering how desperate for company she would have to be before she would go to Tom rather than letting him come to her.

"Has your date abandoned you again?" Brad, the celebrity chef, grinned down at her, his partner David stood beside him.

Courtney shrugged, and didn't bother to correct him on the 'date' issue.

"David and I were wondering if you could help us with something," the blond man continued. "It's about what I let slip earlier."

"The dolphins," explained David, slurring his words slightly. He had clearly gotten over his earlier reluctance to discuss business matters with Courtney, and assumed the expression that some men acquire when explaining a subject they happen to be an expert in to a drop dead gorgeous woman. His breath smelt of scotch. "We're having trouble with the mercury in the dolphin meat, but we've settled the lawsuits and we're experimenting with new mercury extraction processes. However, there's the PR angle to consider – "

"David thinks that dolphins are just too cute for people to

eat. You're a girl." Brad said. "Girls like cute things. What do you think?"

"Oh yes. I love cute things." She smiled suggestively. "Sometimes I just want to eat them up."

"And you haven't seen the things I can do with a piece of meat," the chef boasted, winking at her.

"We just won't be able to do the same thing we've done with sharks," said David, and Courtney's ears pricked up. "I mean, can you see even the edgiest supermodels and rock stars agreeing to be photographed in Brad's restaurant eating dolphin fin soup? Don't be ridiculous. Even if it were made legal, can you see us serving it at the next royal wedding or state dinner, as we did with the shark fin? We'd never be able to manufacture that kind of popularity."

"With my recipes –"

David talked over Brad, "Dolphins are almost as intelligent as humans, it'd be like asking people to eat a relative" – Courtney had, but that was another story – "whereas a shark is just a rather stupid fish."

Well, that wasn't fair. "Maybe sharks are just intelligent in a way you can't understand," said Courtney. "They pretty much have a sixth sense."

"They're psychic?" David looked concerned.

"They can sense electromagnetic fields." Still no sign of recognition from either of the two men; she'd have to explain further. *If you're going to kill an animal, you should know it more intimately than this,* Courtney thought. *Like learning a man's name before you kill him.*

"The Ampullae of Lorenzini, those little black, jelly-filled dots on a shark's skin? They sense electromagnetic currents in the water. Scientists have suggested that they use them to navigate, or possibly to hunt, tracking the electric impulses in their prey's muscle movement."

David assumed the shaken, re-evaluating-my-worldview

expression that some men get when a gorgeous woman surprises them by explaining something she just happens to be an expert in. She hadn't realised how much she appreciated the way Tom Chen really listened to her.

Brad simply looked bored. "There was just one more question we wanted your help with."

"Oh yes," said David. "This one caused us quite a bit of debate. Which of us gets to take you to our hotel room tonight?"

Courtney smiled through closed lips. "Gentlemen. Let's take this discussion outside." She gestured towards the glass doors leading to the pool and small harbour area.

Both men looked disappointed, their hotel rooms being in the opposite direction.

"We could take a boat out," tempted Courtney. "It's quiet out on the water, we can... talk."

"I'm not sure we're supposed to take those," said David.

"I'm sure a man like you didn't get to his position without breaking a few rules on the way," she smiled seductively. "Let me go get us a bottle of something with bubbles in it, and I'll meet you by the boats."

On her way to the bar, Courtney passed the wind power C.E.O. and the fossil fuels hipster kissing passionately in a corner. She couldn't see Tom Chen anywhere.

* * *

DAVID SNORED IN the corner of the speedboat, swaying gently with the rocking of the waves.

Unable to speak over the loud engines for much of the journey, the trio had turned off the *Orca's* engine in a remote part of the harbour in order to get to know each other a little better.

"Did you see that?" Courtney asked. "He just fell asleep! I

thought I was more interesting than that."

"Rude bastard." Brad patted his leg invitingly. "Come sit over here and I'll make it up to you."

Courtney complied, stepping over David's feet and the ropes coiled in the hull floor.

Brad looked at the woman in his lap through half-lidded eyes, slowly running his hands up and down her body and underneath her dress.

"How any man could lose interest with a woman like you around, I don't know."

Courtney licked and nuzzled Brad's neck and spoke into his collarbone, her breath hot on his neck. "I agree. I'm quite offended."

"It must be all that scotch he drank after dinner."

"Or it could have been the Zopiclone I put in the champagne."

"Mmm." Brad made a languid sound of agreement, but then his hands stopped moving suddenly. "What?"

"The Zopiclone. It's a sleeping pill. A strong one." The men hadn't noticed that Courtney wasn't drinking.

"Why would you do that?" despite his alarm, Brad could feel a yawn coming on. He lent back in his seat, but Courtney clutched his shoulders firmly, her legs tightening around his middle.

She grinned, showing, for the first time, her smile in all its glory.

As a deep lethargy crept into his muscles Brad stared into the maw of something from his nightmares, rows of white teeth, filed to sharp little points, bright and shining like a knife in an alley.

"I was hungry." She licked her tongue over her teeth and bent towards his neck.

* * *

THE NEXT DAY, the debate titled *The Ethics and Politics of Shark Fishing* did go ahead without Brad Starland and David Hashimoto-Smith, but in a rather one-sided fashion.

Panicked *Earth Life* organisers managed to piece together that the two men had left the hotel unaccompanied during the previous evening's welcome dinner, but nobody had seen them since.

Neither had sent word that they would be absent from the debate, but Brad's reputation as the *enfant terrible* of the culinary world led many to speculate that the two men had secreted themselves somewhere with a few bottles of scotch and a large quantity of recreational drugs. While setting up the conference room one volunteer was heard to suggest, a little too close to the microphones, that checking Sydney's brothels might yield fruitful results.

Courtney wasn't worried, per se, that her part in Brad and David's disappearance would be discovered. She had been caught before, of course, or she wouldn't be with the W.N.F. Any aberrations since then were usually blamed on her handlers, with some temporary limitations put on her own freedoms. She did find herself worrying about the implications for Tom Chen, however.

Without the presence of Brad and David, Courtney and Tom watched as the remaining panel members, the Regional Director of Greenpeace, China, and a United Nations Environmentalist with a fetching green mohawk, utterly failed to disagree on anything for an hour.

They failed to contradict each other's proof that shark fishing had developed to a globally unsustainable level, they failed to argue against the notion that shark fisheries regularly used methods going against international statutes on animal cruelty, and while there was a very exciting moment where the Greenpeace Director's figures on the DNA testing of shark meat for endangered species seemed to slightly contradict the

314

figures brought by the U.N. representative, it turned out that Greenpeace had failed to carry the one.

As for the audience, it was hard to tell who was most disappointed by Brad and David's absence: the animal rights activists who lost the opportunity to debate shark fishing with two of its foremost supporters, or the Starland fans who missed out on getting their cookbooks (or tablets, or chests) signed by the handsome celebrity chef himself. In fact, the only person that Courtney could see enjoying himself was Tom, smiling and nodding enthusiastically throughout.

Many of the audience members who came for the shark fishing talk also stayed in the conference hall for Tom Chen's presentation: *Natural Born Killers: Surveillance, Conservation and the Mind of a W.N.F. Subject.*

The programme description promised a talk which linked the work of the W.N.F. with the changes in conservation in the twenty-first century – the move from keeping animals locked up in cages, to keeping tabs on them in the wild.

The link had been made many times before, but Tom presented a new take on it.

"It's well-known," he said, "That removing the apex predators from large ecosystems causes untold amounts of damage. And do we not exist within the largest ecosystem of all?"

Not only did Tom fall into the small camp of W.N.F. thinkers who considered violent criminals a valuable part of the human ecosystem, if carefully controlled, he almost seemed to be putting forward the theory that killers were another species entirely, something that had evolved to predate on humanity.

When it was Courtney's turn to come to the stage, Tom told the audience, "I've demonstrated how it can be a useful exercise for us, scientifically, to think of the W.N.F.'s charges not as criminals, but as mutations or even an entirely different species from man itself. But it can also be useful for our charges themselves to think in this manner. Let me and my lovely assistant demonstrate." Tom winked at Courtney, and gestured for her to sit at the table beside him. "Or maybe, as her handler, I'm her lovely assistant – who can tell?"

Courtney stalked gracefully towards the front of the stage. If Tom had not prepared her for this part of the presentation she might have found the machine on the table alarming. Similar to a lie detector in design and metrics but better suited for the stage, (talk show hosts adored them) the machine would chart her emotional and physical reactions to questions posed by Tom, making them visible to the audience.

Tom kept talking as he strapped Courtney's arm to the machine, and fitted sensors onto her forehead.

"Many of our killers have complained that they find W.N.F. surveillance humiliating and dehumanising, even though it allows them to exist outside of a prison environment. Reports pertaining to all but a few of the failures we've had, subjects lost to suicide, escape and uncontrollable rages, have featured a common theme, complaints about this loss of privacy. In fact that particular word, *dehumanising*, turned up in interviews with over 77% of these lost candidates.

"As most of you familiar with our work will know, we rigorously evaluate the health of our charges through monthly psyche tests and therapy, both with the handler figure and outside of that relationship.

"In all this testing Courtney has scored the highest we've seen in tests regarding her satisfaction with the W.N.F., her violent urges and the probability of her attempting to escape. She is by far our healthiest, happiest subject. Let me show you why."

Tom addressed his subject. "Courtney, do you see yourself as human?"

"No." The machines registered barely a flicker; she was telling the truth.

"What are you?"

"Something more." Teeth in the night. A sharp fin in the water. They'd accused her of cannibalism, but it couldn't have been that. Were they really her species?

"Courtney has never claimed to find her treatment dehumanising because, in truth, she does not see herself as human." Tom addressed her again. "Courtney, are you angry with me, for watching you?"

"No."

"Are you angry with the W.N.F.?"

"No."

"Does it seem strange, what we do? That we have cameras in your home, that we study you?"

"Strange? No." They were the wary herd watching for movements in the grass. The nervous silver flicker of the shoal looking for dark shapes in the water. That was why they watched her. "It seems natural."

The audience murmured, and Tom Chen smiled. Finally, they saw in Courtney what he could see. The future of the W.N.F.

"Courtney, when did you last kill?"

She thought of Brad's body beneath hers, his blood on her teeth.

She thought of Tom being led away in handcuffs, like her previous handler. She thought about how inconvenient it would be having to get used to a new handler. Their idiosyncrasies. Hers.

She wondered if, for someone like her, there was a difference between affection and just being used to someone. She wondered if it mattered.

"My twenty-fifth birthday. Six years ago. My father's business associates. We were swimming off his yacht, and one of them cut himself on a coral reef. His blood was in the water, and then there was... a lot more blood in the water."

317

The mess had been too big for even her father to clear up, so, heartbroken, he'd called the W.N.F.

Tom's machines never wavered. She was telling the truth.

* * *

THAT EVENING, UNDER cover of darkness, Courtney took the steps underneath the hotel pier to where the *Orca* was tied to the jetty.

Also tied up were Brad and David, trussed and gagged in the bottom of the boat like two landed tuna. She'd covered them with a tarp during the day but with the half-hearted attempt the hotel staff had put into looking for the two men, she needn't have bothered.

They were still breathing, just. The hole where she'd taken a chunk out of Brad's neck seemed to have stopped bleeding, but his frantic movements when he saw her seemed sure to start it up again. David's eyes rolled back in his head as he moaned hysterically behind his gag.

Her bag thunked heavily when she dropped it next to his head. He stopped groaning.

This time, Courtney took the boat in the opposite direction: through the harbour and towards the sea, to Watsons Bay. Despite Brad and David's insistence on captaining the boat last night, she knew perfectly well how to handle one. She'd grown up around boats.

What she didn't know was that she was being followed.

She passed a few larger vessels but kept out of their way. Without any lights on the speedboat, she doubted they noticed her presence at all.

When she found a quiet, sheltered spot near Watsons Bay, she turned off the engine. The suburb sat on the southernmost rocky outcrop that protected Sydney Harbour from the ravages of the Tasman Sea. Sharks had been spotted in the area that week. She hoped they would be back tonight.

Courtney went into her bag and took out several large, heavy objects. No knives, she'd never needed them, not since she had her teeth filed, against her father's wishes, as a teenager. Daddy had had the dentist sued.

She tied the ten kilogram weights to the men in the boat, wrapping more of the good, strong mooring rope that she'd first used to tie them up around their feet and ankles. She threaded it through the holes in the weights, remembering her father teaching her boating knots. The hotel might or might not notice the loss of the unmarked and unbranded weights from their gym, but it was unlikely they'd ever wash up on shore, or be connected with Brad and David's disappearance.

Weights attached, she pulled David's head into her lap and addressed the two men for the first time since setting sail. "By rights," she began, "I should cut off your arms before I throw you in. It's what you do to your catch. They die on the sea floor, finless, suffocating, or eaten by their own kind."

"But," she sighed, "we can't have your limbs floating about and scaring the tourists. Better to do it this way. Maybe you'll attract some sharks, though." She bent over David like a lover, searched for the artery in his neck, the one she'd purposely missed on Brad last night, so as not to lie in front of Tom's machines, and then she bit down, hard.

Out of practice, she didn't move in time and the arterial spray hit her in the face, full-on. But that, she thought as she chewed thoughtfully, that was fine, because she could wash before she went back to the hotel, and she was surrounded by water, wasn't she?

David would die soon.

Already his face was pale and a little waxy. She licked her lips delightedly, kissed his forehead and dropped him, head first, into the harbour waters. Red bubbles blossomed around his neck and shoulders. She huffed a little with exertion when she picked up the weights and helped his feet into the water.

The splash the weights made when they hit the surface, and the sound of Brad screaming behind his gag, brought a light flashing suddenly over Courtney's head. She ducked under the lip of the boat, horrified, and attempted to kick Brad into silence. It didn't work.

Was that a torch? She had thought she was alone. She'd counted on it.

She gave Brad a harder kick, which either shocked or concussed him into silence.

A voice called out across the water. "Courtney?"

It was Tom Chen.

He hadn't seen her yet, the torchlight flashing cautiously around the bay.

Heart pounding, she dipped her hands over the opposite side of the boat, frantically, uselessly washing the blood from her face. A dark swirling in the water below made her suspect that sharks had got to David already.

"Courtney?" The torch had found her. She turned and blinked into the glare guiltily.

What should she do? Should she turn herself in?

Should she draw him close, kill him too? Could she bring herself to do that? Or hurt him, just stop him somehow and then go on the run in this country, with its laws and its punishments and its prisons?

As she tore through the possibilities in her head Tom's boat edged ever closer.

"Hi, Courtney. Whatcha doing out here?" he asked as if he'd found her out in the park for a stroll.

"Thinking," she answered, truthfully. She smiled flirtatiously and held his gaze locked with hers, putting off the moment he'd see her other passenger.

"About what?"

"About what to" – *do with you* – "do next."

Their boats bumped together, and Courtney's started rocking side to side. Tom started to speak, but closed his mouth and stared. Instead of slowing down, the rocking seemed to be speeding up, becoming more and more urgent.

Courtney's first thought was the sharks below, but she turned and saw Brad, awake and manoeuvring himself into sight, hands still tied, legs still weighted.

"Woah now," Tom put up his hands placatingly and spoke gently to the bound man, "don't capsize her." Courtney, adrift on a sea of indecision, absently found herself wondering if the 'her' referred to her or the boat.

"Tom, I can explain –"

Behind the gag, Brad grunted in outrage. *No, she really couldn't explain*, was what he seemed to be implying.

Tom bent and began tying their two boats together. As he carefully stepped over into Courtney's vessel, she realised he was as calm as she had ever seen him. They must give them training, she thought, on what to do in situations like this. Catching your W.N.F. charge red-handed. She wished she had had some preparation, she still felt utterly paralysed by it all. Shock. Fear. Uncertainty.

"Here, hold this." Tom handed her the thick ropes tied around Brad's torso and she took them automatically, taking orders because she didn't know what else to do.

"Now," said Tom, crouching at Brad's feet, but still addressing Courtney. "I sense I've crashed your party a little. Don't let me get in the way. Act natural!"

"What do you mean?"

"I mean act naturally. Do what it's in your nature to do," he sighed. "You are a killer, Courtney, and this man deserves to die."

"That's… not what you're supposed to say."

"You're right. Perhaps a better demonstration of my personal commitment to the cause *is* called for."

Tom pushed his glasses up the bridge of his nose, then coldly and decisively picked up the weights attached to Brad's feet and dropped them into the water.

Suddenly Courtney was holding all of Brad's weight – the sea wanted him, it was dragging him from her, sucking at his feet as the ropes around his body dug into her hands.

Over the sound of Brad screaming into his gag, Courtney shouted "I don't understand!"

"I'm trying to help you, Courtney. And we can do some good here. We can do it again, too!"

"You're not going to turn me in?"

"Heck, I'm as guilty as you. Aside from my obvious complicity," he glanced quickly at Brad's feet dangling in the water, "why do you think I arranged for us to get out of the country? Who sat you, the serial killer shark enthusiast, next to the shark fisherman at dinner? I gave you the ultimate alibi: you swore in front of hundreds of people that you hadn't killed for six years."

Courtney realised she had been manipulated. And realised, almost simultaneously, that she did not mind. So what if he'd used her to further his environmentalist agenda. She liked sharks. And so he thought she was some kind of next stage on the evolutionary ladder, here to wipe out dangers to the environment like Brad and David – should she become irritated with his fawning over her she could always report him to the W.N.F. at home in the U.S., and get a new handler.

And he was right. It had been six years before today. The thought of waiting that long again before she felt their flesh between her teeth…

Brad's screaming reached a new pitch. That and a strong tugging from the dark waters below made Courtney suspect a shark had just decided to make the celebrity chef its dinner.

"What did you mean we can do it again?" she asked.

"There are other countries out there where your cameras

won't be allowed. Other conferences. Other bastards like this one. What do you think? Shall we do this?"

Courtney smiled, pointed teeth glinting momentarily in the moonlight, and let go of the ropes.

Rise of the Übershark

ROBERT SPALDING

A BUFFET OF wind shook the aircraft. One hell of a storm had to be brewing outside to create that kind of reaction in the largest plane ever to fly.

Caldwell noted the probable strength of the storm as her suit was rocked, but dismissed it quickly. She wasn't going to be up here for much longer.

System checks were her main priority and so far everything was showing green.

Her weapons were fully loaded, fuel was at maximum.

The screen that comprised the front of her cockpit was fed by two external and rotatable cameras mounted into the head of her suit. The picture was clear. As the other systems booted up the HUD came to life. Each of her team-mates glowed with a green tinge, something that would show up on her HUD as long as they were within sensor range. The movement of the cameras gave her a 200 degree field of vision. She was going to need it.

She turned her head inside the cockpit and the cameras reacted, enabling her to check on the rest of her team.

Twelve other Brodies were visible to her right and when she looked left she could see the remaining five members of the squad. Each of the mechanised battle-suits was going through the same motions.

It was hard to suppress a smile. Before the Rise she had been a bit of an *otaku* and seeing the Brodies move fulfilled every little piece of fangirl in her. She had her very own Gundam, an Eva surrounded her. In most ways this was a dream come true.

In reality she could feel the itch of fear between her shoulder blades.

"Check in," the gruff voice of Hoop, the company's Master Sergeant, came through the commlink.

The squad checked in: "All green."

"Drop point minus two."

Caldwell's breath caught. Two minutes to the drop. The fear-itch began to fade, replaced by the thumping of her heart as adrenaline flooded her body.

They were flying at thirty thousand feet, well out of the range of any weapons they knew Jaws possessed.

"Intel says we have a large shiver exactly where we thought. They are closing in on what used to be Chesapeake Bay. Everything suggests they are going for D.C." Hoop gave the squad a moment to reflect on the importance of what they were heading into.

"It might not be the capital anymore, people, but I'll be damned if I'm gonna let any tuna-breathed psycho-cyborgs destroy what was once the foundation of the American dream. Are you?"

The roar of anger from the squad flooded the comm band for a second, Caldwell adding her own voice to the scream of rage.

"Exactly. Lock up people, we got a red light."

The bay flooded with red lights and Caldwell locked the arms of her Brody into position, facing forward again. The automatic system swung her to face the cargo bay door as it opened.

Her breathing began to quicken and she fought to keep it steady. Six of her squad were in front of her as the light went green.

The jetlines went off in sequence, shooting each mech out of the enormous plane so as to not collide with one another. Within three seconds all eighteen of them were in the sky, plummeting towards the flooded Earth below.

*   *   *

As THE FALLING mechanised assault suits passed under the cloud layer, Caldwell felt her breath catch. She had known what she was going to see, but knowing and seeing were two very different things.

Below her should have been green land, a few towns.

Instead there was nothing but blue.

The sea levels had risen, thanks to Jaws and his efforts at the poles.

How many had died in the flooding? How many more had escaped the deluge only to discover that the sharks had evolved, become smarter?

What must have the first person to see a Great White with a life support system and rocket pods either side of its dorsal fin thought, as the shark leapt at them from the water ?

The most efficient killing machine on the planet had become smart and inventive.

And no one knew how.

Not just the Great Whites though, all sharks, from Hammerheads to Tigers. Every single one of them had adapted, been fitted with armour and weaponry.

Hammerheads had covered their hammers with metal and added some kind of insanely fast propulsion system. They would slam into ships and cut through them like a bullet through paper.

So many dead, the sea had become off limits to mankind once more. All that time conquering their fears and trying to master the oceans and now the true owners were expanding their territory.

The Brodies were the latest and most successful attempt to fight back.

Aircraft had been the first thought, but Jaws would disappear into the deep, beyond the penetrating power of conventional weaponry. Nukes had been launched, but very few. The nuclear subs had been among the first casualties, then the silos near the sea had been flooded.

Even with the greatest threat humanity had ever seen, no one was willing to use ICBMs, just in case the other guy got a little twitchy and fired one at you when you had been aiming for the latest report of a shiver.

The Brody was the latest step in something that had originated in Japan, but they barely had time to get a working prototype up and running before the seas claimed most of the country.

Germany had stepped up to the plate, turning their great industries to work. At first they had some successes, but they had thought too small, suits not much bigger than a man. Easy to mass produce but too easy for Jaws to shred if they attacked *en masse*.

It was America that had perfected them. Taking the Japanese designs and German precision and filtering that through the brain of G. Jack Dolan. He was from Texas and had grown up watching anime as well. He knew that it had to be bigger, bigger than anyone else dared dream.

Which was how the twenty seven foot tall mechanised war suit that Lucy Caldwell – originally from Miami, now of Kentucky – was piloting came to be hurtling through the air at terminal velocity.

*   *   *

"Caldwell, open your damn chute!"

Hoop's voice cut through her reminiscences, her HUD was beeping insistently. She was four seconds late opening.

She activated the chute. The sudden deceleration was compensated for by the cockpit and the jolt was nothing like as violent as it should have been.

Her HUD displayed the landing zone with a superimposed red marker over the blue sea. Automated systems kept a close eye on the positions of her team-mates, thruster jets continuously manoeuvring the team away from each other to keep from accidental collisions.

They were aiming for a moving point, a few hundred metres behind the shiver. Hopefully they'd take Jaws from behind and do some serious damage before they were even noticed.

That plan went to shit less than three seconds later as a rocket ejected itself from the water and closed in on Able.

Caldwell watched the rocket shoot towards her team-mate, saw him detach his parachute as soon as his systems recognised the danger, but it was too late.

Able's Brody was engulfed in the explosion and fire covered the parts that weren't blown away.

She shut down Able's comm feed as soon as he began screaming. It had been one of Jaws's incendiary rockets, containing something like napalm that would burn even underwater. As Able's broken mech hit the water she allowed herself a moment to hope that he'd drown quickly.

"Detach, detach, detach!" Hoop's voice commanded.

The entire squad let loose their chutes and dropped the last fifty feet into the water, hoping to avoid any more of the rockets.

Caldwell hit the water hard, coming in at a slight angle which twisted the Brody onto its side. That fluke probably saved her life. A beam of superheated water cut through where her feet would have been if she had hit straight.

Barely a thought later and her HUD was translating the heated water into coloured beams so that Caldwell could track the incoming fire.

A tiger shark, with a lens mounted under its mouth and metallic body armour around it, swung her way and fired again.

She activated the manoeuvring thrusters and twisted the Brody out of the way. The searing beam of water missed by millimetres, the sensor on the left foot registering the high temperature.

Before the tiger could fire again, Caldwell kept rolling and fired her boomer.

The weapon was built into the Brody's arm and worked like a cannon without a projectile. Instead the shockwave fired out in a controlled burst that could break bones and had been proven powerful enough to stop Jaws from being able to swim.

She was on target, the tiger jerked as the shockwave struck, breaking its bones and tearing muscles. It lost all its forward momentum and began to twitch as it started to sink.

It always struck Caldwell as funny that she had effectively killed a shark by leaving it to drown.

A second blast from the boomer ripped sections from the armour and made sure its weaponry was destroyed.

She didn't have a chance to enjoy her kill as the proximity alarms rang out. She searched her screen for the incoming attack.

A hammerhead was racing towards her, its jet thrusters moving it through the water at twenty-five knots. Its reinforced hammer, covered in the strange metal the sharks had somehow created – smelting it over black smokers – was strong enough to carve through the hull of a battleship; it would cleave straight through her if it made contact.

Caldwell twisted, the Brody mimicking her movement,

and the hammerhead shot underneath her.

She aimed her boomer at it but could only watch in shock as it slammed into Topher, cutting him in half.

The shark was already gone into the dark by the time his Brody exploded.

Topher's green marker winked out on her HUD and only now did she realise that over half of her team were no longer represented. They had been in the water less than a minute and only seven of them remained, including her.

The realisation shocked her into inaction. This was a rout, a disaster of the highest proportions. They were supposed to be the Elite, the shock troops that were going to take the war back to Jaws. Instead they had been intercepted and were getting annihilated.

Two more team members screamed their last and as the signals vanished Caldwell came back to life.

She was still alive, heavily armed and in the deadliest war machine mankind had ever created. She felt a scream of rage and defiance build in her chest and held it there, letting it fuel her mental recovery.

"Who's alive? Who's still in this fight?" Hoop's voice bellowed over the comms. "If you're green on the screen then you are a motherfucking fighting machine! Get moving and make me some sushi!"

It was enough to get Caldwell moving again. She located Hoop's signature and started heading his way.

The proximity warning sounded before she had time to cover more than a third of the distance there had at first been between them. Caldwell twisted to face the threat head on. Her systems locked on and identified the target.

"Fuck."

It was a bull shark. The damn thing was covered in scales of armour, which, it was suspected, were part of a mechanised system that increased the beasts' already dangerous strength.

Caldwell manoeuvred into a fighting stance.

She fired the boomer twice, both shockwaves just missing as the bull shark twisted out of the way. She thought a couple of the scales buckled, but couldn't confirm before it was on her.

Bull sharks liked to ram and slam, beating their opponents into submission.

The Brody was too slow to intercept the first attack and Caldwell was thrown around in her harness, swallowing a yell of pain at the blow.

The bull came back for another round and Caldwell punched out at where she anticipated it was going to be.

At the last moment, the bull used its superior underwater manoeuvrability to dodge away, just as Caldwell had expected. She activated the livewires.

The Brody splayed its punching hand out and the fingers detached, shooting out like bolas, trailing the livewires behind them. Momentum pulled them around the bull's body and in moments the fish was wrapped tight in the diamond-hard carbon tube wire.

"Dodge this one."

Caldwell fired the boomer again, at close range into the bull's side. Scales crumpled and fell away.

She retracted the livewires, pulling hard against them as she did so. The cables raced back, cutting their way through the shark. As the fingers slotted back into place, the bull fell away, trailing great gouts of blood. It wasn't dead, but it was dying and out of the fight.

She started heading towards Hoop again and was horrified to see that only he and one other remained besides herself. Even as she registered the last name, Shaw, something huge popped up on her HUD right beside him. Then both blips were gone.

"Hoop? Did you see what got Shaw?" she was racing towards the sergeant as fast as she could.

"Fucking whale shark. I think Shaw self-detonated. Took it with him."

Caldwell didn't want to believe that. Whale sharks didn't like coming this close to shore. If one had, then who knew what else might be heading towards them.

"I'm coming to you," she told Hoop.

"Negative. I've got two Great Whites and three Hammers all tuned in to me. I'll be dead before you're close enough to help. Drop, Caldwell. Go deep and survive this. Find some other way to hit them."

Caldwell bit her lip hard enough to draw blood. She knew she should obey the order, but leaving Hoop alone to face that many Jaws on his own felt so wrong.

"Caldwell?"

"Yes?"

"In my next life I'm going to live on top of a mountain where there's no water deeper than a puddle."

"Roger that."

Then Hoop's signature blipped out, along with three of the red targets around him.

Caldwell found herself in a moment and place of calm. Nothing had her in its sights.

She turned off all her exterior lights and cut the thrusters. Playing dead, she let the Brody drop towards the sea bed.

Down there she could find somewhere to hide.

And plan.

*　　*　　*

THE COCKPIT HAD felt cramped but comfortable when Caldwell had climbed in. Now it was a coffin, close and suffocating.

It had been thirty minutes since Hoop's death. In that time she had sunk to the bottom of the new sea. Amazingly it turned out that she had conducted her battle some hundred feet above a flooded town. Now her Brody was sheltering in a strangely intact barn.

She was keeping most of her systems powered down for now. Jaws seemed to be good at tracking electronic signals and if she was found here, it would be a short fight and one that she would certainly lose.

Her HUD remained blank; with all targeting and sonar systems off, it had nothing to show her except power and oxygen levels. They were too easy to watch and slowly lose your mind over as they crept down to zero.

"I will not sit here and die." she told herself for the tenth time, and for the tenth time her fingers moved to hover over the sonar switch.

For the tenth time she didn't press the button.

She couldn't make herself do it. If she pinged then the fight would almost certainly start again. She should do it, this was what she lived for, or so she had told herself a thousand times.

She was a shark killing machine.

Except she wasn't.

She was a tin of shark food that would just put up a bit of a struggle before the lid popped off.

"I will not sit here and die," she told herself, even though she knew that she probably would.

*　　*　　*

Hoop had been dead for an hour and a half. The rest of her squad slightly longer than that.

"I will not sit here and die."

Three hours ago she had been checking her systems, preparing to dive out of an aircraft and kick some Jaws ass.

That hadn't quite worked out how it was supposed to.

Caldwell chuckled to herself.

"I will not sit here and die."

*　　*　　*

SOME TIME AGO now, when she was a little girl, the only metal you had seen on sharks had been in video games.

The coastline had been pretty much the same for her grandfather as it was for her. Sharks hadn't developed higher level intellect yet. They hadn't supposedly enslaved other aquatic species to do their bidding.

And no one had ever thought that an underwater mechanised battle-suit would be the last resting place of Lucy Caldwell.

"I will not die here."

She heard the steel creep back into her voice, but couldn't press the switch.

Not yet.

*　　*　　*

"PRESS IT, YOU fucking pussy!"

Caldwell had been screaming at her hand for five minutes now.

At the back of her mind was the understanding that people did not normally scream at a body part to work properly. But then normal people did not spend over five hours crouched in a metal suit, in a barn, under one hundred feet of water waiting to be discovered by sharks with advanced weaponry, did they?

No, they did not.

"Find out Find out who's out there you goddamn princess!"

Her hand pushed the button. One insult from her early days in the service was the last straw; she would not be thought of as a scared girl. She was a fucking soldier and she deserved to be there!

The HUD flashed into life.

"Well shit," Caldwell mused. "I guess I am going to die here."

Her screen was filled with red blips – at least fifty. Three were much larger than the rest, more whale sharks she supposed.

The thing that was threatening to remove her veneer of cool was the enormous one that was creeping onto the screen. It had to be the size of a submarine.

There had been reports of megalodons sighted, prehistoric sharks that were supposedly the largest fish ever seen.

This made them small. If she had the resources on board she could have compared the profile to a blue whale, but she was quite certain it was a good ten to fifteen metres longer than they were supposed to grow to.

Was she the first to see it? She suspected so – information about Jaws was not classified. Humanity had banded together in the face of the threat from the seas, and sharing information about enemy capabilities without restriction was seen as the key to survival.

"So I get to name it. *Charcaradon Fuckinhellis*." She allowed herself a small chuckle. "How about Übershark? The shark to which all other sharks aspire to one day grow up to be?"

The Brody did not reply. No one replied.

The fear struck her then, but not for her own life.

She was the only one who knew this Übershark was

heading towards the shore. How many people were going to die in the wake of this *thing*?

The Brody could warn the surface, start evacuations and maybe get some kind of response ready, but she would have to surface for that. And surfacing meant turning systems on, which meant certain discovery.

Could she do it in time?

Her mind hardened and she whispered her goodbyes to the world above, to her grandfather and little sister, to her comrades in arms and all the children yet to be born.

She turned the Brody back on and jetted her way through the barn door even as the battle-suit's weapons systems were still cycling up to speed.

*   *   *

ATTACK WARNINGS BEGAN screaming at her as soon as she hit open water. The main body of the shiver was ignoring her, but the Übershark and two of its whale shark convoy were turning towards her.

The whales were slower than the Über. The damn thing moved like a pike, despite its size.

Caldwell slammed the thrusters to maximum, not caring if they burnt out, as long as she made it to the surface.

The readings on the HUD said she wouldn't.

The Übershark was accelerating, and it was faster than her. She couldn't just race it.

She fired a wave of proximity mines towards the oncoming attackers and twisted away, moving laterally but still continuing her ascent.

Shockwaves buffeted the Brody as the first of the whales hit the mine wall and were reduced to so much chum.

The second moved away, looking for a new angle of attack.

Only then did she realise the Über had circled her trap and was diving straight down, straight towards her!

Looking up she saw metal teeth in a metal mouth and a gaping maw that could swallow her whole.

Caldwell rocketed sideways, out of the Über's path, blasting with the boomer as she did so. The weapon made no visible impact on the Über, as far as she could tell as it passed her. A huge wave of turbulence sent her jerking around in her harness inside the cockpit.

She saw no flesh. The entire monster was encased in the strange metal that the sharks had somehow created.

A realisation came upon her. The Übershark was wearing the Jaws equivalent of a Brody!

Maybe it lived so deep that it needed the armour to keep the pressure consistent around its body. So the Über had constructed a mechanised survival/battle-suit so that it could join the war.

Caldwell checked that her systems were recording everything, an action which nearly killed her.

She was so fixed on the nightmare size of the Über that she had forgotten about the other whale. Explosions surrounded her Brody, denting the armour and rattling her brains as the shockwaves from the whale's explosive ordnance blasted into her.

The whale itself slammed into her left leg, her slight twist as a result of the previous attack the only reason it didn't hit her dead on and smash the Brody to pieces. The blow was enough to rip open the leg just below the hip.

Before water could fill it and damage the electronics the automatic emergency protocols kicked in. A severing plate sliced through the hip joint, cutting off the leg and sealing the battle-suit.

Caldwell was glad she was in a newer model. Older ones did not contain their pilots in the cockpit, instead their arms and legs were inside those of the Brody.

After the first assault on Jaws City, when so many of the few soldiers that had survived had come back as amputees, a redesign was demanded.

The blow spun Caldwell around, her damaged leg falling away before she even had a chance to reorient herself.

As she did so she saw the Über circling below her, watching as the whale turned to make the kill.

"Try my other shoe." Caldwell muttered, pointing her right leg at the oncoming whale "It's explosive."

The targeting systems sang out a lock and she fired, the torpedo ejecting itself from her right heel, right into the head of the oncoming shark.

The closeness of the explosion dented the Brody and sent her spinning away. But even as Caldwell fought to regain control, off balance as the suit now was, she smiled grimly at the chunks of shark meat that flew past.

Alarms sounded before she could begin to congratulate herself.

Tilting the Brody so she could look down, Caldwell saw a huge cloud of mud and filth rising from the sea floor towards her. The huge red blip that denoted the Übershark was moving back and forth at tremendous speed below her. It must have gone low and used the wake of its passing to create the dirt cloud which was now rising to envelop her. She could not see it in the city block-sized cloud, only the electronic sign on her HUD gave an indication as to where it was.

"Clever bastard aren't you?" It was creating a smokescreen for itself, blocking out her visual cues.

The lateral motion of the blip stopped, but the depth indicator next to it began to decrease at a terrifying rate, it was coming up through the cloud, straight towards her!

Cursing the loss of her leg which threw off her manoeuvring systems, Caldwell tried to thrust herself out of the path of the oncoming monster.

The cloud billowed and the enormous mouth burst from it. She saw the teeth clearly this time. They were almost as long as the average man was tall, so sharp she could imagine them splitting the very molecules of the water through which the monster raced.

It saw her movement and adjusted course – the fucking thing was aiming to swallow her whole!

Waiting until the very last moment, until the dark pit of doom was almost upon her, Caldwell felt her heart thumping in her chest and smelt the stale sweat reek filling the cockpit. Her every sense was fully alive now, as though her body was reacting to imminent death by trying to take in as much life as it could.

The dark void filled her entire screen.

Slamming the lateral thrusters on hard, Caldwell was jolted as the Brody rocketed sideways, past the maw as it slammed shut. She punched out with her left hand, activating the electroknux. A shock of electricity passed into the Über, but the damn thing didn't flinch. Instead it curved around in an impossibly tight turn and came back for her.

Caldwell screamed – fear, frustration, anger, all mingling into a primal challenge – and she fired everything she could activate in time.

Short burst lasers glanced harmlessly off the Über, but the bomblet missiles detonated with enough force to divert it away from her, even as the boomer shots missed it.

The shockwaves from the missiles rebounded and threw the Brody into a spin, shaking Caldwell down to her bones.

The Über disappeared from her screen. Had she scared it away?

Realising that now was her chance to send the transmission, Caldwell raced for the surface, fifty feet away.

All clear.

Forty feet.

Nothing approaching.

Thirty feet.

The Über appeared at the very edge of her screen.

Twenty-five.

It had already crossed a third of the distance between them.

Twenty.

Was it coming faster? There was nothing extra she could push.

Seventeen.

With a sob Caldwell reversed direction, shooting back down. The Über shot past where she should have been and she started for the surface again.

Fifteen feet.

The Über dived past her and off her screens into the murk again. Caldwell swore.

Ten feet.

It was rocketing up from the depths like a missile.

"I'm so tired of this shit."

Caldwell flipped the Brody so that she could see the beast coming for her.

This time she had a plan. A crazy, utterly impossible plan, but it was the only thing she could think of.

As the Über reached her floating suit, Caldwell activated the toe thrusters and flipped herself over in the water. She reached out and gripped hold of the armoured snout.

The Über must have been confused by her move. It kept rising, unable to adjust its course.

The snout burst from the water and Caldwell launched her Brody up and away from it even as the beast was diving again, not much more than a foot of it having cleared the surface.

With a whoop of victory she slammed the transmit button so hard she thought she might have broken it.

The burst transmission was sent.

All of her alarms were sounding now as she fell back towards the water, lacking the graceful mobility the Brody had underwater. In the air it was a tumbling mass of metallic limbs.

Something jolted the Brody so hard that Caldwell screamed as she felt something in her back pop.

She watched through tear-filled eyes as her other leg flew away, sliced clean off by the razor-sharp dorsal fin of the Über.

As the Brody slammed into the water, uncontrolled, Caldwell screamed again at the pain in her back.

Had she ruptured a disc? It was agony to move. If her hands hadn't already been clamped to the controls, she wasn't sure she would have been able to grasp them.

"Get a grip!" she hissed at herself through teeth gritted against the pain.

The Über's blip was heading her way again, more sedately this time. Did it know what she had done and felt the urgency was gone? Or was it merely toying with a crippled foe, building up the anticipation of the kill?

Rotating the Brody so that her screen gave her a visual, Caldwell wondered if Jaws even considered the human race a foe. Maybe they simply thought of humans as prey. Perhaps that was the reason for the melting ice caps and the flooding. Humans were prey that didn't come into the water, so Jaws had brought the water to them.

Checking her ammunition, Caldwell sighed. She had plenty of boomer rounds that did nothing to the Über. Mines it had avoided with ease. Her lasers were damaged, and no more use than the boomer anyway. She still had her livewires, but they weren't long enough to go around the Über even once.

The electroknux on her other hand hadn't seemed to do anything either. All she had left was her self-destruct. It was not a cheery catalogue of weaponry.

She watched the Über take a meandering path towards her, coming in then darting away, daring her to attack again.

"Come on, you big bastard, I've got nothing left!" Nothing except one last ditch, suicidal move.

The Über flicked its tail and raced towards Caldwell's floating coffin, mouth open wide.

It swallowed her whole.

Caldwell had expected the crunch of those huge fangs ripping into the Brody. When it didn't happen she was so shocked she delayed activating the self-destruct.

The Brody tumbled down the metallic gullet of the huge fish.

"Detonate in the stomach," she told herself. "Rip it apart from the inside."

The Brody slammed into something hard.

Caldwell rotated the external view and was shocked to see she had hit a huge door. The underwater microphones mounted to the Brody picked up a grinding sound and when she looked towards the mouth, the way she had come in, she was shocked to see another door closing.

What was this? Why would a shark modify its insides in this way?

The inner door started to open and hundreds of crabs came rushing through the opening, each one trailing a thin wire.

"What the fuck?" her mind recoiled at the sight. Sharks in battle armour had become common place, but this vision was a step too far for her.

Even as her brain tried to catch up, the crabs raced over and under the Brody. Trussing it up like a hog on barbecue day.

As the crabs scuttled away, something pulled on the wires holding the Brody and dragged her into the dark space beyond the door.

What Caldwell saw was beyond her understanding. There was no flesh to be seen, only metal walls, each lined with electronic consoles. Her closest mental image was the bridge on a submarine. Except this bridge was completely run by squids, or were they octopi?

She couldn't remember the difference.

She watched as tentacles flickered over controls, and strange writing scrolled across wafer thin screens.

In the centre of the room, one of the creatures was floating above several controls in the floor, deftly manipulating them with all of its tentacles.

Finally Caldwell understood, and she began to laugh , her hysterical sobbing chuckles echoing around the tiny space of the cockpit.

The sharks were not the enemy. They were the muscle.

How had sharks built their armour? It was a question that had plagued mankind since the war started. What tools did they use to smelt and shape the metal? How did they manage the intricate wiring involved in their technology when they had nothing except their mouths to manipulate tools?

The answer was obvious. It should have been seen so long ago.

They didn't.

All of their armaments and armour had been built for them. They weren't the masters of the sea, enslaving other races. They were the muscle. Hired or enslaved, what did it matter?

The creatures that ruled beneath the waves were the ones who had the ability and dexterity to manipulate tools.

And she had just sent her comrades proof that there was a massive shark that commanded the forces.

What a joke.

The Masters of the Oceans were crossing over to her. She saw cutting tools held in several tentacles and interest in their dark, bulbous eyes.

For a moment she wondered what they wanted with her.

Then she realised it didn't matter either way. Once they began cutting, she would be dead.

Still laughing, tears of terror rolling down her cheeks, Caldwell triggered the self-destruct.

SWIMMING WITH THE FISHES

STEVEN SAVILE

THIS IS HOW it happened.

The truth.

The whole truth.

Nothing but.

It's not a pretty story.

It started with the consigliere putting out the word. And the word was cod. Yeah, I'm not shittin' you. Fish wars. Big money in fish. You wouldn't think it. Well I wouldn't, I'll be honest.

The consigliere, that's me. They call me Jaws because I do all the talking for the boss. I've been around the block a few times, clipped a few deserving souls and a few who could consider themselves unlucky. But that's the nature of the game, you upset the wrong person at the wrong time, and it doesn't matter whether you're a deadbeat or a district man, honour's got to be observed. You ain't getting a pass.

I met the headhunter down on the waterfront. He took the envelope without a word and the deal was sealed. I liked the guy. He was old school. He'd given us precise instructions and we'd prepared the place, got a nice bag of cement mix ready to help take the body down to the bottom of the bay. It was a message job. Little Joe wanted it done properly. Little Joe was the boss. The capo. The don. It was also his style of killing.

Four in the face, two in the eyes, two in the mouth. No coming back from that, even in Nyxon.

If you don't know the place, well, that's hardly surprising, it ain't on any map I've ever seen. It's a compound more than a city. The high walls keep us caged up like wild animals. But we adapt and survive. We're the sharks of this world, quite literally. You've got The Strip, which is all bright lights and big dreams, and at the far end, Necro Park, which is basically a dead end. The Coliseum's not been the same since the showdown a few years back with that monster wrangler damn near blowing the place to hell, lots of new people have moved in, looking to fill the power vacuum. That's always the way. With the competition pushing up daisies, the turf was always going to be ripe for exploitation, and Little Joe was a shark. Shark's circle, then at the first sight of blood in the water, strike. It's just what they do.

Anyone who thinks the Red Coats run this place hasn't got a clue about what really goes down on the streets.

Little Joe runs this town now.

What Little Joe wants, Little Joe gets.

And if Little Joe wants you dead and most definitely not coming back, then, well you get the picture. Forget taking it to the mattresses, he'll take it to the ocean bed.

The headhunter, an old fashioned Shoal Man, turned his back on me and walked away. I almost felt sorry for the little fish he was off to see, but sentiment's got no place in a business like ours. Start feeling sorry for someone and they'll find a way to turn it around on you so it bites you in the ass. Me, I just keep my head down, no swimming against the current. So what if the boss wanted to squeeze more juice out of the guys who owed him? You stick your hand in a shark's mouth you expect to get bitten. Of course, this was all a bit different because this goombah had tasted the forbidden fruit and it really didn't matter if he was a friend of ours anymore. Now he was chum.

"Six o'clock," he said.

I nodded.

They were the only words that passed between us. He didn't need to say any more. Six o'clock meant be back here with the cement to make a nice heavy pair of size sixes for our boy. Two sixes. Midnight. Better than crapping out if you're a gambling man, I guess.

He clambered back into the hitmobile and split. He drove a white merc with fins. All the Shoal men did.

I stood on the water's edge for a while, looking out at the big river. Time was this place was a vital part of the economy of the town, but it was a long time since the last ship had sailed down the river. As consigliere I'm a big fish in this town. I watched the birds nestle on the perimeter wall. Three Coribrae. Crow men. Right now they were in their feathered form, but that didn't make them any less creepy. They were carrion birds, always hanging around where they knew dead meat would wash up. They bobbed around on the wall, beaks tapping away at the concrete like metronomes. Sometimes I'd see them in their emaciated half-man half-god knows what form hanging out around the Aqualung, that's Little Joe's casino down on The Strip, and I'd know that something big was going down. It didn't matter if you were a Hyde, one of the Vamps, a Werewolf brother, the Trolls, Zombies, Pookas, Woodwose, Wyverns, Gargoyles, Moth Men, Goblins, even bloody Earth Spirits, you name it if the Coribrae turned up, it was a case of come in number seven, your time is up so you just don't bother fighting.

They weren't a good omen.

I'm not a superstitious man. I didn't think they were for me. Why would I? I'm the consigliere. I'm untouchable in this town.

I needed to get back to the square. Little Joe was waiting,

and one thing my boss isn't is patient.

I turned my back on the water, refusing to think about the cod, and made the drive back to The Square. We're talking the single most valuable piece of real estate in Nyxon—Monster Town as the Brotherhood of the Hand like to call it. Anything to demean us freaks—The Square's what folks call the streets around Necro Park. It's split into four distinct subdivisions, each about a mile and a half long, with casinos, clubs and all the best dens of iniquity on both sides of the street. North side is Blood Vampires' territory, south side is Werewolves' land. Little Joe controls the west side, and yeah, there's a joke in there. We've heard it plenty of times before, given we're sharks, what can you do? Sometimes that's just the way the dice roll.

I pulled up outside the Aqualung. The neons were bright. Frankie was on the door. He's a made man. Literally. A little bit of this, a little bit of that, a few bolts to hold it all together. You don't piss off Frankie. He's liable to snap you in two then harvest a few organs to upgrade his body if you get on his wrong side. Frankie nodded to me. I nodded back as he stepped aside to let me into the Aqualung.

The whole place was rigged up to look like some underwater paradise, with our forbidden fruit over on the stage area posing as Venus on a Half Shell. Her name's Mina. She's a siren. Got a voice like a foghorn. Only siren I've ever met so I have no idea if it's par for the course of if she's just not very good. If she's a decent representative of her species, I cannot begin to understand the legends, I mean that girl *brays*. No matter what she's packing in the clam shells, no way some mook's gonna want to go off the deep end for her dulcet tones unless he's stone deaf.

Little Joe's office was out back.

I could smell swordfish on the griddle as I walked along the passage by the kitchen towards the offices. Visiting the boss always makes me hungry.

I knocked on the door three times and waited for my summons.

Little Joe's anything but. It's one of those ironic nicknames people think are funny, like calling you Tiny when you're six five. He was out of the tank, the aqualung this joint takes its name from around his laughing gear. Little Joe's a shark. A Great White. He's the most ruthless monster in this godforsaken town. The engineers had rigged him the most elaborate harness, giving the boss wheels so he could roll around the room and vent his frustration when things weren't going his way, and a vocalizer than transformed his bloodthirsty thoughts into words.

There was a film of red in the water filling his bulbous helmet. He'd been feeding. It was always good to visit the boss when he had a full stomach. Even so, he looked at me like I was dessert.

I nodded low, bowing and scraping in his presence. It's all about showing the proper amount of respect. You need to know your place in the food chain. Little Joe's the apex predator, he feeds on me, I feed on guys like Frankie.

"Is it taken care of?" the Great White asked, bubbles venting around his words.

"As good as, the headhunter's taken the job, even saw the damned birds out by the wall. They know what's going down."

"Good. This is important, Jaws. No one messes with Mina. We need to make an example of this wise guy, don't want anyone thinking we're going soft. There's too much at stake."

The boss was making a joke about the whole stake thing. We'd been moving in on Blood Vampire territory over the last couple of months. He liked his wordplay. I wasn't going to be the one to tell him just how poor it was. I mean, the fact he could talk at all was downright eerie. I mean, he's basically just a big fish. Not that I'd ever say that to his face, either. I had enough problems worrying about the Cosa Nosferatu working out my secret and feeding *me* to the sharks.

I should probably confess at this point, I'm not a good guy. I mean, really not. But in my defence, I'm swimming with the big boys and just trying to stay alive most of the time. Sure, I do bad things for Little Joe, like framing the guy who is about to get whacked by the headhunter tonight because of my indiscretions. Yep, I've got hidden shallows. It's a miracle of bread and fishes proportions that I can stand here and look Little Joe in the beady black eyes given I've been making the beast with two very horny backs with his precious Mina for about three months now.

I'm practically one of the family, he just doesn't know it.

Workwise, I go both ways. Haven't got a choice. I dunno which would be the bigger betrayal in Little Joe's eyes, the fact I'm dipping my wick in the company ink, or the fact that I'm working with the Brotherhood of the Hand in a sting to bring the whole organized crime racket down in Nyxon and have been for about three months.

Spot the coincidence of dates?

Yeah, ain't no such thing as a coincidence, meaningful or otherwise. You give someone leverage over you, you're screwed. Some wrangler found out about Mina and knew they'd got me over a barrel. Instead of feeding me to Little Joe, they flipped me. Problem is, the Blood Vamps flipped me too. I'm like a politician, flip-flopping around out there. Or like a suffocating fish.

So here I am, playing all three sides in the Cod War. Not as glamorous as it sounds, believe me. In fact it stinks like week-old fish bones to be blunt.

See, food's very tightly controlled. The Brotherhood don't want the wrong kind of stuff in circulation, anything that might rile the populace up and make them hard to control. You've got to understand, they feed us this genetically modified slop

350

that has all sorts of appetite suppressants in it. We don't get fresh stuff. Ever. Unless it's contraband. Forget drugs, fresh food beats Lucy and her Sky of Diamonds and Mother's Little Helper every day of the week in here.

Little Joe's got a good line in cod. He smuggles it in from outside. I don't know how he gets it over the wall. It's not my job to know. It's just my job to make sure the deals go down without a hitch.

Little Joe circled the room, his wheels squeaking as his dorsal fin knifed through the air. Round and around. I waited. I knew the boss had something on his mind. I needed to play it calm, which, believe me, wasn't easy.

I can't tell you how many times I'd imagined taking the statue of Poseidon off his desk and using the trident's tines to shatter the glass helmet that kept Little Joe alive. But knowing my luck they'd get him to the mercy room fast enough—or at least into a fish tank, and it'd be me in the cement shoes instead of my good friend Cornelius, the poor sap I'd just painted that big red target on the back of.

Finally Little Joe stopped circling. He'd scented blood.

"Tell me something, Jaws."

"Whatever you want to hear, boss," I said.

"What's it like out there today?"

"On The Strip?"

"Yeah."

"Edgy," I said. "People are nervous. They know something's gonna go down, but no one's talking."

"And what about you? You nervous?"

"Never, boss," I lied. "What have I got to be nervous about?"

"Nothing," Little Joe said. "We've got a shipment coming down the river at six. I need you to arrange a distraction. Don't want any of the Brotherhood sniffing around."

Six.

Just the kind of coincidence I didn't believe in.

"Sure thing, boss. You got anything in mind?"

"Something spectacular. We need all eyes focused on The Square."

"I think I've got just the thing."

"Don't tell me, just do it."

"As you wish."

"And, Jaws?"

"Boss?"

"Don't disappoint me, there's a good man."

"Wouldn't dream of it, boss."

"I know. You don't dream, do you, Jaws?"

He was right, of course. It's part of my condition. I don't sleep much, and I never dream. Dead Men Don't Dream. Oh, did I not mention that? Yeah, they killed me first time back in 07, but you can't keep a good man down. Okay, yeah yeah, I know I've already admitted that I'm not a good man, but saying you can't keep a zombie down is kinda redundant. I'm decaying a bit under these sharp Italian threads, and the expensive cologne is struggling to deal with the sickly sweet stench of rot, but such is death.

"I don't, boss. I'm all about the here and now."

"And that's just the way I like it, Jaws. Imagination is a bad thing. Thinking for yourself is a *really* bad thing. One thing about us sharks you should know, Jaws, we swim in straight lines, if you catch my drift?"

I had no idea what he was talking about. "Absolutely, boss. Straight lines, no imagination, don't think. Got it."

"Good man. Now make sure my fish is on ice."

I nodded, and left Little Joe wheeling about his office. He knew. I was convinced of it. That was the only thing that could explain the rather laboured threat at the end there. What was the worst that could happen? He could kill me. I've already done that once. It wasn't so bad. Okay, it wasn't pleasant, but worse things happen at sea.

So, I needed a distraction. Something big and it had to go down in the centre of town. Or, let me rephrase that, I needed a sit down with my handler and a fake plan. Time to show Little Joe who the real shark was round here. I mean, I'm consigliere, everyone dances to my tuna. Or in this case, my word is cod.

I shook my head. There are only so many fish puns a dead man can make before they go off.

Making sure I didn't have a tail, I headed over towards Viva Tequila, the nearest thing to a cop bar we've got in Monster Town.

The marquee above the old cinema advertised one of the classics, *Zombie Whore: A Love Story*. Not that it was much of a love story. The President of the United States winds up in flagrante delicto with an undead hooker, only to have his pacemaker stop pacing and winds up becoming one of us. We like to keep it simple in Monster Town, and there's nothing simpler than the hate for Norms most of us feel. It's very much an us and them mentality. They're frightened of us, some of us happen to find them very tasty. Circle of life, my friend.

All eyes turned on me as I walked into Viva Tequila. I'd like to say it's not often a dead guy walks into a bar, but that's pretty much an everyday occurrence in this part of town. What isn't every day is when the dead guy just happens to be Little Joe's consigliere. Then, especially in a cop bar, all heads turn.

She was over at the bar. Suzie Quan. I knew Suzie's Q's story. She's a looker for sure, sultry, curves in all the right places, almond eyes and all those other clichés of the Orient. Thirty something. Used to be a detective out in LA until her brother was iced. She took it bad. He was a victim here, one of the human sacrifices that went down in the Coliseum a few

353

years back. I think she's here as some sort of penance for failing to keep him safe. She's a guard now, got herself a Gargoyle named Cesar as a sidekick. He's her version of a police dog.

"Jaws," she said, pushing an open bottle of beer towards me.

Behind the bar Hector Rodriguez towelled out a glass pitcher and did that wonderful thing barmen across the world did, made himself invisible. In Hector's case, literally, given his genetic predisposition for slipping off the electromagnetic spectrum and disappearing before your very eyes.

"Suze," I said, sitting down beside her.

"What can I do for you?"

"Get me out of here?"

"Not an option, you know the rules. Only Norms outside the wall."

"I know, Monster Alienation Act, yeah, yeah, we're all evil and must be kept under lock and key lest we rampage."

"I don't make the rules."

"You know that doesn't help right? 'I'm just doing my job?' The last refuge of the fascist bigot."

"Careful, Jaws, you don't want to fall out, do you?"

She was right, the last thing I wanted right now was another enemy. "Sorry, Suze. Bit of a sore spot. I know you're not all like that."

I offered a wry smile. I didn't tell her the number of times I'd been tased by a trigger happy Redcoat. I'm sure it was on a file somewhere.

"It's happening tonight, Little Joe's got a shipment coming in down the river, wants me to cause a distraction, make sure your mob are looking the wrong way."

"What have you got in mind?"

"Something big," I said, draining the bottle of beer in one long swallow. One thing being dead gave you was a hell of a thirst. No one ever talks about that.

"I don't like the sound of that, Jaws. Reassure me."

"What if I said the world parlay?"

"You're planning on calling a sit down with the Blood Vamps? Are you crazy?"

"I'm going to tease them with the promise of a marriage with Little Joe. After what went down between them and Gévaudan I think they'll be tempted. But Little Joe's going to scent blood in the water. I'm counting on it going tits up, Suze. I'm thinking big warehouse, lots of guns kind of thing. With a bit of luck Little Joe will try and end the Vamps."

"That's a dangerous game you're playing."

"The fun ones always are," I said without the slightest trace of irony.

"What time's the ship coming in?"

"Six," I said.

"Can you pull it off?"

"That remains to be seen," I said. "But if anyone can, it's me."

"So what do you need from us?"

"I need you to pull Mina out. Little Joe's going to go ballistic. I don't want her becoming collateral damage if this game of ours goes south."

"I'll make sure she's safe."

"I'm counting on you, Suze."

"Where's the meet going down?"

"I'm thinking Tanaka's."

She nodded her approval. Tanaka's was a halfway house for stuff coming into town. It's got good security for what is essentially a repurposed bonded warehouse against the wall. Arturo Tanaka is a dealer—he's got his finger in every pie, which is unsurprising seeing his demonic form is gluttony. He's one of the good guys though, for his kind. I've never understood why he dresses like a priest. Maybe it's something to do with the unholy appetites he's forced to battle every day?

"Good choice. I can make sure the place is clear. Wouldn't want any nasty surprises."

Of course this was only partly true. I was counting on Suzie Quan doing the right thing, which would make her the nasty surprise. With any luck the meet would turn into a good old-fashioned massacre of the Valentine's Day variety.

We wouldn't be anywhere near there. I'd got other plans for Little Joe.

"We good?"

"We're good."

I left her to it. Before I'd made it half way out of my stool the barman began to rematerialize, the tumbler in his hand thoroughly wiped clean now. He nodded to me. Sometimes I forget one of the peculiarities of his invisibility is that he sees *everything* when he's gone. And I mean everything. Even those colourful little pictures we imagine in our mind when we're enjoying seeing our boss die a particularly lurid death. He wouldn't say anything. Barmen had their own version of Omerta. Shooting his mouth off is bad for business.

I walked out of there knowing my biggest problem was making sure I got the Blood Vamps to Tanaka's on time. And I knew just what I had to say.

I crossed The Strip.

Necro Park was dark already. The place gave me the creeps. But then, being dead, I had a pretty good idea what was going on down in the catacombs beneath the park. It made anything we had going on up here pale in comparison, but that's a story for another day. Assuming I would get to die again another day.

The denuded trees swayed in the breeze, their branches casting shadowy skeletons across the ground. I could smell the Jekyll Juice junkies huddled together under them. Don't ask me why anyone would want to put that shit into their veins. I'm quite happy in my skin. I've never felt the urge to burst out of it.

I reached the Coliseum. There were half a dozen Blood Vamps on the doors. They only come out at night, obviously, but from sundown until sunup they rule this town. And they know it. They don't go in for the classic garb, either. This mob were all in distressed leather jackets, hair slicked back, aviator shades over their bloodshot eyes.

"Jaws," one of them said, seeing me approach.

"Bella," I said. Belladonna, in point of fact. She was the worst of a mean bunch. She smiled a smile every bit as predatory as my boss ever had. "I need a word with the Caldura, if she'll see me."

"She's not your biggest fan right now."

"I'm hoping to make it up to her."

"That'll take some doing."

I shrugged. "How about a deal offering control of the west side?"

"You on the juice?" Bella said, shaking her head.

"That's for Caldura to decide, not you, Bella."

"And yet, without my say so, you aren't getting within two hundred yards of her. I guess that's what they call an impasse?"

"What do you want?"

"World peace," the vampire said, then cackled. "But I'll settle for a nice tasty bite. You can sort that out, can't you? Make it so a Norm wanders down the wrong avenue late at night? A girl's got her appetites."

"Tall, short, fat, thin, blond, brunette, just let me know and I'll see what I can do." I said, happy to sell some unsuspecting Norm as a main course.

"Just gorgeous," she said, licking her lips. I should have known she was a Sapphic sister.

"Consider it done. Now - Caldura?"

"She's expecting you."

Bella stepped aside to allow me through. Not so long ago this had been Vlad's place, but times move on, and the old man was an anachronism now, out of time, out of place, and more importantly for him, out of blood. This new breed supped on something called Antigen™, which comes in a tasty range of eight different flavours. You guessed it, O+ O- A+ A- B+ B- AB+ AB-. It's bottled by age, the younger the donor and the rarer the blood type, the more expensive the drink. The Brotherhood bring in it through Tanaka's and make an equally tasty profit off the stuff. I'm old school. Bella's old school. She prefers her bribes with a pulse. I'm happy to oblige.

A lot's changed since Caldura's taken control. She's put an end to the sacrifice bouts for a start. She's also forgone a lot of the trappings of her monsterdom. No thick red velvet drapes, no sleeping in a coffin, no grave dirt scattered across the floor in her office. She's all about modernity. Everything is bright and shiny now, hence the shades.

She met me in the middle of the dance floor.

I didn't recognise the song that was playing.

I wasn't really listening to it, to be fair. I was far more interested in watching her sinuous movements as she moved towards me.

I stood my ground as she danced around me. It's not as sexy as it sounds, believe me.

"I can smell your fear," she breathed, trying to sound all sultry and slutty as she did.

"That's my deodorant," I said. "Eau de Boneyard."

"And how," she said, drawing it out slowly, "is the delightful maiden on the half shell?"

"Leave her out of this," I said, feeling sick to the stomach.

"Is she in this? I was just being polite. Give me one good reason why I shouldn't put an end to your wretched existence once and for all, Jaws?"

"You'll want to hear what I've got to say."

"That's the best you've got?"

"I'm banking on curiosity keeping this cat alive," I admitted.

"Then say your piece. If I like what you have to say, I'll consider keeping you alive a while longer."

"Get yourself to Tanaka's tonight, Seven O'clock. Little Joe thinks it's going to be a parlay. Get there early, set up an ambush, take the entire shark crew out once and for all, take control of the West Side. What's not to love?"

"And you intend to deliver him to us?"

"Absolutely."

"Why should I trust you?"

"Because I've got everything to lose."

"Ah, yes, the lovely Mina. True love lurks behind the great betrayal, yes?"

"Isn't that always the way?"

"Seven o'clock?"

"Yes. I'll deliver him to the door. What you do once he steps through it is none of my business."

Sometimes it's good to be underestimated. Creatures like Caldura think they're so clever, that there's never been a bigger badder monster on the block, they tend to forget about the little Peter Lorre character lurking in the background. I've made a career out of staying alive long after I stopped breathing because of it.

I knew her type. She was greedy. She believed the old adage about the enemy of my enemy is my friend. It was rubbish, there was no friendship there. None. And of course she thought she had something on me. Knowledge is power. Mina was her leverage. She wanted Little Joe gone and she was determined to use me to make sure he disappeared.

Just this once I was happy to be used. With their territories combined it would mean she'd be in a position to move on the hairy shapeshifters down south and push for control of all the

359

territory around Necro Park. I didn't need to be able to read her mind to work that out. I could see the flicker of ghost light in her dead eyes. I'd got her.

"Just make sure he's there."

"Trust me," I said, and made a sharp exit.

Places to go, people to kill. You know how it is.

It was all starting to come together. Suzie Quan would be in place at Tanaka's, ending the Blood Vamps in a hail of holy water-filled silver hollow points (taking no chances). That just left the small matter of the Great White aqualung-breathing crime lord to take care of, and then true love would be mine. It didn't sound so daunting if I said it quickly.

I wasn't going to be able to get Little Joe out of the Aqualung. I knew that much. So I needed to empty the place if my little coup was going to be successful. That's where being the consigliere comes in handy. People listen when Jaws opens his mouth. I headed back to the club and passed the word about the shipment coming in, all hands on deck, we needed to get the cod on ice and into our warehouses before it went off.

The boys did what they were told without question. If they'd looked up and noticed the line of damned Coribrae perched precariously on the old telephone wires outside the club they'd have guessed what was going down. But a smart foot soldier keeps his head down. That's how he stays alive.

I was all too aware of the birdmen as I gave the orders. Then I needed to get Mina out of there. I didn't want my little siren seeing what was about to happen. I still had visions of her being sweet and innocent, no matter how many ancient mariners she'd chowed down on. She wasn't happy about it, but she followed the boys out.

That just left me and the big fish in the club.

I could hear his squeaky wheels grinding as he rolled back

and forth, back and forth. I knew it'd take the boys a couple of hours to unload and get back here. That gave me plenty of time. I thought about reaching out to the headhunter and calling off the hit on my old friend, but in the end decided against it. He might not be guilty of taking a good old bite out of the forbidden fruit, but he was guilty of plenty of other stuff over the years. He'd earned those cement shoes.

Of course, when he'd been down there long enough, I'd fish him up and make him my number two. I've got a soft spot for the old mook.

But first things first, taking care of business. Or as Little Joe liked to call it, *bidness,* heavy on the cliché.

The aromatic torment of swordfish reminded me that Axel was in here somewhere, taking care of the grill. I went looking for him and then sent him on an errand, much to his disgruntled grumbling. He tried the whole Iron Chef thing on me, shouting about how this was his kitchen and he was lord of his domain. I only said one line; it was enough to scare the crap out of him. "I want to rustle something up."

Admittedly, it might have been the way I was holding the bloody huge meat cleaver in my hand as I said it, and the meaningful glance towards the gas burners, rather than the actual words but he got the message, took off his bloody butcher's apron, folded it and laid it on the counter before bailing out.

I put the apron on. After all, these threads were expensive. Imported. Not the kind of stuff you found in Monster Town. Didn't want to get them covered in blood.

Next step, I made sure the door was locked. I didn't want to be disturbed.

Crossing the dance floor I ducked into the DJs booth and added a little musical accompaniment. Just because we're murderers doesn't mean we have to be savages. I picked Sinatra. *Fly me to the Moon*. Close enough.

The meat cleaver would have to do. I'd have rather had a wood chipper, but beggars, choosers and all that.

One good thing about the music was it drowned out those damned squeaky wheels. You'd think Little Joe would have invested in a little WD40.

A second voice joined Frank's dulcet tones. I stopped dead in my tracks, captivated by it. I couldn't move my hands. My feet weren't much use, either.

My little Venus on the half shell came wandering down the corridor, happily singing to herself. It didn't sound like her at all. It was beautiful. Properly beautiful. Like butterflies in winter time, something that didn't belong together, and I realised then that I'd never heard her sing properly. This was *her*, the real Mina, the siren she kept hidden from us for our own good, and as she walked along the narrow passage with her teeth bared, she was irresistible.

She didn't knock. She just opened the door and walked into Little Joe's inner sanctum.

The Great White was wheeling round in circles, bubbles venting in his little aqualung. I almost felt sorry for him.

See, we'd both made the classic mistake. We'd underestimated the dame. We'd just assumed she was window dressing in *our* story. It's a male thing. We are just dumb enough to believe the world revolves around us. She kept singing long after the music had stopped.

I looked at Little Joe.

He looked at Mina.

She looked at me.

A classic love triangle.

It was always going to end in tears.

I mean, seriously, the two-bit hood, the great white gangster and the siren? How could it end any other way?

The tone of her song shifted. It took me a moment to realise what was happening as she scaled towards the glass-shattering high note, tears streaming down her cheeks.

Higher and higher.

I felt the longest single note I'd ever heard vibrate through my body. My skin didn't creep so much as *thrum*. And then it happened. The first hint of it was the sharp *crack*, like a gunshot beneath Mina's song, and then another and another as the aqualung that allowed Little Joe to breathe out of water was lined with spider-web cracks. It took a moment for the pressure to build up behind the glass and then the entire helmet exploded, glass shards flying everywhere. It wasn't pretty. Little Joe was still strapped into his frame, bucking and writhing as he struggled for breath, choking on the air.

It was a long and torturous end for the shark.

And throughout it I was powerless to move, held immobile by the sensuous melody coming out of my love's mouth. That was when I realised just how dangerous a woman really was. Yeah, I'm a slow learner sometimes. I couldn't take my eyes off Little Joe as he very slowly died, dorsal fin twitching, tail lashing about, thumping on the floorboards, like a referee counting out the last ten seconds of a fighter's life. And then it was over.

"Make yourself useful," Mina said to me, all business. She was a different woman. It took me a second to realise she meant the cleaver in my hand.

After a lifetime of underestimating her, I wasn't about to make the same mistake again. I nodded as she unclasped that stupid clamshell bra she wore like armour and tossed it over the back of the chair, like she was discarding her secret identity. Humming to herself left me alone with the dead shark.

I set to work butchering Little Joe immediately. And I don't mind admitting I enjoyed myself. I'd fantasised about hacking the evil bastard up for months.

Sure, it hadn't exactly gone to plan, but the big fish was dead, even if it wasn't me taking over with some grand *Et Tu Brutus* knife in the back.

There was no doubting who was in charge in this man's world. And that was when I realised the absolute genius of her act.

It *was* a man's world. Every single monster Little Joe had surrounded himself with - XY chromosomes, like the cliché mobster he was. We were absolutely helpless to resist her the moment she opened her mouth. But that's men for you. Always thinking with our egos instead of our brains.

I hacked away at Little Joe, making him into a nice little pile of steaks. It took a while, and was messy work. By the time I was done the place reeked of *fish*, which wasn't a great smell. Even if I hadn't won, I was alive, and technically, was now screwing the boss, which could have been a worse outcome. It's a position of power, even if it's reverse doggie style, with me on the receiving end from now on. I figured we were due a celebration. I mean, in the last few hours we'd stitched the Blood Vamps up, leading those Sapphic bloodsuckers into a hail of bullets courtesy of Suzie Q, smuggled in enough fresh fish to keep our bellies full for a long time, and executed the perfect coup, almost bloodlessly. Tonight, Monster Town was ours. But then, Monster Town always belonged to the monsters.

The only thing that remained was to get rid of the body without getting the damned Brotherhood on our back.

Thankfully, I'm a man with a plan.

I'm always thinking three steps ahead. And it's always about pleasing people. Keeping my guys onside.

Besides, it helped that killing always made me hungry.

When Mina returned, she'd changed into a crisp white shirt she'd taken from somewhere inside the club, and a pair of black trousers. Her hair was swept up in a tight bun and she'd removed the stage makeup Little Joe made her wear. She wasn't going to be going under that spotlight again.

She didn't look like a sensual singer men would hurl themselves off cliffs for. She looked like one of the sharks that circled at the bottom waiting to feed on the fools that jumped off those same rocks.

"Smells good," she said, looking at the first few steaks of Little Joe on the griddle. "I could eat a horse."

"Shark'll have to do, unless you want to order take out?" I held up Little Joe's head. "What do you want to do with this?"

She looked at it. I half expected her to say she was going to have one of the boys leave it on Gévaudan's pillow tonight. Send the shapeshifters a message. The Aqualung's under new management and all that. That, or have me hang it from the office wall like a hunting trophy.

She surprised me. "Toss it out back for the birds." That was about the most humiliating thing she could have done. It spoke volumes for the way she intended to run the show.

I nodded, flipping another couple of steaks on the griddle. The smell was amazing. Nothing like quality meat cooked straight from the kill. All those natural juices locked in. I had potatoes on the boil, freshly churned butter ready to slather them in, and a nice marinara source on the bubble.

"The boys will be back soon." I turned the seared steaks over and gave the sauce a quick stir. It was so hot over the oven I was working up a sweat. "Let's hope they've worked up an appetite."

AMBERGRIS

KIT COX

WHEN THE YOUNG Queen Victoria attained the throne she ruled as she saw fit, taking neither council nor guidance from those who had made her early years so fraught with rules and suppression of thought. This freedom allowed her to make many strange decisions that would have been crushed beneath the opinions of more grounded, apparently worldly wise counsellors and allowed her to act on her very private, yet totally legitimate fears. To this end she set up the outline for a regiment of monster hunters, thinking, of course, that the specially trained men and women were to keep the Kingdom free of the sort of beasties that were waylaying her expansion plans towards a safer Empire.

She was not alone in her beliefs as her husband Albert shared both personal and learned experience of the world she so feared becoming public knowledge. With this in mind she gave Albert full command of her Monster Hunters, a position that gave almost everyone the impression he had little say in the running of the country, because all his aims and goals were carried out with the utmost secrecy.

Things therefore had become complicated when the supposed death of her husband had led to the creation of the Royal order of Dragons. Far more clandestine than the previous regiment of glorified big game hunters, the Dragons had slipped easily into the royal affections and quietly assumed a role of unofficial police force. It did not take them long to move operations from the simple cull of all who fell beneath the moniker of 'Monster' to the actual suppression of anything related to the beasts and marauders.

It was because of this additional vision that Major Jack Union, one of the Dragons' most gifted and forthright agents, found himself, for two months of every year, aboard the deck of Her Majesty's ship the ironclad torpedo ram *HMS Polyphemus*. Generally the monsters of the world were unknowingly destructive, bringing them momentarily into the public eye or else they had an agenda that sparked interplay between their needs and those of humans. But whatever the case, they were all unique and in that uniqueness there lay money.

For example, the sterilised shells of the highly poisonous Snark fetched a tidy sum with collectors, whilst its poison could earn more per ounce than saffron. Unbeknownst to most, the feathers of the giant Jubjub bird have been seen to grace the hats of only the finest Parisian ladies, bringing gasps at their stunning beauty and size from onlookers unaware of the loss of life that would have accompanied their collection.

Harmless you might think, but when a market builds then people start to cultivate and breed the beasts in which the profit lies so as to keep that same market alive or in the worst case scenarios, countries become war zones because they harbour the only source of a commodity. It is for these reasons that the monster trade was considered a crime by the Royal Order of Dragons, and they came down hard on all traffickers.

*   *   *

THE BOAT MOORED alongside the *Polyphemus* was a fine sailed whaler straight out of Cornwall. The grizzled crew were not happy to be moving their hard-won cargo from their large, safe hull to become the seized property of a military vessel and the captain, who was stood on the wooden deck, was pleading whole heartedly with the Major before him for the right to keep his bounty, or at the very least the chance to pay a duty to attain legal ownership.

The two figures couldn't have looked more different. The Captain was an old man slumped from the weight of his many years. His colourful clothes were hardwearing and patched many times. His grey hair sprouted from under a peaked cap with no real shape and his face was more straggled, wiry beard than skin. The Major, however, was as upright as a member of the military could be; his back straight, his shoulders wide and square. He was outfitted in a sombre, dark blue uniform, the only true colour coming from the broad red stripe on the trouser legs and the many patches and insignia denoting rank and unit. His hair, held beneath a naval boxed cap, was neat and brown, the beard clipped down to a simple vertical stripe on the chin, the moustache waxed and curled, the two combining to give him the look of a French musketeer. Although the lines on his face showed the beginnings of age, his eyes held only fire.

Major Jack Union wasn't a big fan of depriving people of their livelihoods and he was a firm supporter of all men who found a trade from the sea as they could single-handedly crush any believable truth from a monster sighting just by telling the tale, which made Jack's job all the easier. However, the current seized goods were not to be destroyed but instead to be acquired by the Dragons in developing other ways to fight their foes, and this didn't sit well with Jack at all. If there was a need, then buy it from the struggling workers; don't just take it by force under the veil of an unlawful possession. Jack may have been an officer but at heart he was a common man. It had been luck and knowledge that had taken him from the ranks, and not the usual route of privilege and money.

In this particular seizure they were after Leviathan products, a trade that had existed for many years amongst whaling communities but had always been written off by landlubbers as fishermen's tales.

The Leviathan was as whale-like as any monster could be, but could reach lengths of two hundred feet and more. Their bodies were covered by a giant shell, much like that of the turtle and when they slumbered they would do so for years, floating on the surface of the sea like small islands. The unwary would make these islands into makeshift homes, to relieve the constant movement of the sea or simply to moor up and investigate. Over the many years of slumber, birds would make colonies upon them and bring seeds in their guano, leading to small fruit-bearing trees, a large draw to men trapped at sea with nothing to eat but hard biscuits and salt-cured rations. Eventually the great beasts would wake and dive back beneath the waves, taking all that was upon them to the bottom of the sea. When they weren't becoming traps for those seeking land, Leviathans would cruise the shipping lanes, drawn by the spices of the Persian traders. As a result they became a threat to shipping and a concern for the Dragons.

The Leviathans of the sea were therefore more likely to be found in the waters of Persia but any manner of things could cause them to stray off course and into colder waters. In this particular case it appeared that extreme old age had led one of the island-sized beasts to work its way into the waters off the south coast of England and die. The whalers had not killed the beast but word had certainly got around the community of the great bounty that was ready for ships with empty hulls and fast sails. A harpooned whale could bring a tidy profit, but a Leviathan could give enough oil, blubber, ambergris and ivory to keep a village solvent for a hundred years.

The halted whaling ship had simply raced the fleet of other boats to the carcass, its crew seizing what they believed to be most valuable commodity, before departing at the same speed to avoid any nasty confrontations. They had certainly not been expecting to be run down by a steam-powered ship of Her Majesty's Royal Navy, bristling with torpedo tubes and adorned with an iron hide.

The rumours of the carcass had also reached the ears of Jack. He knew any ships moving at speed away from the scene would be worth investigating and it had been a good hunch as the hull of the whaler had been full to bursting with foul-smelling ambergris, expecting to make a killing on the market. The waxy balls of digestive residue would mature to a heavy musk laden binding agent much prized by the perfume industry.

The Captain's pleas were becoming pitiful and he soon realised the Major was simply humouring him, with his polite questioning of ownership, to find the location of the carcass and the gathered fleet of other scavengers. The realisation brought the Captain's rage to the surface and a stream of colourfully foul language slipped effortlessly into his angry rhetoric. Jack simply looked up from his charts into the hurled abuse and told the irate man it was time he left the ship. The older Captain was truly taken aback; he was never spoken to like a petulant child dismissed to bed and he would have continued the rant – maybe to the point of coming to blows with the Major – had it not been for the fact that something in the man's eyes unsettled him and he realised retreat was the better part of valour.

The Captain turned to face his loyal ship mates, arranged behind him in an ungainly clump of shifting awkwardness on the military vessel's deck, and he knew at once from their faces there was no argument left that could sway the resolve of the notorious Major. He jostled his men before him and stalked past the *Polyphemus's* crew, who were roping the many barrels of his precious cargo securely on deck. With one last look at his stolen bounty, he boarded one of the many planks joining the two ships together; one ancient and wooden with a great history, the other new and iron-clad with its history all before it. Halfway along the centre board he turned to face the stoic Major, the distance bringing his bravery and anger rising again like the turgid green sea beneath him, curling waves flecking his boots with white froth as the ships rose with the swell.

"I shall bring you down, Jack Union. You are known and you are watched. There are others who control this sea besides the British Empire and we shall bring you down!" he shouted, his righteous indignation rising. "You have not heard the last of me!"

And, as if he had challenged the gods themselves, the sea between the vessels erupted with the head of a titanic shark, so vast and ancient that even the monster hunter retreated backwards in shock.

A Megalodon, a colossal shark that had lived alongside the dinosaurs and now considered to be only viewable as a detached jaw in the museums of the world, tore through the sturdy planking that had been used to lash the two boats together. And as wood splintered effortlessly at its sudden violent appearance, the captain disappeared into its great savage-toothed maw.

Jack could see the look of horror that swam momentarily across the Captain's features, not quite able to comprehend what was happening. For a brief moment it seemed like the Captain would slide unhindered down the creature's giant throat, like Jonah himself, but a last minute survival instinct saw the man lunge for any fleeting freedom.

Clawing himself up between the rows of dagger-like teeth with the speed of a man many years younger, the Captain scrambled to escape, his face contorted into a mask of maddened purpose. The action was altogether foolhardy, and doomed to failure, as the relic of a bygone age closed its mouth on the detritus of wood and rope that had snagged around its impossibly endless gape.

The Captain's arm became trapped as a hardened, bone-crushing tooth passed through his flesh, pinning him in place like a stuck pig. The jaws rolled against each other, allowing the serrated teeth to saw through the mouthful of flotsam before opening again to reveal the terrified face of the still conscious Captain, a face that broke at once into a blood-curdling scream as the inevitable realisation dawned. The scream fell short as the teeth closed and ground again, this time finding the Captain's fragile head and exploding it like a ripe melon, in a shower of ichor, bone fragments and shapeless cap. Then, without ceremony, the colossus dived back beneath the waves as suddenly as it had risen.

The sudden descent of such a giant distorted the water as if it was falling away into a vast pit and the two boats tipped alarmingly inwards, spilling sailors into the sea from both vessels. The great canvas-swathed masts of the whaler covered the smoke stakes of the ironclad, bringing huge clouds of thick grey smoke down onto the decks.

The toughened oak masts, unyielding against the metal funnels, creaked and bowed before the dry sails blackened and burst into great leaping flames that rose high above the stricken ships. The heavy ropes used to bind the planks, that still remained attached to strong anchoring points on both ships, suddenly pulled taught across the deck smashing lifeboats, whaling schooners, and shredding carved handrails like matchwood. The interlocking boats were pulled upright and came crashing together as the beast beneath the waves remained snared like a line-caught tuna. Then, with a lurch, everyone still standing was thrown from their feet as the adjoining craft were suddenly propelled forward through the sea at great speed.

Jack rolled onto his back and grabbed a metal ring set into the deck, mainly to stop himself spinning over the side with the erratic movement through the churning sea, but with a

372

certain element of just needing something to hold whilst he cleared his mind.

His thoughts were instantly for the crew of the whaler. The planks keeping the craft apart were strapped there by careful design, as the rocking movements of the iron-armoured naval vessel upon the sea, against the wooden structure of the Cornish whaler, would have been devastating if they had been lashed side by side. This safety precaution had not only been lost but was being aggravated by the great skipping leaps they were making across the waves. And as if this was not enough, the now burning canvas sails were falling onto the vessel below. There were scarce minutes left in the ancient whaler's seafaring life.

With some effort Jack was on his feet. "Get those men across!" he bellowed at the petrified faces of the remaining mates of the doomed whaler. Jack was already shouting to his own crew in order to be heard above the disintegrating wooden hull that seemed to crack and pop as if the wood itself was burning like the sails. To the naval men who rushed forward to help the whalers, it was as if they were to pluck the men from the gates of hell itself.

The mates did not need to be told twice and in a harmony of shouts both crews, united by catastrophe, were inspired to action. Hands grasped arms and flapping shirts in an effort to stop any from tipping back into the waves as they made the jump from the collapsing wooden ship, which rose and fell with each crashing wave. The ships parted with a random nature that stole more than one leaping sailor into the sudden gulf that opened before them but those men still had a chance for survival, clutching at the floating debris. It was the ones who fell as the boats came crashing back together, leaving just a smear of their passing that brought urgency to the watchers with outstretched arms, and made other men leap further than they ever thought possible.

Soon the whaler was empty and the deck of the naval ship was covered with seasoned men hunkering down like scared children. Jack edged to the side of the *Polyphemus* and was rewarded with a gush of salty spray as the hull suddenly gave on the wooden vessel and water rushed in, tipping her burning sails away, and almost instantly beneath the waves with a hiss. For a moment they slowed and swung alarmingly from side to side, as if the sinking boat was acting as an anchor spinning them around. Then an audible snapping could be heard as the weight of the waterlogged vessel became too much for the ropes holding it, and she finally broke free.

A command to duck was shouted by a heavy Cornish accent as the thick ropes sprang from the water like salmon and sailed across the *Polyphemus* at head height. Men wise to the ways of the sea had obeyed the command, even though it sprang from unseen lips and so only the deck furniture became victim to their passage, but the simple action seemed to unite the crew as one.

Without the weight of two vessels impeding it, the creature hidden beneath the swirling green found its pace again. This time they moved faster than any vessel has ever skipped across the brine, the rush of wind taking Jack's naval cap from his head and casting it out across the ship's vast wake.

The naval commander appeared at his wheelhouse door, a slight man with a full red beard. He was clearly no longer in control of the vessel and finally felt it justified leaving the controls to rectify the situation. In his hands he clasped an axe of great weight and clarity of blade. He balanced himself on legs long used to the sea, matching the swell of the ship with a strange plunging gait and advanced on the ropes still hard-tied to his vessel, yet snagged deep in the mouth of the vast Jurassic beast and pulling all towards who knew what fate.

He was surprised to be stopped by the shouts of the Major. "Leave the ropes be, man!"

The commander was officially hampered in his actions by the shouted order of his senior officer but he was still in charge of the welfare of his crew and vessel so protested.

"We shall be lost if we don't cut ourselves free, sir," he said with as much gravity as he felt he could bring to the statement.

"And if we do, we are letting that beast charge unhampered and hungry towards the gathered whaling community of most of the south of England." The Major's voice remained calm but contained enough self-belief to be obeyed.

The commander looked in the direction they were travelling and could picture the masses of opportunistic fishermen trying to scrape a living from the sea, unaware of the death that was barrelling towards them. He came from a long line of seafarers and could see the faces of everyone he had known as a child; especially those lost at sea just trying to earn a crust. The men on board his vessel were at least safe and dry so he lowered the axe to use as a crutch to aid staying upright against the strange galloping motion.

"We don't have a chance of stopping it, sir. It was strong enough to pull two ships. At most we can put the ship in reverse and hope to tire it out before it reaches the carcass. Hope the people can get away from its feeding frenzy."

The commander found he was talking directly to the Major who appeared at his shoulder looking toward the sea that showed no sign of the Megalodon beyond the several taut towing ropes that disappeared some distance before the ironclad into the cold water.

"You're thinking too small, Commander. I wasn't planning on tiring the blighter out. I want to lure it back towards us and kill it. I've got a far greater chance of doing that if I can keep pace."

The Commander gave the Major a concerned look. He had been at sea with him for many weeks now and knew the resolute officer didn't often say things lightly, but the task ahead seemed impossible. They had only seen the creature for a brief moment and already one ship was lost and many lives with it.

"How exactly do we do that, sir?"

Jack cast his eye about the vessel as if seeing it for the first time in weeks. He had simply thought of it as an uncomfortable home for the majority of his time, a base of operations that just happened to move where he needed to be, but now he reappraised it as a weapon.

"This vessel is armed with a front firing torpedo tube and ships ram. Commander, it's simple. We get the fish to try to eat us and let this vessel's weaponry finish it off. I'm not saying there's not going to be a risk. Firing the torpedo to explode so close to the ship or possibly even jammed in the tube could sink us and we don't even know if the shark won't sink us first. It made light work of the whaler and I don't think it was even trying. Just keep us on a steady course and I'll do the rest."

With that the Major was gone, back amongst the men who were finally coming to terms with the speed they were moving at through the waves, and slowly getting back to their feet to watch the spectacle unfold. They watched him lift the lid on one of the mismatched barrels and reel from the putrid smell. The barrels, for the most part, were sound, but a need for storage for the bumper harvest had led to a selection of containers not fit for purpose being used. It was these that had leaked their load, and already the deck of the *Polyphemus* was slippery with a waxy liquid that smelt like dead fish and vomit.

The Major had been trying to work out why the shark was heading straight for the carcass and why it had surfaced so briefly to attack the captain of the whaler. At first he thought it must be the attraction of the rotting beast but now he was sure it was the ambergris. The leaking barrels would have left a trail from the whaler all the way back to the dead Leviathan and the moving of the cargo had soaked the area between the ships with a heady, waxy mix. The Megalodon had not been attacking, it had simply surfaced from the depths attracted by the concentration of musky smells rich in the water. Its destination had been the carcass, but on finding only boats it was now headed straight for the food source, a trail of musk helpfully guiding it by the nose.

"Right, you men. I need the trained crew to go below deck and get us weapon ready, and that includes the front torpedo. Take any extra crew you need to make up for lost souls.. The rest of you, this isn't a passenger liner so start levering open these barrels and emptying them over the front of the boat. I don't care how much you get on us just as long as you get more in the water."

The crew of the *Polyphemus* sprang into action rushing below deck, following a quick head count to ascertain numbers. The rest of the gathered men looked confused, not really sure if they should be taking commands from a man who not only chose to deprive them of their cargo but planned to empty it into the sea.

"Unless of course you want me to use you as bait?" That last comment struck a chord and had the hardened seafarers rushing about the deck to carry out the Major's orders, forming a human chain to pass the perfume fixative towards the heavily armoured prow, there to be tipped into the swirling waters. It felt to most as if they were burning money to go faster.

Stood on the front of the boat the entire time, Jack watched the ropes that pulled them, keeping an eye on the chunks and liquid bile that was sloshed into the sea, before placing a hand on the shoulder of the whaler closest the prow, halting the last few barrels from being tipped over. Below him a steady metal creaking accompanied the slow winching of the armoured ram as it was secured in a raised position, exposing the deadly torpedo tube beneath.

The barrel tippers looked confused as to why they should have stopped dumping and whispers went along the line as all eyes watched the uniformed man before them suspiciously, until they realised the boat was slowing.

Eyes moved out across the rolling waves. A fair distance off a small V-shaped wake formed on the water's surface and the ropes went lax as the great, sail-like dorsal fin rose from the sea, approaching the ambergris-soaked vessel at speed.

The gathered men started moving away, slowly at first, but soon it became a rout as they headed for the stern of the ship, leaving the Major standing alone at the prow, like a figurehead. His hand was raised in signal to the Commander watching from the wheelhouse, a speaking tube connecting him to the sailors in the fully-armed torpedo room.

Jack watched as the great beast swam effortlessly towards them, no longer impeded by the ship's dragging weight, and he could not have been more impressed at the fluid motions; a creature of death designed exclusively for its environment. Its vast back broke through the waves, sending the beaded water sliding across its heavily-scarred body. Truly the beast was a fighter.

Jack could see its dark eyes for the first time since the shark had taken the Captain and snagged his vessel. They were everything he had hoped they would be. They weren't lifeless, as so many would say. They knew life in all its myriad forms and knew how to take every single one in a heartbeat. The Megalodon came surging up out of the waves, its mouth agape. Jack held his stance, fighting the instinct to run and hide, knowing that one false move would cause the ironclad's weapon to miss the great beast they had lured straight to them. Then, with no sign of emotion, he dropped his hand.

"FIRE!" screamed the Commander, who realised his breath had been held the entire time, almost stopping the words from coming.

378

The torpedo room reacted as fast as possible, every man aware that he was below deck in a possibly doomed craft. Those precious seconds saw the front of the ship disappear into the monster's gullet, vast teeth rushing towards the still motionless Jack. Then, from below his feet, he heard the whoosh of the torpedo, its vibration running through his bones, and a heartbeat later the blast erupted from deep inside the colossal beast.

For a moment it merely glowed crimson before suddenly ripping apart, as the shark exploded in a shower of meat and muscle that peppered the churning sea. The head twitched, eyes rolling as if unaware its body was gone and its powerful tail was sinking beneath the waves. Its mighty jaws chewed ineffectually at the prow of the *Polyphemus*, the raised ram keeping it a hair's breadth from Major Jack Union. As its brain died and its eyes failed, the last sight it saw was the single figure of the British officer stood unphased before it.

Once the giant creatures of the sea had been the kings of the planet, but others had escaped from the cradle of the water and evolved into the creature now stood quietly on the deck, eyes dark and emotionless. And deep in the dying predator's brain, the Megalodon felt that it was making way for a greater class of monster.

SILENT WATERS, RUNNING DEEP

GARY McMAHON

THE FIRST THING I noticed when I entered the house was the damp chill. It was cold outside; winter was coming on fast. Inside, the radiators were cold, the pipes behind the walls were silent, and I didn't feel like taking off my coat.

"Please, come through into the lounge."

Bruce Fincher was small and thin. He was one of those men who always looked on edge, even when he wasn't. I glanced at Doris. She smiled nervously. I wasn't worried about her really, but I was concerned that her lack of experience might make her say something wrong.

We followed Fincher through into the untidy lounge. The room was big – much like the rest of the house – and filled with junk. I don't think he'd thrown anything out since his mother died, and she probably hadn't had a clear out for decades.

"Sit down," he said, motioning towards a long sofa.

"Thanks," I said, picking my way across the room. Doris followed me. The veins on her throat were standing out. They always stood out. It drew attention to the small butterfly tattoo she had there.

"Would you like some tea? Or a coffee?"

"Maybe later, Bruce. Is it okay to call you that? Bruce?"

He grinned. "Yes, of course."

"You know why we're here?"

"I think so."

I opened my folder and glanced down at the case notes: Bruce Fincher, aged forty-two. A shut-in, never got over his mother's death five years ago, had tendencies to talk a lot about hurting himself. A neighbour called and said that he'd threatened suicide.

"How are you feeling, Bruce? Are you okay? Nice and calm?"

"I'm sorry. I know I made a nuisance of myself. I was never going to do anything…I just got sick of that nosey bitch next door and thought I'd give her a scare."

"Mrs Jones…" I glanced again at the case notes. "She says you were waving around a noose and shouting something about hanging yourself."

He shook his head. "I know. That was… silly."

I looked at Doris. She was slightly pale, taking down a lot of notes. She smiled at me, nodded. She was fine.

"You know you can't do things like that, Bruce. That's why we're here, to assess whether or not you're a danger to yourself."

He sighed. "I'm not a danger to myself… not me."

I raised an eyebrow. "Sorry?"

"It's not me that's the danger."

"How do you mean, Bruce?"

Doris stopped taking notes and leaned forward on the sofa. I glanced at her legs, admiring the short skirt and the fair, downy hairs on her shins.

Bruce coughed. "It's the shark."

At first I thought I'd misheard him, that he'd said something completely different from what I thought.

"What's that, Bruce?"

He licked his lips. His hands were bunched up in his lap. "The shark. It's trying to kill me."

"Did you say shark, Bruce? Is that what you said? A shark's trying to kill you?"

He nodded. "I know it sounds crazy… you'll probably section me now. But that's what happened. It's what's been happening. The shark is hunting me."

"Hang on…let me get this straight. I don't understand. You claim that a shark is after you?"

He nodded again.

"Where? In the park – the lake? Down by the coast? You never leave the house. You've not left this place in ages, Bruce."

"No, not at the lake. In here. In this house."

I didn't know what to say.

"It swims through the rooms, hunting me. If I'm very quiet, and if I lie very still, it swims on past me."

"What kind of shark?" It was the first thing Doris had said since we got here, and I felt like screaming at her to shut up and not encourage the delusion.

"Thank you." Fincher smiled at her, warmly. "It's a hammerhead."

Doris went back to her note-taking.

Something I'd seen in the notes on the way here snagged in my mind. I flicked through the sheets in the folder until I got to the right spot. A badly photocopied newspaper report, just a few lines: a tiny space-filler of a story. Two years ago a man had been seen around town wearing a mask. A shark mask (it didn't say which species). Bruce Fincher had been questioned, but nobody could prove that he'd ever left the house. Not long afterwards, the sightings of the man in the mask stopped.

"Okay, Bruce. I see."

"You see what?"

"I see. I hear you. I know what you're saying."

"I'm saying that I'm being hunted by a hammerhead shark."

"I know. I know you are."

"But you don't believe me."

"No. I'm sorry, Bruce, but that's impossible. You know as well as I do that sharks live in water. They can't survive on dry land."

"That's correct."

"So how come you claim to have one in this house?"

"That's easy."

I waited.

"That's because it's an imaginary shark."

I tensed the muscles in my cheeks, closed my eyes for a second and then opened them again. "An imaginary shark is hunting you through the rooms of your house?"

"Yes, that's right. It's coming for me, getting closer each time. Soon it'll get me. It started off as a flicker of movement in the corner of my eye, and then it became the *idea* of a shark. Now it's almost real."

"Do you want to know what I think?" I glanced again at Doris's legs. "I think this is like the noose. I think you're trying to put a scare in us, just like you did with your neighbour. Is that what you're doing, Bruce?"

He smiled, but there was no warmth or humour in it. "No."

"Do you still have that mask?"

His eyes widened. "What mask?"

"The shark mask. The one you used to wear – the one you hid behind when you used to go outside. Do you still have it?"

Slowly, he shook his head. "No. That wasn't me." He didn't look too convinced. He lowered his gaze, perhaps ashamed.

Doris let out a breath. She crossed her legs, causing the skirt to ride up even higher at the thigh. I caught Fincher looking at her legs. He looked away, stared at the wall to his left.

"Okay, Bruce. I think we're done here. You aren't a danger to anyone, are you?"

"No. I'm fine."

I stood and handed him a business card and a flyer. "Listen, if you start to feel like you need company again, there's no need for this kind of performance. Ring these people. They'll talk to you. They might even send somebody out to see you, if things get too bad. Think about going out, joining one of the groups we've recommended to you in the past. It isn't healthy to spend so much time indoors, all by yourself."

He was staring at the card and the flyer. Doris got to her feet and approached him. "Goodbye, Bruce," she said, reaching out and touching his shoulder. "Everything will be okay." He glanced up at her and smiled.

In that instant, I thought he looked like a shark: hungry, relentless, without pity. Then the illusion was gone.

*   *   *

As I DROVE through the dark streets, Doris sat in silence in the passenger seat. The silence tightened, like a rubber band being pulled at both ends, and finally I was forced to break it.

"You shouldn't have done that."

She turned to me. Half of her face was in shadow. "What did I do wrong?"

"You encouraged him in his fantasies. You can't do that to them. We're there to assess them, and that's all. We can't get involved with their fantasies. We can't reinforce them. It's dangerous…"

"I'm sorry."

"It's okay." I took one of my hands off the wheel and let it fall onto her thigh. "You're still training. That's what I'm here for, to guide you."

It started to rain. Light spatters of rain against the car windows, distorting the view like television interference.

There was movement in the darkness: a brief flicker. Then it was gone. I was reminded of what Fincher had said about the idea – the concept – of a shark slowly becoming real.

"I'll get better."

I squeezed her thigh. "You are getting better. You're going to make a good social worker. You just need to learn how not to make it personal. Keep that distance between yourself and the client. That's the trick… keeping a distance."

I glanced at her. She nodded.

"Fancy coming back to my place for a drink?"

She nodded again.

My flat was a mess but she didn't mention it and I made no apologies. Since my wife had left me, things had fallen apart. My external environment had come to resemble my inner landscape: everything was in ruin.

I poured two glasses of wine and we sat side by side on the sofa. Doris put down her glass and I drank from mine. Within minutes we were grappling on the floor, her legs wrapped tightly around my waist, my hands crawling all over her.

"We said we wouldn't do this again…" Her voice was weak, unconvincing.

"I'm sorry," I said.

"Don't be." She lunged at me, her teeth snapping the air. She laughed. I felt terrified, and then, the next instant, I was filled with elation.

We made love right there on the carpet, still clothed, knocking over the wine glasses with our feet. It didn't last long; it never did. When it was over, we rolled apart, adjusting our clothing without saying a word.

I got up, went to the kitchen, and poured two more drinks.

"So what's his story," said Doris, as if what had just happened had not just happened. "What was all that stuff about a shark mask?"

I went to the table and grabbed the file, turned to the

385

appropriate page. "A couple of years ago a man in a shark mask was spotted stalking young women in the park. He didn't do anything, just watched them. Bruce Fincher was one of a handful of men questioned about the incidents, due to a past history of bothering women, but as far as anyone could prove he was just a slightly nutty recluse. He wasn't spoken to again because the incidents stopped."

She leaned back on the sofa and took a long, slow mouthful of wine. Her skin looked like plastic under the low lights: a near-perfect replica of itself. "How did you know it was him?"

"I didn't," I said, "until tonight, when I asked him about the mask."

"Very clever…" Her smile was cruel.

I put the folder back on the table and moved to the window, looked down at the street. There was a man standing on the corner, in the shadow of the empty building on the other side of the street. I told myself he wasn't wearing a hammerhead shark mask, but I couldn't be sure. I turned away; when I turned back, there was nobody there.

"Shit," I said. "I must be tired."

"When did you last have a proper night's sleep?"

I shrugged. "Sleep? What's that?"

*   *   *

IT WAS TWO days later when I heard about Bruce Fincher's death. That night, after Doris and I had left, he took out the noose he'd been brandishing earlier, tied it to the stair banister, and hanged himself. What disturbed me most about the suicide was that he was wearing a mask when they found him – that of a hammerhead shark.

I was suspended from work for negligence. They didn't call it that but we all got the implication. Doris was teamed up with another case worker to finish her probationary training. I started to drink heavily again, just like I had when my wife walked out the door. I didn't drink to forget; I drank so that I could remember. When I was drunk, the little details came into view, rising from the depths of memory like things long hidden: my wife's crooked front teeth; the soft skin between Doris's toes; something swimming in the shadows in Bruce Fincher's house when we'd gone to visit him. All these images became muddied, meshing into a single monstrous entity inside my mind.

I'm not sure how much time passed, but eventually I got a call from Doris.

"How are you doing?"

"Not good. I miss you."

"You miss fucking me."

"That, too."

"Listen, I need you to come over. I have someone I want you to meet."

"I'm not sure I can leave the house right now… I haven't been outside for at least a week."

"It's important. Remember that last case we worked on together, the Bruce Fincher suicide?"

I nodded, then realised that she couldn't see me. "Yes."

"There's a girl. She works in a lap-dancing club off the Skinner Road. I've been seeing her because she has problems, and she doesn't want to lose her daughter to the childcare agencies. Anyway, she told me something. Something weird."

I was holding a glass of neat vodka. I took a drink, savoured the harsh flavour. "Is there a point to all this?"

"This girl: Miranda. She works in a peepshow joint three nights a week to make some extra cash. She has this regular punter. He comes in and watches her dance. Just sits there on the other side of the glass booth, not asking for anything, feeding the machine to keep the shutters up. He wears a shark mask: a crude replica of a hammerhead."

The floor tilted, pitching me off my feet and onto the carpet. I sat down heavily, wondering if there was any sense to all of this. Some kind of memory twitched at the back of my mind, straining to be noticed. I glanced towards the bedroom, wishing that Doris was in there; wishing that I wasn't in the flat on my own.

"Are you still there?"

"Yes," I said. "I'm still here." But I had no idea where I really was. No idea at all.

I hung up the phone and poured my drink down the sink. On shaky legs, I went to the upstairs bathroom, showered, and shaved off the straggly beard I'd been cultivating without even knowing. In less than half an hour, I was on the road. I hadn't driven in months. I could barely remember the sequence involved in the approach to a junction or a roundabout. The groups of cars were like schools of fish and I kept having the thought that something was silently pursuing them.

When I got to Doris's place I sat in the car for a few minutes just to clear my head. All her lights were on, as if she was trying to fend off the darkness. I got out of the car and walked to her door, knocked without giving myself a chance to change my mind.

The door was opened immediately. She looked great, had lost a little weight and changed her hair.

"Come in." She stepped back and I followed her inside, along a narrow hallway and into a downstairs room.

A skinny woman with dyed blonde hair and wide eyes was sitting in an armchair. She was rubbing her fingers together, as if she were cold.

"This is Miranda," said Doris.

"Hello, Miranda."

She nodded. Her eyes were huge; she didn't seem to need to blink.

"Tell him," said Doris. She sat down without inviting me to do so, or offering me a drink.

"This man. He comes and watches me dance. He wears a mask, like a shark. One of those with the hammer-shaped head." Her accent was eastern European. I guessed that Miranda wasn't her real name.

"Does he do anything else?"

She shook her head. "He just watches, and then he leaves. Doesn't even have a wank."

"I told the police," said Doris. "They weren't interested. That's why I called you." She looked at Miranda. "Tell him the rest."

Miranda glanced down at the floor, then back up at me. "I have seen him outside the club, in the car park. He... watches me."

I stood and walked over to the window, placed my hands on the radiator. It was hot but I could barely feel the heat. I turned back towards the two women. "That's all? He just watches? He hasn't approached you?"

"No. He watches. That is all."

Doris was fidgeting on the sofa. "I've seen him, too. Out there." She pointed to the window. "Two nights ago, he was standing on the opposite side of the road, in the shadows. I'm sure it was him... I'm sure."

"Did you tell the police about that, too?"

"Of course I did."

"And?"

She stood, walked towards me but stopped about a foot away. "They laughed at me. They think I'm overreacting because of our recent error of judgement."

I turned again to the window, half expecting to see someone out there, but the street was empty. I wondered how I would have felt if I'd seen myself out there in the shadows, wearing a mask. Was madness contagious, like a disease? Had Bruce Fincher planted some kind of virus inside my brain, something that was achieving a form in the real world?

*   *   *

THAT NIGHT WAS the first time I saw the shark. I woke in the darkness and felt as if I were underwater, suspended in the depths. Slowly, I got out of bed and walked across the room. The bedroom door was open; something large and sleek and graceful swam past the doorway. Its great pectoral fins cut through the thickened air; its massive head was shaped like a huge flat hammer, the eyes black and unblinking, the open mouth filled with rows of sharp teeth.

I stood where I was, rooted to the spot, and hoped that it would not return. I stared at the open doorway, too afraid to do anything else. I stood like that until daylight.

*   *   *

MIRANDA'S BODY WAS found in an alleyway between a kebab shop and a lingerie store. According to the details Doris told me, she had been torn apart. Her stomach was ripped open; the skin of her arms and hands had been shredded down to the bone. It looked like the result of an animal attack, but nobody could take a guess at what kind of animal might have caused such injuries.

But I knew what kind; the kind that doesn't survive on dry land.

"I'm scared," said Doris. We were standing in my kitchen, drinking coffee, with all the lights on. I hadn't touched alcohol for two days. My hands were shaking. My vision was blurred. I no longer knew who I was meant to be, what I was supposed to do. I wasn't even sure what the fuck we were so afraid of.

"It'll be okay."

"Will it?"

390

"I don't know."

She shook her head, her eyes filled with disgust. She hated me for being the only one she could rely on, and she hated herself for having to come here to feel safe from some vague threat neither of us understood.

"What do we do?"

I stared at her. She was wearing a black t-shirt and a pair of distressed jeans. Her hair was a fashionable mess. She didn't have any make-up on. I wanted her so badly that I could taste her. "I don't know, but we'll probably be safer together than we would be apart."

"Is that your clumsy way of asking me to stay over?"

I smiled, but my teeth felt too big. The smile probably looked more like a snarl. I watched over her shoulder, staring at the doorway. The lights were on out there, too, but I kept glimpsing movement when I wasn't looking directly into the hallway. I wasn't sure how long I could put up with this. The shark was after me. I could sense it nearby.

Doris walked over to me and put her arms around my waist. I clasped her tightly. Hate rose from her like a vapour. We moved apart and I walked over to the window. It was like looking into a fishbowl: the darkness rippled like water; the streetlights were submerged strands of glowing kelp.

We went to bed but didn't make love. Doris kept brushing against me, but she would come no closer than that. I waited until she was snoring lightly, and then I got out of bed and went into the spare bedroom.

I opened the wardrobe door and reached up onto the top shelf, where I kept the box. I took down the box and opened it.

The mask was inside, where it always was.

I'd first worn it two years ago, when my wife left me. I'd hang around the park watching women, enjoying the look of confusion and then fear on their faces when they saw me. Or had that been Bruce Fincher? I could no longer tell the difference. The boundaries between the two us of had ceased to exist. Bruce Fincher had become the shark had become me…

The mask was a hiding place, a safety barrier from behind which I could watch the world. I'd stopped wearing it out in public after I saw the police hanging around in the park. But I wasn't stalking those pretty little fishes, not really. I was just practising for the time when I would get to hunt bigger and better prey.

Like that girl Miranda.

I put on the mask and felt like I was sinking beneath deep, dark waters. I swam around the house, seeing everything through new eyes. Bruce Fincher's shark wasn't imaginary. It had always been there, for as long as I could remember. When he had looked at me, I saw recognition in his eyes. I'm not sure why he killed himself. Perhaps he had a premonition, and knew how things would turn out. Maybe it scared him enough to end his own life. Or perhaps he had his own shark and it had finally caught up with him.

I swam back upstairs and into the main bedroom, where Doris was sleeping on a bed of seaweed. Her body lolled gently with the movement of the currents; her hair was splayed out around her head like the dark fronds of some undersea flora. I circled her a few times, causing her body to shift. Sand, disturbed from the seabed, drifted up past my eyes.

I got closer to my prey with each slow revolution of the room.

I opened my mouth. I could taste her fear on the tide, even as she slept.

It was time to feed.

YOU ARE THE SHARK

AL EWING & SARAH PEPLOE

THERE WAS A right crowd.

Older boys, spitting *fuck*s and *shit*s, but excited, not cruel. She leaned against the COOL JEWELS opposite the new machine, watching them, their wispy, zitted backs. Occasionally the close-packed bodies would shift enough for a flash of bright, electric blue-white from the screen.

Sometimes red.

And sprouting above the heads of the tallest, the top of the new machine, the name of it. Serrated, silver-red letters, blood dripping at the edges, video-nasty.

One of the boys turned to look at her, and she waited for the sarcastic *Alright sexy?* or whatever it would be, but it never came. There was a shift in the pack and his head whipped straight back to shout – Left! No, *left*! Fucksake.

A jingly scramble for change. She eased herself up onto the little stool in front of the fruit machine. They'd put those in recently. So you could get comfy. There was a thin old man in a flat cap sat on one of them, right at the end, as far away as he could get. He sat, thumbing his ten pees wearily into the SUPER SHUFFLE, and cast angry, fearful looks at the mob, willing them away. Once or twice he looked over at Scouse in his booth, a little silent plea to authority. Scouse shrugged, the once. Didn't bother after that.

One by one, the boys got bored, broke from the pack, left. The old man let out a little soft breath, but didn't manage a smile. Even when nobody was playing, the new machine would let out a shrill little electric shriek – a death scream – and he'd flinch, and scowl.

Now she could see it properly.

It was the mirror opposite of the fruities it was parked between. It had a bright plastic casing where they had plain black, a sunken, murky screen instead of their wheels of gold and lemons and cherries. It would've fitted in better round the corner, with the grabbers and the tuppenny waterfalls, and the huge open doorway showing that triple stripe of front and sea and sky.

But anywhere, it would have turned heads. The picture on the casing alone – a frothing wave buoying up a cartoon blonde in a red bikini, shrieking in terror, begging for help from a muscleman with a cigar and a harpoon.

And between them, a shark.

A great white. You'd know it anywhere like a vampire or a zombie. Barbed teeth and mad dot eyes. She thought of her Dad doing *Jaws* in a crap American accent – *He don't seem to be alive till he bites ya, and those black eyes roll over white* – and dug her thumbnail into her wrist.

If she'd just seen the picture, she'd have thought she'd have to be the muscleman. But there was the name above it, the video-nasty name, dripping blood. That was what had kept her looking. Waiting. That name.

She'd gotten off the stool and walked up to it without really noticing. It had an instruction panel, but there was a COAL NOT DOLE sticker over it. But it didn't need instructions, not really.

There was a slot with 1 GAME x 10p next to it, a joystick, four arrows, one player button, two player button, a button fringed with teeth. Next to that button, one word – BITE.

It didn't need instructions.

She'd got change from Scouse when she'd come in.

Someone's birthday, he'd said, and she'd felt like doing something but she'd just took the ten pees. She thumbed one in, listened to it clatter, pushed the button with the little man on.

The machine screamed at her. The screen brightened. Counted down.

And told her its name.

3

2

1

YOU ARE THE SHARK

*   *   *

IT DIDN'T LOOK like one.

It was blocky, flickery, a cross between the kind of fish she'd've drawn in Reception and the white bit of houndstooth check. Open mouth like Pac-Man. But the fin was unmistakeable.

She pushed the joystick right, up, sending the white block-blob gliding through the blue of the screen. More white pixels floated lazily around her, little pipe-cleaner men.

Swimmers.

She let them live at first, not twigging that just bumping up against the swimmers didn't do anything. It wasn't like Pac-Man, he was always chomping away of his own accord. But with this you had to make the choice, had to do it, you had to –

She brought her hand down on BITE hard enough that Scouse looked up from his booth. The pipe-cleaner man burst in a firework of red. Red blocks hanging in blue water, a white 30 floating up to the surface, the clean purity of it making the red seem redder, bloodier.

It could have been any number.

395

And then some black pixels came in from the south-east and harpooned her. You got three lives, but she didn't wait. She thumbed the rest of the ten pees in without a thought.

*   *   *

SHE'D GOTTEN THE quid at breakfast.

She'd been scooping Hartley's onto her toast like it was ice cream. Her dad would've had a go at her, but in a funny way – *Bloody hell, chuck, I'm not made of jam!* Karen looked but said nothing. She knew she wouldn't. She clenched up with hate for herself, being able to have all the jam she fucking wanted. Before, she'd been trying to switch to just marge on her toast, no sugar in the tea. But now she wanted it all back.

– Right, Karen said briskly, zipping her handbag up. – Got your key?

She nodded, mouth clotted with jam.

– You gonna do today? See your friends?

Nod.

– Are you. Karen glanced at the clock. – I mean. Are you alright?

She swallowed.

– Yeah thanks.

– Ok. Well. She unzipped her handbag and reached into it. – Get yourselves some chips or something.

Karen put the thick gold coin down on the table, then shouldered into her jacket and looked out of the window, or at the window. At the reflection of the table, the mug and plate and jar, the chair, the girl. She had a jabbing urge to grab the jam jar like it was her mug and tip the lot down her throat. She didn't. Karen went. The door clicked shut.

*   *   *

SHE HAMMERED THE button three times BITE BITE BITE, swooping left to right like a dive bomber. Red clouds filled the screen. She didn't see pixels anymore.

X2, x3, 30-60-90. If you got them quickly you got more.

Lives were a line of white triangles at the top, on the left. Fins. Score on the right. At a thousand, you got another fin. She'd got that twice, but lost it right away.

None of the boys had got an extra fin at all.

The black pipe-cleaner men only came when you started eating, so you could let the swimmers build up first, crowd the screen. Wait for them to get together. BITE. BITE. 30-60, missed the third. Back to 30. Too slow.

Eat five and that was level one. Level two was ten swimmers and two black frogmen. Ten was the most swimmers on the screen at one time, but for level three you had to eat fifteen and there were three frogmen all shooting harpoons, deadly little black bars. She'd got to level four once, but only once.

When she'd run out of ten pees, she'd gone down the laundrette and poked the slots with a pocket-knife. She got twenty pee that way. It went straight in the machine.

Wait. Wait. Pick the right – there, move, BITE-BITE-BITE-30-60-90-120-150-LEVEL COMPLETE. She flushed red, grinned despite herself. Blue and red shining in her eyes. The black frogman appeared on the lower-right, stock still. Too late to save anyone.

She looked around, checking if anyone saw. The man in the flat cap glanced back at her, mouth a thin line. He gave an almost imperceptible grunt of disapproval and went back to his machine. GOLD BUG, this time.

Scouse was reading the paper, tapping fag ash into a mug.

It didn't matter. *What we're dealin' with 'ere is a perfect engine,* she thought in her Dad's voice, and turned back to the screen. She was back in her starting position at the bottom left. Above here, groups of white pixels drifted. Lazy.

Unsuspecting. Eight of them now, nine…

She ran her tongue over her teeth. Grinned. Wait. Wait. She was learning.

She was getting better.

*　　*　　*

IT WASN'T ALWAYS that easy. Karen couldn't keep giving her quids, and she was on lates mostly anyway so they hardly saw each other. Sometimes the laundrette would be barren. She would scour the prize trays of the tuppenny waterfalls for a forgotten coin, and use that to win four more. But sometimes she'd misjudge it and her copper would end up trapped in there with the rest, waiting for someone else.

She went to see Emma at the kiosk.

– Will you pay me a quid if I work an hour for you?

– Jog on, I only get a fiver for the whole day.

– Fifty pee? Forty pee? She clutched the sticky window ledge. – Brian and Paddy are under the pier.

A snort. – You're mad you. Forty pee then.

– Ok.

Emma vaulted over the counter and handed her the stupid little cardboard hat.

– You'll have to wait till five for me to get paid though. If I sub it out the till I'll get murdered.

– Ok.

Maybe ten people came by for the whole hour. Just as well as it took her a while to get the hang of the Mister Softee.

– Ooh, said her last customer. – That's twice the size that the busty girl does 'em. We like you, love. He made the click-click winky noise, but it was more of a squint that he did. – You can stay.

He handed one of the 99s down to knee-height, and they

walked down to the beach together, him and his child, the skirt of its swimming costume bouncing on each concrete step.

She stared into the strawberry sauce bottle.

Ten minutes and Emma came back in the same way she'd gone out, knocking the hundreds and thousands over this time. The lid was on.

– You got any spray?

She shook her head.

– Is it really obvious?

She nodded her head. Emma flicked her a double V-sign and chuckled.

– Fuck it. Probably've wafted by the time old horror bollocks gets here. She got them each a cherry Panda Pops – To match my eyes, she trilled in a posh voice – from the very back of the fridge, so it wouldn't be obvious that two were missing.

They sat on the floor together.

– Sup then, motormouth?

– Not much.

– What's the forty pee for?

– This game. In the Nugget.

She wanted to tell Emma more, but found that when she thought about it, thought about talking about it, it all dried up. All the words she had for it seemed flat and simple. Even the name, You Are The Shark – it just sounded stupid. If it had been a film, or something on telly, she could've tried – talked around it, stumbled towards it – but it wasn't. It wasn't something you could talk about like that.

It wasn't even making it sound stupid. It was making it sound boring, that was what stopped her.

– It's dead good, she finished feebly.

– That all?

– Yeah. You?

Emma nodded, looking away for a moment at the jar of hundreds and thousands on the floor. Then it came out, sudden as a sneeze. – When my nan died, it's… I know it's not the same, but…

She shrugged. It could be the same. Emma hated her own dad.

Emma was doing that tilted-head thing now, like people did just before they said *it's ok to cry*. It was a lie people kept telling her, like they were helping. She'd cried loads. It didn't help. It didn't change anything. It was like shitting, or periods. Something her body did.

– Shit intit, said Emma after a while.

– Yeah.

They drank their Panda Pops.

*   *   *

– Morning.

She said it quietly, almost under her breath. The man in the flat cap looked at her, nodded once, went back to his machine. Today it was LUCKY SEVENS. Almost on cue, there was a clatter of coins in the trough, and his old mouth twitched, once, not quite a smile. He made a small, satisfied noise, picked the coins out one by one and immediately fed them back in. She looked at him, and wondered what she looked like when she was playing.

Then she faced the machine. Took a breath.

The first of the ten pees clattered quietly into the slot and she felt another deep breath creep into her lungs, that strange excited calm stealing over her, that focus. Already lining up white swimmers on a background of blue sea. Three. Two. One.

And wait.

Wait.

Now.

Her fingers hammered down. The machine screamed. X2 x3 x4 x5 LEVEL COMPLETE, instinctive now, quick as thought, quick as no thought.

Then on to the next level, and that started the same way, the same wait, same screams, same quick fast hammering biting flashing left to right x5 x6 x7 x8 BITE BITE BITE and she had to stop, slow herself down because the black-pixel frogmen had come on the screen with their pixel harpoons, and it was like a mist had lifted. Feeding frenzy, dying away.

She could hear her breathing. Hear her heartbeat.

She forced it down. Go slow, now. Dodge and weave. Wait for them to fire, then move out of the way of the harpoons and into the stragglers. One burst red between her jaws, then the other, and that was it.

Level three and she'd not died once. Better – there were three fins in the top left corner of the screen, one up on when she'd started. 1590 points up on the right. *Not a bad record for this vicinity.* She bit her lip to stop herself laughing even as her eyes stung.

Level three, the one she'd died on so many times at the start. Again, she waited. Longer, this time, feeling more like a sleek cold predator every second. Waiting and watching, the white pipe-cleaners clumping up, breaking apart, swimming in their own separate patterns that would come together just so, in one moment of perfect vulnerability. All ten of them, together.

She gritted her teeth, slapped the stick right and up, hammered the button, and all ten burst one after another in a second, a red firework, a digital shriek, a cluster of numbers merged together. Her breath caught as another fin lit up in the corner of the screen. It was brilliant. It was perfect.

She was perfect.

Three black sentinels swam onto the screen, too late, too slow. She glided through the water, a sleek, deadly thing, not blocky at all, as five new swimmers joined them, five white meals. She took them each in turn, savouring every tinny scream. The man in the flat cap scowled into his reels, brow knotting, but she didn't notice him.

Level four. Level five. She sank into the rhythm of it. More swimmers, there to be eaten, quickly in their gatherings, then more cautiously once the panic had started, in ones and twos and threes.

More frogmen. She'd struggled with them before, but they shot where she was, not where she would be. She knew how to handle them now. Keep moving. Keep swimming, never cornered, never trapped, the black lines of pixels crawling through the space you leave. Level six. Seven. Eight.

She'd reached a plateau. Six was as many frogmen as there ever were, enough to kill her, sometimes, to stop her moving for a moment. But there were always ten more trusting swimmers at the start of the level, slowly clumping together like a blood clot, waiting for her. There was always another fin, another life.

Thirteen. Fourteen. Fifteen. Always the same level, the swimmers and the frogmen, the quick frenzy and the slow chase. The predator and the prey. It didn't have an end. It wouldn't ever end.

A gang of boys wandered in, shouted something she didn't hear, had a go on the bandits, shouted something else at her, wandered out. Unimportant, peripheral. The man in the flat cap drew his coat around him, pocketed the one-pound-ten profit he'd made on his day's work, and shuffled past her, muttering. Gulls called as the sun went down on the sea. She kept moving.

Even when Scouse said he had to pull the plug, that he

had a home to go to, she ignored him, kept moving, kept biting. She looked up at a line of fins across the top of the screen, crashed into a score full of zeroes, meeting in strange shapes of negative space, digital wreckage. So many lives. – I'm not finished…

But the screen was already dark, and the button she was hitting was just dead plastic. Scouse shrugged. – Sorry love.

– Okay, she said, looking to the door. Afterimages floating in the night outside. Instinctively, she felt in her pocket.

Three ten pees, untouched.

*   *   *

KAREN WAS IN the kitchen, pale and furious.

– Where were you?

– Playing.

– Playing?!? Don't give me that – she really wanted to say *shit*, you could tell – where have you *been*? Down the pier with Patrick White and that lot?

– No. In the Nugget.

– What, all this time? It's – love, it's not *nice* in there at night. There's all sorts of… It's not *safe*.

– I was safe.

– What?

– I was the shark.

– Stop bloody mumbling!

Karen stepped forward suddenly, then stopped. Her hands went to her head, clutching her hair. I do the wrist thing, she thought. Karen does the hair thing.

– I'm sorry, Karen said. – I'm sorry. Oh Christ, I said I wouldn't do this. What happened? Lovey? Why are you - did something happen?

– No.

She had to say. She had to say it to someone.

– I was playing on a machine. An arcade machine. All day. This game where you're the shark and you eat all these people and they try and get you. Like in Jaws but, but they didn't get me, I got further than all the boys did, I got as far as you could go and it just kept going and I kept playing and.

She was crying. She couldn't tell when that had started. It was just coming out of her between the words, all these rasping, whooping noises that sounded like her Dad at the end, at the very end.

– And I kept going. I kept going. I stopped dying.

– Oh love. Karen was looking into her eyes like a keyhole. – Oh God. Her hands quavered free of her hair and flew forward, into hers.

And then they were kneeling together on the lino, ruining Karen's work shirt.

*   *   *

NEXT MORNING, KAREN pulled a sickie and they went to the old caff on the pier, both of them still puffy and raw.

They'd talked all night. She'd said so much to Karen, stupid things that made her sound about three years old. Like he can't really just be gone, forever, so it's all going to turn out to be pretend. Like the dreams she kept having where her throat was full of dirt and stones. And the really bad, evil stuff, like hating him for being dead, and the jam. And Karen listened to all of it, and answered all of it. And had some of her own, to listen to and answer. They hadn't really stopped talking.

Karen got them cappuccinos.

She'd seen other people have them and they'd made her think of the washing up, but it turned out they were alright. Karen sipped hers and looked out the window, still sniffing slightly.

– Used to be the centre of the universe when we were kids, this place. I remember once me and your Dad –

Karen juddered to a halt and shook her head, like it wasn't a story she should tell.

So she put her cup down and her hand next to Karen's and said – It's alright, and that was enough. Karen went full steam ahead into the story, because Frank, he wasn't some old bit of paper you had to lock up in the dark in case it turned to dust. He was big and real. He was in his sister's voice and his daughter's head, he was in their jawlines and eyebrows.

He was getting barred from this caff when he was fifteen for breaking up a fight with a sugar bowl. Coming up the beach with amber and ammonites cupped in his hands like sweets. Knowing what all the Shipping Forecast stuff meant.

Doing bits from *Jaws*.

*   *   *

FRIDAY, SHE WALKED into the Nugget and just four swoops got her 5 coins from the tuppenny waterfall. Too easy, sometimes. Then left and up the step and –

She almost bumped into the old man, who was sat in her usual place, except it wasn't anymore. Now it was a TENSATION. Now it fitted in with all the others, all playing their little jingles, sending out their glowing promises of melons and plums and fivers. There was a little stool.

She managed a *sorry*, surprising herself with how strong and steady her voice was, and shored herself up against Scouse's booth.

– Ah ey, said Scouse, faintly sad like he wished he could've found a moment to break it to her gently.

– When'd it go?

– Yesterday.

She nodded.

– Stopgap, that, love. Sorry. I know you got fond of it.

She shrugged.

– There's one in the main bit where you kill all them big alien dragons. You could have a go on that.

– Yeah, okay.

She stacked the coppers on top of TENSATION as she passed it, headed into the main bit. Once she was out of Scouse's sight, she walked out of the arcade, across the road, down the steps. Onto the beach.

There was a sharp, cold wind coming in off the sea, and she walked as fast and straight as it pleased her to walk, till her trainers were sludgy, then stopped and lifted her face into the sea wind, and the sun.

It was alright. It didn't matter. She could go and go and keep going. She could glide and dodge and snap, forever.

Three.

She was a perfect engine.

Two.

She could taste the salt.

One.

ABOUT THE AUTHORS

Kit Cox, and his alter ego Major Jack Union, create stories in an alternate history where monsters really do hide in the shadows. Kit writes in his Victorian-inspired study, surrounded by monster relics and jet packs. An illustrator who wanted more than the thousand words, his pictures supposedly spoke, to tell his stories, Kit turned to the stage, acting and writing. He owns a retro space suit, Le Matt Revolver and is fully prepared for the Zombie apocalypse. Umbrellas are his natural enemy. You can follow him on Twitter @JackUnion1885.

Al Ewing is best known as a comic-book writer, having worked on *Mighty Avengers* and *Loki: Agent Of Asgard* for Marvel Comics, and *Zombo* and *Judge Dredd* for 2000AD, among others. He's also known for his prose work, including a trio of Pax Britannia novels for Abaddon Books, and his critically-acclaimed novel *The Fictional Man* for Solaris. He can be found on Twitter @Al_Ewing.

By day, **Toby Frost** lives the life of a mild-mannered law reporter. By night, he is the author of five comedy science fiction novels about the misadventures of Captain Isambard Smith of the British Space Empire, published by Myrmidon books. He has also written several short stories and the Warhammer 40,000 novel *Straken* for Black Library. He is currently working on a fantasy novel. His website is at www. TobyFrost.com.

Jenni Hill has written short stories for several anthologies and is also working on a fantasy novel. She lives in London with her husband and their several million books, but you can find her on Twitter at @Jenni_Hill.

Kim Lakin-Smith is a Science Fiction and Dark Fantasy author of adult and children's fiction. Kim's short stories have appeared in numerous magazines and anthologies, including the 2011 British Science Fiction Association shortlisted, *Johnny and Emmie-Lou Get Married* (Interzone Issue 222). Her novel, *Cyber Circus*, was shortlisted for both the British Science Fiction Association Best Novel and the British Fantasy Award for Best Novel 2012. *Cyber Circus's* twin novella *Black Sunday* has been selected for *The Mammoth Book of Dieselpunk*, Prime Books 2015. You can find her at www.kimlakin-smith.com and on Twitter as @theginfairy.

Andrew Lane trained as a physicist and spent 29 years providing scientific advice to the British Army and the Royal Air Force, but he has always had a parallel career as an author – a career which is now his full time occupation. He has, over the past few years, written eight books for the Young Adult market concerning a 14-year old Sherlock Holmes. He has no direct experience of sharks, but he once threw up on a dolphin. Oh, and he actually went through the same operation as he describes in his story, except that the surgeons were taking something out rather than putting it in. You can find him online at www.youngsherlock.com.

David Lee Stone was born 'David Cooke' on 25th January, 1978 in Margate, Kent. He has produced series fiction (writing variously as David Lee Stone, David Grimstone and Rotterly Ghoulstone) for many publishers worldwide, including Disney, Hodder and Penguin. *The Illmoor Chronicles*, which have been translated into many different languages, are currently published in six volumes by Hodder in the UK and Open Road Integrated Media in the USA. They comprise three standalone novels and a linked trilogy. Short stories from the series are currently published on Amazon by Dead Guys Shoe Ltd, including the original Illmoor short *Dullitch Assassins*, which first appeared alongside stories from Terry Pratchett and Tom Sharpe in Peter Haining's comic fantasy anthology *Knights of Madness*, published by Orbit, Penguin and Souvenir Press. David lives in Ramsgate with his wife and two children. He writes a daily blog at www.blokecalleddave. co.uk.

Gary McMahon is the award-winning author of nine novels and several short story collections. His latest novel releases are *The End* and *The Bones of You*. His acclaimed short fiction has been reprinted in various Year's Best volumes. Gary lives with his family in West Yorkshire, where he trains in Shotokan karate and cycles up and down the Yorkshire hills. You can find him at www.garymcmahon.com.

Jonathan Oliver is the award-winning editor of *The End of the Line*, *House of Fear*, *Magic*, *End of the Road* and *Dangerous Games*. He is also the editor in chief of Solaris, Abaddon Books and Ravenstone, and the author of two fantasy novels. He lives in Abingdon with his wife, two daughters and their cat, Fudge. Find him online at jonoliverwriter@blogspot.com and @JonOlivereditor.

Den Patrick was born in Dorset and shares a birthday with Bram Stoker. He lives and works in London and is the author of the *The War-Fighting manuals*, *The Boy with the Porcelain Blade* and *The Boy Who Wept Blood*. Find out more at www. DenPatrick.com.

Sarah Peploe was born and raised in Norwich. She has since headed West/North, working as a student, a librarian, a life model and various breeds of office and retail monkey in the process. Her short stories have appeared in Hic Dragones' *The Hauntings* Anthology, Cassiopeia Magazine, Murky Depths, Flash, 330 Words and one of Tiny Owl Workshop's Krampus-themed Christmas crackers. She illustrated the poetry collections *Ghosts at the Dinner Table, He is in the Stars, Livid Among the Ghostings* and *SALT/LOVE* for Manchester-based performance poet Anna Percy. She also produces comics as part of Mindstain Comics co-operative, including *Celeriac: Vegetable Spawn of Cthulhu, Convention*(with George Joy)and *Grunt8790*(with Steven Burton). She lives in York. Sundry yatterings @peplovna.

Josh Reynolds is a freelance writer of moderate skill and exceptional confidence. He has written a bit, and some of it was even published. His work has appeared in anthologies such as Miskatonic River Press's *Horror for the Holidays*, and in periodicals such as Innsmouth Magazine and Lovecraft eZine. In addition to his own work, a full list of which can be found at joshuamreynolds.wordpress.com, Josh has written for several tie-in franchises, including Gold Eagle's Executioner line as well as Black Library's Warhammer Fantasy line. And if, after finishing *Deep Red Bells*, you're interested in reading more about Charles St. Cyprian and the Royal Occultist, make sure to check out www.royaloccultist.wordpress.com.

Richard Salter is a British writer and editor living in Toronto, Canada. His debut novel, *The Patchwork House*, is a ghost story with a time travel twist. He co-edited *Fantasy For Good*, a charity anthology featuring huge names in the genre such as Piers Anthony, Neil Gaiman, George R R Martin and Michael Moorcock, which benefits the Colon Cancer Alliance. He has written short fiction for Doctor Who and Warhammer, and has a story in *This Is How You Die*, the sequel to the popular

Machine of Death. Find out more atwww.richardsalter.com.

Steven Savile has written for Doctor Who, Torchwood, Primeval, Stargate, Warhammer, Slaine, Fireborn, Pathfinder, Arkham Horror, Risen,and other popular game and comic worlds. His novels have been published in eight languages to date, including the Italian bestseller *L'eridita*. He won the International Media Association of Tie-In Writers award for his Primeval novel, *Shadow of the Jaguar*, published by Titan, in 2010, and the inaugural Lifeboat to the Stars award for *Tau Ceti* (co-authored with Kevin J. Anderson). *Silver*, his debut thriller reached #2 in the Amazon UK e-charts in the summer of 2011. It was among the UK's top 30 bestselling novels of 2011 according to *The Bookseller*. The series continues in *Solomon's Seal*, *WarGod*, and *Lucifer's Machine*, and is available in a variety of languages. His latest books include *HNIC* (along with the legendary Hip Hop artist Prodigy, of Mobb Deep) which was Library Journal's Pick of the Month, the Lovecraftian horror *The Sign of Glaaki*, co-written with Steve Lockley, and has recently started writing the popular Rogue Angel novels as Alex Archer, the first of which, *Grendel's Curse*, is out in May. He has lived in Sweden for the last 17 years. His online presence can be found at www.stevensavile.com.

Laurel Sills co-edits holdfast magazine with Lucy Smee. Holdfast is a free, quarterly online speculative fiction magazine, which is bringing out its first print anthology in 2015.She used to be in a touring band but gave that up in order to be able to afford regular meals. Laurel now works in publishing and holds a Master's degree in creative writing from Goldsmiths University. She was also on the judging panel for the British Fantasy Society Robert Holdstock award for Best Fantasy Novel 2014. Go to www.holdfastmagazine.comand follow her @laurelsills and @holdfastmag.

Robert Spalding lives in Sussex, quite near the seaside but he never goes for a paddle. He had stories published by *Whispers of Wickedness* near the turn of the Millennium but then went radio silent for a few years due to what he describes as, "Purely mundane reasons." He recently had *Men with False Faces* published in *Terror Tales of the Seaside*. This story marks the beginning of what he hopes will be a series all set in the same world. He occasionally blogs and posts short fiction at www.robspalding.wordpress.com and you can follow him on Twitter @robspalding.

David Tallerman is the author of the comic fantasy novels *Giant Thief*, *Crown Thief* and *Prince Thief*, and the absurdist steampunk graphic novel *Endangered Weapon B: Mechanimal Science*. His first short story collection, *The War of the Rats and Other Tales*is due for release in August from Spectral Press; his first novella, *Patchwerk*, will come out early in 2016 from Tor.com. David's short science fiction, fantasy and horror has appeared, or is forthcoming, in around seventy markets, including Clarkesworld, Nightmare, Lightspeed and Beneath Ceaseless Skies. He can be found online at www.davidtallerman.co.uk and wwww.davidtallerman.blogspot.com.

Amy and Andy Taylor are a married couple from Twickenham who until now have written separately and individually; *Shirley* is their first collaborative piece. Amy's last short story, *The Count*, was featured in Limehouse's 2011 anthology *Bloody Vampires*, while Andy has recently been writing short and feature length films. Amy's background is literature and theatre; Andy's is radio and film. Perhaps it is unsurprising that Amy loves to write character driven prose, while Andy is drawn to high-concept screenplays. *Sharkpunk* provided the opportunity to indulge both passions. To find out more about Amy and Andy's writing, both individual and collaborative, please visit www.lynwoodloveday.wordpress.com. Follow Andy Taylor on Twitter @ProducerAndy.

C L Werner was a diseased servant of the Horned Rat long before his first story in Inferno! magazine. His Black Library credits include the Warhammer Hero books *Wulfrik* and *The Red Duke*, *Mathias Thulmann: Witch Hunter*, the Grey Seer Thanquol and Brunner the Bounty Hunter trilogies. In the Time of Legends series he has penned the *Black Plague* trilogy and *Curse of the Phoenix Crown*, the final volume in the War of Vengeance series. *Deathblade* is his contribution to the Warhammer 'End Times' event, featuring the dark elf tyrant Malus Darkblade. His first full-fledged foray into the gothic sci-fi universe of Warhammer 40k occurred in 2012 with *The Siege of Castellax*. He is the author of *Moving Targets*, a novella set in Privateer Press's Iron Kingdoms featuring the iconic heroes Taryn and Rutger. In the sci-fi Old West of Wild West Exodus, he contributed *An Outlaw's Wrath* in the Jesse James trilogy as well as some short fiction for an upcoming anthology. Samurai warrior Shintaro Oba has previously appeared in several anthologies published by Rogue Blades Entertainment. More recently, his short fiction has been featured in anthologies like *Kaiju Rising*, *Fantastic Futures 13*, *Marching Time*, *A Grimoire of Eldritch Inquests* and *Sharkpunk*. An inveterate bibliophile, he squanders the proceeds from his writing on hoary old volumes – or at least reasonably affordable reprints of same – to further his library of fantasy fiction, horror stories and occult tomes. To find out more, visit www.vermintime.com.

Ian Whates lives in a quiet Cambridgeshire village with his partner, Helen, and Honey, a manic cocker spaniel. Ian is the author of six novels to date, most recently *Pelquin's Comet*, released in April 2015. Also, the Helen, a manic cocker spaniel, and a tailless black cat. He *City of 100 Rows* trilogy (Angry Robot), and the *Noise* duology (Solaris). Sixty-odd of his short stories have appeared in various venues, two of which were shortlisted for BSFA Awards, and his second collection *Growing Pains* (PS Publishing) appeared in 2013. Ian has edited some two dozen anthologies and in 2014 one of these, *Solaris Rising 2*, was shortlisted for the Philip K. Dick Award. He has served a term as Overseas Director of SFWA and spent five years as chairman the BSFA, stepping down in 2013. In his spare time Ian runs multiple award-winning independent publisher NewCon Press, which he founded by accident in 2006. Find out more at www.ianwhates.co.uk.

Alec Worley was a projectionist and a film critic before he got to write for legendary British anthology comic 2000AD, for whom he's written *Judge Dredd*, *Robo-Hunter*, *Age of the Wolf* and *Dandridge*. His prose credits include the *Judge Anderson: Rookie* series for Abaddon Books. His lifelong love of sharks began when he saw *Jaws* at the age of 7 and fell off his chair in fright at the bit with Ben Gardener's head. More recently he achieved a lifelong dream of going cage-diving, which he did off the coast of Guadalupe, Mexico. He got pooped on by a Great White. You can visit him online at www.alecworley. weebly.com.

ABOUT THE EDITOR

Jonathan Green is a writer of speculative fiction, with more than fifty books to his name. Well known for his contributions to the Fighting Fantasy range of adventure gamebooks, he has also written fiction for such diverse properties as Doctor Who, Star Wars: The Clone Wars, Warhammer, Warhammer 40,000, Sonic the Hedgehog, Teenage Mutant Ninja Turtles, Moshi Monsters, LEGO and Judge Dredd. He is the creator of the Pax Britannia series for Abaddon Books and has written eight novels set within this steampunk universe, featuring the debonair dandy adventurer Ulysses Quicksilver. Jonathan also the author of an increasing number of non-fiction titles, including the critically-acclaimed *YOU ARE THE HERO – A History of Fighting Fantasy Gamebooks*. To find out more about his current projects visit www.JonathanGreenAuthor. com and follow him on Twitter @jonathangreen.